PRAISE FOR *L*

Named a Book of the Year finalist by *Foreword Reviews*.

"TOP PICK! . . . Acker whips up a winner with appealing characters and a plot wound as tight as a ticking bomb. The high stakes strike to the heart of today's fears. Action in and out of the courtroom tops off this exceptional read."

—RT Book Reviews

"Chilling! This work takes you into the world of the past, present, and possible future, seeping with espionage, deadly secrets, germ warfare, all mingled together for one exciting ride. Fast paced, brimming with mystery and suspense, this is surely a read you will not be able to put down. A real page turner."

—Midwest Book Review

"Move over, John Grisham! In *Dead Man's Rule*, Rick Acker takes readers of legal thrillers into a world of legal technicalities, international terrorism, and biological weapons . . . Acker writes in a straightforward style that compels the reader to read just one more chapter—again and again . . . Acker foreshadows with skill and unwinds the story artfully all the way to a powerful climax."

—Christian Book Previews

"*Dead Man's Rule* . . . delivers the gripping tale of Dr. Mikhail Ivanovsky, an eccentric Russian scientist who is trying to prevent the spread of a lethal 'Ebolapox' virus. The virus could wipe out entire cities within days and spread across a nation before the populace knew what hit them . . . It's a legal thriller with all the trimmings—courtroom drama, murder, near-death experiences, shocking discoveries, and gripping story lines . . . Acker tells a good, strong story with excellent use of some devices that make fiction fun and effective . . . compelling and powerful."

—Randall Murphree, *AFA Journal*

"[A] fast-paced book with subtle references to faith and doing what is right . . . This would be a good addition for those readers who shy away from traditional Christian fiction as too 'preachy.' I liked the book very much."

—Church and Synagogue Library Association

"I've read a lot of thrillers, and this one was truly excellent. It's a nice blend of Grisham and early Clancy—a legal thriller with bullets. The courtroom scenes are compelling without getting into tedious legal detail, and the fight scenes have plenty of zip. As a novelist myself, I had to admire Acker's use of the written word. He really does a terrific job of creating a strong storyworld (the Chicago legal scene and Russian mafiya) with solid characters (loved the Russian ex-FBI agent) and a plot that moves. I don't often read a book a second time, but I'm rereading this one. I give this book an A+, which is rare in my grade-book."

—Randy Ingermanson, physicist and Christy
Award–winning novelist

"The author paints an elegant fiction that is quite close to reality."

—Nwadiuto Esiobu, PhD, professor of microbiology and
federally funded bioterrorism countermeasures researcher,
Florida Atlantic University

DEAD MAN'S
RULE

ALSO BY RICK ACKER

When the Devil Whistles

DEAD MAN'S
RULE

RICK ACKER

Waterfall
PRESS

This is a work of fiction. Names, characters, organizations, places, events, and incidents are either products of the author's imagination or are used fictitiously.

Text copyright © 2016 by Rick Acker
All rights reserved.

No part of this book may be reproduced, or stored in a retrieval system, or transmitted in any form or by any means, electronic, mechanical, photocopying, recording, or otherwise, without express written permission of the publisher.

Published by Waterfall Press, Grand Haven, MI

www.brilliancepublishing.com

Amazon, the Amazon logo, and Waterfall Press are trademarks of Amazon.com, Inc., or its affiliates.

ISBN-13: 9781503934801
ISBN-10: 1503934802

Cover design by Cyanotype Book Architects

Printed in the United States of America

For Anette

Some malady is coming upon us. We wait, we wait,

*And the saints and martyrs wait, for those who shall
    be martyrs and saints.*

*Destiny waits in the hand of God, shaping the still
    unshapen.*

—T.S. Eliot, Murder in the Cathedral

PROLOGUE
A RELIC OF WAR

November 16, 1985

They were late.

Alexei Zinoviev glanced at his watch and looked both ways down the dark, empty street. He swore nervously in Russian. As agreed, he stood on the north sidewalk, halfway across the Madison Street Bridge.

A bitter November wind knifed down the Chicago River and caught him full force, whistling eerily as it blew through the grated steel of the bridge. He ducked his face into the collar of his greatcoat and cursed again.

I'm much too exposed out here—and not just to the wind. He looked at his watch again. *I'll give them five more minutes.*

He couldn't really blame them for being late. He had called them only an hour ago, and they had been expecting a meeting in Berlin, not Chicago. He had told his CIA handlers to meet him in Berlin. He had bought a ticket to Berlin under an assumed name. He had even paid an acquaintance who matched his general appearance to sit in his seat on the Aeroflot flight.

He chuckled softly as he remembered the surprise in his CIA contact's voice when she heard that he was actually in Chicago. He also relaxed a little—if the CIA hadn't known he was here, the KGB almost certainly didn't know either.

The CIA and KGB also wouldn't know that he had visited a local bank before arranging this meeting. Chicago's large Russian community included many who had secrets of their own. And many of those secrets were kept locked away in safe-deposit boxes—so many that the bank employed a vault teller who spoke Russian. The teller had understood perfectly when Alexei insisted that the entire vault—not just the little aisle of booths—be empty when he put his package into the box. That was for the teller's sake as much as for his own, though of course Alexei didn't say so.

So I'm looking out for bank tellers now? He snorted in the chill autumn air. *I must be getting soft.*

Well, he could afford to get a little soft—or he could afford it after tonight, anyway. Obtaining information for the Americans had been a profitable little side business over the years, but this deal would be anything but little. After this, he could retire, bribe his way into a secure *dacha* on the Black Sea, and live like a king.

There would be negotiations, of course, but Alexei did not expect them to last long. He knew his handlers would recognize the value of what he had and would quickly get authorization to pay a reasonable sum for it. He could only guess at just how reasonable that sum would be. He was quite certain, though, that it would be enough to keep him in comfortable excess for many years.

A bland gray sedan turned from Wacker onto Madison and slowed down as it approached the bridge. Alexei rubbed his hands and smiled with relief and anticipation. The Americans would have to pay a premium for leaving him standing in the cold for twenty minutes. But then, what could he ask for that he wasn't already entitled to as payment for his package? This entertaining train of thought derailed when he noticed that the sedan's right rear window was down. That could mean only one thing.

Alexei's plan had been good, but not foolproof—and the decoy he'd sent to Berlin turned out to be a fool. Vladimir Yazov had never been to Germany before, so instead of holing up in his hotel room as instructed until he got the "all clear," he had decided to entertain himself at a midtown nightclub, or what passed for one in East Berlin.

At the club he'd met a pretty blonde East German named Ilsa, who spoke Russian with a delightful lilt. She had somehow managed to buy a red Italian dress that clung to her figure and matched her bright-red nails and lips. After several hours of drinking and dancing, Ilsa and Vladimir had careened out the front door of the nightclub and headed down the narrow, shadow-filled street in the direction of his hotel. It was cold, but he was happy and drunk and oblivious to the chill. He had his arm around Ilsa's waist, and they talked and laughed loudly, their voices echoing down the empty road.

As they passed a large, windowless parked van, its lights suddenly went on and its doors flew open. Half a dozen armed men spilled out. They grabbed Vladimir and threw him to the ground. Two of them pinned him to the cold, wet pavement while two others searched him. A third pair pointed large pistols at his head. As soon as he saw the guns, he stopped struggling and lay limp. They weren't wearing uniforms, but he had no doubt that they were Stasi, East German secret police. "What do you want?" he asked.

With ruthless efficiency, and without a word, they took his money belt and wallet. They then turned him over, handcuffed him, and pulled him roughly to his feet.

As they shoved him into the back of the van, Vladimir caught a glimpse of Ilsa standing on the sidewalk. She was talking casually to one of the men. "Help me!" he yelled to her, but she ignored him.

The doors slammed shut and the van pulled away from the curb. Vladimir found himself sitting on a bench across from two stone-faced men with pistols in their hands. "What do you want?" he asked again.

Silence.

"Where are you taking me?"

More silence.

The back of the van was cold and drafty, but he began to sweat. "Look, I'll tell you anything you want."

Alexei jumped back from the rail between the sidewalk and the street just as the car reached him. Three shots—probably intended for his head—caught him in the chest and side. There was no sound of gunfire to attract attention, just three shrouded flashes and the soft *zip zip zip* of bullets leaving a silencer. Alexei stumbled and fell.

"Hurry!" a voice urged in Russian from the front seat of the car. A tall, dark-haired man jumped out of the right rear door, still holding a Makarov pistol. He shoved the weapon into his jacket and quickly searched Alexei's pockets. As he knelt to frisk through Alexei's pants pockets, Alexei's hand suddenly grabbed the man's arm and held it in an iron grip. His other hand shot into the man's jacket and pulled out the Makarov.

Zip! Zip! The would-be assassin, his eyes now vacant, fell heavily to the sidewalk beside Alexei.

Alexei got to his knees, gritting his teeth against the pain. Broken ribs, probably. He congratulated himself for having decided to wear his new Kevlar vest. He hadn't brought a gun because carrying one could get him arrested. And that might lead to an Interpol inquiry that would have most unfortunate results. Not that it mattered—he had a gun now.

Another man was getting out of the driver's side of the car. Alexei aimed at his head and pulled the trigger.

Nothing.

Alexei glanced frantically at the pistol and saw that a split shell casing had jammed the action. It would take several seconds to clear—seconds that he didn't have. The other man had his gun out now. Alexei needed a diversion or he was dead. He pulled the safe-deposit-box key out of his pocket and shouted, "Here's what you want!"

He tossed the key over the man's head, knowing that it would almost certainly fall through the grated surface of the bridge and into the river below.

The man's eyes momentarily left Alexei and followed the arc of the flying key as it glittered in the streetlights.

Alexei turned and pulled himself up on the bridge railing, gasping in pain as the jagged ends of his rib fractures grated against each other. His groans brought the other man's attention back to him.

Seeing his quarry escaping, the man fired two quick shots into the back of Alexei's head.

Alexei collapsed on the railing for an instant and then began to slide over it. The driver ran around his car and tried to grab the corpse, but he was too late. It disappeared over the side, then splashed loudly into the Chicago River.

The man looked down at Alexei's dead face. It stared back up at him as the body drifted downstream. His orders had been to kill Alexei and search his body for any containers or papers. Well, his partner had done that—or he had started to, anyway, before Alexei had unexpectedly come back to life. The agent grimaced—that had been sloppy.

He thought about jumping into the river and trying to tow the body to shore, but he saw the pale rings of ice around the bridge pilings and knew that the cold would probably kill him. Besides, the police or Alexei's CIA contacts could show up at any minute. He glanced down the street and saw a pair of headlights about a half mile away, coming toward him. That settled it. He bundled his partner's body into the car and drove off.

The key fluttered gently to the muddy river bottom. The current tumbled it along for a few yards and then drove it into the soft silt. More silt collected around it, slowly turning it into an unrecognizable lump of mud, eventually hiding it entirely and forever.

Half a mile away, Alexei Zinoviev's package sat undisturbed in its safe-deposit box, to become a relic of a war that would end in a few years. Like the key, it was hidden and entirely forgotten. But not forever.

Chapter One
The New Client

This doesn't look promising, Ben Corbin thought as he eyed the potential new client sitting in his lobby. The short, wiry man looked like he was about seventy, and the suit he wore was at least twenty years old. A thick shock of unruly gray hair crowned his large head. The man's thin, age-spotted hands clutched a dilapidated and overstuffed briefcase in his lap.

Ben didn't need more clients, he needed more *paying* clients. In the six months since he had opened his own law practice, he hadn't had any trouble keeping busy. The world, he had discovered, was full of people who wanted to hire a lawyer, but only a fraction of those people had both the desire and the ability to pay their legal bills in a timely fashion. That hadn't been a problem at Beale & Ripley, the thousand-lawyer firm where Ben had spent the first seven years of his career. He had gone up to his fortieth-floor office every morning, worked hard for ten or twelve hours a day, and cashed a fat paycheck twice a month.

The Law Offices of Benjamin Corbin had opened six months ago last week, and the past half year had been a mixed bag. Ben had won two trials but had been paid for only one of them. And the firm's expenses were, of course, higher than they had projected. Not a lot, but enough to make their finances uncomfortably tight.

Ben knew he was probably too busy to take the old man's case, even if the man could and would pay. In fact, Ben knew he really should be preparing for a court hearing he had in less than an hour. The hearing wasn't particularly important, but the case was. Ben represented a small company called Circuit Dynamics whose trade-secret software had been stolen—or so Ben hoped to prove—by several car-part manufacturers. If Ben won, the damages would be at least $50 million, and Ben would get 10 percent of that under a partial-contingent-fee agreement he had with his client.

He glanced at his watch. The old man had been referred by one of Ben's more reliable clients, Cathy Pugo, so Ben had to at least talk to him. He swallowed his doubts and strode across the lobby with a smile on his face and his hand out.

"Hello, I'm Ben Corbin." He shook the man's hand warmly.

"Mikhail Ivanovsky," the man said with a sharp nod. "Pleased to meet you, Mr. Corbin."

"Likewise," replied Ben. "Please come with me." He led his guest into the firm's conference room. It was small, but the table and chairs were beautifully finished solid oak. Ben also took pride in the fact that the paintings on the walls were both originals, though they had come from the Starving Artist gallery west of the Loop. "Can I get you anything to drink?"

"Tea with sugar," said Ivanovsky in clear but thickly accented English.

Ben picked up the phone and dialed. "Susan, could you bring in tea and sugar for Mr. Ivanovsky? Thanks." He surreptitiously glanced at his watch again as he sat down at the table. "I have twenty minutes before I need to leave for court. What can I do for you, Mr. Ivanovsky?"

The old man reached down into his battered briefcase and pulled out a stack of papers. "I need you to get some things that are in a safe-deposit box. I bought these things, but they will not give them to me," he explained opaquely.

"Who won't give them to you?" asked Ben.

"The bank which this box is in. American Union Bank." He riffled through the sheaf of papers and handed several to Ben. "Box number 4613 in the LaSalle Street American Union Bank building."

Ben glanced quickly at the papers, which consisted of a map of downtown Chicago with the location of the bank helpfully marked with a red X, some handwritten Russian notes, and a letter from the bank refusing Mr. "Ivansky" access to the box. "They say their records show that the box belongs to a man named Nikolai Zinoviev," Ben observed.

"This lies!" Ivanovsky pointed to the letter. "This Zinoviev, he sold it to me for $5,000 last week."

Ben noticed that Ivanovsky hadn't handed him a contract for the sale of the box. "Did he sign any papers showing that he sold it to you?"

Ivanovsky hesitated. "Not yet."

"Have you asked him to?"

"Yes."

"What did he say?"

"He said he would sign papers from the bank to show that this box is mine, but then he did not do it. Now he will not sign."

"I see," Ben said. Now they were getting somewhere. "Were there any witnesses to the conversation where Mr. Zinoviev agreed to sell it to you?"

Ivanovsky frowned and looked down at his hands. "No, we were alone."

"Did you actually give him the money?"

"Yes, yes." Ivanovsky shuffled through his papers, happy to be able to prove something again. "Here is the receipts, here is the bank statement showing my account before, and here is another statement showing my account is much lower now."

Ben's secretary, Susan, came in with a mug of tea and a sugar bowl for Ivanovsky. He thanked her and dumped four heaping spoonfuls of sugar into his mug. Ben's teeth hurt as he watched his guest drink. "By the way, what's in the box?" Ben asked.

"Jewelries."

"What kind of jewelry?"

Ivanovsky put down his mug. "Okay, here is what happened. I was at Saint Vladimir Church two Sundays ago and I talked to this man, and he told me about a man who died in 1985 and maybe he put some jewelries in this box at American Union Bank on LaSalle Street. This man who died, his brother lives in Chicago now, so I telephoned the brother and asked if it is true. This brother is Nikolai Zinoviev, who is called Nicki.

"I said to Nicki Zinoviev, 'A man told me that when your brother died, maybe he left jewelries in a safe-deposit box at a bank. I maybe would like to buy these jewelries.' He knew nothing of this box and was very surprised. He said, 'You are a very lucky man, Ivanovsky, because I must pay some money to a man today and my bank is closed so I cannot get my money. Because of this, I will sell whatever things are in this box to you for $5,000, but you must pay in the next two hours.'

"American Union Bank is also closed, but I think maybe these jewelries are very valuable, so I take this risk and say yes. I gave him $5,000, and he said we will go to the bank the next day and fill out necessary forms and show the bank papers so we can take the things in the box. But now he says no."

Ivanovsky's monologue seemed oddly preplanned to Ben, and he had a vague feeling that there was more going on here than this man was telling him. Ben thought about asking more questions but decided against it. Did he really need to get to the bottom of whatever was going on? Or, more importantly, did he need to do it now? Not really. After all, he hadn't even taken the case, and he probably wouldn't. He decided to let it slide, at least for the time being. He glanced at his watch again. He had eight minutes. "Did he say why he won't give you the jewelry?"

"He says now we have no deal. He says he has sold the jewelries to someone else."

"So you want your money back?"

Ivanovsky shook his head. His bushy gray hair and spindly neck made him look like a dandelion flopping in the breeze. "No. I want the jewelries."

"But you said—"

"The jewelries are still in the box. The bank is still looking at the papers Nicki gave them."

"Okay, I think I have a basic grasp of what your case is about. The real problem I see is money. This isn't a very large dispute, and litigation is expensive. No matter who you hire, you'll almost certainly spend more than $5,000 on lawyers. Are you really sure you want to file suit over this?"

Ivanovsky didn't hesitate. "Yes."

Ben shrugged. "Okay. And you don't just want your money back. You want the jewelry, right?"

"Yes."

"Well, that will mean not just filing a complaint, but also moving for an immediate temporary restraining order, or TRO, to keep Mr."— he checked his notes—"Mr. Zinoviev and the bank from giving it to someone else. TROs only last ten days, so whether you win or lose the TRO motion, you'll need to file a motion for a preliminary injunction that will prevent them from doing anything with whatever is in the box. The trial on the preliminary injunction may come within ten days, but what usually happens is that the parties agree to extend the TRO—if it's granted—and hold the preliminary injunction trial a little later. That way they can do some discovery before jumping straight into a trial. Still, the trial will probably come within a month, which is about two years sooner than in a regular case.

"My old boss used to describe this type of case as 'litigating with your hair on fire,' and that's what it feels like. You'll be constantly running, from the moment you start until the end of the trial. You'll also be spending lots of money, because your lawyer will be working for you pretty much full time for the whole month." Ben did some quick calculations in his head. "It would probably cost you at least $20,000 to get through the preliminary injunction trial. The case won't end then, but the work and the bills will probably drop off."

Ivanovsky went a little pale. "I—I do not have so much," he mumbled, searching through his bag. "I have only $5,000 with me." He pulled out a stack of traveler's checks and showed them to Ben with a downcast look on his face. "I have some money saved, and I can get the rest from my pension and from selling some things, but not right away. But next week I will pay. Is this okay?"

Ben was stunned and felt a little sorry for the old man. He was clearly burning through his retirement nest egg to get whatever was in that box. "Uh . . . yeah, sure. I would only need $5,000 up front. Just bring me a bank statement showing me that the rest is there."

Ivanovsky started to countersign the checks.

"No, no. Wait," Ben said quickly. "I'm not sure I can take your case. Remember how I said you'll need a lawyer who can work on this full time for a month? I've already got a busy month ahead of me. I wouldn't want to take your case and then not have the time to represent you as well as you deserve."

"But you must!" Ivanovsky said with sudden fierceness. "This is a very, very important case. When I told Mrs. Pugo I needed a very good lawyer, she said, 'Call Ben Corbin, here is his number. He is a good lawyer, Mikhail, the best that you can afford.' So you must take this case." He paused. "I need you."

Ben knew he was running late without looking at his watch. "I have to leave for a hearing now—I apologize for running out so quickly—but I'll take a close look at my calendar, and I'll call you tonight to let you know whether I can take the case." Ben was already thinking about the *Circuit Dynamics* case by the time he closed the door behind Ivanovsky.

Mikhail Ivanovsky took the elevator to the ground floor, walked out of the office building, and turned left. He walked north for a block and a half, then abruptly turned and walked back south for three blocks, intently looking at the other pedestrians as he went. Then he caught a cab to Union Station.

He got on his train, but got off two stops before his station. He watched with great care as the other passengers got off, noted where they went, and then waited alone on the platform for half an hour. When the next train came, he acted as if he were waiting for another train. When the doors were about to close, he leaped in, barely avoiding getting his arm caught. Seats were available, but he stood in the unheated, drafty vestibule for the rest of the trip. When the train reached the next stop, he got off, looked up and down the platform, and then jumped back on.

He got off again at the next station—his actual stop—and walked toward his apartment building. He stopped halfway there and stood in front of a storefront display for several minutes, staring in the window at the reflection of the street behind him. Then he walked briskly around the block twice, once going clockwise and once counterclockwise. Finally satisfied, he went home.

Ben knew he was losing the hearing. The defendants had sent Circuit Dynamics a document request asking for copies of all its tax returns since the day it was incorporated. This, of course, was highly intrusive and had nothing to do with whether the defendants had stolen Circuit Dynamics' software. Ben had objected to the request, and the defendants had filed a motion to compel, which Ben and defense counsel were now arguing in front of Judge Patrick Ryan.

"This isn't discovery, Your Honor, it's harassment," Ben insisted. "My client's tax returns are private documents that have no bearing on any issue in this case. I therefore ask the Court to deny defendants' motion."

Judge Ryan had nodded several times while Ben's opponent argued, but he looked at Ben with an expression of withering skepticism that is only truly mastered by trial-court judges and grade-school principals. He ran his fingers through his thin white hair and sighed. "Mr. Corbin, I'm going to grant the motion, and you're fortunate I don't sanction you as well. In a trade-secrets case, the plaintiff has to turn over lots of private documents, as you should know by now. Your client has ten days to produce the records."

"But Your Honor, these records have nothing to do with—"

"I've made my order, Counsel," Judge Ryan said flatly. He turned to his clerk. "Call the next case."

Hiding his disgust, Ben slipped the motion papers into his briefcase and strode out into the hallway. As he waited for the elevator, he found himself standing next to the lawyer who had just defeated him, a man named John Weaver. Weaver was a partner in a big litigation firm, which he seemed to think made him a courtroom heavyweight—even though he had never actually tried a case. He was the number-two lawyer on the case. That meant he made most of the decisions prior to trial. Steve Rocco, a well-known senior litigator, was the number one, but he wouldn't get significantly involved until the case got close to trial or settlement. "I never heard back from you on our settlement offer," Ben said evenly.

"That should tell you something, shouldn't it?" responded Weaver with a sardonic half smile. "I'll get you a formal response, but I can tell you what it will be. Frankly, your $25 million offer is laughable. We may offer a few thousand as a nuisance payment to make this case go away, but that's it."

Ben had expected something like that. "You're that sure you're going to win?"

"Yeah, I'm sure," Weaver said as the elevator doors opened and both men stepped in. "Your client's case is totally baseless."

"So was your motion, as we both know."

Weaver smiled but said nothing.

"But look what happened," Ben continued. "You can't be sure of anything in that courtroom. Judge Ryan is like a barroom drunk waving a gun around. Today it was pointed at me; tomorrow it may be pointing at you, and neither of us knows where it'll be pointing when it goes off. Your client faces liability of up to $100 million, and there's no way you can honestly tell them they have a seventy-five-percent chance of winning." The elevator jerked unsettlingly, then came to a stop. "Think about it," he said as the doors opened. "I wouldn't laugh too hard at $25 million if I were you."

Weaver chuckled. "But you aren't me, are you?" he said as they stepped out into the crowded courthouse lobby. "And you sure aren't Steve Rocco. Look, I said I'll get you a formal response to your offer and I'll do it, but you and your client will need to seriously rethink your position if you really want to settle this case."

The two lawyers parted ways as they walked through the banks of steel-and-glass doors surrounding the Daley Center, Chicago's massive high-rise state courthouse. A wide stone plaza sprawled immediately to the south, watched over by an ominous fifty-foot-tall sculpture by Pablo Picasso. The city of Chicago was quite proud of the statue but not quite sure what it was supposed to be. The prevailing theory among art critics was that it was the head of a woman. Ben had always thought that was questionable at best. The statue was black-and-gray steel, and it had wings, a long beak-like snout, and an empty ribcage. Several of Ben's clients had commented that it looked like a hungry vulture, which they found to be a particularly apt guardian for a hive of lawyers.

The city put the plaza to good use, and today it held a bustling farmers' market. A maze of stalls sold apple butter, gooseberry preserves, maple syrup, gourds, fresh flowers, and anything else that could legally be grown for profit in the Midwest. The chatter of rural sellers and suburban and urban buyers reminded Ben pleasantly of a county fair.

He spent twenty minutes wandering around the market, making an effort to shake off his irritation at the judge's ruling and Weaver's arrogance. He gradually relaxed as he walked, and he was actually in a good mood by the time he finished paying for a half dozen ears of sweet corn.

◆ ◆ ◆

"Will it be a problem to give them the tax records?" asked Noelle.

"Not really," said Ben. He and Noelle were sitting on their back deck, finishing a delicious dinner of grilled pork chops and the corn Ben had bought. They sipped iced tea and enjoyed the unseasonably warm October evening. The rich golden light from the low sun gave everything it touched a soft glow, bringing out the auburn highlights in Noelle's brown hair and making her deep-blue eyes strikingly luminous. Ordinarily, Ben would have said something nice to his wife, but tonight he was distracted. "Nothing in them has any impact on the case—a point that Judge Ryan completely ignored."

"Is that what's bugging you so much?"

Ben didn't answer right away. He thought for a moment, gazing at the row of oaks at the back of the yard, their red leaves beginning to thin as autumn took hold. "Well, I hate getting criticized by a judge, particularly when he's wrong," he said after a moment. "But what really bothered me was Weaver not taking me seriously."

"He'll learn his mistake in court," said Noelle.

Ben shrugged. "I hope so." He paused again. "You know what? Seven months ago, if I'd been in Weaver's shoes, I would have thought the same thing he did. I wouldn't have been pompous enough to say it, but I would have thought it. Maybe that's what's really eating at me; I'm afraid I'm becoming something I don't respect."

"What do you mean?"

"I left Beale & Ripley because I wanted to do something better. I was tired of always representing big corporations that used my cases as leverage in their business strategies. Even my big courtroom victories didn't have much real meaning."

She nodded. "I remember. You used to joke that your job was 'to redistribute wealth from the rich to the rich.'"

"Exactly, except it wasn't really a joke. I was 'kidding on the square,' as Uncle Mike used to say. That's why, when the time came for me to make a run for partner, we prayed about it. Would I spend even more hours in the office and out entertaining clients? Or would we give up the security and comfort of big-firm life so I could go out on my own and you could open your own accounting practice?"

She cocked her head and wrinkled her brow. "Yes, and we did exactly what we thought God was leading us to do. So why did you stop respecting yourself all of a sudden?"

"Look at me." Ben spread his arms. "I'm running around hustling nickel-and-dime cases to make my rent. I'm just a small-time solo practitioner. When I left Beale & Ripley, I wanted to take cases that would make a difference in people's lives. The only one I've got that fits that bill is *Circuit Dynamics*, and I just took a shot from the judge who'll be trying the case."

Noelle bit her lip. "Um, speaking of paying the rent . . ."

Ben winced. "Are we past due?"

She nodded. "The check from Anderson Engineering bounced, so I couldn't pay Chicago Properties. I called Ed Anderson and told him I was going to break his kneecaps if he didn't have a good check in my hands within twenty-four hours. He said he's bringing over a new check tomorrow morning, but even if it's good, it won't clear for at least another day after that."

Despite the bad news, Ben couldn't help smiling at the thought of his five-foot-four, 110-pound wife threatening to take out the knees of the burly engineer. "And by then we'll be past the grace period and we'll get hit with another $500 penalty, right?"

Noelle nodded.

Ben closed his eyes and sighed. "Any bright ideas?"

"We just don't have $3,000 free right now. We could try to take out a loan, but that would be hard to do on such short notice. Also, we could easily spend $500 on transaction costs and interest." She thought for a moment. "Is there any work you could do that could raise some quick cash? What about that guy the Pugos referred? What kind of work did he want?"

"Well, he wants a TRO and a preliminary injunction," Ben explained reluctantly. "He's willing to pay a $5,000 retainer."

"Terrific! That'll take care of the rent and leave enough extra to pay for the new computer we wanted."

Ben frowned. "This is *exactly* the kind of work I'm trying to get away from. It's just a two-bit little breach-of-contract case, but it could take up a lot of time over the next month, and I really need to focus on *Circuit Dynamics*. I was going to call this guy after dinner and tell him I couldn't take his case."

"Ben, we need that money. What if the Andersons bounce another check? Chicago Properties has already threatened to evict us once. You can't focus on *Circuit Dynamics* without an office."

Ben stared out into space, his jaws clenched in anger and frustration. The only way he was going to get more good cases was to do a good job on *Circuit Dynamics*, but he couldn't do that unless he gave it enough time and attention. But if he gave *Circuit Dynamics* the time and attention it deserved, he wouldn't be able to pay his bills—which would also prevent him from doing a good job. He felt trapped in a vicious cycle of mediocrity. He blamed his deadbeat clients for putting him in this bind, and he blamed himself for working for obvious (at least in hindsight) deadbeats, and particularly for not making them pay up front. But he didn't really have a choice. "Okay," he said at last, "I'll take the case."

Chapter Two
Hair on Fire

Ivanovsky was waiting outside Ben's office when the Corbins arrived at 8:05 the next morning. He wore a threadbare overcoat and a knit hat pulled down over his ears. When he saw Ben, he started toward him in a slightly shuffling walk, holding his battered briefcase in front of him with both hands. "Good morning, Mr. Ivanovsky," said Ben. "I hope you haven't been waiting long. I wasn't expecting you this early."

"I wanted to be here so you could start suing as soon as possible," Ivanovsky explained. "I have this money for you," he added, gesturing to the briefcase.

"Okay, good," said Ben as he unlocked the door. "Come on in." He was afraid the man would start handing him wads of cash in the hallway and quickly ushered him and Noelle into the lobby. "This is my wife, Noelle. She and I share offices, and she helps me run my practice."

Ivanovsky nodded to Noelle and shook her hand. "Pleased to meet you," he said. "Will you be working on the case too?"

"Nice to meet you too," she responded. "I'm not a lawyer, I'm an accountant. I handle the firm's finances."

"Oh, then I should give these to you," he said as he pulled out a sheaf of traveler's checks. "I need to sign these in front of you so Mr. Corbin can start on the court papers."

◆ ◆ ◆

Seven hours later, Ben was just finishing the first draft of a complaint and a set of TRO papers. He stopped typing and frowned at the computer as if it had let him down. The TRO argument didn't convince him. And if it didn't convince him, there was no way it would convince the judge.

The problem was that Ivanovsky was trying to enforce a contract. Courts typically don't grant TROs in contract cases because the proper sum of money is enough to make good nearly any breach of contract. If the plaintiff will be entitled only to a monetary judgment at the end of the case, the reasoning goes, it doesn't make sense to issue orders restraining the conduct of contract violators.

The only way Ben could think of to get around this rule was to show that money alone could never fully compensate Ivanovsky—and the only way to prove that would be to show that whatever was in the box was unique and could not be replaced no matter how much money he got. And that meant Ben needed to talk to his client.

Ivanovsky picked up the phone on the first ring. "Ivanovsky."

Ben identified himself and explained the situation. "So, Mr. Ivanovsky, I need to prove that the contents of that box are one-of-a-kind items."

"They are. I will put my hand on the Bible and swear it."

"Good, but you'll need to do more than that. You'll need to explain *why* they're unique. Can you describe any of these pieces for me?"

Ivanovsky was silent for several seconds. "I have never seen inside the box, but the man I talked to at Saint Vladimir—he said he thought the jewelries were very old and very extraordinary."

That might work, but more detail would be better. "Do you have the number of the man who told you that?"

"He is now in Russia and cannot be reached," Ivanovsky said firmly.

"Okay, can you give me any more details?"

"No. I told you, I have not seen inside the box." And that was all Ben could get out of him.

Ben finished the papers at 4:30.

At 4:55, he called American Union Bank's legal department to warn them that he was seeking a TRO and to ask them not to let anyone into box 4613 until the court had ruled. The bank officer readily agreed.

At 5:05 (after the bank had closed), Ben prepared to call Nikolai Zinoviev to alert him that they would be seeking a TRO against him at 8:30 the next morning. Ben technically didn't have to notify his opponent, but few judges would grant a TRO unless the opposing party had been given a chance to be heard.

Ben hesitated before dialing. These calls were never fun, but they could be useful. Defendants generally had no idea they were being sued until they got the TRO call, and they often went ballistic. If Ben played his cards right, however, he could sometimes talk defendants out of opposing a TRO, particularly in little cases like this.

After four rings, the answering machine picked up. "Hey, this is Nicki Zinoviev," announced a reedy male voice with a Russian accent. "I'm not here right now, so leave me your name and phone number and I'll get right back to you."

"Hi, Mr. Zinoviev. My name is Ben Corbin, and I represent Mikhail Ivanovsky. He has sued you for possession of the contents of a safe-deposit box, and I'll be appearing in front of Judge Harris at eight thirty tomorrow morning at the Daley Center to request an order preventing the box from being opened for the next ten days, so we can sort this all out. I'm having a set of the papers messengered to you tonight. You can appear in court tomorrow morning if you want, but you don't have to. As I mentioned, all we'll be doing is seeking an order to keep the box unopened for the next week and a half. Feel free to call me if you have any questions." He left his office number and hung up. Maybe that would keep Zinoviev out of court tomorrow morning, maybe not.

At 6:10, Ben and Noelle headed home for the last quiet evening they would have for a long time.

At 8:15 the next morning, Ben and Ivanovsky sat on one of the hard, plain wood benches at the back of Judge Alfred Harris's courtroom. His court had the same utilitarian steel-and-oak decor as all the courtrooms in the Daley Center, though it was larger than most. At least fifty lawyers and their clients packed the spectator benches behind the railing that split the courtroom in two. More sat at the two counsel tables in front of the railing and in the jury box, since no juries were needed for the emergency-motion call.

The lawyers were a Whitman's Sampler of the local bar: plaintiffs' attorneys in sport coats and questionable ties, buttoned-down defense-firm lawyers in dark suits, and a surprising number of pillars of the bar in three-thousand-dollar Armanis making country-club conversation with each other. The clients were a mixed bunch too, but their faces all wore the same nervous and uncomfortable expression.

"Do you see Nicki Zinoviev anywhere?" Ben whispered to his client.

Ivanovsky scanned the courtroom and shook his head. "He's not here."

"Good." Ben would still have to convince the judge to issue a TRO, but with any luck this would be an easy victory.

Ivanovsky v. Zinoviev was near the end of the emergency-motion call list, so they would be waiting for quite a while. Ben didn't mind. Judge Harris had a mercurial temper, and watching other lawyers go first would give Ben a pretty good idea what kind of mood the judge was in this morning. Also, although Ben didn't expect Ivanovsky to have to testify, it would be good experience for him to watch other witnesses on the stand and see how a courtroom worked.

"All rise," the bailiff ordered as Judge Harris entered through a door next to the raised dais that held his bench, a large piece of furniture that looked like a cross between a pulpit and an oversized desk. The judge was a tall, thin, olive-skinned man of uncertain ethnicity. He kept his ancestry vague to avoid being claimed by one of the city's numerous racial and ethnic bar associations—and pigeonholed by the others. He was almost completely bald, and Ben would have assumed he shaved his head were it not for the strip of short iron-gray hair that adorned the back of his head just above his neck. It was a perfect mirror image of his thick mustache.

Judge Harris was a sharp jurist who ran his courtroom well and did not suffer fools, gladly or otherwise. He worked through the pile of motions efficiently, ruling promptly after hearing the minimum-necessary argument and evidence. He seemed to be in a generally good mood that day, overlooking the minor gaffes and excesses of the attorneys appearing before him.

His mood changed, however, when he reached the motion immediately before Ben's. A flock of dour defense lawyers and bar luminaries stood up when the case was called, and crowded around the right-hand counsel table. A cluster of high-profile plaintiff's attorneys coalesced around the left table. After they had all stated their names for the record, Bill Corcoran, a well-known plaintiff's attorney, stepped up to the podium.

Judge Harris held up his hand. "I've read the papers and the legal authorities cited by both sides, Mr. Corcoran, and there's no need for argument. Your petition is denied."

Murmurs arose from both tables, and the defense lawyers started to get up, but Corcoran was not so easily dissuaded. "Your Honor, if I might be heard on this matter. This is an awkward issue that—"

"It *is* awkward—for you," interrupted the judge. "That's why you lost. Now, do you have anything to add to what's in your papers?"

"We have several witnesses in the courtroom, Your Honor, who are ready to testify—"

"To exactly what is in their affidavits, correct?" interrupted the judge again, his irritation showing in his voice.

There was a history here. Corcoran and Harris detested each other. They had clashed before Harris took the bench, and Corcoran had contributed heavily to Harris's opponents each time he had been up for reelection. Making matters worse, Corcoran was not used to getting slapped down by judges and did not take it well. "I am entitled to make my record, Judge, and I could do so very quickly if I could speak without interruption."

Judge Harris glared at him. "Mr. Corcoran, your record is adequately made by your papers. Hearing you and your witnesses regurgitate what I have already read will do nothing but . . ."

Ben was distracted by a nudge in his side, followed by whispering in his ear.

He turned to Ivanovsky and whispered back, "Write me a note, we're—"

"Mr. Corbin," the judge said loudly from the bench, "you know better than to talk in my courtroom!"

Ben's face turned hot and he felt like a fourth grader caught whispering in class. "Yes, Your Honor. I apologize."

The judge turned back to lecturing Corcoran. "A TRO is an extraordinary remedy. I do not grant them lightly or often, and I never grant them unless I am convinced they are absolutely necessary. This is a commercial dispute, Mr. Corcoran, and I am not going to impose a TRO simply because your client believes the defendants have violated their contractual duties. I have seen very few cases in which a contractual breach could not be remedied by an adequate application of money, and you have not convinced me that this is such a case. Now, I have a courtroom to run, so please step away from the podium so the next case can be called."

Corcoran did not move. "If the Court would just grant me five minutes to—"

Judge Harris's face darkened and the veins in his neck bulged. "If you do not step away from that podium by the count of three, there is a gentleman here with a pistol"—he pointed to the bailiff—"who will take you to jail. One . . . two . . ."

Corcoran reluctantly stepped back from the podium, his teeth clenched with suppressed fury. Judge Harris stood, and so did everyone else in the courtroom. "We'll take a five-minute recess and then finish the call."

Terrific, Ben thought as the judge walked out. *Now he's in a bad mood, irritated with me, and unlikely to grant a TRO in a contract case. At least this should be uncontested.* After the judge left, Ben turned to his client. "I know I never told you this, but never, ever talk when court is in session. Now, what did you want to tell me?"

"He is here. Nicki Zinoviev. He walked in three minutes ago, and he sits over there." He nodded toward the bench across from theirs.

Ben glanced over. A man wearing a double-breasted black suit with a matching black shirt and tie was doing his best to look nonchalant, but his eyes were wary. A gold watch showed at the end of his left shirt-sleeve and a heavy gold bracelet adorned his right wrist, as did what looked like the end of a tattoo. He had long, thinning black hair slicked back into a short ponytail. Ben counted three earring holes in his left ear. "He looks like a drug dealer," he whispered back to his client.

"He is a drug dealer."

"Are you sure?" Ben asked.

Ivanovsky nodded.

Ben smiled, planning ways to use the information on cross-examination. "Any convictions?"

Ivanovsky shrugged. "I do not know."

Ben was about to follow up with more questions when another man walked in and sat down next to Zinoviev. Ben stared in surprise. "I wonder what *he's* doing here," he said softly.

"Who is he?"

"Anthony Simeon. He's one of the ten or twelve best litigators in Chicago. I'd think this case was a little beneath him."

The judge came back in and nodded to the clerk. "Line twenty-four, Ivanovsky versus Zeen . . . Zeeno . . ."

"Zinoviev," supplied Anthony Simeon in his rich baritone as he approached the podium, giving the clerk a friendly smile. The clerk smiled back.

Simeon was close to seventy, but his perfectly coiffed gray hair, perpetually tanned face, and vigorous, engaging courtroom manner made him appear twenty years younger. He was a thickset man of medium height, but he had an outstanding tailor who made him look burly rather than overweight. He had an impressive book of a business, though he tended to look at his clients' bank balances a lot more closely than their ethics.

Both the bench and the bar respected Simeon, but they did not particularly like him. Not that anyone actually *disliked* him—he was cordial and had a legendary sense of humor—but the general feeling was that he was best kept at arm's length. He was a man of many acquaintances but no close friends: a polished gentleman brawler with a tendency to play hardball with friend and foe alike. That made him an unreliable ally and earned him the sobriquet "the Velvet Dagger."

The two lawyers stated their appearances for the record, and Judge Harris immediately started questioning Ben. "Why should I issue a TRO here?"

"To preserve unique property, Your Honor. My client is entitled to a safe-deposit box containing one-of-a-kind jewelry that Mr. Zinoviev is now attempting to—"

"Surely this jewelry has a monetary value. What did your client pay for it?"

"Five thousand dollars, Your Honor, but—"

The judge held up his hand and looked at Simeon. "Is your client willing to post a five-thousand-dollar bond?"

Simeon glanced back at his client, who in turn looked at two men sitting in the back of the courtroom. One of them nodded. "Yes, Your Honor," said Simeon.

The judge turned back to Ben. "Problem solved, no?"

"I'm afraid not. We're talking about one-of-a-kind items of jewelry here that can't be replaced by any amount of money."

"You keep saying 'one-of-a-kind,' but that's just a phrase from your client's affidavit. What exactly is in the box that's so unique?"

"As described in Mr. Ivanovsky's affidavit, he only has secondhand reports that generally describe the jewelry. He has never been able to look inside the box himself, so—"

"So you can't carry your burden of proof on this point, can you?"

"I think we have, Your Honor," Ben replied, putting as much certainty in his voice as he could muster. "Under the law, it's sufficient for purposes of a TRO to allege uniqueness. This is an emergency proceeding with no time for discovery. Once we've had an opportunity to look in that box, we'll be able to provide more detail."

"That's my point. If you don't know what's in the box, you don't know whether you're entitled to a TRO. And if you don't know whether you're entitled to a TRO, you certainly aren't going to persuade me to issue one."

Ben was about to lose, and he knew it. He decided to take a chance. "Your Honor, there's one person in this courtroom who knows exactly what's in that box, and that's Mr. Zinoviev. I ask the Court's permission to call him as a witness."

The judge turned to Simeon. "Counselor?"

"Your Honor, my client will be happy to testify when proper notice has been given, but it is highly unfair to ambush him like this. It is Mr. Corbin's duty to present the Court with evidence sufficient to justify issuing a TRO—as Your Honor just noted, an extraordinary remedy—and he has not done so. If he had wanted Mr. Zinoviev's testimony, he could easily have included a notice or a subpoena with the TRO papers he served last night. He hasn't done that either. We can produce Mr. Zinoviev for deposition in the next few days, and Mr. Corbin can take his testimony then."

"And in the meantime, he'll be free to dispose of that jewelry, right?" observed the judge.

"A TRO can only issue on a proper showing, Your Honor. In the absence of that showing, there's no reason to prevent my client from disposing of his property as he sees fit."

"Your Honor, the only way I can make the showing you requested is to put Mr. Zinoviev on the stand," Ben interjected.

The judge looked at each of them thoughtfully for a moment. "Mr. Simeon, you are correct that there is no basis to compel your client to testify at this hearing, but Mr. Corbin is also correct that he can't make his TRO showing without Mr. Zinoviev's testimony. Since Mr. Zinoviev is sitting in this room right now, I'm reluctant to deny a TRO just because he hasn't been identified in advance as a witness. So I'll tell you what I'm going to do. You can either let your client take the stand now or I can make certain assumptions about his failure to testify and issue a TRO that will last until twenty-four hours after his deposition takes place. You choose."

"May I have ten minutes to discuss this with my client?"

Judge Harris glanced at the clock on the wall. "You can have five."

The judge went into his chambers and Simeon, Zinoviev, and the two men from the back bench filed out into the hall.

Ben guessed that Simeon would put Zinoviev on the stand rather than agree to a TRO. Otherwise, the judge might suspect that Zinoviev's unvarnished testimony was bad for his case and needed to be polished before his deposition. Also, as a practical matter, it was easier to get a judge to continue a TRO that was already in place than to enter one *ab initio*.

Ben spent his five minutes scribbling down notes for his cross-examination and asking Ivanovsky terse, whispered questions: "Who were those men in the back of the courtroom?" Ivanovsky didn't know. "Did Zinoviev have any criminal convictions, whether for drug dealing or not?" Ivanovsky shrugged. "What price had the second buyer agreed to pay for the jewelry?" He didn't know that either. "Who was that buyer?" No idea.

"But you will win?" Ivanovsky asked anxiously.

"I'm not sure," replied Ben. "That'll depend on what Zinoviev says on the witness stand."

"But you must win!"

"I'll do what I can."

The judge reappeared just as Ivanovsky seemed about to say something else. A few seconds later Anthony Simeon and company reentered the courtroom and walked up to the podium. "Your Honor, we have decided to allow Mr. Zinoviev to testify, though we wish the record to reflect our continuing objection."

"So noted," said the judge. He gestured to the witness box. "Mr. Zinoviev."

Simeon sat down at the defense-counsel table and watched with an air of faint disinterest as Ben approached the podium, his heart pounding. He had never done a cross-examination without days of preparation. He also had never done one without first taking the witness's deposition. One of the time-honored maxims of cross-examination is "Never ask a question that you don't know the answer to"—but Ben was about to ask lots of questions that he had no idea how the witness would answer. And he was going to do it on five minutes' notice in front of an unforgiving judge and the toughest opponent he had ever faced.

Ben said a quick prayer, took a deep breath, and smiled at the witness. "Good morning, Mr. Zinoviev. I'd like to ask you a few questions about safe-deposit box 4613 in the American Union Bank on LaSalle Street. Did you sell the contents of that box to Mikhail Ivanovsky?"

"No."

"Did he give you $5,000 last Tuesday?"

"He loaned it to me, yes. I tried to pay it back, but he wouldn't take it. He insisted that I give him the box instead."

"Why did you ask Mr. Ivanovsky for a loan?"

Simeon stood up. "Objection, relevance. This is getting pretty far afield, Your Honor. Mr. Zinoviev is here to answer questions about the jewelry in that box, not his personal finances."

The judge nodded. "Sustained. Mr. Corbin, at some point you'll have to convince me that your client had a contract to buy that jewelry, but today your examination is limited to whether that jewelry is unique and irreplaceable."

"Thank you, Your Honor," Ben said as Simeon sat down. "Mr. Zinoviev, have you ever looked inside that box?"

"Yes."

"What's in there?"

He shrugged. "Some old pearl earrings, my brother's passport, a few papers, a couple of watches. Nothing special or one-of-a-kind."

"What kind of watches?"

The witness thought for a moment. "A Seiko, I think. A Rolex, too—or it says it's a Rolex, anyway. Some of the gold is rubbing off, and I don't think that happens with real Rolexes." A chuckle ran through the courtroom. Zinoviev grinned and leaned back into the witness chair.

"Anything else?"

"That's it."

"Have you had the jewelry appraised?"

"No."

"Do you have any idea which piece is most valuable?"

He shrugged again. "Probably the Seiko. It looks almost new. The earrings might be worth something, but the pearls are pretty small."

"You recently sold this jewelry, correct?"

"Correct."

"To whom?"

"A trading company. I don't remember the exact name."

"Are those gentlemen back there affiliated with this company?" Ben pointed to the two mystery men sitting in the back of the courtroom.

Zinoviev sat forward in his chair and it creaked. "I think so."

"What are their names?"

Zinoviev glanced at them nervously. "I think one of them is named Anton and the other is Josef. I don't know their last names."

"Did you let them look in the box before selling the contents to them?"

"Yes."

"Did you let Mr. Ivanovsky?"

"I told you, I never agreed to sell the jewelry to him, so no."

I walked into that one, thought Ben, kicking himself. "How much did you sell the jewelry for?"

"Objection." Simeon stood again. "This is all outside the scope of this hearing."

"Overruled," said the judge. He glanced at the clock. "But do try to wrap this up in the next few minutes."

"I will," said Ben. He was running out of questions, in any event. "How much did you sell it for?" he repeated.

"I don't remember exactly."

"Do you remember generally?"

"Not really."

"When did you agree to sell the jewelry?"

Zinoviev hesitated. "Last Thursday."

"So you sold the jewelry last Thursday, but you have no idea how much you sold it for, right?"

"Objection," interjected Simeon. "He's arguing with the witness."

"And he's winning," said the judge, who was now watching with interest. "Overruled. This is well within the bounds of permissible cross-examination."

Asking questions about the men on the back bench seemed to make Zinoviev uncomfortable, so Ben decided to do it again. He pointed at them. "Do you think Anton or Josef might have any idea how much they paid you?"

Ben could see tiny drops of sweat glistening between the strands of Zinoviev's sparse black hair. "I didn't say I had no idea how much they paid, I just said I couldn't remember the figure."

"So what do you remember?"

"I think it was somewhere around $100,000." He was flustered and didn't realize his mistake until the words were already out of his mouth.

Gotcha! "You earlier testified that the Seiko watch was the most valuable of the four items in that box. Would it be fair to say that it accounted for forty percent of the purchase price?"

Zinoviev now sat on the edge of his seat, shoulders slightly hunched as if he were expecting someone to hit him. "I don't know."

"Thirty percent?"

"I don't know."

"But certainly more than twenty-five percent, right?"

Zinoviev sat in miserable silence for several seconds. "I guess so."

"No further questions." Ben returned to his seat, walking on air.

Simeon stood up, but the judge held up his hand. "May I ask a few clarifying questions, Your Honor?" Simeon asked.

"Not unless you can clarify how a Seiko watch can be worth more than $25,000 and not be unique," the judge replied. He didn't wait for Simeon to respond. "I've heard enough to convince me that whatever is in that box is pretty unusual and should stay there until we can have a full preliminary injunction trial, at which point you can ask as many questions as you want. Now, I've got another trial starting in here in half an hour, and I needed to meet with the two sides ten minutes ago to rule on some motions *in limine*. I want you gentlemen to go into the cloakroom back there and work out a discovery-and-trial schedule. Then go to my chambers, and my clerk will give you the next available trial date."

The two lawyers caucused with their clients in preparation for meeting in the little room that opened off the entrance to the courtroom. As soon as they were alone, Ivanovsky grabbed Ben's hand in both of his and shook it vigorously. "You were magnificent!" he said, his voice quavering with emotion. "I thought for sure we were going to lose, especially after I made the judge mad at you for talking. But then you put Zinoviev up there and showed the judge he was lying and he gave us this TRO! Thank you so very much!"

Ben smiled and gently retrieved his hand. "You're very welcome. This is a significant win for us, but it's just the first round. Remember what I said about litigating with our hair on fire? That's what happens now. Do you have any appointments during the next month that you can't cancel?"

Ivanovsky shook his head.

"Good. Wait out here and I'll go see if Simeon is ready."

Ben found the distinguished defense attorney waiting for him in the cloakroom. It might at one time have been used to store coats, but now it served as an informal conference room for attorneys appearing before Judge Harris. It held a well-used round table and five unmatched chairs, the best of which was now occupied by Anthony Simeon. Ben sat down facing him, and they quickly agreed to extend the TRO from ten days to thirty to give them both time to prepare their cases. They then hammered out a schedule of deadlines for the coming month. As they sat waiting for the clerk to finish in the courtroom, Simeon turned to Ben and said, "By the way, congratulations. That was a nice piece of cross out there."

"Thanks, Tony," said Ben, who was still a little giddy from his victory. "It's always nice to get a win, particularly when the competition is so good."

Simeon's smile was both affable and hard edged. "Savor the moment."

Chapter Three
Secret Police

Twenty-two phone messages and forty-three e-mails awaited Ben when he finally reached his office at two forty-five the next afternoon. He had spent most of the morning at Circuit Dynamics, preparing their tax returns for review by John Weaver and his minions. Then he'd spent forty-five minutes taking a slow and construction-intensive drive downtown. After that, he'd wasted two hours cooling his heels with roughly a hundred other lawyers at the "cattle call," where a single judge went through several dozen cases and checked on the status of each one while everyone else waited. Ben had once calculated that the collective billing rate for all the lawyers kept loitering by the cattle call was about $20,000 per hour.

One of the waiting phone messages, from a college friend of Noelle's, piqued Ben's curiosity. A friendly woman's voice with a slight but noticeable Russian accent said, "Hi, Ben, it's Elena Kamenev. Congratulations on your TRO win yesterday. Please give me a call when you get a chance. And say hi to Noelle from me. Thanks!"

Elena Kamenev was a tall, athletic woman who would have been a serious contender for the Russian women's biathlon team in the Lillehammer Winter Olympics, but she'd injured her knee in a fall. Her athletic career over, Elena had decided to settle in the United States and become an American citizen. She had subsequently joined the FBI, which always had openings for native Russian speakers who could shoot. She now lived in Chicago and occasionally had lunch with the Corbins or met them at alumni functions. But Ben hadn't seen her for over a year, and he didn't think Noelle had either.

He played the message twice, then sat back in his chair and stared absently out the window at the empty offices in the building across the street. How did Elena know about the hearing yesterday? Why would she call him and not Noelle? He buzzed Noelle to get her thoughts, but she wasn't in. He wondered if there was any reason to wait to call Elena back, decided there wasn't, and picked up the phone.

"Hi, Elena. It's Ben Corbin returning your call. What's up?"

"Hi, Ben. Thanks for getting back to me. How do you like having your own firm?"

"It can be a headache, but it can also be lots of fun. There's nothing quite like seeing your name on the door when you walk in each morning."

"And how are things going in court? I understand you won a TRO hearing yesterday. Congratulations."

"Thanks. It's always nice to win. By the way, how did you know about that? The FBI isn't investigating me, is it?"

She laughed. "No, no, of course not. We're just keeping an eye on a client of yours."

That couldn't be good news. "Who?"

"Mikhail Ivanovsky. He is a person of interest to us."

"Really?" Ben was genuinely surprised. "What's so interesting about him? Or can't you tell me that?"

"I can't tell you. Sorry."

"Can you tell me why you're investigating him?"

"We're not really investigating him," she explained. "We do routine monitoring of anyone in the US with certain types of backgrounds. We noticed that he had filed a lawsuit and I saw that you were representing him, so I thought I'd give you a call."

"Okay," said Ben, thinking quickly. "So what can I do for you? I assume you've seen the complaint and the TRO filings."

"I read them this morning. We're not looking for anything in particular. We'd just appreciate it if you kept us in the loop about developments in the case."

"Why's that?"

"As I mentioned, your client is a person of interest to us, and Nikolai Zinoviev has a pretty long rap sheet. Any connection between the two of them is something we want to keep tabs on."

"I see," said Ben, jotting down a note to track down Zinoviev's criminal records. "So do you think there might be more to this case than a box full of jewelry?"

"Do you?"

Ben thought for a moment. Zinoviev was lying, of course, but what was he lying about? Just the type of jewelry in the box? Maybe . . . but maybe not. "It wouldn't shock me."

"What do you think it is?"

A box full of drug money, or maybe evidence of a crime, Ben surmised. *Either of those would explain the men in the back of the courtroom.* He had to be careful what he said, though. Elena was a friend, but she was also FBI. And it suddenly occurred to Ben that he wasn't entirely sure his client was clean in all this. "It could be lots of things," he said carefully. "What do you guys think?"

"Nothing really," Elena replied casually. "Like I said, this is just routine monitoring, not an active investigation. I'd appreciate it if you'd send me copies of court papers, let me know about upcoming dates, and that sort of thing. It's nothing I couldn't get from the public record, but it would make my life easier if I didn't have to go dig through the court file every week to find out what's going on. We'll reimburse you for copying and postage costs."

Sounds harmless, Ben thought. "I'll need my client's permission, of course, but I don't see why he'd have a problem with what you're asking."

"Actually . . . he hasn't been that cooperative in the past. He can be a little . . ." She paused, searching for the right word. "Cranky. But if you have to ask, you have to ask."

"I have to ask. I'm sorry, but my first duty is always to my client. So, how are things at the Bureau?" They chatted for several more minutes, sharing news about mutual friends and catching up on developments in each other's lives.

After they hung up, Ben immediately dialed Ivanovsky's number. He knew he probably should have collected his thoughts a little more before calling, but there were some questions he wanted answered *now*.

"Ivanovsky," said a familiar man's voice.

"Hi, it's Ben Corbin. I just got a call from the FBI, and there are a few things I'd like to talk to you about."

Ivanovsky paused for a heartbeat before responding. "What did they want?"

"They asked if we would keep them informed of developments in the case—"

"No."

"—and give them copies of any court filings."

"No."

That sent up a big red flag. Through hard experience, Ben had learned that people who wanted to keep information from the FBI generally had reasons for doing so. "Why not?"

"They are secret police. I never cooperate with secret police. You cannot trust them."

"The agent who called is an old friend of mine," protested Ben. "I've known her for years."

"No," repeated Ivanovsky firmly. "Maybe she is a nice person, but she is secret police. My lawyer must not be informing to secret police."

"We wouldn't be 'informing,'" Ben replied. "She's not asking for anything she couldn't get by walking over to the Daley Center and looking in the court file."

"Let her look in the court file. You must not help her."

Ben took a deep breath. "Mr. Ivanovsky, what is in that safe-deposit box?"

He paused before answering. "Jewelries. I told you this already."

"Anything else?"

He hesitated again. "I do not know. You heard Nicki say in court there is an old passport."

"Why would those men in the back of the courtroom pay $100,000 for some jewelry and an old passport?"

"I do not know."

"That's an awful lot to pay for some jewelry, isn't it?"

"Maybe it is. It depends on the jewelries."

"Is it possible that there's something else in there that would be worth $100,000?"

"Maybe," admitted Ivanovsky. "I told you I have never seen inside the box."

"What might that something be?"

"I do not know!" Ivanovsky shot back. "You are speaking as if you do not trust me."

That, of course, was entirely true. Ben had started the conversation with some suspicions, and now he had more. In fact, he was beginning to have doubts about whether he could continue representing this man. He didn't want to become an unwitting accomplice in some crime. "Mr. Ivanovsky, I can't think of a single good reason not to cooperate with the FBI, but I can think of plenty of bad ones. Before I can continue representing you, I need you to convince me that you have a good reason. I cannot allow you to use my services to commit a crime or a fraud, and if I suspect you're doing that, I have to withdraw from this case. I—"

"No! No! No!" exclaimed Ivanovsky, cutting Ben off. "I am committing no crimes or frauds! I promise this! I swear on twenty Bibles and all holy things!"

"Then why don't you want me to talk to the FBI?"

Ivanovsky didn't respond for several seconds. "You will stop being my lawyer if I do not tell you?"

"Yes, I'm afraid I'll have no choice."

"Okay, I will tell you this thing," he said. "But it is shameful for me and you must promise never to tell it to anyone else."

"Of course not. Anything you say to me stays secret."

"Okay. I will tell you the whole story so you understand." Ivanovsky sighed and his voice calmed. "I began at the university in 1946, one year after the Great Patriotic War against the Germans ended. It was a glorious time for a young fool who did not doubt what he was told. Many countries were becoming socialist around the world. Soviet teachers and engineers and doctors were going to them to help our new comrades rebuild their countries and advance their societies. I thought that we were finally done with war and that we could now stop spending our energy on fighting and begin making a world with peace and enough to eat spreading out from the Soviet Union.

"I decided to study microbiology so that I could someday find cures for diseases afflicting many peoples, particularly poor victims of imperialism. I progressed quickly in my studies and made good marks on all exams.

"Then one day, the professor who taught the class on infectious organisms asked me to see him in his office after the daily lecture. He was a great and famous scientist named Pavel Vukov. So I went to see him. He said, 'Mikhail, you are a very intelligent young man and you can do great service to the motherland.' I asked him what this service was, and he said, 'A great struggle is beginning between world socialism and capitalist imperialism. The war against the fascists was just the beginning to this struggle. It will not stop while both sides still exist. They will use all possible weapons to destroy us, and we must be ready to respond the same way. In the history of the world, germs have killed more millions than all weapons ever created by men. We must harness this power of the germ to protect ourselves, Mikhail. Will you help us to do this?'

"I said yes to Professor Vukov and began working with him right away. Every day after classes, I would spend hours helping him with his experiments and researches."

"Wait," Ben interrupted. "You were part of the Soviet germ-warfare program?"

"Yes," Ivanovsky said, "but I did not make these weapons. I did decontaminations and inspections."

"Okay, uh, please go on," Ben said. He could see why his client would interest the FBI.

"Professor Vukov and I, we became very close and he was like a second father to me. He helped me to get my PhD, and I did many researches for him during five years. We would eat our meals together and I often slept at his house when we had worked late. I would stay in the room of his son who died in the war." His voice suddenly wavered, and he stopped for a few seconds.

Ben said nothing, waiting for his client to continue.

Ivanovsky took a deep breath and mastered himself again. "Then I did this stupid and shameful thing. We were trying to find ways to make our germs resist the decontaminating chemicals used by the Americans. I wanted to do experiments on a new method I had thought, but he said, 'No, it will not work, Mikhail.' I said that the theories of Lysenko predicted that it would work, so we should try, but he said, 'Lysenko is a fraud. Do not waste time on this foolish idea.' Ben, do you know who Lysenko was?"

Ben searched back through dim memories of his single college biology course. "No, I'm afraid I don't."

"Do not be afraid; it is good that you do not know about such a man. Trofim Lysenko was a biologist who had certain scientific theories. These theories were very wrong in many ways and Lysenko was a bad scientist, but Stalin thought his ideas were socialist and progressive. So Lysenko was made in charge of all scientists and his theories were taught in Soviet universities as absolute truth.

"So when Professor Vukov said, 'Lysenko is a fraud,' this troubled me. Had my other professors and my textbooks taught me lies? Or was this great man who was my mentor lying? And I did not like that he had said my idea was foolish.

"The political officer working with our team was a young man only a little older than I. He and I would sometimes drink vodka and play chess together, and I thought he was my friend. I said to him, 'Alexander, may I ask you something?' He said yes. I said, 'Do not repeat this to anyone, but Professor Vukov says that Lysenko is a fraud. Is this true? I must know so that I can do my researches correctly.' He said, 'Professor Lysenko is a great man. It is good that you have told me this, Mikhail.'

"The next morning, Professor Vukov was gone. The head of our laboratory said that Professor Vukov had become an enemy of the revolution and that I should take over his work. The first experiment I did was to test the Lysenkoist idea I'd had. It failed completely."

Dr. Ivanovsky simply stopped talking, and it took Ben a few seconds to realize that he was done with his story. "That's terrible that they did that to Professor Vukov, but I'm not sure I understand what you're saying. You don't want to talk to the FBI because the KGB arrested your mentor?"

"Yes. Secret police are secret police—in America or Russia. They are all secret police."

"But the FBI is nothing like Stalin's KGB," protested Ben.

"They are different and they are the same," replied Dr. Ivanovsky. "Maybe the FBI does not make people disappear for having wrong opinions. Maybe the FBI works for a democracy and not a dictatorship. But they are the same in one very, very important way: it is their job to learn things and do things for the state. It is not their job to help me or you or to be our friends. Maybe they are helping and friendly now, but their help and friendliness go away as soon as being your friend stops helping the state. To give them information is like going into the den of a tiger to feed him. He may be very nice to you for a long time, but one day maybe you run out of food and he will be hungry and looking at you, and then you will wish you had never fed him at all."

Ben decided to try one more time. "All she's asking is that we send her publicly available documents. That seems pretty innocent."

"Nothing the secret police does is all innocent," Dr. Ivanovsky persisted. "I do not know everything they could do with these documents. Do you? Also, if we give them these papers now, it will be harder to say no to them the next time they are asking for information, and who is to say they will be innocent then? No, Ben, it is better not to walk into the den of a tiger in the first place."

The tiger's-den analogy obviously was well established in Dr. Ivanovsky's mind—and probably had been for decades. Ben realized it gave the old scientist a comfortable and clear-cut reason to avoid potential entanglements with law enforcement where he might find himself in over his head. There was little chance he would rethink it based solely on the suggestion of a young lawyer whom he had known for only a few days. "Okay, I'll tell her we can't help her."

Ivanovsky released a breath. "Thank you, Ben."

As Ben hung up the phone, he suddenly felt very tired. He had worked until ten o'clock last night and had headed out the door again at six forty-five that morning. He was beginning to feel it. "Maybe the big-firm life wasn't so bad after all," he muttered as he rubbed his eyes and yawned.

He got up and walked over to the coffeemaker in the file room. The pot held about two inches of poisonous-looking black sludge. "Oops!" said a voice from behind him. "Would you like me to make a fresh pot?"

Ben turned and saw Susan Molfino, his office manager/receptionist/secretary/file clerk, bustling in, nearly hidden by a large stack of folders. Susan was a tiny and tirelessly perky woman with the energy of a toddler on espresso. She never drank coffee and therefore didn't always keep as close an eye on the coffeemaker as she should. She was an otherwise-outstanding employee, however, so Ben and Noelle forgave this flaw—though Ben in particular occasionally suffered for it. Fortunately, there was a good coffee shop less than a block away, and it was open late.

"That's okay," said Ben as he flipped off the machine and poured the syrupy mess into the sink. "I'll just go down to the Mud Hole. I could use a little fresh air anyway."

On his way out of the office, Ben stuck his head into Noelle's doorway and saw that she was back at her desk. "Hey, I'm about to make a Mud run. Want to come with?"

She looked up from a pile of financial printouts and smiled. "Sure. I haven't seen you all day."

The Mud Hole had only three small tables, but it did a brisk takeout business among Chicagoans who knew their coffee. The two brothers from Seattle who ran the place were as passionate and expert in the art of making caffeine-based drinks as any sculptor or painter was at his art. They had even built a hot-sand pit in the back of their kitchen to make true Turkish and Greek coffee. "Hello, Ben. Hello, Noelle," said Brett, the younger brother, as the Corbins walked in. "What would you like this afternoon?"

"I'll have a decaf mocha," said Noelle.

"And I'll have a double Turkish Hammer," said Ben.

"That'll keep you up until midnight," Noelle warned. "Or is that the point?"

Ben sighed. "I've got a mediation statement due tomorrow in the *Bock* case, and I haven't even started it. It's going to be another long night for me."

"That's two in a row, Ben. Is it going to let up anytime soon?"

He shook his head. "I'm overcommitted this month. It seems like I'll be spending half my time on *Circuit Dynamics*, half on *Ivanovsky*, and half on all my other cases."

"Do you need to head back to the office?"

"Not quite yet. Something just happened that I'd like your thoughts on. Are you up for a quick walk in Grant Park?"

"Sure," said Noelle, looking at him with curiosity. "I've been stuck inside all day."

Grant Park is a long strip of green between downtown Chicago and the lakefront. It's bordered on the north by a cluster of upscale apartment buildings, on the south by Soldier Field, and on the west by the business district. To the east are the wide waters of Lake Michigan. The park is a favorite spot for joggers, bikers, open-air-concert organizers, and anyone who wants to escape from the constant rush of business in the Loop. As Ben and Noelle turned from the crowded sidewalk onto a quiet, maple-lined path, Noelle turned to Ben and said, "Okay, so what's up?"

Ben described his conversations with Elena and Dr. Ivanovsky. "And now I know why he's 'a person of interest' to the FBI. He's hiding something, but I'm not sure what," he concluded.

They walked along in silence for several seconds, the fallen leaves crunching under their feet. "Well, do you think he's hiding something problematic?" Noelle asked.

Ben shrugged. "He doesn't have a lot of guile, so I think I can generally tell when he's lying to me. I'm pretty sure he was telling the truth about why he doesn't want to talk to the FBI, but not about what's in the box. Do I think that overall he's hiding something 'problematic'?" He paused for a moment and looked out over Lake Michigan. Its slate-gray surface was broken into choppy waves capped by dirty white foam, harbingers of an approaching storm. "I doubt it. He doesn't seem like the type who would murder the man who used to own the box or something like that. I'd say Dr. Ivanovsky is a pretty good guy, but he's also pretty eccentric. And for some reason he doesn't want to tell me everything about this case."

"You're a good judge of character," commented Noelle. "If you think he's clean, he probably is."

"He's probably clean, at least as far as this case goes. My guess is that he somehow got wind that there's something valuable in that box. Maybe he knows what it is, maybe not. I'll bet Nicki Zinoviev didn't know, but he needed cash right away and he isn't all that bright. So he sold the box to Dr. Ivanovsky without looking inside. Later, he realized that wasn't a good idea and went to the bank to look in the box. Did he see a couple of cheap watches and some junk? No. He saw something a lot more valuable. Something he doesn't want to tell the judge about. Maybe something that has the FBI interested in this case."

"Do you think it has anything to do with Dr. Ivanovsky being a germ-warfare expert?"

Ben kicked a stone down the path. "Good question. That's another thing I'm going to look into. I doubt that's what it is, though. I mean, why would anyone put Soviet germ-warfare stuff in a bank box in Chicago? Also, *Ivanovsky* didn't put anything in the box, and he's the only one we know of here who has anything to do with germ warfare.

"From what Ivanovsky told me, Zinoviev's brother was a smuggler, not a bioweapons scientist. He probably stashed something in the box—maybe extremely valuable jewelry—and died without telling his brother about it. But he told someone, and ultimately Dr. Ivanovsky heard about it. I'll bet his Russian pension isn't that generous, and he plans to supplement it by selling whatever's in the box."

"And that makes you uncomfortable," commented Noelle. "I can see why."

"Yeah, the whole thing makes me uncomfortable." They came upon the stone again, and Ben kicked it hard this time, taking out his frustration on the chunk of limestone. "I'm not sure I can keep representing him under these circumstances. I'm not concerned about breaking any legal ethical rules here, but I don't just want to do what's ethical. I want to do what's right. As a Christian lawyer, is it okay for me to help my client get a treasure that may well be the product of some crime?"

"Well, aren't you just *speculating* that it would be illegal or immoral for him to own whatever's in the box? You won't know one way or the other until you open it."

"True," said Ben. "Besides, the only real alternative I've got is to withdraw from the case and let this Zinoviev guy win. Even if the box is full of stolen diamonds or something, it's not like I have a choice between giving them to Dr. Ivanovsky and giving them to the true owner. As a practical matter, I have to choose between giving them to the thief's brother and possibly giving them to an old treasure hunter."

"And if you find anything suspicious when you open the box, you can call the police then."

"I suppose," said Ben, though he didn't relish the idea of calling the cops on his own client. "It's not like I haven't had clients with secrets before. It just bugs me when I've got a case where all the pieces don't add up as a result. It's hard to be an effective lawyer when that happens."

"But you can keep working on the case, right?" Noelle asked a little anxiously. "I mean, we did accept Dr. Ivanovsky's retainer, and . . . um, we're not really able to give any of it back."

Ben rolled his eyes. "When do I get to start working on the real cases, the ones we opened this practice to handle? We were going to serve Almighty God, not the almighty dollar, remember? And here I am grubbing for greenbacks just to keep the doors open."

"Is that a long way of saying, 'Yes, I can keep working on the case'?"

He sighed. "I suppose so."

Chapter Four
Discovery

Ben sat back and looked at the to-do list he had just typed up for the *Ivanovsky* case. It was depressingly long. Today he had to prepare formal document requests, interrogatories, deposition notices, and the rest of the opening salvo of discovery he would fire at the other side. Anthony Simeon—or, more likely, one of his junior associates—was currently readying the defense's initial broadside, so tomorrow Ben would need to go through his client's documents to get a head start on preparing the responses. He also had to subpoena all of American Union's records about either the box or the Zinovievs.

Hiring a good private investigator was also high on the list. Formal discovery done through lawyers was necessary but not sufficient. It wasn't unheard of for lawyers—or, more often, their clients—to lie or fail to produce damaging documents. An experienced detective could often catch them in their lies, and that could force quick and favorable settlements.

The PI would have to be cheap as well as good, given the size of this case. Strong connections to the Chicago Russian community were also a must. Finding someone who fit that bill could take a lot of looking.

And all of that was just the first week. Next week there would be depositions to take and defend, documents from the other side to dig through, responses to the defense's discovery requests to prepare, and more.

Ben went through his list and put a time estimate next to each task. He had at least twenty hours' worth of work to do this week and thirty-five hours' next week. It was Wednesday evening, so that meant he would have to spend long days on Thursday and Friday just working on *Ivanovsky*.

He pulled out his to-do lists for *Circuit Dynamics* and his other active cases and did time estimates for them as well. *Circuit Dynamics* was going to take about ten hours of his time this week and twenty next week. His other cases needed around five hours of work before Monday and ten hours or more next week. He put down his pen and ran his fingers through his hair. It took at least thirteen hours in the office to get ten hours of billable work done, so that meant that he would have to work from eight in the morning until after nine at night every day until next Friday. He could handle that, assuming everything went smoothly and there were no surprises, but neither of those were safe assumptions in the practice of law. If something went wrong, he would be in deep trouble.

"What's up?" Noelle's voice broke into his deliberations. Ben looked up and saw her standing in his doorway.

"Too much. I was just figuring out how much work I've got to do over the next week and a half. It's not pretty."

"Will it get better after that?"

Ben thought for a moment. "No."

Noelle looked down and shuffled her feet guiltily. "Is there anything I can do to help?"

Ben was about to say no—after all, she wasn't a lawyer—when an idea hit him. He raised his eyebrows and smiled. "Actually, there is. What's your time like over the next few weeks?"

"I've got a stack of spreadsheets to go through and I need to update our books, but other than that I'm pretty free. What do you have in mind?"

"You don't have a law license, so you can't handle depositions, court appearances, and stuff like that. But there are other things you can do. For starters, you can go through documents and interview witnesses, which would be a big help. You can also help me put together discovery requests. We can bill you as a paralegal at, say, a hundred dollars an hour. It would really help me, and Dr. Ivanovsky shouldn't mind. You'll be doing work I otherwise would do, and you'll be doing it at half my rate. Also, I could boss you around, which would be fun."

Noelle smiled and arched her eyebrows. "There's a first time for everything, isn't there? Actually, I like your idea. It'll mean more revenue, which we can always use. Besides, if you're going to be working late every night, I might as well do something useful to stay busy. I've been getting a little sick of doing reconciliations or bookkeeping for half the day and being bored the other half."

Later that afternoon, Ben struck gold. A former colleague gave him a lead on a private investigator, and now he was sitting across the conference-room table from a former FBI agent named Sergei Spassky. The private eye was about six foot two and had a lean, sinewy build that looked almost skinny if he stooped his shoulders. He wore wire-rimmed glasses that hid his dark, quick eyes and made him look more scholarly than streetwise. His short flattop haircut and open face also looked a little out of place for an experienced special agent—which Ben guessed was at least partially intentional.

Spassky's resume was impressive. He had received several commendations from the Bureau and had been the lead agent on several high-profile cases. His references—two of whom Ben knew personally and respected—spoke quite highly of him. He had only recently left the FBI to start his own agency, and his rates were well within the budget Ben and Dr. Ivanovsky had discussed. He seemed like a good candidate.

"Sure I know Elena Kamenev," Spassky said in response to Ben's question. "She and I never worked together, but she had a reputation as a good agent. She's a great shot. Two years ago she beat me out for the Chicago shotgun-marksmanship title. She's also a SWAT-certified sniper."

"But I see you beat her in the handgun category," Ben replied, looking at the man's resume. "What's this 'Possible Club' you're a member of?"

"That means I got a perfect score on the handgun range at the FBI National Academy."

"Pretty impressive," said Ben. "Hopefully that's not a skill you'll need on this case. How many investigations did you handle involving Russian immigrants?"

"At least two dozen. There weren't too many of us who could speak Russian without an accent, so we tended to get a lot of Russian crime cases."

"You don't have an accent in English either," observed Ben. "How did you manage that?"

"I was born and raised in America, but my parents came over from Russia in the sixties and we always spoke Russian at home."

Ben checked the language item off his list. "Ever hear of Nikolai Zinoviev?"

"No."

"How about Dr. Mikhail Ivanovsky?"

"No."

Ben looked over his resume again and decided to hire him. "Congratulations, Sergei. We're going with your agency for this investigation. Dr. Ivanovsky will be your employer on this case, and Mr. Zinoviev is the target of your investigation." Ben went on to briefly explain the case. "Any questions?"

Spassky shook his head. "The case seems pretty straightforward. You want me to do a background check on Zinoviev, right? Pull his criminal record, credit reports, that kind of thing?"

"Right. I'd also like you to try to identify Zinoviev's new buyers and those guys in the back of the courtroom. We'll need to hit them with subpoenas in the next few days."

The detective jotted down some notes. "What did they look like?"

Ben stared at the table for a few seconds, trying to remember. "One was a big guy with a scar on his forehead. The other one was about average height, maybe five ten. The big one had black hair and looked like he was around forty. The other one had gray hair and looked ten or fifteen years older. Their names were Anton and Josef, but I don't know which was which."

"How were they built? Skinny? Fat?"

"They both had on overcoats, so I couldn't really tell. I don't remember either of them being particularly thin or fat, but the big guy looked pretty strong."

"Facial hair? Tattoos?"

"The smaller one had a mustache. I think the other one was clean shaven. No tattoos that I saw, but they had their coats on the whole time."

"Were they wearing black?"

"Yeah," said Ben in mild surprise, "and so was Zinoviev. How did you know?"

"Russian *mafiya* types and *mafiya* wannabes generally dress in black." Spassky wrote down a few more notes. "Okay. Anything else you can tell me about either of them?"

Ben thought for a moment. "Nothing I can think of right now. If I remember something else, I'll give you a call."

Spassky opened his briefcase and put his pen and notebook away. "Thanks. I'll start working on it this afternoon."

"How long do you think it'll take?" asked Ben. "I'd like to be able to subpoena those guys in the next couple of days."

Spassky stared into space for a few seconds, apparently making some mental calculations. "Putting together a background file on Zinoviev shouldn't be too hard, but getting names and addresses for everyone you want? That could be tough. With a couple of breaks, I could do it in two days. I'll do what I can, but I don't want to get your hopes up."

Ben appreciated the man's honesty. "That's all we ask. Welcome to the team."

Sergei Spassky made a couple of quick calls to start the processes that would produce Nikolai Zinoviev's police file (he had no doubt there would be one), credit report, and so forth. That was so routine he could have done it in his sleep. Tracking down Zinoviev's buyer and the two men Corbin had seen in the courtroom would be harder, and doing it in two days would be harder still. Sergei smiled. It would be a challenge, and he liked few things better than a good challenge.

His first stop was a construction site on the North Side. Workmen had gutted an old warehouse building and were now rebuilding it into a mix of small shops and expensive loft apartments. Sergei stood outside, watching the construction and listening to the men carry on loud conversations in Russian and Polish over the noise of the machinery.

After several minutes, a large man with a sport coat, tie, and improbably good hair emerged. He made a beeline for Sergei and shook his hand, saying in Russian, "Sergei Kirilovich, what brings you to see me?"

Sergei noticed the respectful use of his patronymic and caught the hint of nervousness in the man's voice. He smiled inwardly. Yuri Filimonov had been known to hire workers whose skills were impeccable but whose immigration papers were not. Federal law-enforcement officials were generally—but not always—willing to overlook this circumstance in return for Yuri's willingness to provide information from time to time. "What can you tell me about Nikolai Zinoviev?"

He made a dismissive gesture with his left hand. "Nicki? Small-time drug dealer, heroin from Central Asia mostly. The word is that he shoots his own smack, which is stupid and cuts into profits. He's just a *shestyorka* doing odd jobs for some local smugglers and drug runners. He's nothing, but his brother was something, and Nicki mostly lives off his contacts."

"Who's his brother?" asked Sergei, a little surprised that there was a Chicago-connected Russian criminal who was "something" but whose name he didn't know.

"His name was Alexei. High-end smuggler. He died before your time. They found him in the Chicago River."

Sergei made a mental note to look into that. "Who are Nicki's contacts?"

"I don't know," the contractor said, his eyes darting sidelong at Sergei. "Business has been very heavy, and I don't talk to people as much as I used to. Sorry."

Sergei turned back to the warehouse. "It looks like business has been good to you, Yuri. I see you've hired a couple of new carpenters. What are their names?"

"Pasha and Janko," he answered warily.

"What are their last names?"

"You're not FBI anymore."

"So? Does that mean I've forgotten ICE's phone number?"

He glared at Sergei. "There can be no leaks."

"Of course not."

"So what happened with that investment-fraud case where those *kidali* were ripping off old ladies? It got out that I talked to you guys, and I nearly got killed!"

"You know that wasn't me," Sergei replied evenly. "And as you pointed out, I'm not with the Bureau anymore." He looked at Filimonov expectantly.

The burly contractor returned Sergei's gaze for a moment, then shook his head and muttered an oath. "Nicki works with the Brothers. They do import/export business and maybe other stuff. I don't know much about them, but I think they're old friends of Alexei's. I never deal with them, and I don't know any of their names. And that's *it*! I don't know anything more!"

Sergei looked him in the eye and decided he was telling the truth. He smiled and patted Filimonov on the back. "Thank you for your help, Yuri. Have a nice day."

Filimonov's face relaxed. "You won't be making any calls?"

Sergei's grin widened. "About what?"

Nicki Zinoviev's criminal file arrived on Sergei's desk the next morning. Zinoviev had emigrated from the Soviet Union twenty years ago, possibly because of legal problems there, though of course that wasn't what he had put on his immigration forms. The file said he was forty-two, but he looked at least five years older in his most recent mug shot. *But then, most people do,* thought Sergei, *particularly if they're using.*

Zinoviev had two convictions for drug possession, including one for half a kilo of heroin. He'd been sentenced to two years for that one but had gotten out after eleven months based on good behavior and alleged progress in a drug-treatment program. While he was still on probation, though, he'd been busted for conspiracy to sell drugs and carrying a concealed weapon. He had avoided more jail time by cooperating with prosecutors, but he might have cooperated a little too well—he later picked up a perjury conviction for some of his testimony against his former business partners.

After forty-five minutes, Sergei closed the manila folder and plopped it on the to-be-filed pile. Nikolai Zinoviev was just what Filimonov had said he was: a retail-level dealer and gofer with a drug problem. Turning state's evidence in the conspiracy case would have ended his career (among other things) if he had been in the mafia or the Russian *Organizatsiya*, but Russian and ex-Soviet crime in the United States was much less organized than it was in the former Soviet Union. There were no real loyalty rules here, so Zinoviev's betrayal simply meant that his remaining colleagues would never trust him, confining him to small, low-level roles in any operation.

Sergei had lunch at the Petrograd, a small restaurant of what he called the "borscht and babushka" type: lots of traditional food listed on the cheap laminated menus, lots of middle-aged and older women talking away the afternoon over sweet tea, very little English being spoken.

Little streamers of cigarette smoke rose from most of the tables before blowing away in the currents from the ventilation gratings. The walls displayed the mandatory "No Smoking" signs, but the patrons viewed these as purely decorative—which they were in places like the Petrograd. Sergei didn't mind. The smell of harsh Russian tobacco awakened fond memories of visiting his grandparents when he was young.

He sat down at the counter and called to an elderly, aproned woman standing at the far end. "Good afternoon, Auntie Olga. How are you today?"

"I'm as well as an old lady can expect," she said, putting down some dishes and walking over to him. "But I'm still depressed about the Bears. When are they going to get a back that can actually run the ball?" She looked at Sergei as if she expected him to know the answer.

"Good question. Kozlowski's a good bulldozer if they only need two or three yards, but he never gets much more than that. They could sure use someone with some real speed and evasiveness."

"Maybe," Olga said. "But you are not just here to talk football, am I right?"

She was right. Olga Yanayev was his mother's second cousin, but she was also the widow of one of the top bosses in the Moscow *mafiya* and the mother of two others. Her sons did no business in the United States—otherwise she would have had nothing to do with Sergei except at family reunions. However, she knew most of what went on in the local *mafiya* underworld, especially if it involved dealings with Russia. She and her husband had moved to Chicago when he'd retired, so that they could be near extended family and good hospitals, which he had needed because of his diabetes. It finally killed him two years ago, and he had left her a small fortune of dubious origin. She worked in the restaurant because it was a convenient way to talk to her friends and hear news, not because she needed the money.

"Of course you're right," Sergei said with a smile. "I came for the borscht and black bread too. And for the chance to visit with you."

She left to tend to her other customers and came back a few minutes later with his food. "Here's the borscht and bread. Now let's have the visit." She walked around the counter and sat on the stool next to him and eyed him shrewdly. "Let's be frank. You want to ask me something, and I want to ask you something too. Since you're the guest, I'll let you ask first. What is it?"

"Do you know Nicki Zinoviev?"

She shrugged slightly. "I know of him. He's a small fish for you, isn't he?"

"But not for my client. Nicki broke a contract to sell a safe-deposit box because he got a better offer from someone else. My job is to find out who that someone else is. I think it might be the Brothers. Do you know where I can find their names and addresses?"

"I can get them for you."

"Thanks. Do you know if they're trying to buy something from Zinoviev?"

"I don't know what they're doing. Why would they tell me?"

"I didn't think they would, but it never hurts to ask."

"Sometimes it does," she observed. "Now it's my turn."

"Fire away," said Sergei with a relaxed smile that hid a heightened alertness. She was his auntie, but she was also a very shrewd lady with her own agenda and a remarkable ability to read between the lines. He'd have to choose his words carefully.

"What are the Chechens up to around here?"

"Lots of stuff," he said. "You know that."

The Chechens had been fixtures in the Chicago crime scene for years. When Sergei was still with the Bureau, for instance, he had helped break up a sex-slavery ring on the North Side, allegedly run by Chechens. Recently, there had been a string of beatings, robberies, and murders targeting the Russian community, and a lot of people suspected Chechen gangs. Sergei had heard through the grapevine that the FBI was in the midst of a large investigation aimed at putting a stop to these attacks, but of course he couldn't say that.

Olga looked him in the eye for several seconds. "You know what the problem with those evasive running backs is? If you catch them, they go down hard." She smiled and patted his hand so that he wouldn't take her comment too hard, just hard enough.

Sergei smiled back. He knew she wasn't really threatening him, but he also stopped evading her questions. "You know from the papers that someone's been attacking Russians over the past few months and that it's probably a Chechen gang or gangs. All I can tell you is that law enforcement is aware of the problem and taking steps to deal with it."

"Are the gangs taking orders from Grozny?"

"Not that I know of. Why?"

"My boy Kolya heard that a gang based near Grozny might be trying to put together something here. Not Obshina. Someone else. He heard they were buying a brewery in the western suburbs, but that doesn't make any sense, because they're Muslims."

"Think it might be a cover for a meth lab?"

She nodded. "That's what scares me. If they try to push into the drug market in an organized way, there could be a war. Maybe they're attacking people now to build a reputation for the future."

"If I hear anything that I can tell you, I will," he assured her.

"You're such a good boy," she said with an affectionate smile. They had learned what they needed from each other and the conversation turned to other topics, but a lingering worry remained in the back of Sergei's mind. Criminals from the former Soviet Union, particularly Obshina and other Chechen gangs, tended to be brutal, smart, well educated, and highly effective when organized. In Russia they had corrupted most major businesses and all levels of government so badly that they had become a serious threat to the country's stability. For some reason, ex-Soviet criminals in America almost never organized in gangs of more than half a dozen, which made them much less effective. It would be bad if that changed. Very bad.

"So, Mr. Ivanovsky, you say that you paid $5,000 in cash to Mr. Zinoviev for something you had never seen?" said Janet Anderson, a junior partner working with Anthony Simeon on the *Ivanovsky* case.

Ben took a sip of coffee and awaited his client's response with mild interest. Dr. Ivanovsky's deposition had been going on now for two and a half hours, and he was doing well. Unlike many witnesses, he was doing exactly what Ben had told him to the evening before: listening carefully to Anderson's questions, pausing before each answer to give Ben a chance to object if necessary, and answering the questions directly but without volunteering extra information, even if it were damaging to the other side—which would merely alert them to problems in their case. Also, Ben and Dr. Ivanovsky had practiced most of the questions that the opposing attorney had asked so far, which helped.

"Yes."

"And the reason you weren't able to see it is that American Union Bank was closed, correct?"

"Objection, asked and answered," said Ben, who was a little annoyed that the other attorney was replowing old ground. "Just because the rules give you three hours doesn't mean you have to use it all. If you don't have any new questions, let's call it a day."

Anderson ignored Ben. "You can answer," she said to Dr. Ivanovsky, which was true. If Ben didn't instruct him not to answer (which he couldn't do simply on the ground that Anderson was repeating herself), he had to.

"Yes," he said again.

"Was American Union the only bank closed at that time?"

"No."

"Was your bank closed?"

"Yes."

Ben could see the concealed eagerness in her face and realized that she was about to spring her trap. This was a common tactic in depositions—asking hours of relatively harmless questions to tire the witness and get him off his guard, then trying to ambush him near the end. "You had to pay Mr. Zinoviev within two hours or the deal was off, right?"

"Yes."

"But if your bank was closed, how were you able to get the money?"

"ATM."

Her eyes gleamed. "But ATMs have withdrawal limits, don't they?"

"Yes. I had to go to many ATMs. And then they would not give me more and I still did not have enough, so I must sell some things to secondhand stores and pawnshops. There are many receipts, which I gave to my lawyer."

"You'll find them at Bates numbers IVA000142 to 163, counsel," said Ben, referring to the stamped numbers on the documents they had produced the day before.

There was a pause while she riffled through the stack of documents and found the appropriate pieces of paper. She glanced at them for a few seconds, then said, "Let's take a five-minute break."

Ben and Dr. Ivanovsky went out to the hallway for privacy. "How am I doing?" asked Dr. Ivanovsky as soon as the door was shut.

Ben glanced through the glass conference-room door and saw that Anderson had a calculator out. He smiled. He had added up the receipts two days ago and knew they would come out to $5,064. "Terrific. She's gotten absolutely nothing useful out of this deposition. In fact, I think that last line of questioning was their great hope for destroying your case, and it completely cratered."

"Cratered?" asked Dr. Ivanovsky with a puzzled look. "What does this mean?"

"You know how if you fire a rocket into space and it fizzles and falls back to earth, it makes a big hole in the ground, a big crater? Well, that's what just happened to their theory that you couldn't have gotten the $5,000 to pay Nicki because all the banks were closed."

"Cratered," repeated Dr. Ivanovsky, chortling happily. "I like that word here. Just like the early American satellite rockets. That is very funny. So you think they have no hope of destroying my case?"

"There are no guarantees," Ben said, reciting the rote cautionary boilerplate of every confident lawyer. "Anything can happen at trial, and the other side has very good lawyers. But things are looking pretty good so far. The documents are inconclusive, but they're all consistent with your story. It'll basically come down to your word against Nicki's. I still need to take his deposition, but I think you'll be a lot more believable than him."

The door to the conference room opened and the court reporter appeared. "We're ready to go back on the record."

Janet Anderson was already seated as Ben, Dr. Ivanovsky, and the court reporter resumed their places. "Okay, back on the record at 3:46 p.m.," the reporter said, and started typing again.

"No further questions," said Anderson.

"I have no questions," said Ben.

The court reporter began, "We're going off the record at—"

"Hold on a sec," Ben interrupted. "There's one scheduling matter I'd like to take care of first. Counsel, I need a date from you for Mr. Zinoviev's deposition."

"Counsel, this is something we can take care of off the record," Anderson responded.

"We've tried that," said Ben. "On three separate occasions over the past week, I've tried to get a date from your firm, and you still haven't given me one. That's why I need a response from you on the record."

"I don't know my client's schedule—"

"There's a phone on the credenza behind you. Call him."

"And Tony will be defending the deposition. I don't know his schedule either."

"Call him too."

She glared at Ben. "It is highly inappropriate for you to ambush me like this. We will get you a deposition date as soon as we can."

"You guys have been saying that for a week," Ben replied calmly. Doing this on the record at a deposition was a little unusual and aggressive, but it was hardly inappropriate in light of their stonewalling. "Can you promise to give me a firm date by tomorrow afternoon?"

"This is ridiculous," Anderson said as she shoved her papers in her briefcase and stood up. "This deposition is over. I'm leaving."

As she walked toward the door, Ben said, "Janet, if you can't promise right now to give me a date by four thirty p.m. tomorrow, I'll be in front of Judge Harris tomorrow morning on an emergency motion to compel, and the transcript we're making will be Exhibit One."

Anderson paused as she reached the door. She was a competent lawyer and knew as well as Ben that Judge Harris would be irritated with both of them for wasting his time with their discovery dispute, but that he would probably be most irritated with her. "Fine. I'll have a date for you tomorrow." She gave him a poisonous look. "This is extremely unprofessional of you." She opened the door and stalked out without waiting to hear Ben's response.

Ben smiled and turned to the court reporter. "Off the record."

Eight days later, Ben sat in his conference room, waiting for Nicki Zinoviev and Anthony Simeon to arrive. A box of documents in neatly organized folders sat on the chair beside him. Each folder contained three copies of an exhibit that Ben planned to use in Zinoviev's deposition—one copy for Ben, one for Simeon, and one for the court reporter to attach to the transcript. They included the transcript of Zinoviev's testimony from the TRO hearing, which Ben planned to spend at least half an hour asking about; a contract between Zinoviev and the Brothers LLC for the sale of the contents of the safe-deposit box for $100,000; two different versions of Zinoviev's criminal record (the one he had produced in discovery and the one Sergei Spassky had uncovered); and a number of other equally damaging documents. He also had marked-up transcripts from the depositions of the four members of the Brothers, men who had been in Soviet prison together but were not actually brothers. Unfortunately, they were cagey, well-prepared witnesses, and their testimony had been basically useless. Nicki would be a different story. *This will be like shooting fish in a barrel,* thought Ben in happy anticipation.

He glanced at the clock and saw that Zinoviev and Simeon were fifteen minutes late. Were they going to back out on him? They had fought this deposition as long as they could. Even after Ben's exchange with Janet Anderson at Dr. Ivanovsky's deposition, they had continued to put him off. It wasn't until Ben scheduled an emergency motion to compel and sent a draft of it to Simeon that they finally relented.

And now Ben was beginning to fear that they were at it again. He could already hear the excuses he would get from Simeon's harried secretary: "Mr. Zinoviev had a family emergency, we'll have to reschedule," or "Mr. Simeon developed a scheduling conflict with another case; he'll get back to you with a new date." Ben regretted not having gone forward with his motion to compel. It might have annoyed the judge, but at least there would be a court order requiring Zinoviev to appear for his deposition, and he would be in contempt of court if he didn't.

Ben waited five more minutes, then he walked back to his office and pulled Simeon's card out of his Rolodex and dialed. In case Simeon didn't pick up—and Ben doubted he would—Ben pulled up the draft motion to compel on his computer and started updating it. To his surprise, the attorney himself answered on the third ring. "Anthony Simeon," he said in an odd monotone.

"Tony, it's Ben Corbin. What's going on? You guys were supposed to be here almost half an hour ago."

Simeon took a deep breath before responding. "Ben, I just got off the phone with my client's landlord. He found Mr. Zinoviev lying in the hall outside his apartment this morning." His voice shook and he was clearly rattled. "He's dead. The police are there now."

CHAPTER FIVE
THE DEAD MAN'S RULE

After he got off the phone, Ben sat in his office in shock for several minutes. According to Anthony Simeon, the preliminary cause of death determined by the police was an unintentional drug overdose. Zinoviev had needle marks on his arms and legs, and initial tests showed lethal amounts of heroin in his blood.

Ben remembered how Zinoviev had squirmed and sweated on the witness stand at the TRO hearing. And he must have known his deposition would be worse.

Ben felt a twinge of guilt as he wondered if one of the reasons Zinoviev overdosed was that he was nervous about his deposition the next day and was trying to relax. "God rest his soul," Ben murmured to his empty office.

With a start, Ben realized that the court reporter was still sitting in the conference room, waiting for the deposition to begin. Ben hurried back and told her what had happened. Then he walked into Noelle's office and sat down in one of her chairs. She was on the phone and had a spreadsheet in front of her, but as soon as she saw Ben's face, she said,

"Something just came up. Could I call you back later this morning? Great, thanks."

As soon as she hung up, Ben said, "Nikolai Zinoviev died last night."

Noelle's eyes went round. "What happened?"

"Drug overdose; his landlord found him this morning." He realized the muscles in his shoulders were tense, and he stretched. "I feel bad, but I'm not sure what to do. Nothing like this has ever happened in one of my cases."

"Have you told Dr. Ivanovsky?"

Ben shook his head. "Not yet. I wanted to think about it a little first and decide what I'm going to tell him. My initial thought is to recommend that we offer to put off the trial and extend the discovery and motion deadlines until an executor has been appointed for Zinoviev's estate. It's the right thing to do, and the judge will probably give them the extra time whether we agree or not."

"That sounds like a good idea." Noelle sat back in her chair, still absorbing the news. "Wow. So what does this mean for the case—I mean, other than that everything will get delayed?"

Ben thought for a moment. For starters, Zinoviev's estate would need to be substituted as a defendant. More substantively, his testimony had been critical to his case. Ben mentally catalogued the evidence on both sides of each issue. On Dr. Ivanovsky's side, there was his testimony, which was circumstantially supported by a handful of documents like the pawnshop and ATM receipts. On the defense side, there was . . . well, nothing. Without Zinoviev's testimony, there was simply no way for the defense to rebut Dr. Ivanovsky's case. Ben had been confident before, but now he didn't see how he could lose. "I think it means we win."

When Ben called Dr. Ivanovsky to relay the news, the scientist appeared unfazed by the turn of events but eager to press his advantage.

"Why should we give more time?" he demanded.

"Well, because it's the right thing to do and—"

"But more time makes them more able to fight us, yes?" his client interrupted.

"Yes," admitted Ben. "But even with more time, I don't see how they can win."

"We must win as quickly as possible," Dr. Ivanovsky insisted.

"I never said we would necessarily win," Ben cautioned. "I only said that I didn't see how they could win without Zinoviev's testimony. Anything can happen in the courtroom."

"If the possibility of our winning is higher without giving more time, then you must not give more time. I am sad Nicki Zinoviev is dead, but we must not give up any advantage. We must win. It is very, very important."

Ben decided to try one more time. "Dr. Ivanovsky, I strongly recommend against refusing to extend the preliminary injunction schedule. The judge will probably give it to them anyway."

"Maybe the judge will give time to them. We will not."

Ben sighed. "All right."

Ben frowned as he hung up the phone. He resented Dr. Ivanovsky for compelling him to be rude and inconsiderate to a senior member of the bar. He winced inwardly at the thought of having to oppose a motion for continuance. He also disliked his client's abrasive and peremptory manner in instructing him what he "must" do to win this "very, very important" case. If there was anything important about the case, Dr. Ivanovsky certainly wasn't sharing it with Ben—which was another thing he didn't like. The TRO had been fun, but overall he regretted having taken the case. *Oh well,* he told himself, *at least it's pretty much over.*

He turned his attention to more pleasant matters. The effective completion of the *Ivanovsky* case would free up valuable time for other cases, most importantly *Circuit Dynamics*. Despite Noelle's help with *Ivanovsky*, Ben had fallen behind in his other work. He had needed to get deadline extensions from opposing counsel in two cases, which he hated doing because he then owed them favors. He probably would have needed extensions in three more matters if the *Ivanovsky* case hadn't been resolved. He also worried that he would give his clients and opponents the impression that he wasn't paying attention to their cases, which could cause serious problems with both groups.

Ben put the *Ivanovsky* case out of his mind and had a productive day working for other clients. He pumped out three long letters that he had been putting off and got a good start on a brief that was due in two days. He would be out of the office at a *Circuit Dynamics* hearing and deposition tomorrow, but now he wouldn't have any trouble filing the brief on time, which would save him from having to ask for yet another extension.

Ben's hearing the next morning was at eight thirty, so he headed directly to the courthouse and didn't bother stopping at the office first. He did, however, call Susan from the L, Chicago's extraordinarily loud light-rail system. "Anything interesting?" he shouted into his cell phone over the clatter and roar of the train.

He had the volume on the phone turned all the way up, but he still could catch only about half of what Susan said. Fortunately, he could fill in most of the blanks. "Let's see. Cathy . . ."

Pugo. Ben mentally filled in the missing word as the noise drowned out Susan's voice for a second.

". . . called about the status of the . . ."

Wilson Trucking case, Ben supplied.

"Frank Harbaugh sent you a letter wondering when you could . . ."

Give him the witness list I promised him a week ago.

"And Anthony Simeon hand delivered a petition to substitute a new defendant and a motion . . ."

For a continuance . . .

". . . set for hearing tomorrow at nine."

Ben gritted his teeth at the last item. He wasn't looking forward to that hearing. Judge Harris was likely to continue the trial date and other deadlines for as long as Simeon wanted, no matter what Ben said. And the judge would probably be surprised and annoyed that Ben was opposing the extensions.

"Okay, thanks," he yelled and hung up.

Ben's *Circuit Dynamics* hearing was a status conference at which the judge would review the current progress of the case and set a schedule for future activity. Discovery was mostly done, so Judge Ryan would likely set a motion cutoff in the next month or two, and a trial date a couple of months after that. Two days ago, that would have been a difficult schedule, but now it was definitely doable.

John Weaver was already in the courtroom when Ben arrived. Ben nodded to him and sat down. They were near the top of the court call, so they didn't have to wait long. "Circuit Dynamics versus Johnson Automotive," said the clerk two minutes later.

Ben and Weaver walked up to the wooden ledge that stuck out from Judge Ryan's bench in place of a podium. "All right, gentlemen, where do we stand?"

As plaintiff's counsel, Ben was expected to take the lead in pushing the case forward, so this question was directed primarily to him. "Your Honor, we have completed document discovery and each side has responded to interrogatories and requests for admission. We have three depositions left, but those are all scheduled."

"Anything to add, Mr. Weaver?" the judge asked.

"We want to re-depose the president of Circuit Dynamics, Mr. Schultz, in light of some extremely interesting revelations in the company's tax returns, which were only provided to us a week and a half ago. We have filed a motion seeking to reopen his deposition." He handed copies to Ben and the judge.

"This isn't set for hearing today, Your Honor," said Ben as Judge Ryan skimmed through the document. "We haven't had the opportunity to respond to it."

"And you oppose it, right?" asked the judge.

"Yes, Your Honor."

The judge nodded slowly as he finished reading the motion. He looked at Weaver. "I know this isn't before me today, Counsel, but I've got serious concerns about it. Why are questions about these tax returns relevant to anything in this case?"

"Well, as Your Honor correctly noted the last time we were before you, these tax returns are directly relevant to the issues in the case."

"I said that?" Judge Ryan asked incredulously.

"Actually, Your Honor, all you said was that they were entitled to look at them," Ben interjected. "You never said that they were relevant, and you certainly never said that Mr. Weaver could use them as a crowbar to reopen other areas of discovery."

"That's what I remember too," said the judge. "I'm going to deny your motion."

"But it's not actually before you, Your Honor," Weaver began, now in full retreat.

"Then why did you bring it up and give me a copy? Look, if you want to come back here next week just to hear me deny it again, maybe that's your right. But it seems like a waste of time to me."

"We'd like to at least keep the hearing date for now, Your Honor."

The judge rolled his eyes. "All right. Now tell me what's going on in settlement negotiations—I know you must be having them."

"We made an offer," Ben reported, "but they haven't responded."

"Why not?" the judge asked Weaver.

"They want $25 million, Your Honor," Weaver said with a faint tone of disbelief. "That's not even in the ballpark, as far as we're concerned. If Mr. Corbin's client would knock a couple of zeroes off that number, maybe we could start talking."

Judge Ryan raised his eyebrows. "Counsel, I can't tell you and your client what to do, but I've looked at this case, and I strongly advise you to reconsider your position. As an incentive, I'm going to set this case for trial in sixty days."

"But Judge, we need time for motions—for a summary judgment motion at least," Weaver spluttered.

"Sixty days is fine with us, Your Honor," Ben put in.

"I'd be surprised if you can come up with a meritorious summary judgment motion," the judge said to Weaver. "If you can, file it in the next three weeks. If it merits full briefing, I'll move the trial date at that time. If it doesn't, I can take care of it pretty quickly, and there's no reason we can't have a trial in two months. Talk to my clerk to get a date for trial. Okay, next case."

Five minutes later, Ben and Weaver were standing in the hallway waiting for the elevator. Ben turned to his opponent and said, "The gun's pointed back at you now, John."

Weaver gave a thin smile but said nothing.

Ben went straight from court to a deposition in another case, and he didn't get back to his office until close to five o'clock. He called Fred Schultz at Circuit Dynamics to tell him about the upcoming hearing and warn him that he and their other witnesses would need to clear their calendars for the trial. Then Ben called another client, Eagle Insurance, to report on the deposition he had just attended.

It wasn't until nearly six that Ben finally started going through the pile of messages and mail sitting in his in-box. The motion from Anthony Simeon was the third item from the bottom. Ben never got to the last two documents.

He stopped cold when he read the title of the filing Simeon had sent. It was not a motion for a *continuance*, as Ben had thought. It was a motion for *summary judgment*. Ben was stunned. Opposing counsel was asking the court to cut off all further proceedings—including the trial—and immediately enter a final judgment against Dr. Ivanovsky.

A litigant could only bring a summary judgment motion if, based on the undisputed facts, the other side could not win. Ben didn't see how Simeon could make such a motion, particularly after Nikolai Zinoviev's death. In fact, Ben had been toying with the idea of moving for summary judgment himself.

Ben read through the motion twice, once quickly and once with a fine-toothed comb. Simeon's argument was based on the Dead Man's Rule, an archaic and seldom-used rule of evidence that had made its way into the Illinois statute books. Basically, the rule said that when a lawsuit was founded on an oral contract and one of the parties to the contract died, no one with an interest in the contract could testify against the dead person's position. Thus, because Zinoviev was dead, Dr. Ivanovsky was barred from testifying against him. And because the only real evidence of a contract came out of Dr. Ivanovsky's mouth, Ben's case would collapse—and Simeon would be entitled to summary judgment—if the rule applied.

Ben called Noelle and told her he'd be late—just how late, he didn't know yet. Then he spent the next three and a half hours researching the Dead Man's Rule, looking for some exception or loophole that would let him and his client escape. At ten o'clock, he concluded that there probably was none, though the case law in Illinois interpreting the rule was voluminous and murky.

He sat despondently in the office's small law library, wondering what to do. He would appear in court tomorrow morning and make the best of a bad argument, but he would almost certainly lose. Anthony Simeon was a smart lawyer and Alfred Harris was a smart judge, so Ben had little chance of winning based on rhetoric alone. If he'd had more time, he might possibly have been able to find something by digging through the mountain of Illinois court opinions. Or maybe there were good cases interpreting other states' versions of the Dead Man's Rule. But he didn't have more time. The hearing was only eleven hours away, and he was dead tired.

Ben yawned and kicked himself for not having paid attention to the motion earlier in the day. He could have had Susan messenger it to him at court or at his deposition, but he hadn't. He could have asked her to read the title to him again when he could hear better, but he hadn't done that either.

Oh well. There wasn't much he could do about it now, except stay up all night and run up an exorbitant computer-research bill sifting through cases from across the country. He could do it, but a case of this size really didn't justify that kind of out-of-pocket expense. A decent night's sleep might actually be more beneficial, anyway.

Ben stood and stretched. Should he call Dr. Ivanovsky before leaving? It was ten thirty, but Ben decided that he couldn't let it wait until the morning. There was a good chance that the man's case would end tomorrow, and he had a right to know that.

To Ben's relief, he got the answering machine. "Dr. Ivanovsky, it's Ben Corbin. I'm afraid I've got some bad news for you. Nicki Zinoviev's death may have had some negative consequences for your case. There's an obscure technical rule called the Dead Man's Rule that Tony Simeon is trying to use to throw us out of court. He filed a motion for summary judgment today based on that rule, and it's set for hearing at nine thirty tomorrow morning. I'll let you know what happens, but I have to be honest with you—it does not look positive. I'll be in the office by eight thirty a.m. Call me if you have any questions." Ben hung up, yawned again, and went home.

Ben and Noelle drove in together the next morning. They hadn't been riding together recently because Ben's workload had forced him to go in early and come home late most days. In fact, they hadn't been spending much time together, period—except for time spent discussing discovery requests or document productions, which hardly counted. They were both looking forward to half an hour or so of chatting over coffee during their morning commute.

Then Ben made the mistake of checking his voice mail as they pulled out of the driveway. Eleven messages waited for him—and there probably would have been more if his mailbox hadn't filled up. All were from Dr. Ivanovsky. The first one had come at 6:43 in the morning, when he had presumably gotten Ben's message from the night before. The last one had arrived at 7:32. They were all agitated variations on the same general theme: "I am much dismayed and confused by this news. You said we would win, but now you say maybe we lose! Why this change? It is very, very important to win! Call me quickly!" Around 7:00, he started adding things like, "Why do you not call? I will come to your office and speak to you. You must win today!" Ben was very glad he had never given this client his home or cell numbers.

Listening to the messages took half the trip to the office, and the other half was ruined by the prospect of dealing with an upset and demanding client the moment they walked in the door. By the time he and Noelle arrived at the office, they both thoroughly resented Dr. Ivanovsky.

Once again, they found him in the hallway, wearing clothing that looked like rummage-sale rejects. He paced back and forth, muttering to himself and resembling a deranged vagrant.

"Hello," Ben said as they approached, a polite smile firmly planted on his face. "I just got your messages. You can come in if you like, but I really should spend the next hour preparing for the hearing."

To Ben's surprise, Dr. Ivanovsky did not protest. "Okay. I will wait. We will speak on the way to this hearing. May I have a copy of Mr. Simeon's motion to read?"

"All right. I'll set you up in the conference room. You won't be needing it this morning, will you, Noelle?"

"No, no, that's fine," she said quickly. Ben guessed that she also didn't want Dr. Ivanovsky sitting and talking to himself in the lobby, on display for any visitors who might come during the next hour.

Dr. Ivanovsky didn't disturb Ben, but it wasn't easy for the old scientist. He didn't completely understand the motion—though he understood enough to be very anxious. Losing the case was unthinkable, but now he was forced to think about it. Ben had said in his voice mail (which Dr. Ivanovsky had listened to five times and had largely memorized) that the situation did "not look positive." How bad was it? And what exactly would happen if they lost—would the Brothers get immediate access to the box? Dr. Ivanovsky desperately wanted to go into Ben's office and get answers to these and dozens of other questions, but he knew that would be counterproductive and he restrained himself with an iron will.

Finally, he got up and walked around the conference room. He stared at the paintings without seeing them. He fidgeted with the office supplies that sat neatly organized on the credenza at the back of the room. His lack of knowledge and control of the situation weighed heavily on his mind.

At all critical points in his adult life, Mikhail Ivanovsky had been in control. He had made a point of it. When he'd caught pneumonia and had to be hospitalized, he'd argued with the doctor about his treatment even though he could barely breathe. When his condition worsened, he took over his own treatment—feverish and weak as he was—and managed to cure himself. And when some bureaucrats in the collapsing Soviet Union had tried to keep him and his wife from emigrating to America, he had stormed past a host of protesting functionaries and into the office of the passport-control officer and refused to leave until the man reversed his decision.

Ivanovsky had even guided the lives of those around him at crucial times. When his wife was diagnosed with cancer, for instance, he had researched the type of tumor and its treatment in depth, had handpicked her doctor after several rounds of interviews, and had even stood watching in the operating room during her surgery.

He had decided long ago that even people of goodwill cannot be entirely trusted, and that not all those who seemed to have goodwill actually did. Even the best of them had small weaknesses, corruptions, and lapses in judgment that made them unreliable. Ben Corbin, for instance, seemed to be a good lawyer and a good man, but he had obviously completely missed the legal significance of Nicki Zinoviev's death. What else had he missed?

Dr. Ivanovsky wondered whether he had made a mistake in not handling the case himself. Then he thought of the Byzantine procedural intricacies that Ben negotiated so effortlessly. No, he decided, he could no more represent himself than he could have removed his wife's tumor. But he could be more involved. Ben's performance at the TRO hearing had given him a false sense that everything was under control. Now he knew that it wasn't—and that he'd have to keep a shorter leash on his lawyer.

◆　◆　◆

Ben stuck his head in the conference-room doorway. "Let's go."

Dr. Ivanovsky, who had never taken off his overcoat, quickly grabbed his papers and met Ben in the lobby.

"What's that?" Ben asked, looking at the pad of paper Dr. Ivanovsky held in his hand. It was completely covered by numbered paragraphs of scribbled Russian.

"I have some things to ask you while we walk."

There were a lot of questions. "We're only going a little over a block."

"Okay. I will start now and ask quickly. What is the chance to win? And why?"

The elevator came and they got in. "Less than fifty percent. Why? Because the law in Illinois more or less supports Simeon's position and he's a good lawyer."

"Okay. I read Mr. Simeon's motion, but I still do not understand. Why should this Dead Man's Rule apply to my case when I am not dead?"

"Because the idea behind the rule is that dead men should be protected," explained Ben.

"Yes, but they are dead. How to protect them?"

They stepped out of the building and into the teeth of a cold November wind. Ben pulled up his collar against the blast. "Maybe it's more accurate to say that their heirs need protecting. Dead men make bad witnesses in court, so it would be easy for someone to come in and say, 'I had a contract with Mr. Dead Man to buy his Ferrari for $5,000, but he died before we could write it down.' Mr. Dead Man can't testify, so it will be hard for his heirs to prove there was no contract. The people who made up the Dead Man's Rule hundreds of years ago didn't think that was fair, so they made a rule that prohibits people from testifying about oral agreements they claim they had with dead people."

"But this rule is not fair either!" Ivanovsky objected.

"I know. The law is full of rules that are supposed to make it fairer but do the opposite."

Dr. Ivanovsky said something, but Ben couldn't hear him over the whistle of the wind. "What was that?"

"Why did not you tell me of this rule before last night?" he repeated, watching Ben closely from under his knit hat, which he wore pulled down to his unruly eyebrows.

Ben stared ahead as they walked and didn't answer right away. "Because I didn't think of it," he said candidly. "It doesn't come up often, and I've never run into it before. It's a pretty obscure rule." He paused. "I'm sorry. I shouldn't have gotten your hopes up without doing more research."

Dr. Ivanovsky nodded. "I forgive you. All persons make mistakes." They were crossing Daley Plaza now, and Dr. Ivanovsky hurriedly scanned through his questions. "What happens if we lose this motion?"

"We're done," Ben replied as they walked into the building and got in line to go through a metal detector. "The case is over for all practical purposes. We could try appealing, but it would be virtually impossible to keep that safe-deposit box frozen in the meantime. And from what you've said in the past, I assume you wouldn't want to bother with an appeal under those circumstances."

Dr. Ivanovsky grabbed Ben's arm with surprising strength and looked at him with burning eyes. "You must not lose!"

"Your Honor, all Mr. Simeon is doing here is making a premature motion to bar," Ben argued. "At most, the Dead Man's Rule might allow him to prevent Dr. Ivanovsky from testifying at trial. It does not entitle him to summary judgment in the middle of discovery."

"But you're not in the middle of discovery, are you?" interjected Judge Harris. "As I understand it, both sides have completed their document productions, have responded to interrogatories, and have deposed all the witnesses they want."

Simeon nodded and Ben shook his head. "Your Honor, there are deposition subpoenas outstanding for four witnesses—the members of the Brothers LLC, the entity that attempted to purchase the contents of the box from Mr. Zinoviev after he had entered into a contract with my client. Those subpoenas also call for the production of additional documents."

"We will be moving to quash those subpoenas, Your Honor," replied Simeon. "Mr. Corbin just handed them to me in court this morning, so I haven't had a chance to analyze them in depth, but I don't need to, and neither does the Court. All of these witnesses have already been deposed and produced documents. They didn't know anything about Dr. Ivanovsky's purported contract then, and they don't know anything now. These subpoenas are nothing but a stalling tactic to avoid summary judgment."

That was at least partially true, Ben had to admit. He decided to try a different tack. "We just got this motion yesterday, and trial is less than two weeks away. We haven't had time to respond. Mr. Simeon can make his motion to bar at the proper time and on proper notice, and the Court can rule on this issue if it comes up at trial. In the meantime, we're entitled to finish our discovery and put on our case."

"Mr. Corbin doesn't have a case to put on, Your Honor," retorted Simeon. "That's the point of our motion, and that's why we ask you to rule on it today. There are two crucial points that he does not and cannot dispute. First"—he held up a finger—"the Dead Man's Rule prevents Dr. Ivanovsky from testifying. Second"—another finger—"without Dr. Ivanovsky's testimony, the plaintiff has no case. Mr. Corbin understandably would like the Court not to rule on this motion today, but the only ground he cites for delay is his hope that additional discovery will somehow uncover a new keystone to his case to replace his client's inadmissible testimony. It will not, and even Mr. Corbin cannot articulate why he thinks it would. Further delay will only waste the time and resources of the Court and the parties. We ask that the Court enter summary judgment."

"Anything further, Mr. Corbin?" asked the judge.

Ben had already run through all of his points twice during the half-hour oral argument. Doing it again would irritate the judge. "No, Your Honor. We believe the Court should deny the motion or at least put it over until trial."

"Okay, here's my ruling. I'm going to grant the motion and enter summary judgment in favor of the defendant and against the plaintiff. I am not a fan of the Dead Man's Rule, but I am bound by it. It's clear that the rule bars Dr. Ivanovsky's testimony. It's also clear to me that the remaining admissible evidence is not sufficient to allow the plaintiff to prevail at trial. Normally, I wouldn't enter judgment without a full briefing, but frankly I don't see what more briefing would contribute, given the clarity of the law and the facts in this case. Summary judgment is therefore appropriate."

Ben had expected to lose, but it still stung. The judge looked at him as he continued to rule from the bench. "However, Mr. Corbin, I realize that this motion only got dropped on you yesterday and that you haven't had a chance to adequately respond. Mr. Simeon was right to bring this issue to my attention promptly, but you still got sandbagged. I'm not unsympathetic to that fact, so I'm going to hold the effect of my ruling in abeyance for seven days. That will give you a chance to file a motion for reconsideration if you can find valid grounds for one. I don't think they exist here, but I'm willing to let you try.

"Thank you both. Draw up an order and bring it back to my chambers for me to sign."

The judge got up and left Ben and Simeon to haggle over the exact wording of the order. As the two lawyers sat down to write the judge's ruling on one of the blank forms from the clerk's table, Ben glanced over at his client. Dr. Ivanovsky's face was slack and deathly pale. He was shaking.

Chapter Six
A Prayer for Those Who Have Not Died

By the time they returned to Ben's office, Dr. Ivanovsky had started to recover from the shock of losing and was peppering Ben with questions again. Ben told him that they had two options. First, they could file the motion to reconsider suggested by the judge, though Ben didn't think that would work. He hadn't had time to research the Dead Man's Rule exhaustively, but he doubted that there were any major arguments that he hadn't already uncovered. A motion that merely rehashed and expanded on the points he had made that morning would likely lose.

The second option was worse. They could file an appeal in the First District Court of Appeals, but to succeed they would have to convince the appellate court to keep the TRO in place until the appeal could be fully briefed and heard, which the court was unlikely to do. Then they would have to *also* convince the appellate court that the highly respected Judge Harris had made a mistake, which was even less likely.

"So no matter what we do, we probably lose?" asked Dr. Ivanovsky after listening to his choices.

"I'm afraid so."

Ivanovsky pulled off his cap and started wringing it with white-knuckled hands. "Can we win if we give this Judge Harris some money?"

"What? No, no. First we would lose, then we would go to jail. Besides, I don't practice law like that."

"But I have read about Chicago judges," persisted Dr. Ivanovsky. "The papers say that—"

"Don't believe everything you read," Ben said, cutting him off. He was having renewed doubts about representing this man. "There are some dirty judges in the system, but I've never seen or heard of any judge I know taking a bribe. And even if I thought a bribe would work—which I don't—I wouldn't do it. In fact, you could probably go to jail just for asking me to bribe a judge."

Dr. Ivanovsky looked down. "I am sorry. I am talking crazy because I am afraid to lose."

"Don't worry about it," Ben replied. "I don't like losing either, but I'm afraid that's what's going to happen. Nicki Zinoviev's death probably also means the death of your case."

Dr. Ivanovsky's head remained bowed, and he folded his hands on the conference-room table. He sat silently like that for some time, then his shoulders began to shake again and his breath came unevenly. Ben suddenly realized that his client was praying and weeping. After an unnerving minute and a half of silence, Dr. Ivanovsky said in a ragged voice, "Why did Nicki have to die?"

"I . . . uh, I'm sure he would be touched by your concern and . . . and your prayers."

"I do not pray for the dead," Dr. Ivanovsky said hoarsely. "I pray for those who have not died. We have failed—I have failed. And now many will die. Nicki was only first."

The muscles in Ben's stomach and shoulders clenched. "What do you mean?"

Dr. Ivanovsky took a deep breath and looked up. His face was wet and blotchy, and his eyes were streaked with red. "I have lied to you. There are no jewelries in the box. There is death."

"What do you mean?" Ben repeated.

"Very deadly microorganisms, I think," Dr. Ivanovsky said, looking down again. "Or maybe a receipt for the freezer where these are stored. There probably is also notes saying how to make more."

Ben was instinctively certain his client was telling the truth. *I should have known,* he realized with cold despair. Dr. Ivanovsky's odd monomania about the case, his unusual background, the vague but strong sense that both sides were lying—all the uncomfortable aspects of the case that Ben had been pushing out of his mind for the past few weeks. It all now made perfect and terrifying sense. "How do you know all this?" he asked.

"Before I came to this country, I was first deputy commander of the decontamination unit at Biopreparat, the Soviet program for making germ weapons. When sometimes accidents and contaminations happened, the facility director would call me. I was very busy, but I remember especially one time."

His voice steadied. Talking about it seemed to calm him, though it had the opposite effect on Ben. "The director of this small research facility on an island in the Aral Sea called to me. He said, 'I am in the quarantine section of the hospital here. Everyone from the facility is here too. A viral organism came into the air system. We do not know how.' I asked him, 'What is this organism?' and he told me, 'It is a smallpox variant with Ebola genes introduced. Based on our symptoms, it is much like blackpox, except the infection rate is very high and symptom progression is much faster. We will take notes as long as we can so you have records.'"

"So you could have the records?" asked Ben. Then he realized what the statement must have meant, and a chill ran through him. "Oh."

Dr. Ivanovsky nodded. "They knew they were dying. They had made this disease to be very, very fatal and to have no cure. So they knew."

"Why would they make a disease with no cure?" asked Ben.

"If we can cure diseases, so can our enemies and the disease is not so good a weapon. So we made diseases with no cures."

"But what about your own people? Weren't you worried that the diseases would get back to them?"

Dr. Ivanovsky shrugged. "This is always a risk, but we took steps. Such diseases only go on long-range missiles and bombs, so the sickness is very far away from us. Also, disease can only come back if people carry it. If the germ is strong enough and fast enough, no one can carry it back to us. And even if it comes back, we have very good decontamination units," he added with a touch of pride. "Such units cannot cure diseases, but they can make buildings and vehicles clean after"—he paused—"after the disease is over."

"Were they all dead by the time you reached them?" Ben asked.

"Yes," he said in a strained voice. "They were in rows in the hospital refrigeration room, except the last two. They were on beds. I have seen many deaths, but . . ." His voice trailed off and he stared blankly at the wall. "Ebola, it . . . it degrades the tissues and there is much bleeding through the eyes and the skin and . . ." Again his voice trailed away. He shook his head and took a deep breath. "The disease they made is fast, which was good. Twelve hours after symptoms begin, victims are in coma. Next day, they are dead."

Ben shivered. "How did the virus escape?"

"Now you come to the question I asked many, many times. For one person to have an accident in a sealed room—this happens. For two or three persons to maybe die from leaks or contaminated equipments, this happens once or twice. For viruses to come into the air system and the whole facility to die, this never happens. My team and I, we read the notes and other documents from the facility, trying to understand this. We tested all virus-holding equipments for leaks, but we found no leaks. We examined every centimeter of the air system for malfunction or leak, but there was nothing.

"But we found another thing: one container and lab notes were supposed to be there, but they were not there. This is not unusual. Scientists lose things or give them to other scientists very often, especially in the end of the Soviet Union when there were not enough supplies. So maybe this happened here, but there was no one I can ask if this is true. I began to think that maybe there is a connection between these facts. Maybe everyone is dead to hide what happened."

Ben saw where this was going. "Was it Nicki Zinoviev's brother?"

"I think yes, now," replied Dr. Ivanovsky. "But in that time I did not have theories about who did this thing. We developed films from the security cameras. There was no picture of a person breaking in, but the pictures showed every day a man bringing supplies to the island. It was the same man in all pictures, except on the day the contamination happened.

"I knew we must find this man very, very fast. Maybe he was guilty and killed these persons and stole this Ebolapox and notes. Maybe he was not guilty, but was infected and dead and infected more persons. It was very necessary to find him.

"I went to the supply base making deliveries to the island and talked to the commander. He was very scared, but I believe he said the truth. The man making deliveries every day was sick on the day when the contamination happened, so the commander sent another man who was new. The commander showed me his picture and his documents. He has all necessary papers, but the picture does not look like the one from the security films. Not very different, but different. 'Where is this man?' I asked. 'He is dead. A terrible death,' the commander said. 'How did he die?' I asked. The commander said, 'His truck crashed and there was a fire.' I examined this body. It was very burned, but there was no Ebolapox on the pieces of unburned skin. We did a full autopsy and found no Ebolapox in the blood. Also, we found this man did not die from burning. His lungs had no burns, so he was dead before the fire."

"What killed him?" asked Ben.

"Broken skull, but it was broken in back, not in front where the head hits the car. So we now called to Biopreparat security, and very fast they come with KGB. They talked to us for three days while we decontaminated the island and did more autopsies on the persons from the facility and took samples from them for production."

"What do you mean 'samples for production'?" Ben asked, not entirely sure he wanted to know the answer.

"This was always done in Biopreparat," explained Dr. Ivanovsky. "If a disease kills a person—and especially if it kills all persons who are infected—we know it works. Otherwise, we only know it works on monkeys and rats, which is very different. So we took samples from the dead persons to produce in a factory laboratory the exact organism that killed them. Sometimes we named it for the person who died. For example, there is a virus named Variant U for a Dr. Ustinov that it killed. But this one is called Variant D for Dracula, because it makes blood come through the skin." Ben winced. "This name was from the persons in the facility that wrote it in their notes. They made this joke when they were dying because they were brave and scared, I think."

"Wow," Ben said. He was only beginning to absorb the magnitude of what his client was telling him. "So you think Variant D is in that safe-deposit box?"

"Yes. Well, not Variant D—it would die if not frozen. But I think there is in the box a receipt for a commercial cold-storage facility where it is. And also notes on how to make this organism."

"But how did it get to Chicago? And why did it stay here all these years without being found?" asked Ben.

Dr. Ivanovsky shrugged. "This I am not sure of. After we finished the decontamination, we left the island, but the KGB stayed. They never spoke to me of this thing again. One time I called to a KGB agent I met on the island and asked him what happened. He said, 'This is a state security matter that you must not speak of.' So I never did until now."

"Everything you tell me is confidential, of course," said Ben. "But about the safe-deposit box—"

"Yes, yes. So after some years, the Soviet Union ends and Biopreparat becomes much smaller. Many people I know are gone and I am now old, so I retire and come to this country. I was having tea with my friend after church on a Sunday, and we were remembering the old KGB. My friend said to me, 'The KGB one time even killed a man in Chicago. This was before you came, Mikhail.' I asked him, 'You are sure this is true?' He said, 'Oh yes, it is true. The Americans think it was *mafiya*, but I know a *mafiya* man here and he says it was KGB, not them.' Then he also said, 'I even have some newspaper stories about this thing that you can read.' He went into his basement and came back with some old pieces cut out of newspapers. One of them had a picture of the dead man, but with his eyes made to look like they were open. My friend said, 'That is him,' but I knew this face. It was the man I saw on the security films from the facility."

"You're sure it was the same guy?" interrupted Ben, hoping Dr. Ivanovsky was wrong. "After all those years, you remembered exactly what he looked like?"

"The contamination that happened on this island made a very big impression on me. So many dead and in such a way, and this Variant D Ebolapox maybe stolen. Yes, I remember exactly the man's face and many other things."

"Okay. So what did you do then? How did you find the box?"

"I asked my friend how this *mafiya* gangster knew KGB killed this man. He said, 'This gangster I know, he knows the dead man's brother, and the brother told him.' So I asked, 'Who is this brother?' And he said, 'Nicki Zinoviev.' Zinoviev is not the name in the newspaper pieces, but they also say police found passports containing different names with the body, and maybe all of them have false names.

"It is very, very probable this man was CIA and stole Variant D for America. I now think, 'Did he give Variant D to America before he died?' So on the next day, I talked with an American government microbiologist I know who is at Fort Detrick, which is where the Americans do such researches. Of course, he will not tell me if America has Variant D, so I do not ask him this. I ask him about treatment and decontamination procedures in case of terrorist biological attacks, and we talk for a long time about different organisms. When we are done, I know that America has no procedures for organisms like Variant D. If America had Variant D, it would also have decontamination and treatment procedures for it."

"I thought you said there was no cure," Ben broke in.

"Even if there is no cure, there is always procedures," explained Dr. Ivanovsky, "even if it is only for decontamination, containment of outbreaks, and handling of bodies.

"So this container with Variant D and lab notes never came to the American government," he continued. "So now I think, 'Where are they?' This is when I called to Nicki Zinoviev. I told him that his brother had carried a package belonging to me but that he died before he could give it to me. He asked, 'Why do you come to me only now after so many years?' and I said, 'I did not know his true name until now.' Then he said, 'I know of no package.' I said, 'I will give you money for this package.' He said, 'This is good, but I still know of no package. If I find one, I will tell you.' This gave me an idea. I said to him, 'If I look for things belonging to your brother and I find some things, will you promise to sell them to me for reasonable prices?' He said yes, and he told me the false names his brother used.

"So I called to many storage facilities and banks to see if this Alexei Zinoviev had lockers or safe-deposit boxes there. First they would not tell me anything because I am not Alexei Zinoviev, even though he is dead. Then I got a paper from Nicki Zinoviev saying that they should answer these questions—"

"You didn't tell me about this," Ben interrupted. "That's an important document."

"It said nothing about jewelries, of course, so I did not want to show it to the judge," replied Dr. Ivanovsky. "Maybe it would make him think it was not jewelries in the box."

"He probably thinks that already. That document helps to show that there was a contract between you and Nicki. If I'd known about it and we'd produced it in discovery, there's at least a chance we would have won today." That chance wasn't particularly large, but Ben decided not to mention that. It was time Dr. Ivanovsky learned a lesson about the dangers of sharing information selectively with his lawyer.

"I did not think of this," admitted a crestfallen Dr. Ivanovsky. "I am sorry. Can we use it now?"

"Maybe. The judge will be angry, and he may well bar us from using it, as a sanction for intentionally withholding it during discovery." Ben glanced at his client's morose face and slumped shoulders and decided not to push the matter further. "Get it to me as soon as you can and we'll talk more after I've had a chance to look at it. But I interrupted you—what happened next?"

"Mostly you know already. I found this box at the American Union Bank, which Alexei Zinoviev had rented under one of the false names and paid much advance rent, maybe because he worried he might go to jail. There were many papers to sign, because Alexei was dead and Nicki was the only one left from his family and the box key was lost. Nicki said to me to take care of all these things and he will give the box to me, but I must pay him $5,000 right away. So I paid him $5,000 and I took care of these papers so he can get in the box, but then he says we have no deal. I think it is because he looked in the box and showed it to his gangster friends who will give him the $100,000 he said in the court, or maybe even more."

"And if they get it, who knows what'll happen?" Ben sat in silence for several seconds, considering the possibilities. Sergei Spassky had reported that the Brothers ran a lucrative smuggling operation under the cover of their import/export business. Who would they ship this particular item to? North Korea? Al-Qaeda? Some new enemy that hadn't yet entered America's nightmares? "We need to tell the FBI."

"No!" Dr. Ivanovsky almost shouted. "Did you not hear what I said? The American state killed all those persons in the facility and the delivery man! The American state brought Variant D here and put it in this box! Then they lost it in some way before they could study it or make a weapon with it. I thank God very, very much that this happened. I will not now give it to them!"

"You would rather give it to the Brothers?" asked Ben incredulously. "You'd give it to them, but not your friend at Fort Detrick?"

"The man at Fort Detrick I would maybe trust with this, but he is ordered by generals that I do not trust. Nuclear bombs were discovered by scientists but taken by generals to kill many persons. Scientists are tools of generals, Ben, and generals always want new ways to kill persons."

Ben couldn't believe his ears. "I'd trust generals before I'd trust the Brothers. Imagine what would happen if they decided to use Variant D for extortion or sold it to terrorists."

"I already imagined this," said Dr. Ivanovsky with a drawn face. "I imagine it now. This is why I gave money to Nicki Zinoviev—so I could destroy what is in this box. And this is why I gave so much money to you to win this case." Ben squirmed inwardly as that shot went home. "Thousands, maybe millions, of persons would die if terrorists use Variant D, but with generals it would be much worse. Generals have never in all history had weapons they do not use sometime. Remember,

Ben, American generals used nuclear bombs against cities. They are the only ones to ever do this. I will not give Variant D to them."

"But that was during a war," protested Ben, "and they've never used bioweapons."

"You think there will be no more wars?" retorted Dr. Ivanovsky. "And it is not correct that Americans never used bioweapons. One big example of these weapons was when Americans gave blankets with smallpox to Red Indians during a war. Very, very many of them died."

Ben studied Dr. Ivanovsky's resolute, almost defiant face and knew there was no way he was going to change the old man's mind. Ben also needed time to think more before making his next move. He was playing a game whose rules he did not know and which he must not lose. "Okay. Well, I don't think there's much more for us to talk about right now. I need to get to work on this motion for reconsideration, and you need to send me that document—and anything else I haven't seen that is at all connected with this case."

Dr. Ivanovsky nodded sharply. "I will do this right away. I will call to you tonight to ask how this motion is progressing."

Ben walked back to his office and stood in front of the window, staring down the street. The gray early-November clouds were dumping snow on the city. Not the fluffy, soft, snow-globe kind, but the hard, granular kind that stings when carried on a sharp wind like the one blowing now. The snow made a sizzling hiss as it drove against the window before swirling away.

"So what do I do now?" he asked himself.

His immediate impulse was to call the FBI. If Dr. Ivanovsky was telling the truth—and Ben strongly suspected he was—then this was obviously no longer something he could handle on his own. In fact, it was something he had neither the ability nor the desire to handle at all. The entire situation should be handed off to law enforcement as soon as possible.

An ugly thought occurred to him: Would calling the Bureau cost him his law license? The attorney-client privilege ordinarily prohibits attorneys from revealing communications from their clients, but maybe there was an exception for this kind of situation.

He pulled his ethics treatise out of the bookshelf and found his answer. To his relief, Illinois—unlike some other states—contained a specific exception to the privilege that allowed a lawyer to tell authorities if his client intended to commit a crime. And Ben was pretty sure that Dr. Ivanovsky would be committing lots of crimes just by getting possession of Variant D, regardless of what he did with it.

But the more he thought about calling the FBI, the less it seemed like a good idea. Although Ben didn't know much about criminal law, he thought that the Bureau could probably get into the box if they wanted to. But would they want to?

The local FBI office had been the target of harsh public criticism in the past couple of months for obtaining terrorism-related warrants based on secondhand and, in retrospect, faulty intelligence. There had been high-profile raids and arrests, followed by awkward questions in the newspapers, followed in turn by an internal investigation that had led an embarrassed and furious local US attorney to drop all charges. Two agents had been fired and others transferred, and several of the arrestees had already filed lawsuits against the government.

So even if the Bureau could technically get a warrant, they might well insist on interviewing Dr. Ivanovsky first. He would probably vigorously deny Ben's story. Would a gun-shy FBI then be willing to stick its neck out by asking for a warrant? Ben doubted it.

Talking to the FBI also risked destroying Ben's relationship with Dr. Ivanovsky. The man had told Ben his story in confidence and would likely view Ben's breach of that confidence as a betrayal. That confidence was qualified, of course—as Ben had warned his client. Still, Ben strongly suspected that Dr. Ivanovsky would fire him if he found out that Ben had leaked information to the government.

Another option would be to fire Dr. Ivanovsky as a client. He had lied to Ben and was using him to commit a crime, either of which gave Ben firm ethical grounds—and possibly a duty—to withdraw. It would be a clean, simple solution. He could walk away from this suddenly disturbing case and back into a life where the most important thing he had to think about was how much money he could wring out of the defendants in *Circuit Dynamics*.

Then what happens? he asked himself bitterly. Dr. Ivanovsky might try to hire another lawyer, but he likely wouldn't have enough money to do so, based on the bank statements he had shown Ben. Besides, he might not be a great fan of the legal profession after Ben pulled out at a crucial juncture. So Dr. Ivanovsky would probably wind up representing himself against Anthony Simeon. Ben had no doubt how that contest would play out. And then there would be nothing to do but scan the papers for reports of people bleeding through their eyes.

He shivered and watched the monochrome sky slowly darken into a long, cold night. If he kept litigating the case as he had, he would probably lose and the Brothers would get Variant D. If he talked to the FBI, the most likely outcome was that they wouldn't search the box but would talk to Dr. Ivanovsky—and Ben would be lucky to stay on the case, let alone win. If he withdrew, Dr. Ivanovsky would probably wind up fighting and losing the case alone. There were no *good* options, and Ben could not tell which was the least bad.

He closed his eyes and prayed silently, asking for guidance and pleading that the horror in the box would never escape. When he opened his eyes, the sky was completely black. He sighed and ran his fingers through his hair. "So what do I do now?" he asked again.

Chapter Seven
A Voice in the Night

Ben called Sergei at eight o'clock the next morning. Last night, while retelling Dr. Ivanovsky's story to Noelle, it had occurred to him that it wouldn't be a bad idea to have a PI try to verify at least some of the details before making any decisions. Noelle had agreed. She had also pointed out that Sergei was ex-FBI and would have a much better feel for how the Bureau would react. And Sergei was covered by the attorney-client privilege, meaning that Ben could talk to him without violating any duty of confidentiality that he owed Dr. Ivanovsky.

When Sergei didn't answer his office phone, Ben called his cell. "Hello. Sergei Spassky."

"Sergei, it's Ben. I need your help on a follow-up project to the Zinoviev investigation. It's urgent."

"What is it?"

Ben hesitated. "It's pretty sensitive. I'd rather not discuss it over the phone."

Sergei paused. "That serious, huh?"

"Yes."

"Okay, I'll be right over."

Ben suddenly realized that there was no reason why his phone would be bugged and his office wouldn't. "I'll meet you on the street," he said quickly.

Twenty minutes later, Ben spotted the detective coming out of a nearby parking garage and walked over to meet him. "So what's going on?" Sergei asked.

Ben kept an eye on the other pedestrians as he and Sergei walked along the street. He recounted his conversation with Dr. Ivanovsky. "So I need to know two things," he said after finishing his story. "First, is he telling the truth? Second, what would the FBI do if I told them?"

"And third, has someone bugged your phone or your office?"

"That too."

"I'll come by this afternoon and check your office and phones. I don't have the right equipment in my car. What would the Bureau do if you told them?" He paused thoughtfully. "Well, for starters they'd probably go get a warrant and search the box."

"They would do that? Even after the al-Fawaz mess?"

"Yeah. Getting a search warrant is pretty easy these days, particularly if there's a legitimate national-security concern—and this sounds a lot more legitimate than what went on in that al-Fawaz case. Dr. Ivanovsky's background and allegations ought to be enough, even if we don't give them his name."

"And whether we give his name or not, they won't have any trouble guessing it's him, will they?" asked Ben.

"Nope. They'll pull him in for questioning no matter what's in the box. He tells a pretty scary story."

The moment that happened, Dr. Ivanovsky would fire him. If the box held the Variant D sample and the notes—*and* if there were no more surprises—then it would be worth destroying his relationship with his client. But this case had produced a lot of surprises so far, and Ben didn't want to burn any bridges if there was even the smallest chance that he would need them later. Besides, there was no immediate risk that anyone would get into the box.

Ben frowned. "He won't take that well. Can you think of a way to check out his story without having the FBI interview him?"

"That could be a problem," Sergei conceded. He walked in silence for several seconds, staring at the sidewalk. Then he stopped and looked up with a smile on his face. "Nicki's brother. If he really was running some kind of op for the CIA, there'll be a file on it somewhere."

"You think we can get it?"

"No, but I think just raising the subject will be enough. If there's something there, they'll be calling me to talk, and I can simply point them to the box without ever raising Dr. Ivanovsky's name."

Ben smiled with relief. "I like it."

"And if there's *not* something there, you probably don't want to be calling the Bureau in the first place."

Sergei was busy with an industrial-espionage investigation all morning and part of the afternoon, but he couldn't help thinking about Dr. Ivanovsky's story. Was it true? Ben seemed to think so, but he hadn't spent nearly as much time with secretive Russians as Sergei had. Sergei knew that a lot of strange and worrying things had gone on in the Soviet Union, and he had no doubt that Dr. Ivanovsky had been involved in some of them. But that didn't necessarily mean that he was telling the truth about this alleged Ebolapox virus or Alexei Zinoviev. Sergei had dealt with people like this before, and in his experience they were not particularly reliable. The Soviet system had encouraged habitual lying and concealment, especially among those who worked in its secret programs.

He grabbed a late lunch and called a friend from the Bureau as he ate. "Hi, James, it's Sergei. I'm trying to run down information on a possible CIA project from 1985."

"So why are you calling the FBI?"

"Because the Agency shares its database with you but not with me."

"You know I can't give you classified information."

"Of course not, but not everything in there is classified. I'd call Langley, but you know how those guys are. If you ask them what time it is, they'll tell you it's classified, particularly if you're FBI. I'd rather not spend a month doing FOIA paperwork just to find out there's nothing there."

"I hear you. Okay, if you're not looking for classified stuff, it shouldn't be a problem. What do you want?"

"I'm looking for a guy named Alexei Zinoviev, Z-I-N-O-V-I-E-V. Was he involved in a CIA op in 1985?"

Sergei heard the sound of typing, then several seconds of silence. "Man, this thing is slow," commented James. "You'd almost think they don't want us searching their files."

Sergei chuckled. "By the way, how do you like working with those guys?" James and a few other FBI agents had been posted to the CIA to facilitate information flow between the two organizations.

"I just got my security clearance, so they'll actually let me touch their computers now. I used to have to write down the search request on a form and have one of their people do it. They're good guys by and large, just a totally different mind-set."

The rules requiring information sharing among the various intelligence agencies were particularly galling to the CIA. The Agency viewed the FBI as a bunch of glorified cops. In their view, FBI agents were—at best—excess baggage, and at worst, simpleminded police detectives who would screw up delicate intelligence-gathering operations.

Part of the problem was the different missions of the two organizations: the CIA's principal goal was to collect and analyze information; the FBI's was to enforce the law. If the Agency discovered an international crime ring, for instance, it would want to learn everything it could about the players, their methods, their connections to foreign governments, and so forth. The FBI would want to start arresting people. And once the arrests started, the intelligence sources generally vanished.

"Here we go," said James at last. "The only stuff we've got on Zinoviev comes out of our own files. Nothing from the Agency. If they have anything, it should be in here, but I'll ask them to do a file search anyway."

"Thanks."

"By the way, this guy looks like a real winner. According to our unclassified stuff, he was a smuggler who got himself shot to death by someone with an East European piece—probably a Makarov. No witnesses or arrests. Typical."

"I know," said Sergei. "It's amazing how bad people's vision and hearing get during Russian-on-Russian crimes." Russian immigrants were generally distrustful of authority, particularly law enforcement, an attitude many of them had learned the hard way in the Soviet Union.

"No kidding. By the way, he has a brother you might want to talk to."

"*Had,*" Sergei corrected.

Sergei finished his lunch and headed back to his office at a brisk walk. He would bring his debugging equipment to Ben's offices, do a sweep, and hopefully be back behind his desk by two thirty, which would give him time to get through a stack of files before going out for dinner and the Bulls game with some friends that evening.

About halfway back to the office, Sergei suddenly realized he had left his briefcase—which held his cell phone and several sensitive files—in the restaurant where he had eaten lunch. He spun around and started jogging back. As he did so, he noticed a man about a half block behind, staring at him. The man froze for a split second, then turned quickly and looked into a display window full of women's shoes.

"Amateur," Sergei muttered as he ran. He was irritated that he was being tailed, but even more annoyed that he hadn't realized it sooner.

On impulse, Sergei stopped as he passed the man and said, "Never freeze. Never stare."

The man mumbled something inaudible, and Sergei patted him on the back and ran on.

By the time he reached the restaurant, Sergei regretted having spoken to the man. It was a stupid, impetuous move that had made him feel good, but it was almost certainly counterproductive. Now the tail would be more careful, and he would have a special motivation for beating the detective who had humiliated him.

Fortunately, the busboy had found Sergei's briefcase and it was waiting for him at the front desk, its contents undisturbed. As expected, Sergei didn't see the tail again as he walked back to his office. The man's employers wouldn't use him for street surveillance anymore, at least not on foot.

And just who might those employers be? he wondered as he unlocked his office door. He could think of half a dozen candidates off the top of his head, but none was more likely than any of the others. The only way to know would be to put the tail under surveillance, which would have been hard half an hour ago. Now it would be virtually impossible.

◆ ◆ ◆

Ben stared blankly at his computer screen, lost in thought. The "paper" Dr. Ivanovsky had received from Nicki Zinoviev was a badly typed letter that stated in its entirety:

> *To Wom It May Concern:*
> *I am Nikolai P. Zinoviev. I am the hair and executor of Alexei Zinoviev (a/k/a Vladimir Nikolaev, Ivan Kuzmin, Peter Romanov, Yuri Sokolov), who is dead since 16 November 1985. If you have things belonging to Alexei Zinoviev, you can tell Mikhail Ivanovsky.*
> *Very Truely Yours,*
> *Nikolai Zinoviev*

Dr. Ivanovsky had also sent a form order from Alexei's long-closed probate estate appointing Nicki executor of the estate, which banks had no doubt required before they would accept the letter.

Ben was trying to think of a good argument for why the letter and order helped prove that there was an oral contract between Nikolai Zinoviev and Dr. Ivanovsky. It was hard work. So far, the best he could come up with was that the letter showed that Dr. Ivanovsky had been prospecting for lost assets belonging to Alexei. In that context, the $5,000 transfer from Dr. Ivanovsky to Nikolai only made sense as a payment for an asset Dr. Ivanovsky had located—and the only asset fitting that description was the safe-deposit box.

"Pretty thin," Ben admitted to himself as he scrolled through the draft motion for reconsideration. All he had really shown was that a contract for the sale of the box was consistent with the known facts, but so was a loan or a contract for the sale of some other object. Without the seller's or the buyer's testimony, Ben couldn't actually *prove* that Zinoviev had sold the box to Dr. Ivanovsky, a fact that Anthony Simeon would be sure to point out.

"How's it going?" Noelle asked from behind him.

Ben swiveled his chair around and saw her leaning against the jamb of his office door. "Okay. This *Ivanovsky* motion is going pretty slow."

"Is he still calling every hour?"

Ben grinned. "You've been out of the office all day; how did you know?"

"Lucky guess."

"I explained to him that the less time I spend on the phone with him, the more I can spend on this motion. I'm also having Susan screen my calls. That's helped, but I'm still having a rough time."

Her face grew serious. "Are you going to win?"

He leaned back, stretched, and ran his fingers through his hair. "Maybe."

"Not *probably*?"

"Nope." He didn't really want to talk about it anymore and changed the subject. "Sergei Spassky was here this afternoon. He checked the office, and we're bug free."

"Did he find anything on Zinoviev's brother?"

"It looks like he was a smuggler, but not a CIA agent. They don't have any record of him."

"How'd Sergei find that out?"

"He didn't give me the details, but I think he managed to have someone search the CIA's database."

"Pretty impressive." She paused as she considered the implications. "So what is that? Good news? Bad news?"

"Yes," Ben said with a wry smile. "The good news is that it looks like Dr. Ivanovsky might not have been telling the truth about Variant D."

"And the bad news is that he might not have been telling the truth at all."

"Right. That doesn't necessarily make him a liar. There might be a bug in the CIA database. Or Dr. Ivanovsky could've been mistaken about the picture in the paper. Or he might be delusional."

"Or he might be a liar."

"Yeah, he might," admitted Ben. "I kind of doubt it, though."

"Why?"

"He doesn't lie well, for one thing. And I just can't believe that the display he put on was fake. If it was, he deserves an Oscar."

"He has turned out to be full of surprises, hasn't he?" said Noelle.

"He has, but I really think he believed what he was telling me," Ben said with a shrug. "Whether he was right or not is another question."

"Well, what do you think?"

"For one thing, I think there's not much point in going to the FBI, at least not until I've got something more reliable than a completely unsupported secondhand story. Beyond that . . . well, I don't know what to think. Which is part of the reason I'm having trouble writing this motion. Here I am in the middle of the case, and I don't know what's really going on. In fact, I know a lot less than I thought I knew the day after I took the case. It's frustrating."

"But does that directly affect this motion you're writing?" asked Noelle.

Ben thought for a moment. "I guess not. The motion will be the same whether the box holds fake watches or real bioweapons. I suppose I can only do what I have in front of me, and today that's this motion. If I win, then I can worry about what's in the box and who exactly is after it." He paused. "Actually, I'd probably worry about that more if I lost."

"Me too. Don't lose."

"So you think you're being followed?" Auntie Olga asked as she wiped down the long Formica counter.

"I know I was yesterday," Sergei replied, lifting up his coffee cup and saucer as she reached him. "The tail is compromised, though, and he knows it. I haven't seen him since, so my guess is that there's someone new and more careful out there today."

"Why are you sure your tail knew he was compromised?"

He didn't want to talk about his stupid stunt, so he gave a nonchalant shrug and said, "Well, after years of FBI experience, I could just tell."

Olga looked at him oddly, but all she said was, "All right. So how can I help?"

"I'll arrange to walk past here three or four times over the next day, and each time I'll let you know I'm coming. Just look out your window for a minute or so after I pass. If you see the same person each time, that's my new tail. I'll stop in for lunch tomorrow, and you can tell me what you saw, okay?"

"Okay."

That afternoon, Sergei went to his barber, an elderly gentleman who did one style (the flattop) well and therefore gave it to anyone who sat in his chair unless they specifically instructed him otherwise. On the way back to his office, Sergei took a route that went past the Petrograd. He also went to an indoor shooting range about a half mile away, to keep from getting rusty with his nine millimeter. The L or the bus would have been faster, but his walk took him past Olga Yanayev's window going both ways. The next morning, for good measure, he went to a Russian bakery a block and a half from the Petrograd and bought some fresh, but overpriced, *prianik medoviy*, a type of honey cookie he had loved since childhood.

A few minutes after noon, he walked into the Petrograd and sat down on a stool at the end of the counter, where he could see out of the restaurant's large plate-glass window but couldn't easily be seen from the street. Olga came over half a minute later with water and silverware. "Thanks," said Sergei. "Did you spot my friend?"

"He just went into the Starbucks across the street," she said as she arranged his place setting. "White guy, maybe forty or forty-five, black hair, a little on the short side."

Sergei studied the customers at Starbucks. "Hat and a tan overcoat?"

"That's the one. By the way, don't count on tracking him based on what he's wearing: he changed clothes at least once yesterday."

"So he's more professional than the last guy," Sergei said, nodding approvingly. "Good. This should be fun." It had been years since he'd done countersurveillance, and he relished the challenge. "He must have someone to cover for him while he's changing. Did you see anyone else?"

She shook her head. "Just him." She put her hand on Sergei's arm and looked him in the eye. "And this isn't 'fun.' This is business. I have seen men dead because they played games in situations like this and lost."

He patted her hand affectionately. "So have I. Don't worry, I know what I'm doing. I'll be careful."

Ben slouched in a chair at one of the little tables at the Mud Hole, drowning his sorrows in espresso. Noelle sat across from him, listening as he explained what had just happened in Judge Harris's courtroom.

"So wait, why did the judge throw out that letter?" she asked.

"Because we never produced it in discovery and we didn't have a good reason for withholding it. I was afraid this would happen. Judges hate it when parties hide stuff."

"But was Dr. Ivanovsky really hiding it from them? This Zinoviev guy signed it, after all, right? Wouldn't he have a copy?"

"You'd think so," said Ben. "But Nicki's dead, and if he had a copy, he didn't give it to his lawyers or tell them about it—or so Tony Simeon says. I don't think it really mattered to Judge Harris, though. He kept coming back to the fact that we were obligated to produce that letter and didn't do it. He said that the law doesn't permit litigants to play hide-the-ball, even if their opponents happen to know where the ball is." He took a sip of his coffee. "Actually, he's probably right."

"So what does this mean?" asked Noelle. "Can you still win the case?"

"Theoretically, yes. This was only a motion to strike; the motion to reconsider isn't up until day after tomorrow. But the judge struck the only new evidence I've got and everything in my motion that refers to it. All that's left is a rehash of the arguments and evidence I used in opposing Tony's summary-judgment motion. Judge Harris didn't buy it then, and I'm not really optimistic that he'll buy it the day after tomorrow."

"Have you committed it into God's hands?"

"Of course—just like I did with the motion I lost today."

Sergei's apartment building had a fire escape in back, which proved useful. When he arrived home that evening, he quickly changed into a black sweatshirt and black jeans and grabbed his compact camera and telephoto lens. He unlocked his gun cabinet and took out his Beretta 92 Elite nine millimeter (the best general-purpose handgun in his armory) and his quick-release belt holster. Then he slipped out his back window and slid down the fire escape—acutely aware of the noise he was making—and dropped to the ground. He ran around the side of the building just in time to see his tail's car pulling away from the curb a block and a half away.

The tail would probably recognize Sergei's customized black Mustang, which his friends had dubbed "the Black Russian." So he had asked a friend to rent a car and park it behind the building. He ran back to it, found the keys hidden under a tire, and drove down the alley leading to the street. The alley was a maze of dumpsters and parked cars. It took time to navigate in the day and was impassible to the uninitiated at night. Sergei drove as quickly as he dared, nearly killing a neighbor's cat in the process.

When he reached the street and looked down it, he saw what looked like the tail's car almost five blocks away. That was too great a distance to do reliable surveillance, but the streets were empty and well lit, and he didn't want to risk getting caught. Besides, if he lost the car, he could always try again tomorrow. At the next stoplight, he pulled out his telephoto lens and trained it on the distant car's license plate. He could only pick out the first three characters because a delivery truck partially blocked his view, but they matched the plates on his tail's car. He also confirmed that the make, model, and year of the car were the same. Satisfied, he put away the lens as the light changed.

He felt familiar butterflies beginning to flutter in his stomach, and he smiled. He had done this at least a dozen times before, but it still made him nervous—and it probably always would. A touch of nerves wasn't necessarily bad; it kept him on his toes and prevented him from getting careless. And, as had been repeatedly drilled into his head during his FBI training, "Carelessness kills."

He followed the tail's car into a brightly lit strip mall just outside the city limits. It parked near one end of the long, half-full lot in front of the stores. Sergei drove through the parking lot, turned into the delivery lane that ran behind the stores, and continued along until he reached an alley leading back to the storefront side.

He parked his car and carefully made his way down the short, shadowy alley until he could see the tail's car. It was empty. Sergei froze and the hair on the back of his neck stood up.

Where are you? He glanced around quickly but saw nothing except dark asphalt and the blank walls of the buildings on either side. Great spot for an ambush. He took his pistol out of its holster.

Staying in the shadows, he walked cautiously to the end of the alley, then stopped and crouched behind a dumpster. He snuck a quick glimpse around the edge of the dumpster and got a better look at the tail's car. It wasn't empty after all. A man leaned back in the passenger seat, apparently asleep. So where was the driver?

Sergei heard a man's voice talking in muffled tones, probably five or ten yards from his hiding spot. He peeked around the corner and caught a glimpse of a man standing at a pay phone about twenty feet away. He was facing Sergei, but the phone was between them. All Sergei could see were the man's legs, but he had no doubt that it was his tail. Cell phones, even digital ones, could be monitored with the right equipment. Pay phones could not, unless they were bugged in advance. Professionals in search of an easily accessible and relatively secure line therefore often used randomly selected pay phones.

The man seemed to be leaning into the little half-booth for privacy. Behind him, a steady stream of customers flowed in and out of a store's entrance. His view was completely blocked by the walls of the booth, which gave Sergei an idea. He thought about it for a moment and decided it was worth the risk.

Putting his pistol away, Sergei walked out of the alley and joined the shoppers on the sidewalk. His gaze flicked back and forth between the car and the man on the phone. It looked like the tail, though Sergei couldn't be sure without seeing his face. If the man turned around, he couldn't help seeing Sergei. But if he didn't, Sergei might be able to eavesdrop on him for several seconds as he walked into the store.

The man remained intent on his conversation as Sergei walked behind him. He was speaking quietly, but the curved walls of the phone enclosure reflected his voice outward. Sergei could almost, but not quite, make out what the man was saying. He slowed his pace and listened intently. The man wasn't speaking English, Russian, or any language that Sergei recognized, but the general tone and cadence of his speech sounded vaguely familiar. Sergei was intensely curious now. He wanted to stop and listen, but he knew he couldn't. The automatic doors of the store opened and he reluctantly walked through. Just before they closed behind him, he caught the word *ghaskhi*. He'd heard that before—but where?

As soon as he was inside the store, Sergei turned left so that the tail couldn't see him through the glass doors. He glanced back to make sure no one was behind him, then ducked down an aisle of discount cookware. Slowing his pace, he stared blankly at rows of different-sized Teflon pans as he tried to place the man's language. *Ghaskhi* wasn't Russian, but it reminded him of a trip he'd made to Russia a few years ago. *But why?*

Then it hit him—he'd heard it on TV while watching coverage of the Chechen war. It was the Chechen word for "Russian." He stopped and a chill ran through him. Chechens? Why on earth would Chechens be following him?

"The bugs can go back now that they're done sweeping," the man said into the pay phone. "We don't want to miss more than we have to."

"Yes, sir. They'll be back in when the cleaning service is done tonight."

"Good. How is the surveillance of the scientist going?"

"He is a difficult subject," the voice at the other end admitted wearily, "but at least he hasn't spotted me."

"Yes. We have already lost one good soldier. We cannot afford to lose another." He had regretted the necessity of young Alikhan's fate, but a shadow soldier cannot have a face. If he does, he is compromised. Worse, he risks compromising every other soldier he comes in contact with, and they in turn become dangers to everyone they contact. A fighter whose identity is known is like a plague bearer, spreading his lethal infection wherever he goes.

Unfortunately, there was only one way to stop such an infection. They all knew this; Alikhan had known it before he volunteered. He had accepted his transfer to the martyrdom unit bravely and calmly, and even now he was probably preparing for his mission against the Russian occupiers in Grozny.

The man at the pay phone was sure Alikhan would carry out this task honorably and successfully, but he could have done so much more. A surge of fury rose in his throat as he thought of the loss of his fine young comrade. He wished he could put a knife through the heart of that arrogant Russian detective who had, in effect, killed Alikhan. *That day will come,* he thought, calming himself. *Soon all our dead will be avenged.*

Ben lay in bed, staring at the blank ceiling and listening to Noelle snoring softly beside him. He turned his head and looked at the display on the alarm clock. *1:33 a.m.* He closed his eyes and tried to relax his body and mind. He was dead tired, but somehow he just couldn't force himself to sleep. He opened his eyes again and peered at the green digital readout. *1:46.*

He couldn't stop thinking about the hearing on the motion to reconsider tomorrow morning. *This morning,* he corrected himself. The hearing was only about seven hours away, and he had no idea how he could win. He had considered and rejected every possible argument, and he was left with very little that even passed the straight-face test. He had more or less decided what he was going to say, but it wasn't very persuasive and he knew it. His mind kept trolling through the facts and law of the case, looking for a winning angle that he might have missed somehow. Sleep would do more good than mental fidgeting, but he could not make himself sleep.

A heavy weight of guilt kept pressing down on his mind. *If* he had pushed Dr. Ivanovsky when they were assembling their document production, the old man might have coughed up the now-forbidden

Zinoviev letter. Instead, he had delegated the job to Noelle, who had no legal experience, while he worked on what he thought were more important projects. *If* he had spent more time getting ready for the summary-judgment hearing, maybe the judge wouldn't have ruled against him. He'd put in the time now, of course, but getting Judge Harris—or any judge—to reverse himself was always an uphill battle, no matter how good an argument the lawyer presented. He shifted uncomfortably and rolled over. The bottom line was that *if* he had been faithful in the small things, he might not be facing this overwhelming crisis.

He tried not to think about losing, but he feared it. Or rather, he feared the consequences of losing this case. Three times over the past week, he had woken in a heart-pounding sweat from nightmares that his eyes were bleeding—or worse, that Noelle's eyes were. Lying there in the hopeless hours between midnight and dawn, Ben knew in the pit of his stomach that his nightmares could easily become real. Thousands, maybe millions, of men, women, and children could die horrible deaths because Ben had let himself be distracted from this irritating little case. And now there was nothing he could do to stop it.

He tried to persuade himself that Dr. Ivanovsky was wrong, that the safe-deposit box held nothing more dangerous than smuggled diamonds or drug money. But every time he had almost convinced himself, he remembered his client's anguished face and shaking voice as he described the dead scientists at that lab. Then the horror gripped Ben anew and he was wide awake again.

He prayed. He often prayed for victory, much as an athlete prays before a game, but this was different. Never had he felt so utterly helpless, and never had the stakes of a hearing been so high. He was powerless to undo the damage his neglect had allowed, and he knew it. Only God could do that, but Ben had difficulty believing that he would. It wasn't that Ben lacked intellectual faith, but that he lacked visceral trust. It's one thing to believe in miracles; it is quite another to rely on one actually happening.

Ben had never thought of his law practice as much more than an enjoyable way to make money. In one sense, he always wanted his cases to have some meaning too—otherwise winning wasn't very gratifying. But real meaning, he decided—the kind of meaning that kept him in agonized prayer long after midnight—he could do without. He wanted to change people's lives, but not hold their lives in his hands. He knew, of course, that they were also in God's hands, just as he was. But that truth seemed awfully theoretical right now, and the hearing a few hours away seemed awfully real.

The phone rang, startling him out of his black reverie. He looked at the clock: *2:06 a.m.* The knot in his stomach tightened as the phone rang again. Nobody ever calls at two o'clock in the morning with good news. "Wha—who is it?" Noelle said sleepily.

"The caller ID says 'Unknown Caller,'" Ben replied, "but it can't be a telemarketer at this hour." He reached over and picked up the receiver as the phone rang a third time. "Hello?"

"I have what you need," said a digitally altered voice. It was so distorted that Ben couldn't even tell if it was a man or a woman. "I can prove that there was a contract between Mikhail Ivanovsky and Nikolai Zinoviev."

CHAPTER EIGHT
THE HUNTED MEN

"*Ivanovsky versus Estate of Zinoviev,*" the court clerk announced.

Showtime. Ben got up from his seat next to Dr. Ivanovsky and walked to the front of the courtroom. After last night's sleepless vigil, punctuated by the early-morning phone call, he was operating solely on the combination of adrenaline and caffeine that the litigators at Beale & Ripley had always called *jet fuel.* The reason for the name was that some high-fliers could thrive on that mixture for months straight, while others burned out and crashed. Ben knew which category he fell into—he was focused and full of energy now, but he would be essentially worthless by early afternoon.

"Good morning, Your Honor," Ben said as he approached Judge Harris's bench. "Benjamin Corbin on behalf of Dr. Mikhail Ivanovsky."

"Good morning. Anthony Simeon on behalf of the estate of Nikolai Zinoviev," Ben's opponent said as he approached from the other side of the courtroom.

"Good morning, Counsel," Judge Harris greeted them from his high seat behind the bench. "Mr. Corbin, what do you have to say in support of your motion for reconsideration?"

"As pointed out in our motion—"

"Which I've already read," the judge warned.

"Yes, Your Honor. As the Court knows, one of our central arguments is that summary judgment is inappropriate because there may be additional evidence that could prove the existence of a contract between Dr. Ivanovsky and Mr. Zinoviev without the necessity of my client's testimony.

"That argument was proven true at 2:06 this morning. As is set forth in my affidavit, which was hand delivered to your chambers as soon as court opened today, there is a witness out there who claims to be able to prove that this contract exists. We deserve the opportunity to find that person and establish that he or she is telling the truth. But we can do that only if the judgment in favor of Mr. Zinoviev's estate is vacated. All we're asking for is what the law clearly gives us: the right to finish discovery and present our evidence. Thank you, Your Honor."

"You're welcome," said the judge. "Mr. Simeon?"

"Your Honor, this affidavit is the very definition of hearsay: an out-of-court statement introduced to prove the truth of the matter it asserts. We cannot cross-examine this person who called Mr. Corbin or otherwise test his reliability. We don't even know who he is. Your Honor told Mr. Corbin to file a motion to reconsider if he uncovered new admissible evidence. He has not. All he has is his own affidavit saying, in essence, that he hopes to find admissible evidence in the future. That is not enough.

"Worse, this is hearsay tied to a sandbag. This is the second time this week that the plaintiff has tried to blindside us with undisclosed evidence. The Court rejected my opponent's last attempt to circumvent the discovery rules and should do so again. Thank you, Your Honor."

"You're also welcome." The judge turned back to Ben. "Okay, Mr. Corbin, I'm going to give you the last word."

Ben straightened his papers and collected his thoughts. "Mr. Simeon said that this affidavit establishes nothing but the hope of finding admissible evidence. That is precisely the purpose of discovery, Your Honor. It allows litigants to pursue the hope of finding admissible evidence to support their cases. If that hope remains unfulfilled when all avenues of discovery have been exhausted, then—and only then—is summary judgment appropriate.

"This affidavit does not prove that a contract existed between my client and Mr. Zinoviev, but it *does* prove that evidence exists that can establish that fact. We are entitled to investigate that evidence.

"As to Mr. Simeon's allegation that we sandbagged him, I—"

"That doesn't bother me," interrupted Judge Harris. "I came down on you last time because it looked like you or your client was withholding evidence and playing hide-the-ball. I don't get the sense that that's happening here. What troubles me about this affidavit is how you're going to get this informant's testimony. I don't have any idea how you're going to do that. Do you?"

"Well, Your Honor—"

"And if you don't, why should I keep this case going?"

"We have already retained a top-notch detective to look into this, Your Honor. I was on the phone with him this morning before the hearing. He's a former FBI agent with outstanding credentials and strong connections to the local Russian community. I have every confidence in him. If anyone can hunt down this informant, he can. Again, Your Honor, all we're asking for is the opportunity to try."

"They've already had that opportunity," Anthony Simeon countered. "This sounds like a wild-goose chase to me."

The judge sat in thoughtful silence for several seconds. "I'm reluctant to enter judgment against a party when it looks like evidence may exist that could prove his case. Maybe it is a wild-goose chase, but the law allows him to chase that goose. I'm going to vacate the judgment entered in favor of the defendant."

Relief flooded through Ben and he heard stifled sounds behind him where Dr. Ivanovsky was sitting. With an effort, he focused his attention back on what the judge was saying.

". . . previously set trial date still stands. There will be no continuances. We'll all be back here in five days and, Mr. Corbin, you'll need more than an affidavit to avoid judgment then. You're free to chase your goose, but you'd better catch him by nine o'clock Monday morning."

◆ ◆ ◆

"Do you know who this informant is?" The voice on the phone was smooth and professional, with only a slight Chechen accent.

"I'm sorry, 'Leonid.' We don't," Dmitry Kolesnikov replied, his palms growing slick with nervous sweat as he spoke.

Dmitry hated dealing with Chechens. They were exceptionally brutal, even by *mafiya* standards. For instance, he knew of a gang of Chechen drug runners who had been having difficulty getting paid by some of their buyers. As a remedy, they had caught one of their delinquent customers and vivisected him. Not only that, they had videotaped the whole thing and distributed copies to their other slow-paying accounts with a note saying, "Pay or you are next." A Russian gangster might kill another man in a situation like that, but it would be a clean shot to the head, not a sick exhibition. But with the Chechens, vicious behavior was the rule, not the exception—Dmitry knew a dozen similar stories, some worse.

He and the other Brothers never would have dealt with such barbarians if there hadn't been so much money at stake. "Leonid" and his associates—none of whom the Brothers had ever seen—were willing to pay five million dollars up front and another ten on delivery, over twice as much as the next-highest bidder. Money like that was worth taking a risk or two.

"Do you have any suspects?" Leonid asked.

"Unfortunately, we don't, but if we think of any, we'll tell you right away."

"I can think of four," Leonid said evenly.

Fear clutched Dmitry's heart. "It's not one of us! I swear it!"

"Then find out who it is."

"But how do you know there even is an informant? You know how these American lawyers are—they always lie."

"The lawyer is not lying. How we know this is not your concern. Finding the informant is." The line went dead.

Dmitry paused for a moment, then slowly placed the receiver back in its cradle. "Anton!" he called.

A few seconds later, his colleague appeared in the door. He was a big man with the large, scarred hands of a boxer. "What is it, Dima?" He looked at Dmitry's face. "A call from Leonid?"

Dmitry nodded. "He wants us to find whoever called Ivanovsky's lawyer last night."

"Why should we?" Anton growled. "That wasn't part of the deal. We've done a lot more than we agreed to already. I'm getting tired of those *baklany*."

"They think it might be one of us."

"So?" Anton spat angrily. Then the implication hit him. "Oh."

"Exactly," said Dmitry. "It wouldn't be quick either. Those filthy animals would want to get us to talk first." He shivered. "That cold-blooded snake Leonid never even raises his voice. Those types are always the worst."

"I'd get him first," Anton said. "I'd give him a bullet right here"—he pointed to his pockmarked forehead—"and that's if he's lucky."

Dmitry nodded absently, his brain whirring. "Do we have a traitor among us? Remember how the police were sniffing around a few months ago and then backed off?"

"Because we made sure they didn't find anything."

"That's what we all thought. But what if they *did* find something? What if, instead of arresting someone, they decided to *threaten* to arrest someone unless that someone turned informant? And what if that someone said yes and that's why the police aren't bothering us—for now?"

Anton stared for a second with his mouth open. "I am not an informant!"

Dmitry chuckled. "If I thought you were, would we be having this conversation? No, I don't suspect you. But someone is talking to that lawyer."

Anton looked confused. "Why the lawyer? Wouldn't they be talking to the cops?"

"Of course," Dmitry said patiently, "but there's no reason they can't talk to both the cops *and* the lawyer. If they're going to be double-crossing us, why not make some money in the process—particularly since the police will be shutting down our little business? They tell the police what we're doing to stay out of jail, and they sell the same information to the lawyer. In fact, they probably tell the lawyer first, because once the police know, everyone gets arrested, the story hits the papers, and there's nothing to sell."

Anton nodded slowly as he thought it through. "But who would do this?"

Dmitry shrugged. "Someone who knows about Nicki's foolish deal with the scientist. Someone who can be pressured. How many people fit that profile?"

"Pasha. Josef." Anton was silent for a moment, his brow furrowed in concentration. "I can't think of anybody else."

"Neither can I," said Dmitry. "Let's keep a very close eye on those two. And if we catch one of them, he has an 'accident,' just like Nicki."

Anton looked troubled, so Dmitry added, "I don't like it, but we don't have much choice. And if the lawyer or his detective get too close to finding the informant . . . ?"

Anton grinned like a hockey player, reminding Dmitry of just what a tough, ruthless fighter his colleague had become in the Soviet prison system. "They have 'accidents' too."

Dmitry smiled. "Exactly."

Where to start? Sergei settled in at his desk and reached for a notepad. The thing to do, of course, would be to assign a detective to each potential informant and investigate that person thoroughly. Sergei didn't have those kinds of resources, so he decided to do the next-best thing: pick the most likely suspect and watch him.

And who was the most likely suspect? Probably one of the Brothers, or someone close to them. To Sergei's knowledge, they were the only ones who could know about both the contract and Ben's need for their help.

Sergei had already reviewed all their phone records to see if any of them had called Ben. He also checked Dr. Ivanovsky's records. It wasn't impossible that the monomaniacal scientist was trying to generate evidence to keep his case alive. None of them, however, had called Ben from home or on their mobile phones, and two of the Brothers—Dmitry Kolesnikov and Pavel Voronin—had been on the phone with each other at the time the informant had called Ben.

Two down, three to go.

There was only one man in Chicago who sold digital voice-altering equipment, and Sergei knew him. He picked up the phone (which he regularly swept for bugs) and dialed.

"George, it's Sergei Spassky. I've got a couple of questions for you about some equipment you sold."

"Fire away." George Spender was a former FBI electronics expert who had discovered about five years ago that his skills were a lot more valuable to private buyers than to the government.

"Have you sold voice-altering equipment to a man in his seventies with bushy gray hair and a thick Russian accent? He's about five foot eight, thin, and he doesn't dress too well."

"Doesn't sound familiar. I've sold to Russians, but no one fitting that description."

Sergei crossed Dr. Ivanovsky off his list. "How about a big Russian guy, about forty, with lots of tattoos and some missing teeth?"

"Nope."

"Okay." Sergei drew a line through Anton's name. "Last one: a Russian in his early fifties with a light accent, bald, glasses, and around five ten."

Spender had to think about that one for a few seconds. "Maybe . . . maybe. I've sold to a couple of Russians this month, and one of them might have looked like that. I just don't remember."

Sergei circled Josef Fedorov's name. He now had his prime suspect. "Thanks, George."

After he hung up the phone, Sergei sat in silence for several minutes, considering his next move. After rejecting more aggressive alternatives, he decided on a conservative and straightforward strategy: he would simply put Josef Fedorov under surveillance and wait to see what he was doing the next time the informant called Ben. Sergei was about to call Ben when the phone rang. He picked it up. "Sergei Spassky."

"Sergei, it's Ben Corbin. Good news. I just got a package from our informant. He sent me the minutes from a meeting of the Brothers where they talked about buying the box contents from Nikolai Zinoviev. Nicki was actually there for part of the meeting—and he told them he already had a deal with Dr. Ivanovsky. Plus, all four Brothers signed the minutes."

"Great!" Sergei replied. "I was just about to call you with an update on my search for the informant, but I guess there's no point in that now."

"Yes, there is," Ben said. "I still need someone to authenticate this document in court. All I can tell the judge right now is that some nameless person sent this to me in the mail. I need someone who can testify that this is a real document reflecting a real meeting where Nicki really said those things. I'll need the informant to do that. Otherwise, there's no way I'll be able to get this into evidence."

Sergei could hear paper rustling in the background as Ben talked. "Ben, are you holding that document right now?"

"Yeah."

"Don't. I'll need to check it for fingerprints."

"Oh. Good point." Another rustle. "Okay, I put it down and I won't touch it again till you've had a chance to look at it."

"Thanks. I'm on my way over."

Sergei wasn't surprised to find that the only fingerprints on the paper were Ben's. The informant had used voice-altering equipment on the phone to avoid being identified. He presumably would also be careful enough to use gloves in handling these pieces of paper. The envelope had lots of fingerprints on it, of course, but Sergei doubted that any of them belonged to the informant. Still, he carefully lifted each usable print he found.

Sergei then examined the minutes and envelope for any possible clues. The postmark showed that it had been mailed from downtown Chicago. The envelope was a generic business-size white one, and it contained no hair or other potential identifiers. The paper on which the minutes had been copied was twenty-pound generic copier paper. The stamp was a peel-off sticker, eliminating the possibility of DNA testing of dried saliva on the back. In short, the informant's package was as clean and anonymous as possible.

"Whoever sent this was very careful," Sergei told Ben when he finished his examination.

"Any idea who it was?" asked Ben.

Sergei briefly described his research and his tentative conclusion that Josef was the informant. "I was just going to watch and wait for him to contact you again, but I suppose it's a little late for that now," he concluded.

"Yeah," agreed Ben. "He may call me again, but he may not." He thought for a moment. "In fact, he probably won't. He'll think that by sending me this document, he's given me everything I need."

"So, where do you want to go from here?" asked Sergei.

"I'm going to call Josef and see if I can talk him into testifying."

"Actually, it might be best if I talk to him," said Sergei. "He's obviously afraid of someone, probably the other Brothers. I can talk to him about realistic ways we can give him security. I also speak Russian and have more experience dealing with people like Josef, so I may be able to get a better result. No offense."

"None taken. I appreciate your volunteering. Okay, talk to him, but it has to happen today or tomorrow."

Sergei sat at a small table in a shadowy corner of a food court. Across the street was the old brownstone that held the Brothers' offices. He looked out through the wall of plate glass, waiting for Josef Fedorov to appear. He glanced at his watch. It was 5:25 and the streets were full of commuters heading home. The Brothers didn't keep regular business hours, but frequently they did go out for dinner at around 5:30.

Sergei took his eyes off the street for a few seconds to scan the food court. Three of the tables were occupied and about half a dozen people stood at the counters of various fast-food outlets, but Sergei noted with satisfaction that his tail was not among them. Ditching him had been simple—Sergei had merely gone back to his office after meeting with Ben, dropped off his briefcase, and left. He had taken the elevator down to the basement, where his building opened into one of the pedestrian tunnels that honeycombed the ground under the Loop. He had then taken the tunnel to the nearest El station and caught the train to the Brothers' neighborhood. The tail was probably still sitting outside his building, waiting for him to emerge.

There he was. Josef Fedorov trotted down the steps and disappeared into the stream of pedestrians. Sergei rose from his seat and headed out at a brisk walk, his eyes scanning the crowd for Josef. Losing a target was always a danger in heavily traveled areas.

Sergei caught a glimpse of a black leather jacket like Josef's thirty yards ahead of him and hurried to catch up. Running might attract attention, so he speed-walked with the determined haste of a commuter who was late for his train. He got a better view of the black jacket half a minute later and realized with a start that it wasn't on Josef. He slowed down and angled toward the edge of the sidewalk, glancing up and down the street as if he was looking for a cab.

Nothing. Josef had vanished. Embarrassed, Sergei turned and headed back for the L station, making plans for catching Josef at his apartment building. He glanced in the window of a little hole-in-the-wall bar and grill that he hadn't noticed before and saw a black leather jacket hanging on a chair. *Bingo.*

Sergei walked in and stood by the door for a moment as his eyes adjusted to the smoky gloom after the bright early-evening sun. When he could see clearly again, he noticed that Josef was already staring at him.

Sergei gave him a friendly smile and walked over to his table. "*Dobry dyen*, Josef," he said as he sat down.

"Who are you?" Josef asked in English. His face was white and his voice shook.

"Sergei Spassky," the detective said amicably, "but you already know that. And I'll bet you also know why I'm here, so I'll make this short. We appreciate the information you've provided about the contract between Nikolai Zinoviev and Mikhail Ivanovsky, but we need you to testify at trial."

Josef started to sweat. "Get out of here! I don't know what you're talking about!"

"Yes, you do," Sergei said calmly. "Listen, I understand why you're frightened. We can help with that. We can make security arrangements for you and take care of you."

Josef leaned forward and hissed in Russian, "If you do not leave now, dog, I will kill you."

Sergei's friendly tone didn't waver as he slipped into Russian. "I doubt that. By the way, testifying isn't nearly as dangerous as *not* testifying. Either way, we'll tell the judge that we think you made that call to Ben Corbin and sent him those documents. If you help us, we'll protect you. If not, we won't. It's your decision. Call me or Mr. Corbin." He pulled out a business card. "Here's my number. You've already got Mr. Corbin's."

Sergei got up and walked out, leaving Josef sitting frozen, staring at the card. As Sergei left, he debated whether Josef really was the informant. The man's fear, shock, and outrage had all seemed genuine, but that could mean either that he wasn't the informant or that he hadn't expected Sergei to be able to identify him. Not that it mattered much. Josef would be in almost as much danger if Ben identified him as the probable informant as he would be if he actually testified. Either way, he would need protection, and that meant he would have to cooperate—whether or not he had intended to when Sergei had walked into the restaurant. The detective chuckled as he reflected that even if he hadn't *found* an informant, he had probably *created* one.

He was in an excellent mood as he went back to his office to wait for Josef's call. In fact, he was so busy congratulating himself for outmaneuvering the Brothers that he forgot to reenter his building through the basement. Instead, he got off at his usual El station and walked in through the front door.

Across the street from the grill, Anton watched with growing rage as Josef—that treacherous little *suka*—sat talking to the scientist's detective. They seemed like old friends. He couldn't see Josef's face, but the detective was smiling and gesturing as he talked. Now Josef was leaning forward to tell the man some secret, which made him smile again. They chatted for a minute more and the detective put a small card on the table for Josef, then got up and left.

The detective walked out of the restaurant with a satisfied smile on his boyish face. Anton clenched his large fists and visualized how good it would feel to smash that smile away permanently. But of course he couldn't. He had business to attend to.

Josef picked the card up from the table, looked at it for a few seconds, and put it in his pocket as a waitress arrived with his meal. He ate slowly, paid his bill, and left.

Anton followed him, making sure to stay in the shadows.

Josef started walking back to the office, but he took a wrong turn and walked half a block to a bus station.

Anton waited for half a minute, then followed him in. Josef was standing at a bank of pay phones with his back to Anton, talking quietly. A business card lay on the little stainless-steel counter next to him.

Anton reached into his jacket and fingered his gun. It would be easy to take Josef here. The station was nearly empty, and he could probably get out before anybody could see him. But Dmitry had said that Josef should have an accident, and that was probably right. Anton removed his hand from his coat and slipped out of the station.

He jogged back to the office so he would have time to talk to Dmitry before Josef arrived. After he gave his report, the other man nodded. "You did the right thing. Killing him in public would have caused problems."

Josef walked in just then. "Evening, Dima, Anton. What's up?"

"Not much," Dmitry said. "A little problem came up with that Chechen deal, but we've almost taken care of it."

"Good. Let me know what happens, okay?"

As Josef shut his office door behind him, Dmitry said, "Of course." He turned to Anton and said softly, "Make him disappear."

At 1:35 a.m., the living room of the apartment was dark and silent. The remains of a Chinese takeout dinner sat on the coffee table between the leather sofa and the large TV, sharing space with several sports and news magazines. A Russian novel was propped open on one arm of the sofa, and the previous day's newspaper lay strewn on the cushions of the matching love seat.

A scratching noise outside the window broke the late-night stillness. A dark shape crouched on the landing of the fire escape, bent over a small metal tool similar to the slim-jim device that tow-truck operators use to unlock car doors. The thin strip of metal appeared on the inside of the window just under the latch. It slowly moved up, pushing the latch open. The intruder removed the jimmy and eased the window open an inch. It creaked softly but audibly, so he took out a small aerosol can of oil and sprayed the hinges of the old-fashioned window. After a moment the window started to open again, this time soundlessly.

The shadowy figure popped out the screen, slipped through the open window, and dropped lightly to the floor. He was dressed all in black and wore a black ski mask. At his waist, he wore a belt lined with small pouches. A compact holster with a small pistol was strapped to his right thigh and a sheathed knife was on the left.

Drawing his gun, the man started across the room, hugging the wall as he cautiously made his way out of the living room and down the short hallway. A door stood half-open at the end of the hall, and the dark figure watched it closely as he edged forward. He stood outside the door for several seconds, listening. The stillness was disturbed only by a soft snoring and the faint sounds of the street outside. He looked inside and saw a man lying on his back in a large bed in the middle of the room, his sleeping face lit by the faint moonlight coming in through the window.

The intruder smiled in the darkness and put away his gun. The target had been positively identified, and he was alone and fast asleep. This would be quieter—and more satisfying—with the knife. As he pulled out the long, sharp blade and stepped toward the bed, a floorboard squeaked loudly under his foot.

The target lifted his head off the pillow and caught sight of the intruder in his bedroom. For an instant, both men froze. Then the intruder launched himself toward the bed, his knife aimed at the other man's throat. The man in the bed gave a wordless shout as he rolled onto the floor, his hand feeling for a gun on the bedside table. In his haste and groggy clumsiness, he knocked it off and it fell to the floor with a loud thunk.

The intruder scrambled across the bed and slashed wildly at the figure on the floor. The other man grabbed the intruder's knife arm and pulled him down, slamming his hand into the bed frame. The knife fell to the floor, and the two men grunted and cursed as they struggled in the narrow space between the bed and the wall.

The intruder landed a solid blow to the other man's head and broke free. He reached for his gun, but the holster was empty. The pistol must have fallen out during the struggle. He looked around wildly and saw the knife on the floor behind him. He grabbed it and lunged at his enemy.

A flash and a loud bang broke the dark stillness of the night. A burst of sparks flew from the knife and the intruder cried out as pain shot up his right arm. He staggered back, then turned and ran. A second shot just missed him as he sprinted out of the bedroom. He raced across the living room and dove out the window. He heard a third shot reverberate above him as he slid down the fire escape. Simultaneously, a searing pain blossomed in his left arm as the bullet tore through his triceps. He fell as he reached the ground, and rolled under the edge of the second-floor balcony. Staggering to his feet, he ran to his waiting car to nurse his wounds and fight again another day.

Back in the apartment, Sergei Spassky sat shaking on the floor. He had been fine until he got off the phone with the police. There had been things he needed to do, people he needed to talk to. But now he could only sit and wait and reflect on what had just happened—and what could have happened. He fingered the deep scratch that stretched from his sternum to his left shoulder and did his best not to imagine what it would have felt like to wake up to a knife plunging into his chest. He glanced at the windows and swallowed hard, though he was virtually certain the assassin was long gone.

He decided to do some informal crime-scene investigation to take his mind off of gruesome could-have-beens. Beretta in hand, he got up and walked down the hall, making sure not to disturb anything for the professionals who would arrive in a few minutes. He noticed with grim satisfaction that there were drops of blood on the floor.

He got down on his hands and knees to look at the gun and knife that lay on his bedroom floor. The gun was a Glock 23—a small, reliable, high-powered pistol. Sergei looked at it for only a few seconds; it told him nothing except that his attacker knew handguns.

The knife was more interesting. It was a long fighting knife with a dagger point and a keen edge that ran the length of the blade and partway along the top. It looked like a *Spetsnaz* commando knife, but it wasn't. Sergei was pretty sure that the Soviet military had never used handcrafted leather grips, and the blade appeared to be a custom high-carbon steel alloy. It was a beautiful knife; the only flaw was a large black dent in the grip and finger guard. Using a pencil, Sergei turned the knife over to get a better look. The dent appeared to be fresh. Sergei smiled coldly as he realized that it must have been caused by one of his shots. "I'll bet that hurt," he murmured.

He glanced around the room to see if his attacker had left anything else behind. A small black object in the corner caught his eye. After half a second, his mind identified it as the finger of a black glove. He crouched down for a closer look. The assassin's finger was still inside. Sergei flinched back, then stood staring down at the severed digit. His smile returned as the shock faded and he started thinking like a detective again. *You were careful not to leave any fingerprints, but you couldn't help leaving a finger—and it'll point straight back to you.*

Chapter Nine
Opening Statements

"Any luck?" Ben asked.

"Not yet," Sergei admitted. "I can't find him anywhere. He's not returning calls, his apartment seems to be empty, and I haven't seen him around the Brothers' building."

Ben leaned back and rubbed his eyes. "I thought you said he was going to testify. What happened?"

"I don't know. I talked to him in the restaurant. Then he called me half an hour later and said he thought we could do business. He said he'd make me an offer, but he never did. These *mafiya* types disappear all the time for all sorts of reasons."

"Well, is there anything you can do to find him?" Ben asked, frustration creeping into his voice. "Trial starts tomorrow, and I need him to testify—and I need you to make finding this guy your highest priority."

Sergei looked down at his notes. Candidly, he knew he should have followed up on this sooner than he had. He had viewed the matter as basically closed once Josef had called him, and he had allowed other matters (particularly the intruder who had nearly killed him) to occupy his attention for most of the past two days. It wasn't until yesterday evening—more than forty-eight hours after Josef's phone call—that he'd begun trying to find the man. "I'll keep on it. I know you need him by tomorrow morning at nine."

"Don't stop looking if you haven't found him by then. That's when our trial technically starts, but there'll probably be some motion practice and procedural arguing for most of the morning. I can also put on other witnesses for a while to delay things, if need be. But I will need him, and the sooner the better. Without Josef Fedorov, we're dead."

By three o'clock that afternoon, Ben's conference-room table was completely covered with paper. Noelle had spent most of the afternoon in the file room making copies of potential exhibits. Dr. Ivanovsky had dropped by after lunch, and for once Ben was glad to see him—the doctor was now checking the copies for missing pages and organizing them into neat stacks at one end of the table.

Ben sat at the other end, working on his opening statement. He murmured to himself in the middle of an untidy ring of court filings, deposition transcripts, scribbled notes, and accordion files of document productions, all liberally sprinkled with hundreds of annotated Post-its. He bent over a notepad bearing the latest outline of his statement, muttering and gesturing to an imaginary courtroom. Occasionally, he would fall silent and scribble on his pad or dig through a pile of papers for a document that had suddenly become important to his thinking.

Dr. Ivanovsky was careful not to disturb Ben with questions or suggestions. Indeed, he did not even feel tempted. It reassured him to see Ben at work. He looked like a scientist.

Sergei's tail was gone. Or, more likely, his old tail had been replaced. Sergei wasn't particularly surprised—it wasn't unusual for surveillance operatives to be rotated, particularly when they were observing a cautious subject. Still, it was unnerving. Sergei thought about using the Petrograd trick again, but he didn't have time to do that *and* find Josef. All he could do was try some countersurveillance techniques and try to ignore the feeling that someone was watching him.

Sergei decided that his best bet was to maintain a constant vigil of Josef's apartment and his car, which was parked directly below the apartment. If Josef was still in the area, he would probably come home—or at least come for his car—at some point. But by midnight, he still had not shown himself, and Sergei was beginning to doubt that he would.

It was time to take a risk. Sergei slipped across the street and into the parking lot. He approached Josef's car, staying out of the glow cast by the streetlights as much as possible. Fortunately, the car was in a dark corner of the lot. Sergei pulled out a small flashlight and played its beam over the interior of the car. A briefcase lay on the front passenger seat.

That was strange. Why would he leave his briefcase in his car?

He tried the door. It was unlocked. He got in and quickly searched through the briefcase. It contained a three-day-old newspaper, Sergei's business card, some documents related to what appeared to be a deal to import beluga caviar, a travel itinerary for a flight to Russia leaving two days ago and returning tomorrow, and Josef's passport. It took Sergei a few seconds to realize what that probably meant. He searched the rest of the car at a more leisurely pace, but found nothing relevant to the *Ivanovsky* case.

When he got back to his office, he dug out Ben Corbin's home number and called him, despite the fact that it was nearly one o'clock in the morning. After five rings, a groggy voice said, "Hello?"

"Hi, Ben, it's Sergei. Sorry to call you so late, but I just found out something you should know about. I don't think Josef Fedorov will be testifying at trial."

"Why not?"

"It looks like someone got to him before we did. My guess is that he's dead."

Promptly at nine o'clock, Ben stepped up to the podium, arranged his notes, and surveyed the courtroom. Directly in front of him, Judge Harris sat in a tall black chair behind his massive wooden bench, flanked by his clerk and bailiff. A court reporter sat on a small chair just in front of the bench, typing silently on her stenographic machine. Anthony Simeon and Janet Anderson were at the counsel table to Ben's right, and three of the Brothers (Dmitry, Anton, and Pavel) sat immediately behind them in the first row of seats. Noelle sat at the counsel table to the left of the podium, surrounded by boxes of neatly organized exhibits. Dr. Ivanovsky fidgeted nervously in the first row, and an elderly woman in a long Slavic-looking dress and practical shoes sat next to him. He had introduced her to the Corbins as his wife, a fact they had already guessed. Her name was Irina, and she had a friendly smile and very limited English.

Ben looked the judge in the eye and smiled with a confidence he did not feel. "Good morning, Your Honor. As the Court knows, opening statement is my opportunity to tell you what the facts will show. I am here this morning to present evidence, not argument."

"Which is all that the law or I will permit you to do in opening statement," Judge Harris interjected dryly.

"Yes, Your Honor, but the facts themselves argue more eloquently than I ever could. This is a case about a broken contract. You will hear Dr. Mikhail Ivanovsky"—he gestured to his client with his left hand—"testify that on October seven, he and Nikolai Zinoviev negotiated for the sale of the contents of safe-deposit box 4613 at the LaSalle Street branch of American Union Bank. He will further testify that he gathered $5,000 on two hours' notice and delivered that money to Mr. Zinoviev—testimony that will be corroborated by Mr. Zinoviev's bank records and his testimony in this room at the TRO hearing last month. The Court's earlier rulings will not allow my client to testify as to what happened next, but he doesn't need to. The only inference that can reasonably be drawn from these undisputed facts is that—"

"Objection, argument," interrupted Simeon.

"Sustained."

"Thank you, Your Honor," Ben said. Judge Harris was apparently going to keep him on a short leash despite the absence of a jury. Ben made a mental note to omit the potentially argumentative portions of his opening. "Furthermore," he continued, moving to his next point, "evidence from Mr. Zinoviev's own colleagues"—he pointed to the Brothers—"will independently prove the existence of this contract. They met with Mr. Zinoviev on October nine of this year to discuss a business proposal. And it so happens that they took minutes at that meeting." Ben took out an enlarged copy of the minutes and put it on an easel. "In the very first paragraph it says—"

"Objection," said Janet Anderson. "This document is a forgery, Your Honor. We—" Simeon put his hand on her arm, and she stopped.

"That may be a valid objection if and when Mr. Corbin moves for the admission of this exhibit into evidence," said the judge. "He hasn't done that yet. If you disagree with his version of the facts, tell me your own version in your opening. Don't interrupt his. Objection overruled."

Ben smiled inwardly as his adversary sat in red-faced silence. "Thank you, Your Honor. The first paragraph of these minutes states that the purpose of this meeting was to discuss the purchase of the contents of the very same safe-deposit box that Mr. Zinoviev had already sold to Dr. Ivanovsky.

"The second paragraph says that they agreed on a purchase price of $100,000, 'conditioned on a representative of the Company inspecting the contents of the box and deeming them satisfactory.' We know from

Mr. Zinoviev's earlier testimony that he did in fact show the Brothers the contents of the box and that they agreed to pay him $100,000. We also have the contract that they signed with him.

"But what's *not* in the contract is the last paragraph of these minutes, which I've highlighted in yellow here: 'Mr. Zinoviev disclosed to the Members of the Company that he had entered into a prior agreement to sell the contents of the box to a third party. He agreed that he would be solely responsible for obtaining the release of any obligations under that agreement. He further agreed that payment of the purchase price was conditioned on his delivering full and clear title to the contents of the box.'" Ben paused. "Mr. Zinoviev never received that purchase price. Why not? Because he could not deliver 'full and clear title to the contents of the box.' And why couldn't he deliver that title? Because he had already sold it to Dr. Ivanovsky.

"Mr. Zinoviev no doubt developed a severe case of seller's remorse when he realized that he had sold for $5,000 what he could have sold for $100,000. That gave him a powerful motive to trample on Dr. Ivanovsky's rights, but not the legal ability to do so. We ask the Court to vindicate those rights. Thank you, Your Honor."

Sergei shifted uncomfortably in the metal-and-plastic chair in front of Elena Kamenev's well-used steel desk. Elena sat across from him, mostly hidden by a bulky old computer monitor and several piles of paper. If she hadn't been tall—about five foot nine—she probably wouldn't have been visible at all. As it was, all Sergei could see was the top of her blonde head, her concentration-wrinkled forehead, and her brown eyes focused intently on the screen in front of her.

The FBI was investigating the attack on Sergei because of the possibility that it was connected to organized crime. Several of his current investigations were at least indirectly related to the *Organizatsiya*. The fact that the victim was a well-regarded former FBI agent didn't hurt either. They had established him as a "source," which made it possible for him to participate in the investigation to a certain degree.

As one of the few Russian speakers in the Bureau's Chicago office, Elena had been assigned to investigate. Unfortunately, she wasn't having much luck. She looked up from the computer. "We've run both the fingerprint and the DNA profile through our database and all the police databases. No hits."

"Have you tried Interpol?"

"Of course. We're also working with our legats in Moscow, though that's taking longer."

Sergei wasn't surprised. The Russian police records weren't as thoroughly computerized as the FBI's. Many of them needed to be checked by hand, which could take a long time. Also, the agents working in the legal attaché's office—known as legats—needed to work through local officials, which would take even more time. Understanding the reason for the delay didn't make it any less nerve racking, though. Somewhere out there was a man who had wanted to kill him *before* he had blown off one of the man's fingers. Now that assassin was even more motivated and was probably somewhere planning his revenge even as Sergei sat talking to Elena.

Sergei felt extremely vulnerable and jittery—the perspective of a crime victim was new to him. Elena's eyes flickered down to his lap for an instant, and he realized that he was fidgeting with his pen. He put it down and reflexively covered his fear by making a small joke. "Russians," he said derisively, shaking his head with a mischievous smile.

Elena smiled back. "I know. My life would be so much easier if they could shoot as well in the dark in their apartments as they can at a shooting range."

Sergei laughed. "Mine too." He remembered the wickedly long knife he had found lying on his bedroom floor. "Say, have you asked the Russians to check their military records for this guy?"

She raised her eyebrows. "You think he might be a vet?"

Sergei nodded. "That knife I shot out of his hand looked custom made, but it was the same pattern as the knives the *Spetsnaz* commandos use. Maybe he bought it without knowing what it was, but maybe he was trained with that kind of knife and bought it because he knew how to fight with it."

"Could be," she acknowledged. As she typed, a new wave of unease roiled Sergei's stomach. The possible involvement of criminals with *Spetsnaz* training added a higher level of seriousness to the investigation. They were elite commandos equally skilled in combat and infiltrating enemy—meaning American—society. This would make them excellent hit men, couriers, enforcers, and so on. They would be a most unwelcome addition to Chicago's underworld.

At the end of his opening statement, Ben left the blowup of the minutes on the easel. This was a standard lawyer's ploy that gave Anthony Simeon two choices: he could either take the exhibit down—which would make him look like he was afraid of it—or he could leave it up to distract the judge during his opening. Either way, Ben would gain a small tactical advantage.

"Good morning, Your Honor," Simeon said, setting his notes on the podium before he stepped in front of it. "I have a prepared opening statement, of course, but before I give it I would like to take just a few minutes to respond to Mr. Corbin's remarks." He gestured to the minutes. "This document on which Mr. Corbin lays such great weight perfectly summarizes the central flaw in his case: he has theories, but no evidence to support them. Lawsuits can only be won with evidence, not allegations—and this document is not evidence. According to Mr. Corbin's own admission, he received it one day in the mail, in a blank envelope. He does not know who sent it to him, where the original is, or whether it is genuine or a forgery. We heard him speculate as to the answers he would like to each of these questions, and indeed we can each speculate to our own tastes. But the law does not value speculations—only facts.

"What do the facts show here? They show that Mikhail Ivanovsky gave $5,000 to Nikolai Zinoviev, nothing more. Was it a loan? Was it a gift? Was it the purchase price for some thing or service? It could have been any of those or none of them. We do not know.

"What we *do* know is that the evidence will establish no link between that money and the contents of the safe-deposit box that Mr. Zinoviev inherited from his brother. Tragically, Mr. Zinoviev is not here to tell us his side of the story on this point. As a result, Dr. Ivanovsky is barred from telling his side, a point Mr. Corbin ignored in his opening."

"Objection, argument," said Ben.

"Sustained."

"Thank you," said Simeon in his rich, mellifluous voice. "Once we strip away the plaintiff's inadmissible story"—he gestured to Dr. Ivanovsky—"his attorney's skillful speculations"—he gestured to Ben— "and this foundationless document"—he gestured to the minutes on the easel—"what are we left with?" He walked over to the easel, turned the blowup around, and set it back in its place with the blank reverse side exposed. He pointed to it again. "Nothing."

Elk Grove Village is home to a large collection of light-industrial parks. Low one- and two-story buildings cluster together along small streets in the same way that houses line the roads of residential subdivisions. Much of the town lies under the flight paths of O'Hare Airport, which depresses rents and property values, particularly close to the airport.

At the end of one cul-de-sac less than two miles west of O'Hare, a dilapidated building stood between two vacant structures that were slowly being shaken into ruins by the continual roar of jets taking off and landing. The building had a freshly painted black-and-white sign in front that said "Illinois Industries," though no Illinoisans worked there and what went on inside could hardly be considered industry.

In the back of the building, a row of cots lined a quiet room that served as a combination barracks and hospital. Only one of the cots was now occupied. On it lay General Elbek Shishani, the man who had been tailing Sergei Spassky and who was now recuperating from surgery to repair the damage done to his left arm by Sergei's bullets. One shot had removed a finger from his right hand. Another had torn his triceps nearly in half, three inches above the elbow, and his arm would have been crippled permanently without a prompt operation to sew the muscle back together. Fortunately, they had recruited a skilled medic for this mission, one who had extensive experience treating bullet wounds caused by Russians.

The surgery had gone well and Elbek was expected to recover fully, though he would need to learn to hold a handgun with only four fingers. But that would have to wait. He would be bedridden for the next several days with little to do but think. And remember.

The road that had led him to Elk Grove Village had started almost thirty years ago on the other side of the world. Elbek had been a promising young officer in the *Spetsnaz*, one of the few non-Russians groomed for advancement. In the early 1980s, advancement for a commando had meant a tour of duty in Afghanistan.

He had heard enough stories from returning veterans not to believe the version of the war told by *Pravda* and the TV news. But nothing had prepared him for the reality he'd found. The Red Army and their Afghan allies controlled the cities and most of the larger towns. The privileged few welcomed them as protectors, but the wretchedly poor masses watched them with dark, stony eyes wherever they went. The main roads were safe during daylight hours, as long as they traveled in well-armed convoys, checked continually for mines, and avoided narrow gorges and other obvious ambush locations.

After nightfall, the countryside belonged to the *dukhs*, or "spirits," Soviet slang for the Afghan resistance fighters. Cloaked in darkness, they could creep close enough to Soviet and government strongholds to hammer them with hit-and-run mortar attacks. If the Soviets sent out retaliatory strikes, they found nothing but freshly laid mines and—if they strayed too far from their camps—snipers and deadly ambushes.

In the early years of the war, the Soviets had responded to *dukh* raids with massive artillery barrages and bombing raids of suspected rebel positions, but the *dukhs* had generally vanished by the time the bombers or lumbering howitzers could pound their positions. All this tactic had accomplished was the expenditure of hundreds of tons of ordnance and the annihilation of any Afghan civilians in the target area.

So what to do? The Soviet answer was to send in men like Elbek: highly trained soldiers who could operate alone or in small bands and take the fight to the guerrillas in their caves and mountain camps.

It was a brutal war. Elbek had quickly learned not to show mercy to prisoners, and to expect none if he was captured. He'd also learned that there was no such thing as an "innocent civilian." The old arthritic man sitting outside his hut might well be hiding *dukhs* inside. The frightened young mother and children cowering by the road would likely be out in the fields after an ambush, looking for wounded Soviets to torture and kill.

Afghanistan made Elbek very businesslike about the administration of pain and death. If placing burning coals in the wounds of an injured fighter would make him reveal the location of a secret camp or the identities of the peasants who had helped him, then Elbek had no qualms about doing it. If calling in air or artillery strikes to destroy a village would make it harder for the *dukhs* to operate in an area, then it would be foolish not to do so.

But if the war desensitized Elbek in some ways, it had sensitized him in others. The more he killed, the more of his comrades he saw killed, the more he suffered through grueling missions, the more he wondered what the point of it all was. Not just the point of the war, but the point of *him*. Surely there was a greater purpose to his life than killing people in a dusty, bone-poor scrap of land in the middle of nowhere.

He spoke of his concerns to a fellow officer one night over a tin cup of "vodka," the generic term for the wide variety of home-brewed—and occasionally poisonous—alcoholic beverages the soldiers concocted in illicit stills. The man nodded knowingly. He was a veteran, nearly forty-five years old—an ancient age for an active-duty special-forces soldier in the field. He assured Elbek that every soldier who saw sustained combat confronted the same question. Those who made it found an answer that worked for them.

"What's it all about?" the old vet ruminated. "When you're fighting, it's about the man next to you. He's your brother and you fight for him. When you're not fighting, it's about good friends, good times, good women, and bad vodka." He raised his cup to this impromptu toast and drained it.

"That's it?" Elbek asked as his companion poured another drink. "That's enough?"

"It better be," the man replied, "because that's all there is."

But it wasn't enough for Elbek. He'd gone back to his bunk later that night and had lain awake until dawn.

His mission the next day was routine, but he remembered it afterward as one of the crucial turning points in his life. Bands of *dukhs* had been harassing convoys traveling through a mountain pass ten kilometers away. The Soviets sent two armed Mi-8 Hip helicopters and a top-of-the-line Mi-24 Hind to blast the rebel positions, but a small group of rebels at the top of a nearby peak had fired down on the helicopters with Arrow missiles provided by the Americans. These were not as accurate as the Stingers that would come later in the war, and all had missed their targets. But in trying to evade the missiles, one of the Mi-8s had collided with the Mi-24 and both had crashed, killing twelve men and destroying valuable military hardware.

The air was too thin for a helicopter attack on the peak, which would have been dangerous in any event because the fighters presumably had more missiles. It was Elbek's job to take a small group up the mountain and destroy the enemy position.

The climb had been difficult but straightforward. There was only one approach up the mountain, and it was exposed to Soviet artillery fire and therefore unguarded by the *dukhs*. They had set booby traps, of course, but Elbek and his men had enough field experience to spot and avoid these.

They stopped about fifty meters from the summit and sent two scouts ahead to pinpoint the location of the enemy position. The scouts returned twenty minutes later and reported that the Afghans were camping in a small cave just below the summit. They had set a guard, but he was poorly positioned and could be killed without alerting the others.

Elbek had handled similar situations before. He had the sniper in his squad shoot the guard from a great-enough distance to avoid the sound of the gunshot carrying to the camp. Then the Soviets crept to within twenty meters of the cave. They'd seen no one, but a tiny wisp of smoke curling up from the top of the cave mouth betrayed the presence of the fighters within. They set up two light machine-gun positions covering the entrance to the cave while the scouts searched for the emergency exit from the cave—if a cave didn't naturally have two openings, the *dukhs* would virtually always dig a second one. When the scouts signaled that they had found it, Elbek had given the order for the attack to begin.

His men clustered around the cave mouth on either side and threw grenades into it. Five seconds later, a second group dropped grenades into the bolt hole the scouts had found. The machine guns then fired a burst into the cave mouth. The instant they fell silent, the men went in, checking for any booby traps that the grenades and gunfire hadn't triggered.

Inside, they found five dead rebels and one who was wounded. They also found a cache of six Arrow missiles and launchers, which they destroyed with rifle butts and grenades. They brought the injured man to Elbek, who questioned him in a mix of Pashto and Russian. The man had sat in grim silence, staring at his interrogator with hard, fearless eyes.

Elbek could see that it would take considerable time and effort to pry information out of this man, and his youth and tattered clothes made it unlikely that he knew anything that would make it worth the trouble. He took out his pistol and pointed it at the man's head, but still the *dukh*'s face showed no trace of fear.

Elbek paused. "I'm about to kill you. Why aren't you afraid?"

"You Russians call us 'spirits.' This is truth, but you do not understand," the young man said defiantly in broken Russian. "In my heart I have spirit of a true Muslim. Death is nothing. It is only the door into Paradise. You have no spirit. You are just an animal with a gun."

The *dukh* spat at Elbek, who promptly put a bullet through his brain.

The sun had been quickly sliding down to the horizon, so they'd done a cursory search for anything of value and then scrambled down through the thin, cold mountain air.

They returned to a celebratory welcome at their base. There had been much backslapping and congratulating, but when it was over, Elbek was haunted by the young Afghan's indomitable resolve, condescending eyes, and piercing words.

The memory of the incident on the mountaintop grew stronger rather than weaker as the weeks went by, and Elbek found himself subconsciously almost envying the dead *dukh*. Though nominally a Muslim by virtue of his birth as a Chechen, he had never taken his faith nor his nationality seriously. Now he did. He began to spend all his free time studying books on Chechen history and a dog-eared Russian translation of the Koran that he bought on the black market.

His worried commanding officer took him aside and warned him that reports of his off-duty activities were bound to make their way into his personnel file. He knew that Elbek meant no harm, but others would almost certainly view his choice of interests and reading material as subversive. That would damage his career and could even lead to a court martial and prison. Elbek had to make a choice, the commander had said, between his bright future in the Red Army and the little stack of books he kept in his footlocker. Elbek had thanked his CO for his concern and said he would make the right decision. The next day, he had taken his books and vanished into the Afghan countryside.

Sergei had every confidence that Elena would do a fine job of hunting for his attacker—just as he was certain she would do good work on all the other case files piled on her desk. But she might only be able to spend four or five hours on his case over the course of a week. That wasn't enough for Sergei's peace of mind. Besides, he had his own ideas on how to handle the investigation.

He started by making a tour of his contacts on the edges of the Russian underworld. None of them admitted knowing anything about ex-*Spetsnaz* assassins in the Chicago area. Sergei questioned them closely and found their denials believable—which surprised him. Even if this guy was working for non-Russians, his presence wouldn't go entirely unnoticed in the Russian community. Maybe Sergei's quarry wasn't *Spetsnaz* after all, but then, who was he? He had no US criminal record, which would suggest he was a recent immigrant. But the *Spetsnaz*-style knife probably at least meant that he was Russian, though Sergei had few other clues.

He decided to spend the evening at the shooting range at the Shooter's Palace, a large gun distributor and retailer on Chicago's southwest side. The facilities weren't particularly good or close, but Sergei thought it would be worth the trip. When he arrived, the big parking lot was nearly full, and he had to park fifty yards from the store's entrance.

It was hard to believe that fifteen years ago this had been a struggling little family machine shop and lumber warehouse. The machine-shop owner, a man named George Hanson, had discovered that he could make a lot more money selling guns than he could turning out hubcaps and rebuilt Camaro engines. Within five years, the front half of the warehouse had become a vast showroom doing a brisk business in handguns and assault rifles. The Palace was popular in part because Hanson and his sons sold guns from a wide variety of manufacturers—from cheap, zinc-alloy Saturday-night specials priced under a hundred dollars to top-of-the-line sniper rifles selling for twenty times that amount. Other gun stores boasted at least as wide an assortment, but what made the Palace so popular was the Hansons' willingness to operate on the very edge of the law—and sometimes beyond it. It was a testament to their luck and savvy that none of them had ever been indicted.

Sergei walked around the crowded showroom, jotting things down in a notebook while smiling and greeting other patrons, few of whom met his eye or smiled back. The customers were a mixed bag of people who shouldn't be buying guns: half a dozen obvious gangbangers, lots of teenagers, a low-level Russian gangster, a couple of convicted felons whom Sergei recognized from his days at the Bureau, and a number of unsavory types who looked like they should be arrested on general principles.

The crowd of buyers thinned out noticeably after fifteen minutes, so Sergei headed back to the shooting range. He paid his fee and set up in the only free spot. After a few minutes, he noticed a couple of other shooters talking and glancing his way. He put down his gun long enough to make a couple of notes, but otherwise ignored the men. They left, and, as they walked out, they stopped to talk to another marksman, who also walked out. Ten minutes later, the range was nearly empty.

"Can I help you?" a loud voice addressed Sergei from behind. He took off his ear protectors and turned around. George Hanson was glaring at him, his thick arms folded across his broad chest above an equally broad paunch. His thick, iron-gray flattop was so similar to Sergei's that the detective wondered if they used the same barber.

"What was that?"

"I said, can I help you?" Hanson repeated with just a hint of impatience.

"I think you can," Sergei said with a smile. "You sold a Glock 23 to a man named Eddie Thompson. You recently got an ATF trace request on it."

Hanson shrugged. "I sell a lot of guns. I get a lot of trace requests. I don't remember all of them."

"You might remember Eddie, though. He bought forty-six of your guns over an eight-day period."

"A lot of our customers are collectors."

"Collectors?" Sergei scoffed. "This guy bought twelve identical Glock pistols, fourteen Uzis and AK-47s, and twenty assorted Saturday-night specials. You really think he's a collector? Did it occur to you that he might possibly be a straw purchaser?" Sergei had seen it all too often—lowlifes with clean criminal records who would buy guns on behalf of others (generally felons and minors) who could not legally own firearms.

"Hey, if the government doesn't want people buying more than one gun, they can pass a law, all right? It's not my job to go sticking my nose into my customers' business."

Rick Acker

"But it *is my* job," responded Sergei. "That Glock wound up in the hands of someone who broke into my apartment three nights ago and tried to kill me. He got away, and I need you to help me find him."

"I'm sorry to hear that, but I don't see how I can help. You've already got the name of the guy who bought the gun from my store. There's not much else I can do for you."

"The police and the FBI haven't been able to find him. Maybe you could help. And maybe you could talk to some people who might know who he sold the gun to."

Hanson shook his head. "Like I said, I don't stick my nose into my customers' business. I respect their privacy."

"Okay, no problem." Sergei had expected this. The Hansons' no-questions-asked policy was a big part of their success. "I'll just be in here every night looking for Eddie Thompson and practicing my shooting."

The gun-shop owner clearly didn't like that idea. "No offense, but some of my customers get a little nervous around FBI agents, even if they're retired. You're bad for business."

"I don't know," replied Sergei. "When I walked in, business seemed pretty good for a school night."

Hanson's face reddened. "If you're so scared of this guy, why don't you hire some protection?"

Sergei picked up his pistol, put in a fresh mag of ammunition, and turned to the row of targets. He swept his gun across them, firing rapidly. When he was finished, he turned back to Hanson. "Take a look at those targets and you'll see that I'm my own protection. Eddie's been selling guns to bad people, George, people who might wind up working for your enemies one day. If they scare *me*, they should *terrify* you."

◆ ◆ ◆

Elbek had not walked an easy road after he deserted in Afghanistan. He'd spent long years studying the Koran in a stern, monastic *madrasa*, followed by longer years of fighting. He had taken up arms with Muslim militias in the agonizing civil wars that broke out in Afghanistan after the Soviet withdrawal. As those conflicts had drawn to a close, war had flared in Chechnya and he'd hurried home to join in the fighting.

He had returned to Chechnya as the perfect warrior. He knew Russian equipment and tactics intimately from his time in the *Spetsnaz*. He knew how to fight a guerrilla war from his years in Afghanistan. And, perhaps most important, he had developed the spirit that the *dukh* had spoken of on that mountaintop. Elbek felt in the very depths of his soul that it was Allah's will that he should free his country from the crushing fist of Russian oppression.

The war had gone well for a time. For two years, the freedom fighters had ambushed convoys, bombed barracks, and launched hit-and-run attacks against vulnerable outposts. They fought no significant battles, but they imposed a high cost in blood and treasure on the Russians occupying their homeland. Diplomatic pressure also increased with each new atrocity the Russian Army perpetrated against civilians or prisoners of war. Gradually, the Russians withdrew, first from the virtually ungovernable mountains in the south, and then finally from all of Chechnya.

There was no true peace, but there was a grudging and watchful cease-fire. Elbek, who had risen to the rank of general, lived a happy and peaceful life for the next three years. He married the daughter of a tribal chieftain and retired to a rambling chateau in the mountainous southern border region. Every morning he woke to a majestic view of the Argun River valley below. There he used his reputation and connections to set up a prosperous smuggling operation.

But the war was not over. It was merely dormant, like a deadly disease that abates temporarily and lets its victim hope for recovery before it suddenly reappears to kill him. Troubles gathered beyond Chechnya's borders, and rumors of war reached even Elbek's remote mountain home. Rebels in neighboring Dagestan attacked Russian interests and soldiers. They were inspired by their cousins' success in Chechnya and discreetly aided by the Chechens, though the government in Grozny denied it. The Russian eyes watching Chechnya had grown daily more baleful as the unrest in Dagestan festered and spread.

After a terrorist bombing in Moscow was blamed on Chechen rebels, Russian armored columns punched back into Chechnya with brutal force. The Chechens fought well, but they were vastly outnumbered and outgunned. And this time the Russians did not seem to care what human or diplomatic price they paid for their victory.

It was over in a matter of months. The first tanks rolled into Chechnya in September 1999, and by February 2000 the Russians had pounded the capital city of Grozny into submission.

By the end of April, Elbek's house was a smoking pile of rubble that served as a burial cairn for his wife and infant son. He never learned why the Russians had destroyed his home and family. Was it because they knew he lived there? Or was it simply because his chateau was a large building in an area where resistance was strong? Not that the answers mattered greatly.

Throughout the summer of 2000, he and a gradually dwindling band of fighters had kept up the fight in the sparsely settled wilderness of the Argun Valley, hiding from the helicopter gun ships and picking off careless Russians when they could. They spent the long, hot days resting and planning in carefully concealed caves. During the short nights, they harassed the invaders with sniper attacks and small ambushes.

Elbek had not slept well during those months, despite his increasing exhaustion. He laid awake near the mouths of the caves, gathering news on a small shortwave radio and listening for the *thup-thup* of the ubiquitous Mi-8 helicopters or the occasional scream of an Su-25 *Grach* ground-attack jet.

"If you don't sleep," a voice told him one afternoon, "you won't be able to fight."

He had turned to find his Uncle Hamzat sitting in the shadows two meters away, a fatherly smile on his weathered face. He was nearly sixty, but he had the strength and stamina of a man half his age. A shrewd, well-read, and deeply religious man, he had been one of Elbek's most trusted advisors since the younger man had returned from Afghanistan.

Elbek switched off the radio to talk to his uncle. "It doesn't matter whether I sleep or not. The end will be the same."

"The war goes badly then?"

"It's hardly even a war anymore," he said in a low voice. "The Russians control the whole country. There are some units like ours that keep fighting, but not many. I haven't told the men, because it would only hurt morale."

Hamzat nodded. "They guess more than you know. But even if they didn't, we all know that the Russians are stronger than we are. We can hurt them, but we can't beat them."

"So it always is with Islam and its enemies," Elbek said bitterly. "We are always weak and divided, while they are strong and united."

"Of course," Hamzat had replied. "That's their plan, and it has worked for centuries. They attack one small part of Islam and crush it while they keep the rest in turmoil. The Americans and Jews are masters of this art. Look at how they split off the Arab nations one by one with peace treaties and bribes. If one of them dares to stand up like Iraq did, they pay off the corrupt leaders of the others to do nothing or even help while they smash down the upstart. They know that we are stronger than them if only we unite."

"Which is why they will never let that happen." As if to punctuate Elbek's statement, a formation of helicopters flew by at a low altitude, momentarily drowning out their conversation. "I've been wondering if it's worth keeping up the fight," Elbek confessed. "We kill and we die for no purpose."

Hamzat arched his bushy gray eyebrows. "There are other ways."

Elbek had heard this argument before. He shook his head. "Hitting soft targets never helps. Blowing up a hundred random Russians or Americans may feel good, but all it accomplishes is to give them an excuse to attack us. Look at the Palestinians: all they've done is bomb themselves out of a country and make the Zionist atrocities look justified to the West. The Russians know this—they even blew up their own people to give them a reason to destroy our country."

The commonly held belief among Chechens was that the Moscow apartment bombings that started the second Chechen war had been the handiwork of Russian agents trying to create a justification for renewed attacks against Chechnya.

Hamzat's face was both angry and resigned. "So you want to give up? Just walk away and try to make a living under the Russian boot?"

Elbek stared at the stone wall of the cave without seeing it. "For now," he said, "but not forever. The problem with blowing up a plane or a building is that it hurts our enemies without weakening them. We have to find another way. Hit them hard enough to break their grip on the Muslim world long enough for us to join together."

Hamzat nodded. "Never shoot a bear if you are not sure you can kill it," he said. "Now, how do we kill the bear?"

They spent the rest of the day discussing and discounting various options. Nuclear weapons would work, but only if enough of them could be set off in enough cities. Nuclear bombs were hard to buy and extraordinarily expensive. They would also be difficult to smuggle into the target countries. Chemical weapons were cheaper and easier to obtain or make, but they wouldn't kill enough people fast enough to do more than create a temporary panic.

They finally settled on biological weapons. There were thousands of unemployed scientists in the former Soviet Union with bioweapons expertise. Some of them reputedly were looking for work and had taken "souvenirs" from their labs. A virulent plague could disable an entire people for decades, maybe permanently. Besides, there was a precedent:

Allah had finally stopped the Crusaders by sending the Black Death to destroy them. Perhaps he would do so again through the hands of the Chechens.

Elbek had slept well that night for the first time in months. The path ahead of him was hard and uncertain, but it led to victory—and victory not just for Chechnya but for Muslims everywhere.

Elbek examined his bandages and grimaced as he recalled his ill-fated attempt to kill Sergei Spassky. The skinny Russian detective bothered him, and not just because of the throbbing ache in his left arm and his maimed right hand. Spassky represented the most significant unresolved threat to the Vainakh Guard's US operation. The Brothers had assured him that the detective's investigation had been neutralized, but not before he had identified Alikhan.

Spassky had also managed to evade Elbek's surveillance and talk to the informant, Josef Fedorov, at least once before the man died. That had been enough to warrant a death sentence. Now matters were more serious: the detective had talked to the police and the FBI, but what had he said? Elbek and his commanding officers needed to know. The Russian needed to die—but first he needed to talk. Elbek was very good at making Russians talk. Despite his pain, he smiled.

Chapter Ten
The Show

"I call Josef Fedorov as my first witness," Ben announced.

A murmur of surprise rippled across the courtroom. Several people looked around for Josef—but Ben noticed that Anton and Dmitry did not. After several seconds, it was clear that Josef was not going to appear. Ben continued, "It appears that Mr. Fedorov was unavoidably detained despite the trial subpoena served on his counsel."

As Anthony Simeon stood to respond, Ben noticed Anton give Dmitry what he must have thought was a discreet nudge and a wink. Dmitry ignored him.

"Your Honor," said Simeon, "we have been attempting to communicate with Mr. Fedorov ever since we received the subpoena. We are making every effort to locate him, but we have been unable to do so to date."

"All right," said the judge, "but if he's not here by tomorrow, I'm issuing a contempt citation. And if he's not here by the day after that, I'll issue a bench warrant for his arrest. Is that clear?"

"Yes, Your Honor," Simeon said as he sat down.

"Since Mr. Fedorov is unavailable," said Ben, "I call Anton Brodsky."

Anton conferred briefly with Dmitry, Pavel, and Simeon, then got up and walked over to the witness stand with an apprehensive, sullen look on his face. The bailiff swore him in as Ben arranged his witness outline and notes.

Ben guessed that Anton would be nervous on the stand and planned to keep him off balance. He also guessed that Anton would never admit to knowing about Dr. Ivanovsky's contract, but it might be possible to make some headway indirectly. "May I approach the witness, Your Honor?"

The judge nodded.

Ben picked up a piece of paper and a pen and walked over to Anton. "Please sign your name, Mr. Brodsky."

Anton hesitated for a moment and glanced around the courtroom as if looking for guidance. Then he slowly signed his name.

"Thank you," said Ben. He retrieved the paper and put an exhibit sticker on it. "Let the record reflect that I am marking Mr. Brodsky's signature as Plaintiff's Exhibit Two for identification." He then walked to an overhead projection camera and put the piece of paper under it. The signature projected on the screen looked nothing like the one on the blowup of the minutes. "That's your regular signature, correct?"

"Yes," said Anton.

"The signature you use every day when you sign checks or credit-card receipts?"

"Yes."

"How long have you signed your name like that?"

"I don't know."

"That's not a special signature you invented for us here this morning, is it?"

"No."

"May I approach the witness again?"

The judge nodded and Ben handed Anton a copy of the minutes, which were already marked as Plaintiff's Exhibit 1. Ben then pulled out another piece of paper and arranged it for the camera. The screen showed a close-up of a signature identical to the one on the minutes.

Ben pointed to the screen. "Is that your signature?"

"That is a fake."

"I'm not asking you whether the document is real. I'm just asking whether your signature is. Have you ever signed your name like that?"

"No."

"Those two signatures match each other," Ben gestured to both the screen and the blowup on the easel, "and neither of them matches the signature you just gave me, right?"

"I think that's right," Anton replied uncertainly—as if he sensed a trap, but wasn't sure how to avoid it.

Ben turned down the magnification on the projector so that the whole page was visible. It was the signature page to the contract between the Brothers and Nikolai Zinoviev. "I'm going to mark as Plaintiff's Exhibit Three the contract between Mr. Zinoviev and the Brothers LLC. Do you remember when I took your deposition in this case, Mr. Brodsky?"

"Yes."

"And do you remember that I asked you, 'Is that your signature on the last page of the contract?'" Ben said, reading from the deposition transcript.

"Yes."

"And do you remember what your answer was?"

Anton glared malevolently at Ben. "Yes. I said it was my signature."

"But today you said it wasn't your signature. In fact, you said you never signed your name like that, right?"

Anton sat silently for several seconds, struggling to think of an answer. "I . . . I guess I made a mistake."

You sure did, thought Ben.

In fact, Anton had made the same mistake as Nicki Zinoviev: thinking it's easy to lie during a lawsuit. It isn't. The entire litigation system is designed to ferret out the truth, and any moderately talented attorney will eventually uncover at least some of the lies told by an opponent. Furthermore, each lie must be entirely consistent with all other statements—including previous lies—and all facts known to the opposition. Only witnesses with a perfect and nimble memory have any chance of not getting caught. And getting caught almost always does more damage than whatever fact the witness was trying to hide—judges and juries assume the worst about whatever the lie concerned. They also naturally mistrust everything else the witness says.

All lawyers, even dishonest ones, invariably instruct their clients to tell the truth under oath. Any client who isn't smart enough to take this advice generally isn't smart enough to lie effectively—as Ben had already been able to demonstrate twice in this case.

Ben decided it was time to drive the knife all the way in. "And the reason you made that mistake was because you wanted to hide from Judge Harris the fact that you signed those minutes, correct?"

"No! I . . . This document is forgery, so I could not sign it! It does not matter how my signature looks, this is fake!"

Ben put away his notes while Anton answered. Nothing the man said could make much difference at this point.

"No further questions." Ben sat down. He doubted that even the great Anthony Simeon could do much to repair the wreckage on the witness stand.

"Any direct examination, Mr. Simeon?" asked Judge Harris.

Simeon stood, but didn't leave the counsel table. "I'm not certain, Your Honor. I have one or two questions about the transcript." He turned to the court reporter. "I'm sorry, miss. At my advanced age I don't always catch everything people say. Did Mr. Brodsky testify that he heard Dr. Ivanovsky and Mr. Zinoviev verbally agree to any contract?"

The court reporter skimmed through the transcript. "No, he was never asked that question."

"And was he ever asked if he had personal knowledge of any such contract?"

She checked the transcript again. "No, sir."

"Thank you." He turned back to the judge. "No, Your Honor, I have no questions for Mr. Brodsky."

Ben's self-satisfaction evaporated. That was the most effective non-examination of a witness he had ever seen. Simeon had not only shown that Anton's testimony did little to establish the existence of a contract, he had done it in a way that prevented Ben from asking any rebuttal questions. Any further questions he asked the witness would be limited to the subject matter raised by Simeon in his questioning—but he hadn't actually questioned Anton, so there was nothing for Ben to follow up on. All he could do was sit there and admire his opponent's work. The Velvet Dagger had just struck again.

"All right," said the judge. "You may step down, Mr. Brodsky." He glanced at the clock and turned to Ben. "Mr. Corbin, it's 4:40. Can you finish your next witness in twenty minutes, or shall we call it a day?"

Ben doubted he could do another witness that fast. "Let's call it a day, Your Honor."

"Okay," said the judge. "I have some hearings and a motion call in the morning, so we'll start after lunch tomorrow. This trial is in recess until one o'clock tomorrow."

Sergei got a call from Ben as soon as trial was over for the day and went to Ben's office, where they spent two hours getting ready for the next day. They went over the background of Pavel Voronin, whom Ben planned to call as his next witness. They also teed up a couple of areas for investigation the next morning. Pavel was the Brothers' bookkeeper, but Ben had picked up hints from the documents that he might be something more.

After they finished, Sergei strolled down Dearborn Street to the garage where he had parked his car. He called his voice mail as he walked and found a message from Elena waiting for him. "Hi, Sergei. I got a call from George Hanson that I'd like to talk to you about. Also, I think I've got some info on your nine-fingered friend. If you get this after six, call me at home." She left both her work and home numbers.

Sergei glanced at his watch. It was seven o'clock. He hesitated—he didn't like to call people at home, but she had invited him to. Plus, he really, really wanted to know what she had found. He dialed her home number.

"Hello?" Elena said.

"Hi, it's Sergei. I got your message. What's up?"

"I got a package of documents from the military archives in Moscow. Very interesting. Do you have time to look through them?"

"I'm tied up tomorrow, but I've got some free time tonight."

"Okay. The file's at the office. I'll meet you down there and let you in."

"Thanks," said Sergei. "By the way, I haven't had any dinner, so I'm going to pick up some Chinese on the way. Can I get something for you?"

"Some sweet-and-sour pork and a side of rice would be great."

"Done. Dirksen Building in thirty minutes?"

"See you there."

An hour later, they sat side by side at a little table in the FBI cafeteria, poring over old documents and using chopsticks to chase the remaining morsels of stir fry and rice around their foam plates.

"Are they sure they matched the prints right?" Sergei asked.

Elena nodded. "I had our own lab check it, and they're sure it's a match."

"Really?" said Sergei, shaking his head with surprise and disbelief. He looked at the file again. "Most of this does fit the profile, I guess—*Spetsnaz*, urban warfare school, combat experience in Afghanistan. It's just that—"

"—he's been dead for years?" Elena finished.

"Yeah, that generally rules someone out as a suspect."

"That's one of the reasons I wanted you to look at this. Tell me what you think of this page that I've flagged."

Sergei turned to it and read carefully. "Hmmmm. No body, no eyewitnesses, no details on manner of death—just 'killed in combat.'"

He sat back and thought for a minute. "You know, one of my uncles was in Afghanistan. I asked him once how many of his unit died, and he said he supposed that fifty-three of them did. I asked him what he meant by 'supposed.' He said that a lot of times they weren't able to get bodies back after a fight. The Afghans would run off with them and do all sorts of unpleasant things with the corpses. Since the mujahideen didn't take prisoners—or didn't keep them, anyway—the soldiers just figured that anyone who disappeared during combat must be dead."

"I hadn't heard that," said Elena, "but I was thinking along the same lines. This Elbek Shishani was a Chechen, right? And his personnel records say that he had been acting erratic toward the end and was getting more religious. Maybe he decided to defect using some battle as cover."

Sergei nodded and flipped through Elbek Shishani's file again. "Based on this, I'd say you're right, but what's he doing in America? Any insight from George Hanson?"

"Actually, yes. He gave me a call this morning out of the blue. He said he had a security video from his parking lot that he had 'forgotten' to give us and wondered when he could drop it off. One of his boys brought it over this afternoon."

Sergei laughed. "Amazing what a good citizen George can be when he's properly motivated. Have you looked at the tape yet?"

"Yeah. All it shows is Eddie Thompson entering and leaving the store and getting picked up by someone in a light-colored Ford Taurus. The license plate isn't visible, even with digital enhancement. I—"

"Where's the tape?" Sergei interrupted.

"It's back in my office."

He got up. "Are you still on the ninth floor?"

"Yeah," she answered as they walked back to her office at a rapid pace set by Sergei. "What's the hurry?"

"I think I may be able to give you the license plate number for that car," he answered as they arrived at her office.

Elena grabbed the tape off her desk and they walked down the hall to a conference room with a VCR, where she popped the tape in the player. It showed a black-and-white night view of the parking lot outside the Shooter's Palace. The quality wasn't great, but it was better than most security videos. That surprised Sergei—Hanson hadn't struck him as the type to go the extra mile on customer safety. One of their better customers must have gotten mugged out there.

"There's Eddie." Elena pointed to a man standing on the sidewalk outside the Palace and holding several boxes. "And here comes his ride." A light-colored sedan pulled up. Eddie got in and the car drove away.

"Replay that last five seconds," Sergei said, walking up to the screen. Elena replayed it.

"There!" Sergei pointed at the car's rear bumper. "See that scuff? The car that was following me had a scuff just like that on the rear bumper, and it was a late-model light-gray Taurus." He grabbed a notepad from the tabletop and hastily scrawled a series of letters and numbers. "Here's your plate number."

Elena glanced at the notepad. "Okay, we'll check it out." She tore off the top sheet of the notepad and clipped it to the front of a set of documents. "Sounds like this guy isn't content to just watch you anymore. Any idea why not?"

Sergei shrugged. "I don't even know why he was following me in the first place. Is there an arrest warrant out on him yet?"

"We should have one by tomorrow morning. We'll also do a search on that plate number tonight. Between that and the sketch you helped us do on Thursday, we should be able to snag this guy soon."

When court convened the next afternoon, Ben opened by calling Pavel Voronin, the Brothers' accountant, to the stand.

"Do you go to many monster-truck rallies, Mr. Voronin?" asked Ben.

Pavel's appearance fit the cruelest stereotypes of his profession: bottle-bottom glasses, thin shoulders, ultraconservative three-piece suit, and a bald head with a bad comb-over. "What?" he asked after a few seconds of silence.

"Do you attend many monster-truck rallies?" Ben repeated.

"No."

"Do you like to go deer hunting?"

"No. I . . . uh . . . I have never gone deer hunting."

"How about bass fishing?"

"I have never done that either."

Anthony Simeon stood up. Judge Harris looked at him. "I assume you're going to object on relevance grounds."

"I am indeed," replied Simeon.

Ben had, of course, expected this. "I'll tie all this up in the next couple of minutes."

"You'd better," said the judge. "Objection overruled without prejudice."

Ben turned back to the witness. "What I'm trying to figure out, Mr. Voronin, is why every couple of months or so you make weeklong road trips through small towns in Iowa, Wisconsin, and Illinois. I thought maybe you had some hobby that took you out there, but I guess not." Ben reached over and picked up a stack of documents from the counsel table. "Those were business trips, weren't they?"

Pavel's face turned pasty white. Ben obviously knew things that hadn't been disclosed in discovery. *But you don't know how much I know, do you?* thought Ben. *And you can't make up your mind whether to tell the whole truth now. Since you're a cautious little geek, I'm going to guess you'll decide truth is the safest option.*

Pavel swallowed, his Adam's apple bobbing in his reedy neck. "Maybe partially."

"The Brothers LLC maintains accounts at banks in each of the towns you visit. Isn't that true?"

He hesitated, now seeing clearly where Ben was going. "We try not to put all our assets in one place."

"And on these trips, you make deposits into each of those accounts. Isn't that also true?"

"I think that's right."

"And the deposits are always less than $10,000 per account?"

"I don't remember every deposit I've ever made for the company."

"That's okay. I've got the bank statements right here. These are collectively marked for identification as Plaintiff's Exhibit Four. May I approach the witness?"

The judge nodded.

Ben handed copies to the judge, the witness, and Simeon. "Please look through these, Mr. Voronin, and tell me if you see a single deposit of $10,000 or over."

Simeon stood again. "I renew my relevance objection. Opposing counsel is obviously trying to establish that the witness has violated US currency-transaction-reporting laws. While that may pique Mr. Corbin's curiosity, it has no bearing whatever on the issue before this Court."

Judge Harris turned to Ben. "For purposes of *this* case"—he looked ominously at Pavel—"why should I care whether the witness has been smurfing?" *Smurfing* is the illegal practice of evading federal reporting requirements on currency transactions of $10,000 or more by making multiple transactions of less than $10,000.

"Two reasons, Your Honor," replied Ben. "First, it impeaches the credibility of the witness by establishing that he engaged in criminally dishonest conduct. The second reason will become clear when I am through with this line of questioning."

The judge considered for a moment. "You may proceed, but I'm not going to let this go on for much longer."

"Thank you, Your Honor," said Ben. Turning back to Pavel, he continued, "Did the Brothers authorize you to open these accounts and make these deposits, or is that something you did on your own?"

"They authorized me to do all these things," said Pavel. "And we were breaking no laws."

"How did they authorize you?"

"We had a meeting and passed a resolution."

"Is it this resolution?" Ben pulled out his next exhibit and handed around copies.

Pavel looked at it briefly. "Yes, this is the one."

"And the four of you passed that resolution because this was a significant business decision, correct?"

"Yes."

"In fact, you told me during your deposition that your company passes resolutions authorizing all significant business decisions, didn't you?"

"I think so."

Now let's see if you'll tell the truth one more time. Ben pointed to the minutes on the easel. "And there's the resolution authorizing the contract with Mr. Zinoviev, right?"

Pavel sat silently for several seconds, his eyes darting furtively between the other Brothers and Ben. "I . . . No, that is a fake."

"But there was a resolution authorizing the contract with Mr. Zinoviev?"

"I think so."

"Do you know why that resolution wasn't produced in discovery?"

"I do not know."

"Was it because you didn't want my client and me to see it?" asked Ben, again pointing to the blowup.

"No! I told you, that is a fake!"

"Is that your signature on it?"

"It looks like my signature, but I never signed it."

"No further questions."

Ben picked up his witness outline and sat down. That had gone as well as he could have hoped—or almost as well, anyway. The accountant had been on the brink of telling the truth about the minutes, but he backed away at the last second. Ben wished he could think of a way to push him that last step, but he'd used up all the ammo he had. Oh, well.

Anthony Simeon took Ben's place at the podium. "Mr. Voronin, did you ever hear Nicki Zinoviev and Dr. Ivanovsky agree to a contract for the sale of the contents of safe-deposit box 4613 at the LaSalle Street building of American Union Bank?"

"No."

"Did you ever hear them agree to any contract at all?"

"No."

"Have you ever heard them speak to each other at all?"

"No."

"No further questions."

"Any rebuttal, Mr. Corbin?" asked the judge.

"Yes, Your Honor," said Ben as he approached the podium. "Mr. Voronin, do those minutes say that Mr. Zinoviev and Dr. Ivanovsky came to a meeting of the Brothers and agreed to a contract in front of you?"

He looked at the minutes for a few seconds. "No."

"It says that Mr. Zinoviev 'disclosed to the Members of the Company that he had entered into a prior agreement to sell the contents of the box to a third party.'" Ben picked up a sheaf of papers. "Did he do that?"

Pavel looked anxiously at the documents in Ben's hand, obviously worrying that Ben had another unpleasant surprise for him—which was precisely why Ben had picked them up. "I don't remember."

"The Brothers entered into a $100,000 contract to buy the contents of a safe-deposit box—a contract that would completely evaporate if

Nikolai Zinoviev had already sold those contents to someone else. And you don't remember whether he told you he had done that?"

"No."

Nuts. "No further questions."

The upstairs dining room at the Italian Village was decorated to resemble a quaint outdoor Italian piazza at night. It was almost entirely dark, lit only by strings of small lights along the walls, a faint glow coming from the starry dark-blue ceiling and the candles on each table. Ben could barely make out Irina Ivanovsky smiling quietly in the shadows, but her husband leaned forward into the candlelight. His face was clearly lit and seemed to float disembodied over the dinner table.

"You are winning very well, Ben," remarked an ebullient Dr. Ivanovsky, who had insisted on treating the Corbins to dinner. "And the judge is very, very angry with them because Josef Fedorov does not appear. I was worried when the trial started, but now I think this judge will give us the victory." He nodded in agreement with himself. "Yes. I think we will win."

Ben took a cautious sip of the top-shelf vodka his client had ordered for them. "Thanks. I hope we win, but . . . Well, don't get your hopes set on it."

"I thought things were going pretty well," said Noelle, who sat beside Ben. "Is there some problem?"

"The same basic problem we've had since Nicki Zinoviev died: Dr. Ivanovsky can't testify under the Dead Man's Rule, and without his testimony we don't have any evidence that there was a contract."

"But we have these minutes that speak of the contract," protested Dr. Ivanovsky around a mouthful of veal.

"Yes, but we don't have any evidence proving that the minutes are genuine," explained Ben. "Both of the witnesses so far have claimed that the minutes are fake."

"But they were lying," said Noelle. "And you caught both of them at it. Did you see the look on the judge's face when he realized that Voronin guy had been smurfing? He also wasn't real pleased by Brodsky's new signature."

Ben smiled. "No, he wasn't. And yes, they were lying. The problem is that their lies don't prove the authenticity of the minutes. I'm having great fun beating these guys up on the witness stand, but so far I haven't been able to make much progress in proving that there was a contract."

"I see," said Dr. Ivanovsky, his wizened face now thoughtful and slightly downcast. "Is this why Mr. Simeon does not say many things?"

Ben nodded. "He just sits back and watches while I put on my show. Then he gets up and says a few words to remind the judge that it's only a show and that I haven't really proven anything. Then he sits down again and waits for the next act."

"So when does the show stop?" asked Noelle. "When do you think you'll be able to start proving there was a contract?"

Ben took a deep breath and let it out slowly, gazing up at the faux Italian night sky. "My best hopes were these first two witnesses. There was a chance that I would be able to trick or pressure them into admitting that those minutes were real. But it didn't work. I got in some good shots, but neither of them cracked.

"Presuming Josef Fedorov doesn't magically appear, the only two witnesses I've got left are Dmitry Kolesnikov and you." He nodded to Dr. Ivanovsky. "Kolesnikov is a clever, slippery guy. I got nothing useful from him at his deposition, and I doubt I'll get any more tomorrow. As for you, I'm expecting the judge to cut me off before you can say anything useful."

"If the judge cuts you, then what happens?" asked Dr. Ivanovsky, his face anxious and drawn in the flickering light from the candle.

Ben gave a small shrug. "Then the show's over and we go home."

CHAPTER ELEVEN
A MATTER OF LAW

Shamil watched the target park his car and go into the building. The night-vision binoculars gave the man's face a strange greenish glow, but Shamil was used to it and had no trouble making a positive identification. He watched until the man's light went out, then handed the binoculars to his subordinate, Umar, before clambering into the back of the windowless delivery van to get a few hours of sleep. "Let me know if he comes out. Otherwise, wake me at five thirty."

"Yes, sir."

The floor of the van was cold and uncomfortable, but no worse than the caves of the Chechen highlands. Still, Shamil had trouble sleeping. He never could relax on the night before an operation, and this time was no different. He lay awake for more than an hour, mentally rehearsing the plans for the morning. He finally forced himself to sleep by reciting over and over the specifications for the AK-104 assault rifle, which a deranged drill instructor had forced him to memorize in boot camp.

It seemed only a moment later when Umar shook him awake. He quickly assembled his gear in the dark, not risking a light that might be visible from the building. He swallowed a couple of ration bars and some lukewarm coffee from a thermos, then quietly opened the rear door of the van. That was when he got his first unpleasant surprise: a carpet of new snow lay on the ground.

He briefly considered aborting the mission, but decided against it. He could mask his footprints well enough by keeping to the edge of the alley, where the snow was thinnest.

He ran lightly along the narrow strip of nearly bare concrete beside the retaining wall that formed one side of the alley, then crouched down between the wall and the target's car.

Then he waited. More snow fell, covering the faint prints he had left and turning his black commando coat a dusty gray.

The sky began to lighten, and the everyday noises of a waking city increased. Car and truck engines coughed to life, followed by the wet whiz of vehicles driving through the slushy street at the end of the alley. A jet roared overhead. Tires squealed and two irate male voices held a brief but pointed conversation. Another jet thundered into the sky.

Still, Shamil waited. He stretched and kneaded his cold arms and legs as best he could to keep the muscles loose, but it wasn't easy.

Then he heard the sound he had been waiting for. The door on the building opened and feet carefully descended the snowy steps, making soft scrunching noises as they went. Just a few seconds more. He took off his right glove and pulled his pistol out of its holster inside his jacket, where he had kept it warm and dry for maximum reliability.

The steps reached the car and stopped. He heard the sound of car keys, meaning the target's hands would be busy.

Now. He stood up from behind the car and pointed his gun across the vehicle. He had meant to explode to his feet, but his muscles were cold and stiff and he moved a bit more slowly than he had intended. Too slowly. By the time he reached his feet and had his gun ready, the target had ducked behind the car and had pulled out his own gun, which was pointing at Shamil's chest through the car windows.

"Bang, you're dead," said the target.

Shamil put away his gun and cursed as Umar got out of the van and several more men emerged from the building. General Shishani, his left arm in a sling, gave a black-eyed frown from the steps. "Let's go inside and talk about what went wrong."

"Yes, sir," Shamil said glumly.

The men all trooped back inside and gathered in the cafeteria, where they sat around small tables and looked toward their leader. Umar got some hot tea for himself and made a cup for Shamil, who accepted it with a nod and a tight smile.

"Shamil, tell us what happened," said the general.

"I was stiff from the cold and squatting for so long. I couldn't move fast enough."

"Yes. And?"

Shamil's frustration boiled over. "And he knew I would be waiting for him."

"You think the test of your plan was unfair?"

"Permission to speak freely?"

"Of course."

"It was not fair," Shamil said in a tightly controlled voice. "The Russian will be wary, but he will not know the time and place where we will strike. Arzu did, and that made the test unfair."

There was murmuring in the room, but General Shishani showed no emotion. "Your plan must be good enough to pass unfair tests. If you can capture a man who knows when you will strike, you can capture a man who does not. There will be unexpected problems when you execute your plan, and it must have a sufficient margin for error to account for them. My plan did not." He held up his four-fingered hand, then pointed to his wounded arm. "You must do better, and I know you will. We will test you again tonight."

◆ ◆ ◆

Ben arranged his notes on the courtroom podium and looked up at Dmitry Kolesnikov, who sat waiting in the witness box. "Mr. Kolesnikov, is that your signature on Plaintiff's Exhibit One?" Ben asked, pointing to the minutes.

Dmitry studied the document briefly. "Yes, I believe it is."

"I . . . Thank you," said Ben, a little stunned.

"As you pointed out in examining my friend, Mr. Brodsky, we use the same signature block for all company documents. It would be easy—"

"Excuse me, Mr. Kolesnikov," Ben interrupted, trying to maintain control of the witness. "I haven't asked you another question yet."

"I was finishing my answer to the last one."

"This is all going to come out on direct anyway," Judge Harris interjected. "I see no reason why we shouldn't hear it now. You may complete your answer, Mr. Kolesnikov."

"Thank you, Your Honor." Dmitry's English was flawless and had only a slight, urbane accent. "As I was saying, it would be easy for someone to cut the signature block off any of our documents, attach it to these fake minutes, and then make a photocopy to hide what has been done. In fact, that is what I believe has been done here. If you look at the area between the end of the text and the signatures, you will see a faint line. Your Honor, may I leave the witness box so I can be closer to counsel's blowup of Exhibit One?"

The judge nodded. "You realize that you're still under oath."

"Of course. Thank you, Your Honor." He stepped down from the box and walked over to the easel. "Here is where the real signatures end and the false minutes begin," he continued, pointing to a faint, intermittent line that Ben had not noticed before. "So yes, I believe my signature on this document is genuine, but the document itself is not. Thank you for allowing me to complete my response to Mr. Corbin's question." He returned to the witness box.

"Do you see this line here in the middle of the text?" asked Ben, pointing to the top portion of the blowup.

"I do."

"Would you agree with me that this line and the line you just pointed out divide the page into thirds?"

"Approximately, yes."

"Would you also agree that those lines are consistent with the minutes having been folded and placed in a business-size envelope?"

"Yes. If one was trying to conceal a forgery of this type, it would be logical to splice the documents at a fold in the paper to mask what had been done. That must have been done here."

"Move to strike everything after 'yes' as nonresponsive."

"Granted," said the judge. "Mr. Kolesnikov, please try to answer yes/no questions with a simple yes or no whenever possible. If you can't give an unqualified yes or no, then it's fine to explain yourself. But if you simply disagree with Mr. Corbin's theory of the case, that is another matter. Mr. Simeon is a very competent lawyer and does not need your help in arguing the defense's version of the facts."

"On the contrary, Your Honor," Simeon said, "I will take whatever help I can get."

"The witness is helping you quite enough without previewing your closing argument," replied the judge.

Ben did *not* like the sound of that. He needed to win this round decisively, but he had a growing feeling that he was being outmaneuvered by Dmitry and would be lucky to come out with a draw—and evidently the judge agreed. He decided to gamble, hoping to shake up the witness in the process. "Mr. Kolesnikov, on the first day of trial, I called Josef Fedorov to the stand. Everyone in the courtroom turned to look except you and Mr. Brodsky. How did you know that Mr. Fedorov would not be walking through those doors?" he asked, pointing to the double doors at the back of the courtroom.

Dmitry went white, but recovered quickly. "He, um, he had mentioned that he planned to leave town, so I did not expect him to arrive at trial."

"Did he say where he was going?"

"Not that I recall."

"Was it inside the US? If so, we can find him and bring him in."

"No, I think he was going overseas."

"Then why did he leave his passport on the front seat of his car?"

Dmitry's eyes went round and he began to sweat. "I—I—" he stammered.

Janet Anderson saved him. "Objection, Your Honor. Assumes facts not in evidence. Also, Mr. Corbin never disclosed this alleged information to us in discovery."

Nuts! Whether by skill or luck, she had made exactly the right tactical move while Simeon sat watching impassively. Ben was confident that he could defeat her objection, but its real value lay in simply having been made. Ben had had Dmitry off balance. One or two more hard questions might have cracked him, and then Ben might have been able to beat him into making some useful admissions about the contract. But now Dmitry would have a minute or so to regain his composure and think through his answer while his lawyer's objection was argued and ruled on. "Counsel, this is cross-examination," said Judge Harris. "Mr. Corbin can assume whatever he wants as long as he does so in good faith, but your discovery objection may have more merit. Mr. Corbin?"

"Your Honor, this information isn't responsive to any discovery they served on us. None of their interrogatories asked us what we knew about Mr. Fedorov's whereabouts or anything like that. Their failure to ask the right questions is hardly grounds for an objection."

The judge nodded. "All right. Based on Mr. Corbin's assurances, I'm going to overrule the objection. If the defense can later establish that Mr. Corbin was being untruthful, I will consider a motion to strike and for sanctions." He turned to Dmitry. "You may answer."

"I didn't know that his passport was in his car, so obviously I have no idea why he left it there," the witness said smoothly. "You'll have to ask him that, if you can find him."

"But he won't be able to answer me, will he?"

"I don't understand."

"Sure you do, because you had him killed, right?"

"Objection!" Anderson leaped to her feet again. "This questioning is highly argumentative and completely baseless!"

"Then why is your client shaking like a leaf?" Ben shot back, pointing to Anton, who sat quivering on the edge of his seat, every muscle tense.

Judge Harris looked down at Dmitry with a grave expression on his face. "Did you have Josef Fedorov killed?"

"No, Your Honor!" Dmitry replied firmly. "Of course not. He is my friend and colleague."

"Do you have any idea where he is?"

"No, Your Honor. I had recalled that he was going overseas, but based on Mr. Corbin's statements, I must have been misremembering."

The judge turned to Anton. "Do you know where Mr. Fedorov is? And remember, you're still under oath."

Anton shifted uneasily in his seat. "No, Your Honor. He was my friend too."

"Why did you say 'was'?"

"I meant 'is.' I . . . I am not so good with English."

The judge regarded him silently for a moment, and Anton looked down at the floor. The judge turned to Ben. "Mr. Corbin, if you have any evidence that a murder has been committed, I urge you to contact the Chicago Police Department."

"We're already in touch with them, Your Honor," Ben said, watching Dmitry carefully. He didn't react. "May I question the witness now?"

"Certainly. I apologize for interrupting your examination."

"I understand completely. If these men have murdered a witness to prevent him from testifying, that is obviously a matter of great importance to the Court." He turned to Dmitry. "Mr. Kolesnikov, did Nikolai Zinoviev ever tell you that he had entered into a contract with Dr. Ivanovsky?"

"He did not."

"Did you ever learn from any other source that there was a contract between the two of them?"

"No."

This wasn't going anywhere. "No further questions."

"Mr. Simeon?" asked Judge Harris.

"No questions, Your Honor."

"I didn't think so," observed the judge, and Ben's heart sank.

Sergei Spassky and Elena Kamenev sat in one of the booths lining the walls of the Petrograd, examining the dinner menus—which were exactly the same as the lunch menus except that everything cost a dollar more and came with stuffed cabbage. When Olga Yanayev came out of the kitchen, she spotted them and walked over. "Hello, Sergei," she said.

"Hi, Auntie Olga. I'd like you to meet Elena Kamenev, a friend of mine from the FBI. She's investigating that break-in at my apartment last week."

"Welcome to the Petrograd," she said, eyeing Elena appraisingly. "What can I get for you?"

They both ordered and Sergei added, "And we'd like your company, if you have the time. I'll buy you dinner."

Olga looked over the restaurant, which had only two other occupied tables, both of which had passed to the tea, cigarettes, and gossip stage of the meal some time ago. Another waitress lounged behind the counter, reading the paper and occasionally visiting the other diners to refill teacups and confirm that they didn't want anything more. "Yes. I'll need to leave when the dinner rush starts, but that won't be for another hour or so."

Olga walked into the kitchen, returning ten minutes later with their food. She sat down next to Elena and turned to her. "So, have you had any luck finding this Chechen animal?"

"We're working on it, but we don't have him yet. But there are a couple of things you can do to help us. First, could you look at this sketch and description and tell me whether it matches the man you saw following Sergei?"

The old woman put on her reading glasses and studied the drawing and written description, her forehead furrowed in concentration. She nodded. "That's him. I'll show this to everyone I know. What's the second thing?"

"As you can see from the description, we think he's a *Spetsnaz* vet and may be looking for work in organized crime, probably as an assassin or enforcer. If you can think of anyone who might have hired—"

"I'll show this to everyone I know," Olga repeated flatly, looking Elena squarely in the eye.

Elena took the hint and moved on to a different topic. "Thank you. Sergei tells me you're from Moscow. So am I; I lived there until I was twenty."

"I thought I recognized your accent," said the older woman, her face breaking into a smile. "What neighborhood?" The three of them chatted for the next hour, reminiscing about Russia and commiserating about the Chicago Bears. Around six o'clock, the restaurant started to fill up. Olga got to her feet and smoothed her apron. "Well, time for me to get back to work."

"Me too," said Sergei. "I've got an appointment to go look at an apartment."

"You're moving again?" asked his auntie. "You've only been in your place for six months. Just moving to a new apartment won't protect you from people like this."

"I'm not moving," replied Sergei. "I talked to Josef Fedorov's landlord. He told me that just before Fedorov disappeared, he said that he would be leaving and that the landlord had better look for new tenants. So he is. I told him I'd be interested in seeing the apartment, and he invited me to come over tonight at seven."

Auntie Olga nodded. "It sounds like he was planning to go to ground after he cooperated with you. He should have done it first."

Elena looked at Sergei with interest. "I actually have a warrant to search Fedorov's apartment for evidence that he was murdered. I was going to execute it tomorrow, but I'd rather have a look without announcing that I have a warrant. That sort of news gets around pretty fast."

"Yes, it does," agreed Sergei.

"Mind if I come with you tonight?"

The landlord was a garrulous old Ukrainian with a gold chain peeking out of his open collar. "So, will you be renting together, then?" he asked as he guided them back to Josef's apartment.

"We're just friends," replied Sergei.

The man nudged Sergei in the ribs. "Too bad for you."

Elena laughed politely, which the landlord took as encouragement. "So, if she's your friend, you'll be inviting her over a lot, then? Maybe sitting out on the porch with her so she can increase my property value?"

"If I do, will you give me a break on the rent?"

The man laughed boisterously and clapped Sergei on the shoulder. "I like you. So, what is it you do for a business?"

Sergei briefly considered giving him a cover story but decided there was no need. It would be pointless anyway—if the landlord was working with the Brothers, he would already have Sergei's description and possibly a picture. "I'm a detective."

"Is she your assistant, then?" Another nudge to the ribs.

"No, we're just friends," replied Elena. "We don't work together."

"She'd be handy to have around, though," put in Sergei. "She's the best shot I've ever seen. Why, she could shoot an apple off your head at a thousand yards in high winds."

The landlord looked at her with surprise. "Really?"

"Actually, I'd probably blow your brains out at that distance if there was wind," Elena said modestly.

The landlord looked at them nervously, his gaze stopping briefly on the bulge in Sergei's coat. He apparently decided they were probably *mafiya* enforcers of some kind and that he had better treat them respectfully—which was exactly what Sergei had intended.

The Ukrainian chuckled uncertainly. "Okay. So, here we are, then." He stopped in front of an apartment door and took a big bunch of keys out of his pocket. His cell phone rang as he opened the door and led them into the apartment. He looked at the number and said apologetically, "I must take this." He stepped to the side of the doorway and answered the phone. "Hello? Can I come down in a few minutes? I am busy now."

As he listened, his smile faded. "Is it flooding right now?" He paused. "How did that happen?" A longer pause. "A toilet is not a garbage disposal, Maria. You cannot just—"

He listened again, then rolled his eyes. "Okay, okay. I am on my way down."

He ended the call and turned back to Sergei and Elena, making an effort to smile. "Call my mobile if you need anything—or please just come to the front office when you're done looking." He turned and hurried out of the apartment.

Sergei laughed softly as he watched the man scurry into the stairwell. He very much doubted they would be interrupted, no matter how long they stayed in Josef's apartment.

The apartment was spacious and pricey, at least for Chicago's Russian neighborhoods. Josef had decorated it with expensive vulgarity. The skin of a Siberian tiger, complete with snarling head, adorned the marble floor in the entryway. The kitchen counter held an impressive array of flavored vodkas and rums of the sort typically found in the liquor cabinet of a wealthy college fraternity.

The bedroom, however, was the pièce de résistance: a huge round water bed in a mahogany frame, three signed Patrick Nagel prints on the walls, a mirrored ceiling, and a bottle of Viagra on the dresser.

In the den, they found what they were looking for: Josef's computer and a file cabinet holding five drawers stuffed with receipts, tax returns, import permits, and other random documents. "Bingo!" said Sergei after a few seconds of leafing through the documents. "If there's anything, it's in here."

He took out a digital camera with a high-volume memory and started quickly flipping through the documents, snapping pictures of anything interesting. "So, how do you know Ben?" he asked.

"From college," Elena answered as she started on another drawer. "Noelle—Ben's wife—was my roommate my junior year in college. We'd been friends since sophomore year; a group of us would do stuff together most evenings, unless we had dates or something. That was pretty often for Noelle. She had a very serious boyfriend who took up a lot of her time."

"Ben?" asked Sergei.

"No. She and her boyfriend broke up over spring break, and she was very depressed. She wouldn't leave the room because she was afraid she would see this guy, who lived in the same dorm we did. Noelle is usually a lot of fun to talk to and spend time with, but not then. All she wanted to do was lie on her bed and listen to depressing music or talk about whether she and her boyfriend were going to get back together. And since she wouldn't leave the room except for classes and meals, I started to get pretty sick of it."

"So what did you do?"

"After this had been going on for about three weeks, I suggested that we go listen to a band at the Grove—that was an outdoor auditorium in the woods behind our quad. Eat some nachos and have a good time. At first she said no, but I insisted and we finally went. We danced with friends for a while, but then I went to get a Coke and found her dancing with some guy when I came back. He had sort of a college pretty-boy look: shoulder-length hair in a ponytail, goatee, gold hoop earring, good tan, tight T-shirt."

"I know the type," Sergei said, shaking his head. He stopped and his jaw dropped. "Ben?"

Elena nodded, a broad grin on her face.

Sergei stared at her for a second before breaking out in laughter. After a moment, he mastered himself. "Okay. Wow. So that's when you first met Ben?"

She shook her head. "Actually, I didn't meet him for about a week after that. Noelle was having fun, so I left her to dance the night away. I asked her about her new catch the next morning, and she told me it was nothing. She said he was fun, but kind of shallow—not a serious long-term prospect. Her exact words were that he was 'perfect' for her right then because she didn't want another serious relationship and he was 'basically eye candy.'"

Sergei roared with laughter. "So Ben 'Eye Candy' Corbin must have cut his hair, shaved, and lost the earring when he went to law school. What a shame. It's amazing how time changes people."

"By the way, that reminds me of something I've been meaning to ask you: What made you leave the Bureau?"

"Money," he replied immediately, turning his attention to a row of boxes along one wall. "Lots of money."

"Really?" she asked, a tinge of disappointment in her voice. "Are you making a lot more now?"

He stopped his work for a moment and glanced over at her. Her long blonde hair, slim build, and stylish trench coat made her look like she had just stepped out of a film noir.

"I only wish," he said. "It wasn't *my* money that made me leave. I had taken an accounting course—just one—in college, so I wound up working on that Inkombank money-laundering case. After that, the Bureau figured I was a perfect fit for all of the follow-up investigations they did. I spent my last six months there going through bank documents and running spreadsheets, and it got pretty old. Nailing shady bankers and accountants is important work, but it's not that exciting. I wanted something that would get me out of the office and"—he gestured to Josef Fedorov's unique decor—"let me see new and interesting places. Also, I didn't join the FBI to go after money launderers."

She had stopped working and turned her full attention to him. "Why did you join?"

"Mostly because of something that happened one summer when I was in college. I was running some errands with my mother when I saw these two big guys arguing with an old lady in a business suit. All of a sudden, one of them punched her in the stomach. She doubled over and the other guy grabbed the back of her head and smashed his knee into her face. She went down and both of them started kicking her in the head and chest. I started to run over to help her, but my mom practically tackled me. 'They're *mafiya*,' she said, and I noticed that no one else was helping the old lady. In fact, everyone had disappeared from the street.

"We heard later that the police were looking for witnesses, but my mom wouldn't call, and she and my father wouldn't let me call." He shrugged and looked down, shamed by the memory. "I joined the FBI because I didn't want people to be afraid like that anymore."

"Were those two guys ever prosecuted?"

"Not for that. One of them is doing a fifty-year sentence for attempted murder and a bunch of extortion counts. The other one died a couple years ago."

He felt exposed, and her wide brown eyes unsettled him, so he changed the subject. He stooped and pulled a white satin shirt out of one of the boxes. "Well, this is evidence of something, but I don't think I want to know what."

Elena laughed. "I'm sure it would look good on you."

"Was that a compliment?" he asked, looking at the shirt. "Or were you trying to make me picture myself as a *Saturday Night Fever* extra?"

She laughed again. "I'll let you decide."

It was nearly six, but Judge Harris had kept them late in order to finish one more witness. That worried Ben. Judges typically did that only when they were convinced the testimony would take just a few minutes. Since the witness in question was Dr. Ivanovsky, and Ben had a lot more than a few minutes' of questions for his client, he took the judge's scheduling decision as a bad omen. "Dr. Ivanovsky, when was the first time you met Nikolai Zinoviev?" asked Ben.

"I met him on September fifteen of this year. A man I know from Saint Vladimir's church said to me that maybe Mr. Zinoviev owned something that I wished to buy, so I called Mr. Zinoviev and he said to meet him. So I met him."

"And what did you discuss at that meeting?"

"Objection, Dead Man's Rule," said Simeon.

"Your Honor, that rule is intended to protect the interests of deceased parties by preventing testimony about oral contracts with them," said Ben. "It is not intended to bar all testimony in which a witness happens to mention a dead man. I recognize that the Court has barred Dr. Ivanovsky from testifying about his contract with Mr. Zinoviev, and I don't intend to ask him about that. But the witness is entitled to talk about his other contacts with Mr. Zinoviev."

"Your Honor—" Simeon began, but Judge Harris held up his hand.

"Regardless of what the Dead Man's Rule may or may not be intended to do, Mr. Corbin," the judge said as he opened a well-thumbed copy of Illinois's civil procedure statutes and rules, "I am bound by what it actually does. Section 8-201 of the Code of Civil Procedure says in relevant part, 'In the trial of any action in which any party sues or defends as the representative of a deceased person, no adverse party shall be allowed to testify on his own behalf to any conversation with the deceased.'" He closed the book and put it down. "That doesn't leave me much choice. I'm bound by my oath of office and the laws of Illinois to enforce the Dead Man's Rule as it's written, whether I like it or not. And that means I'm going to have to bar this witness from testifying to any conversations he had with Mr. Zinoviev." He paused and looked at Ben compassionately, knowing full well that he had just torn the heart out of Ben's case. "I'm sorry."

After they had been in the apartment for about half an hour, Sergei called Ben to give him an update. "There are lots of documents from the Brothers. Import/export licenses—including some forgeries that Elena is excited about—corporate resolutions, contracts, minutes of meetings, stuff like that. Also, it looks like these guys received five million dollars recently from an offshore bank account, and there's nothing to explain why."

"Five million bucks?" Ben whistled through his teeth. "That's a chunk of change."

"No smoking guns, though," Sergei continued. "No letter saying that Dr. Ivanovsky had a contract with Nikolai Zinoviev or anything like that. Is there anything in particular that you'd like us to look for?"

"Yes, but it would take too long to explain it over the phone. I've got an after-dinner meeting with another client that I'm already late for. Do you have time to bring the documents over to my office first thing tomorrow morning? I'd like to go through them with you before I head over to court."

"No problem. How early would you like me there?"

"How about seven?"

"Sure. I'll see you then."

Sergei turned to Elena. "I'm going to meet with Ben tomorrow morning to go through this stuff. Want me to just bring it to the Bureau when we're done?"

"That'd be terrific."

"I'll go tell the landlord that we're leaving—unless you'd like to."

"That's okay. I'll let you do it."

"Really? I think he'd like to say good-bye to you."

"But if I see him again, I won't be able to say good-bye," she said with mock passion.

Sergei chuckled. "I'll try to let him down easy."

"Thanks. I'll meet you out front."

Five minutes later, Sergei met Elena on the sidewalk in front of the apartment building. The night had turned cold, and a chill, wet wind was blowing in off the lake. "Hey, they've got great peppermint cocoa over at Peet's," said Elena. "Could I talk you into some?"

"You just did," he replied.

Sergei tore himself out of bed at six o'clock the next morning. He was still exhausted from staying up until one thirty to print and read the documents he had photographed. Some of them looked more interesting than he had first thought—including some corporate minutes that discussed a contract between Zinoviev and the Brothers. He had meant to get up at five thirty, but he'd slept through his alarm. Now he would have to rush to be at Ben's office by seven. He took a quick shower, dressed, and grabbed a banana as he ran out of his apartment.

A high-pitched alarm went off just as he opened the door. He grimaced, then turned on his heel and ran to the control panel for his new burglar alarm. He had already set it off three times since it was installed last week. He keyed in the pass code and the alarm stopped, but it was too late. Now he would have to wait for the security company to call.

He looked impatiently at his watch as long seconds passed, each one making it less likely that he would arrive downtown by seven o'clock.

The security company finally called and Sergei ran out the door a second time, now with only fifteen minutes to make the twenty-five-minute trip. He tossed the stack of printouts into the backseat and jumped into the driver's seat. He stuck his key in the ignition and turned. Nothing happened. Heart sinking, he tried again. Still nothing.

He popped the hood and got out, hoping that it was a loose wire rather than a dead battery. He walked around to the front of the car, opened the hood, and looked down at the engine. He had just enough time to notice that the wires on the battery had been disconnected—but not enough time to wonder why—before something heavy struck him from behind and he passed out.

"Hi, Elena, it's Ben Corbin. Have you seen Sergei this morning?"

"No. I haven't seen him since he dropped me off at the FBI parking garage last night. Why?"

"He was supposed to meet me here at seven o'clock this morning with some documents. It's seven thirty and he hasn't shown up or called. I tried his office and his cell phone, but he's not answering. That's not like him."

"No, it's not," said Elena, concern in her voice. "I'll look into it and let you know what I find. Call me if you hear from him, okay?"

"I will. Thanks."

Ben hung up the phone and wondered what to do next. Elena would no doubt do a better job of looking for Sergei than Ben could, but there wasn't much she could do to help him with his case. Ever since Sergei had called last night, Ben had entertained the hope that even if Josef Fedorov couldn't testify, his papers could. Those documents were

Ben's last chance of finding some type of admissible evidence of the contract, and it looked like that chance was slipping away.

Ben nervously paced the short hallway of his office. He rarely felt helpless or frustrated in his law practice, but now he felt both. Again. This case held more unpleasant surprises than any other case he had ever worked on. If Sergei had been working for Ben on *Circuit Dynamics* and had not shown up for a meeting, for instance, Ben would have simply assumed that his detective had car trouble and had forgotten to call. But Ben didn't assume that in this case. His gut told him that Sergei was in serious trouble. *Not that there's anything I can do about it, of course,* he thought, his jaws clenched in impotent anger.

That wasn't quite true, he realized a second later—there was one thing he could do: pray. So he prayed silently but fervently for Sergei as he walked back to his office and sat down at his desk.

Noelle came in a few minutes later and found her husband staring out the window. "Still no word from Sergei?" she asked.

"No, and I've got a bad feeling about it. I called Elena, and she said she'd try to find him."

She sat down in one of his guest chairs. "Do you think that assassin might have come back for him?"

"That guy's probably still in the hospital, but he might have friends. And the Brothers might have done to him whatever they did to Josef."

"Especially if they can make those documents disappear at the same time."

"I know." He put his head in his hands and sighed. "I *need* those documents, and I need them before the trial ends. And I'm worried about Sergei. Every time I start feeling good about this case, someone dies or there's some disaster in court and we're in deep trouble again. It seems like each day holds a new crisis where I'm completely out of control and all I can do is pray and hope. This is getting to be a habit."

Noelle reached over and patted her husband's arm. "Praying and hoping aren't bad habits to have."

◆ ◆ ◆

Two hours later, Ben stood at the lectern in Judge Harris's courtroom, bracing himself to try one more desperate gambit. "Your Honor, I move the admission of all of plaintiff's exhibits into evidence."

"Any objection?" Judge Harris asked Anthony Simeon.

"We object to Plaintiff's One. Lack of foundation."

"Your Honor, I believe we've laid a foundation establishing the authenticity of this document. Mr. Kolesnikov conceded that one of the signatures on this document was probably his. Mr. Voronin admitted that the Brothers passed resolutions authorizing all significant transactions and that he couldn't find another resolution authorizing this one. True, these witnesses also denied that Plaintiff's Exhibit One is the minutes of their October nine meeting. However, none of their denials were credible. If anything, they underscored the fact that this is a genuine document."

The judge raised skeptical eyebrows, sending wrinkles up to his gleaming scalp. "But the problem is that you have nothing *but* denials. No one has come in here and said these are in fact the actual minutes of an actual meeting. Without that, I can't let this into evidence. You have raised serious questions about the character and credibility of various witnesses, but that's not enough. A series of unbelievable denials does not add up to an admission. Objection sustained. Does the plaintiff rest, Counsel?"

"For the moment, Your Honor. I—"

"There's no resting your case 'for the moment,' Mr. Corbin," interrupted the judge. "Either you have more evidence to put on or you don't. Which is it?"

"We don't have any more evidence to offer right now, but we may later today. I had expected to receive some documents this morning, but they haven't arrived yet. I would ask the Court for a brief recess, probably not past the end of the day."

"What are these documents?"

"Even though the defense has been unable or unwilling to produce Mr. Fedorov—despite repeated court orders—we have managed to obtain a number of documents from him regarding the Brothers."

"You were able to find Mr. Fedorov?" asked the judge in surprise.

"No, Your Honor, just his documents."

"Are any of them relevant to this case?"

"I don't know yet," admitted Ben. "I need to go through them first."

"And you need to get them before you can go through them," observed the judge, shaking his head. "This is a trial, Mr. Corbin, not some open-ended truth-seeking investigation. When you're done putting on the evidence you have right now, you're done. I'm not going to recess this trial so you can go looking for more. That all has to happen before trial. Now, do you have any more evidence to put in the record, or do you rest?"

Ben stood for several seconds trying to think of some way to buy time, but he couldn't come up with anything. Hopefully, he'd be able to track down Sergei in time to introduce any new documents as rebuttal evidence after Simeon put on his case. "Your Honor, the plaintiff rests."

"The defense moves for judgment as a matter of law, Your Honor," Anthony Simeon said, handing up a stack of papers.

Ben wasn't happy, but he wasn't surprised. The defense always has the option of moving for judgment as a matter of law at the end of the plaintiff's case in chief. If the plaintiff fails to put on any evidence in support of a necessary element of his case, the defendant can ask the judge to end the trial because there's no need to put on the defense case—the plaintiff's case is fatally defective no matter what evidence the defendant presents.

"We can have our response on file in forty-eight hours, Your Honor," Ben said as he leafed through the copy Simeon had given him.

It appeared to make essentially the same points as the summary judgment motion the defense had filed earlier in the case.

"No," the judge said. "The whole point of this motion is that none of us should have to sit through the defense case if your client can't win. If I give you a briefing schedule on this, then Mr. Simeon has to put on his case anyway—and that defeats the purpose of a motion like this, doesn't it?"

"You could recess the trial for long enough for this motion to be briefed and argued," suggested Ben.

"I wasn't willing to give you a one-day recess five minutes ago. I certainly won't give you a two- or three-day recess now. Mr. Simeon, are you ready to argue this?"

"Yes, Your Honor."

"Proceed."

"Thank you. The very first fact that any plaintiff in a breach-of-contract case must prove is, of course, the existence of a contract. The plaintiff here has not done that. There is no evidence in the record of any contract between Mr. Zinoviev and the plaintiff.

"First, let's look at the testimonial evidence. Every time Mr. Corbin has asked a witness if such a contract exists, he has received denials. He may not believe those denials, but as the Court just explained, a collection of unbelievable denials does not add up to an admission. No witness has admitted the existence of the alleged contract.

"Second, the documentary evidence. The only contract in evidence is the agreement between Mr. Zinoviev and the Brothers LLC—a contract that covers the same items that the plaintiff allegedly bought and is therefore *completely* inconsistent with the plaintiff's theory of the case. What else does the record contain? Mr. Brodsky's signature, some bank statements, and a resolution authorizing the creation of bank accounts in various locations. None of that proves the existence of a contract between the parties to this case.

"It's also worth noting what the record does *not* contain." He pointed to the minutes that had just been excluded from evidence. "It does not contain the one document on which Mr. Corbin has founded his whole case. The Court once entered judgment against the plaintiff in the absence of that document, a judgment that was only reversed when Mr. Corbin promised that he would be able to produce a witness to authenticate it. He has not done so. He has produced no evidence that the meeting referenced in that document took place or that Mr. Zinoviev made the statements attributed to him. He cannot even tell you who wrote that document. We move the Court to enter judgment in favor of the defendant."

The judge nodded. "Mr. Corbin?"

"Yes, Your Honor. I have already gone over the unbelievable testimony offered by the defense witnesses, all of which points to the existence of a contract between Mr. Zinoviev and Dr. Ivanovsky. If there is no contract to hide, then why were they lying?"

"I remember their testimony," interjected Judge Harris, "but you'll need more than that to defeat Mr. Simeon's motion."

Ben launched into his last argument, which had only occurred to him that morning while he was waiting for Sergei. "Well, Your Honor, even more significant than the testimony of those witnesses who *did* take the stand is the probable testimony of one who *didn't*. I believe Josef Fedorov is the man who called me that night, and he indicated to us that he would be willing to testify. We subpoenaed him, but he did not come to court. Your Honor held him in contempt, but he still did not come to court. Your Honor issued a bench warrant for his arrest, but even then he did not come to court.

"Mr. Fedorov is a missing witness within the meaning of *Neal v. Nimmagadda*. He satisfies all of the *Neal* factors." Ben ticked them off on his fingers. "First, he was under the defense's control and they could have produced him in court, but they didn't. In fact, it appears that they actively prevented him from testifying. Second, he was not equally available to us. Third, you can bet that if he were going to testify favorably to them, he would have been here. And finally, they've offered no excuse for failing to produce him. We therefore ask that Mr. Fedorov's likely testimony be construed against them."

"Your Honor," rejoined Simeon, "the missing-witness presumption only applies to witnesses controlled by a *party* to a lawsuit. Aside from Mr. Corbin's client, the only party to this lawsuit is the estate of Mr. Zinoviev. There is no evidence whatsoever that the estate controls Mr. Fedorov or is preventing him from testifying. If Mr. Corbin is to be believed, the Brothers—who are *not* parties to this case—are doing that."

The judge nodded. "That's my understanding of the law as well. I appreciate your creativity and tenacity, Mr. Corbin, but I'm going to have to grant Mr. Simeon's motion. There is simply no evidence from which I can conclude that the contract in question exists. Judgment is hereby entered in favor of the defendant. Mr. Simeon, please draw up an order."

So that was it. Ben stood numb, still rooted in front of the lectern. The case was over, and he had lost. Intellectually, he had always known defeat was a possibility, but he had never really believed it in his gut. Now it was a reality, and it struck him like a shot to the solar plexus.

As required by courtroom etiquette, both lawyers thanked the judge. Ben turned around and started walking back to his seat, avoiding Dr. Ivanovsky's eyes. Instead, he looked at the blowup of the minutes, absently reading its familiar words. Then he stopped and read them again, remembering something Simeon had just said. His heart began to pound as he read it a third time with growing conviction that his hunch was right.

He turned to face the judge. "Your Honor, the plaintiff requests leave to call one more witness."

Chapter Twelve
In the Chair

Sergei awoke to find himself sitting in an unpainted metal chair, a bright light shining in his eyes. He groggily tried to raise his hand to shade his eyes, but he couldn't—his arms and legs were tied securely to the chair.

A light breeze chilled him, and he noticed that he was wearing only his underwear. He looked down at the floor and another sort of chill ran through him—he saw a wire crudely soldered to one leg of the chair. It snaked across the floor and up to a surge protector sitting on a worn wooden table. The table also held a pair of pliers, a syringe, and a gun.

A small, almost polite cough alerted Sergei to the presence of someone else in the room, hiding behind the glare of the light. "Let me guess," said Sergei. "The wire and the pliers are to make me talk. The syringe is full of thiopental sodium in case the wire and pliers don't work. And the gun is the final threat in case the truth serum doesn't work."

A hand reached out from the blinding glare and flipped the switch on the surge protector. Electricity coursed through Sergei's body, seizing his muscles and pulling his face into a rictus of agony. His back arched and he clenched his jaws as he tried not to scream.

After a few seconds, the hand switched the current off. Sergei collapsed back into the chair, breathing heavily.

"In this room, there are two rules," said a gentle, even voice with a Chechen accent. "First, you will speak only the truth. Second, you will speak only when spoken to. You broke both of those rules. You were wrong about the syringe and the gun. The gun is your reward if you follow the rules. After you have spoken the truth in answering all of my questions, you will die instantly with a bullet through your head. The syringe is your punishment if you break the rules. It is filled with diluted battery acid, not thiopental sodium. It will take hours, maybe days, to kill you. Now I will ask the first question. What is your name?"

The SWAT team made a tight wedge around a battering ram. They waited outside the door of the small two-story house. Each member wore body armor and held an assault rifle or a shotgun. Elena Kamenev stood behind them, her shotgun ready. She wiped nervous sweat off her palms as she waited for the operation to start. According to the Department of Motor Vehicles, this was the address of the owner of the car driven by Sergei's tail. She dreaded what might lie behind the door.

The commander of the team nodded. The ram sprang forward, smashing in the door. The lead men burst through behind the ram. "Police! Hands in the air!"

The crowd of armed men blocked Elena's view, but she heard a woman shriek, "It's the cops, Earl! Cops!"

A confused sound of running feet and slamming doors came from somewhere farther away as Elena waited tensely outside, watching the corners of the building for fugitives. She heard one of the officers yell,

"Freeze!" as teams of police ran through the house, looking for more occupants.

After about two minutes, the commander emerged. "All right, ma'am. The building is secure. No sign of Mr. Spassky or the suspect you described."

She nodded, both relieved and disappointed. "Any sign of criminal activity?"

He chuckled. "Only in the vegetable garden."

Curious, Elena slung her shotgun over her shoulder and cautiously walked through the door. She found a very ordinary, if slightly tacky, living room, complete with an overstuffed sofa protected by a plastic slipcover. A terrified woman of about fifty-five sat in a chair under the watchful eyes of two policemen as a third questioned her. A simple hair band held her long, straight gray hair away from her anxious face. She wore a rainbow-colored dress that would have been the height of fashion forty-five years ago in San Francisco.

An open door led to a tidy kitchen with pink wallpaper and Formica counters. The water was running in the sink, partially muffling the voices Elena heard through the open window. She found the back door and went out, squinting in the unseasonably warm sun.

The backyard of the house was not large, but it held an impressive vegetable garden and a picnic area. It also had a high privacy fence for reasons that became plain to Elena as soon as she took a close look at the table. It was covered with piles of cured marijuana leaves, some loose and some in plastic bags. It also held a food scale for weighing the crop. A handcuffed man—presumably named Earl—with shoulder-length gray hair and a full beard was arguing with a couple of SWAT team members, or at least trying to. One officer was methodically cataloguing and gathering evidence while a second guarded the prisoner. A third patiently questioned Earl, ignoring his angry outbursts but getting little useful information.

Elena went back inside to see if they were having better luck with the woman. They were. "Here's the receipt," she said in a rapid, edgy voice as she handed a piece of paper to her interrogator. "See? Thirty-two hundred in cash. And it's dated October thirty. It's just like I told you—we haven't seen that car since the day before Halloween. That sticks in my mind because we were worried some kids would egg it or something and we wouldn't get as much for it. So we were really happy when those guys said they wanted to buy it." She laughed nervously. "I guess we shouldn't have been so happy."

The policeman examined the bank receipt carefully and placed it in an evidence bag. "If you sold the car, why is the title still in your name?"

"They said they were going to take care of all the paperwork, but they must not have." She looked anxiously at the officer as he took notes.

Elena stepped forward and held out the drawing of Elbek Shishani. "Is this the man you sold your car to?"

The woman glanced down at the sketch, her hands fidgeting in her lap. "That's one of them. He did most of the talking. There was another guy who was taller and younger. He had a real strong accent, and I don't think his English was too good." She glanced around the room, and it suddenly dawned on her that the small army of heavily armed and armored urban warriors had not come for her and Earl. "Who are these guys?"

"What is your name?" asked the voice for the hundredth time.

For the hundredth time, Sergei said nothing, and another jolt of electricity wrenched him. It passed and he sagged back into the chair, dazed and only half-conscious. He felt the residual tingling in his limbs and absently wondered what the repeated shocks were doing to his nervous system, but he couldn't summon the energy to care. He was going to die in this chair, so what did it matter?

"What is your name?" asked the patient voice again, and again Sergei refused to answer. This time the expected shock did not come.

The voice sighed. "You suffer needlessly, Sergei Spassky." Sergei looked up at the sound of his name. "You are surprised that I know your name? I know many things about you, so there is no harm in telling me. All that will happen is that I will not have to hurt you. Now, what is your name?"

Sergei felt an overwhelming urge to answer, to just give in and stop the pain. It would be so easy. And it would be harmless, just like the voice said. He opened his mouth and was about to speak when he realized that it would *not* be harmless. If he answered this question, it would be much harder not to answer the next "harmless" question. The one after that would be harder still to resist—whether it was harmless or not. The soft-voiced interrogator knew that, and that was why he was asking Sergei these questions.

For the first time in his life, Sergei faced a moment that he could not escape with his glib tongue or his deadly gunplay. He was stripped not only of his clothing but of all his defenses. There was no escape, no ducking and weaving. He either had the strength to resist or he didn't.

He sat perfectly still for a moment, balanced on the edge of a knife. Then he slowly closed his mouth and stared straight ahead with his back straight and his head up, waiting for the next shock. *They'll probably kill me,* he thought with bleak resolve, *but they'll never break me.*

The torturer sighed again, and Sergei saw a hand reach out toward the table from the shadows. He steeled himself, but the hand did not touch the surge protector. Instead, it picked up the syringe. "I am truly sorry that we did not have more time together, Sergei. Things might have turned out differently. I must go shortly, and I cannot leave you here. But before I depart, I will give you one last chance. What is your name?"

The syringe and the gloved hand hovered at the edge of the shadows. Sergei stared at them, unable to tear his eyes away. His heart pounded at the terror of imminent excruciating death and a fog of fear shrouded his mind.

Running feet and voices broke the agonizing silence. A door flew open and Sergei glimpsed a figure sprinting past him. A tense, low conversation in Chechen followed. Then the light went out, and two sets of footsteps walked quickly past him. A door opened and shut, and Sergei was alone in the darkness.

Judge Harris gave Ben a jaundiced look. "Who is this new witness you want to call?"

"Anthony Simeon, Your Honor."

Judge Harris stared at Ben in surprise. Whispers filled the gallery behind Ben's back. Anthony Simeon stopped writing the directed verdict order and looked at Ben with faint amusement in his eyes.

Janet Anderson, however, was not amused. She bolted from her chair. "Your Honor, we object strenuously. Mr. Simeon was never disclosed as a witness. And it's highly improper to call a party's attorney as a witness."

Ben was not about to back down. "*Unless* the attorney personally knows information that can't be obtained from other witnesses. I just realized that Mr. Simeon might have such knowledge, Your Honor. This will take less than five minutes, I promise."

"I can't see what unique factual knowledge he could possibly have about this case," said Judge Harris, "but I expect you intend to enlighten me about that shortly." He looked over at Simeon. "Are you willing to spend five minutes on the stand?"

"I suppose," Simeon said in resignation. "We'll spend more time than that arguing about this."

"Thank you," said the judge. "All right. You have *five* minutes, Mr. Corbin." He took off his watch and placed it on the bench in front of him.

The lead counsel for the defense walked up to the witness stand, was sworn, and sat in the witness chair. It was not a comfortable chair, but he looked comfortable in it.

Standing at the lectern, Ben was anything but comfortable. "Mr. Simeon, when did you first see Plaintiff's One?" he asked, gesturing to the blowup of the minutes.

"When I wrote them, which was probably on October ten or eleven," Simeon said nonchalantly.

The courtroom became utterly silent. Ben stood frozen for several seconds, unable to believe his ears. "I, uh, thank you. Um, did you attend—? Strike that. Under what circumstances did you write that document?"

"I am the attorney for the Brothers LLC. In that capacity, I attend certain of their corporate meetings and draft minutes memorializing them. I wrote these minutes after attending a meeting held on October nine."

"And did Nikolai Zinoviev also attend that meeting?" asked Ben.

"He was there for part of it, but he left about halfway through."

Ben was still dazed, but he tried to concentrate and make sure he asked all the necessary questions. "While he was there, did he make the statements attributed to him—that you attributed to him in these minutes?"

Anderson rose to her feet tentatively. "Objection: attorney-client privilege."

"Let's see about that," said Judge Harris. He turned to the witness. "Mr. Simeon, was Nikolai Zinoviev your client on October nine?"

"No, Your Honor. Mr. Zinoviev did not ask me to represent him until after this lawsuit was filed."

"So nothing he said to you on the ninth could have been privileged. Objection overruled. You may answer the question."

"The answer is yes. Mr. Zinoviev did make those statements."

Ben pointed to the blowup on the easel. "You see the reference to a preexisting contract in the third paragraph of these minutes?"

"Yes."

"Did Mr. Zinoviev say who the buyer in that contract was?"

"Yes. He said it was one Mikhail Ivanovsky."

"Did that cause the Brothers some concern?"

"Not that I recall. Mr. Zinoviev said there was a contract, but that it wouldn't be a problem because he would 'get out of it.'"

"To your knowledge, did he get out of it?"

"No."

Ben heard murmuring behind him as he formulated his next question. "Who retained you to defend this case?"

"Mr. Zinoviev formally retained my firm, but our bills are being paid by the Brothers LLC."

Why are you doing this? Ben wondered as he began to recover his composure. He could have asked dozens more questions, but he probably wouldn't get any better testimony than was already in the record. One of the cardinal rules of cross-examination is to ask only as many questions as absolutely necessary, because every question gives a hostile witness an opportunity to take a shot at the questioning attorney. And Ben had everything he needed. Besides, he half suspected that Simeon was somehow outmaneuvering him yet again, though he couldn't figure out how. "No further questions."

As he walked back to his seat, he glanced at the faces of the audience. To his left, Janet Anderson sat pale and slack-jawed at the defense-counsel table and the Brothers were in a heated, whispered conversation. To Ben's right, Dr. Ivanovsky beamed with the excited glee of a child who has just gotten a long-coveted toy for Christmas. Irina Ivanovsky smiled happily—not quite sure what had happened, but glad that her husband was pleased. Noelle gave Ben a wide, slightly disbelieving grin, amazed at what he had just pulled off. Ben saw, but did not really notice, a young man in the back of the courtroom with dark, intense eyes that took in everything.

"Any questions, Ms. Anderson?" the judge asked.

She looked at the judge, but couldn't seem to make her mouth work.

Anthony Simeon stirred in the witness chair and cleared his throat. "The defense has no questions for this witness, Your Honor," he said dryly.

"You may step down, Mr. Simeon." Judge Harris turned back to Ben as Simeon returned to the defense table. "Does the plaintiff rest?"

Ben rose from his seat. "First I would like to move the admission of Plaintiff's One into evidence."

Ben looked at his opponent, curious how he would react. "No objection, Your Honor," Simeon said casually.

"Plaintiff's One is admitted," said the judge.

"The plaintiff rests," said Ben. He watched Simeon nervously. If he had a trap for Ben, he would spring it now.

"The defense also rests."

The judge arched his eyebrows in surprise, wrinkling his forehead all the way to the top of his shiny head. "Are you sure, Mr. Simeon?"

"Quite sure, Your Honor. Mr. Corbin has already put on all of my witnesses. I have no further questions for them."

"And no documents you wish to put in the record?"

"None, Your Honor."

"All right."

The muttering from the Brothers grew louder. Ben glanced over and saw that Anton was half out of his seat, his red face a mask of rage.

The judge saw it too and decided to cut the proceedings short. "Ordinarily, I would entertain closing arguments at this time, but I don't see how Mr. Simeon could give one in light of his testimony. I will take this matter under advisement and prepare an order of judgment. You can pick it up when court opens tomorrow morning. This court is now in recess." He banged his gavel and walked out of the courtroom at a brisker pace than usual. The watcher at the back of the room also slipped out, though nobody noticed except Dmitry.

As soon as the judge was out of the room, Anton turned to Simeon and seemed about to lunge at him. Simeon didn't flinch. "Hold it!" yelled the bailiff, drawing his pistol.

Dmitry grabbed Anton's arm and said something to him in Russian. Anton continued to glare at Simeon, who looked back at him steadily. Anton pointed at him. "You are a dead man!" he shouted and stormed out of the courtroom, followed by Dmitry and Pavel.

Elbek closed the door to the torture chamber behind him, leaving the Russian detective slumped in his chair. He turned to his aide, a burly man named Yunus. "Now, what is the news from the watcher?" he asked, referring to the man the Chechens had hired to watch the court proceedings from time to time to ensure that they were getting accurate reports from Dmitry.

"He said that the Brothers' lawyer testified and that he said he was at a meeting where Zinoviev said he had a contract with Ivanovsky. The Brothers became very angry. One of them threatened to kill the lawyer when it was over. He was so loud that the watcher heard it through the door."

Elbek digested the news, trying to evaluate how serious it was. "What about the judge? What did he say?"

"He said he would make a decision and that the lawyers could come get it when the court opens tomorrow."

"Did he say anything about what his decision would be?"

"No, sir. I questioned the watcher closely on that."

Elbek paused, evaluating his options. "When does the court open tomorrow morning?"

"I don't know," Yunus admitted. "I will find out."

"Do that. I will need to know in the next half hour. But first, set two guards to watch the Russian. Tell them to keep him alive—I'm not quite done with him yet. He was close to breaking when you came in, Yunus. Very close."

"I'm sorry, sir."

"No, no. You were right to bring me this news immediately. There are things we need to do."

Ben and Noelle started packing up notes, extra copies of exhibits, highlighters, and other trial paraphernalia into boxes. Anthony Simeon and Janet Anderson did the same on the other side of the courtroom. Ordinarily, the lawyers would have exchanged pleasantries as soon as the judge left, but the scene a moment ago with the Brothers left a lingering cloud in the courtroom. They all wanted to leave as quickly as possible—except for Dr. Ivanovsky. He talked excitedly with his wife, laughing and gesturing expansively. After a few minutes, he walked over to Ben, a wide smile splitting his leathery face and tears of joy gleaming in his eyes.

Ben smiled back and put out his hand. "Congratula— "Whoa," he said as his client ignored the proffered hand and enveloped him in a bear hug, planting kisses firmly on both of his cheeks. Ben chuckled and hugged Dr. Ivanovsky back. "Congratulations!"

"Thank you. Thank you so very, very much," said Dr. Ivanovsky when he finally released Ben. "I am so happy." He gestured to the dingy, windowless courtroom. "This is now my favorite place in all America because of that you won today," he declared.

"We haven't won yet," Ben cautioned reflexively. "We don't know what the judge will do tomorrow morning."

"No, but we do have a pretty good idea," said a voice behind Ben. He turned and saw Anthony Simeon approaching. "I'm not going to hug you," he said, extending his hand, "but I did want to congratulate you. Nice work."

"Thanks," replied Ben as he shook the other lawyer's hand. "I appreciate your candor on the stand. I wouldn't have had a chance without it."

Simeon gave Ben an odd half-amused, half-knowing look. "I expect you have plans for dinner," he said, glancing at Noelle and the Ivanovskys, "but if you have time, I'd like to buy you a drink when you're done here."

◆　◆　◆

The phone rang in Dmitry's office, where he, Pavel, and Anton were discussing their next move. "Hello?"

"Hello, Dmitry," said a soft, familiar voice. "This is Leonid. What happened in court today?"

Dmitry had expected this call and steeled himself. "The judge threw out Ivanovsky's case, but then his lawyer put our lawyer on the witness stand. The judge postponed his decision until tomorrow morning."

"I see. Which way do you think the judge will rule?"

"For us, of course," replied Dmitry as confidently as he could. "The judge has already ruled our way twice. I don't see any reason why he won't do it again."

"What did your lawyer say?"

"He's confident too," Dmitry assured him.

"What did he say on the stand?"

"Oh, nothing important," Dmitry said just a little too quickly. "He just talked about a meeting we had with Zinoviev. The minutes from that meeting were on an easel for the whole trial, staring the judge in the face. The lawyer just rehashed what was in them. It was no big deal."

"Then why did you threaten to kill him?"

The question flustered Dmitry badly. He had thought the man in the back of the courtroom had left before Anton's outburst. "We had a . . . uh . . . a misunderstanding about his bill. One of my colleagues got a little upset."

There was a pause. "I understand perfectly. It is very disturbing to pay a large sum of money to someone and then have them fail to perform as expected."

Dmitry could feel beads of sweat forming on his forehead. "Yes. Well, our business should be concluded tomorrow. I'll call you as soon as we have the judge's ruling. I expect we will be delivering the merchandise by lunch tomorrow."

He hung up the phone and looked at Pavel and Anton, who were watching him apprehensively. "We have to run. Now."

Chapter Thirteen
Evening Prayers

Khalid Mohammed approved of his new neighbors. They were quiet, they didn't park in front of his building, and they were observant Muslims. He knew this last fact through an incident the previous week. Dawn had just been breaking and he had been at work early, loading his small delivery truck in back, when he'd heard a tinny, recorded voice chanting the morning call to prayer. He'd looked through a window in the neighboring building and seen two men prostrated in prayer. Feeling guilty, he'd climbed into the back of the truck and prostrated himself between crates of fragrant hummus.

He nodded at the memory. Allah had called him to account that day for neglecting his prayers, using his neighbors to set an example for him. Khalid was thankful for that. As the father of five and the owner and operator of a small Middle Eastern food-distribution business, he rarely had enough time for anything. He often caught himself forgetting his prayers.

He wanted to meet his neighbors, but he had been unsuccessful so far. On the rare occasions when he spotted one of them outside, they seemed to be in as much of a hurry as he always was. He didn't feel comfortable accosting them on the street just to introduce himself.

The day after they had unknowingly shared their morning prayer with him, Khalid took fresh falafels to them as a welcome gift. No one answered the door when he knocked and rang the bell. The bell was corroded and the door appeared to be made of thick wood, so he hadn't been sure whether anyone inside had heard him. He considered walking in and announcing his presence, but instead he simply left the falafels and a friendly note on the concrete doorstep. The falafels and note were gone the next morning, but no one had ever thanked him.

As the days passed without any word from his neighbors, Khalid began to wonder whether they had found the gift he'd left for them—or whether someone else had stolen it from their doorstep. There were vagrants and other disreputable people on the streets, even during the day—though this problem had diminished with the arrival of the men next door. Khalid had seen a particularly aggressive homeless drug addict harassing one of the men as he carried a car battery and some wires into the building one day. Khalid turned away quickly to avoid making eye contact with the addict—a mistake he had made once before—but as soon as he turned his back, he heard a piercing shriek. When he turned again, the addict was limping away quickly while spewing profanity at the man with the battery, who then calmly walked into the building.

The addict hadn't returned, and many other undesirable street dwellers also vanished as word of his experience apparently spread. Khalid approved of this too. A good Muslim is considerate of the poor, of course, but Khalid had always understood the Prophet's maxims on this subject to include an implicit exemption for the obnoxious and ill-mannered poor.

So Khalid was pleased to see one of the men coming out of the building just as he was parking his truck after making the last delivery of the day. The man was about forty or forty-five, a little shorter than medium height, and he had a sling on his left arm and bandages on his right hand. He was too pale-skinned to be an Arab or a Persian. Perhaps he was an Azeri or northern Turk.

Khalid left the truck and walked quickly over to intercept the man before he climbed into his car. Khalid came up to him just as he reached out his good hand for the car door. He saw Khalid out of the corner of his eye and turned with a sudden catlike move that made Khalid pause and hold up his hands.

"I just wanted to welcome you to the neighborhood," he said with a friendly smile. "My name is Khalid Mohammed, and I own a wholesale food business right there." He pointed to his building. "So you see, we are neighbors. Did you receive the falafels I left on your doorstep last week?"

The other man relaxed, but only slightly. "Yes, a gracious gift. Thank you."

Another man burst out of the building and ran to the car. He stopped beside the first man and looked darkly at Khalid. "You'll forgive us, Mr. Mohammed, but we must go," said the first man as he got into the car with his companion.

They sped off, leaving Khalid looking after them and wondering where they could be going in such a hurry. Then he saw the sun hanging heavy and red-gold just over the western edge of the world and it hit him. He smiled and shook his head ruefully. "Evening prayers at the mosque," he said to himself. "Of course, how foolish of me. I can't believe I almost forgot *again*."

He went into his building to pray.

The rays of the setting sun poured through the western windows of the West Lounge at the Metropolitan Club, filling it with a rich, golden light. The club occupied the sixty-sixth and sixty-seventh floors of the Willis Tower and gave a spectacular view of the surrounding city. The forest of glass, steel, and stone towers—the tallest of which ended well below the club's windows—gave way to shorter buildings of brick and concrete and then to a sea of homes and small buildings. The expanse of rooftops stretched to the horizon, broken only by the grid of car-choked streets.

Anthony Simeon had doubtless seen this view many times before, but it was new to Ben, who gazed out the window as he drank a glass of Chardonnay.

"So what made you decide to call me as a witness?" asked his host.

"It was actually a point you made in arguing your motion for judgment as a matter of law." Ben set his glass on the white linen tablecloth. "You said I didn't know who wrote the minutes, which was true. So I looked at that blowup on the easel, wondering who had written it. I realized that there was something I hadn't noticed about the wording."

"And what was that?"

Ben took a sip of his wine. "It was pretty clear that a lawyer had written them. None of the Brothers are lawyers, so I knew it couldn't have been one of them. You represented them, so I guessed that you either wrote the minutes or knew who had. And then I also realized that throughout the whole trial you never once claimed that the minutes were fake, only that I hadn't laid a foundation for them." He paused and looked at Simeon, who had the same amused and knowing look he had worn in the courtroom. "You didn't seem very surprised when I called you. You were expecting it, weren't you?"

"By that point, yes. I had hoped the Brothers would testify differently or that you'd be able to get the minutes into evidence some other way, but—"

"Tony!" a man's voice called from near the door.

They both turned and saw Steve Rocco walking toward them. He was a tall man about ten years younger than Simeon, with a booming voice, a perpetual tan, and suspiciously good hair. Like many good litigators, he would have made an outstanding salesman.

"I haven't seen you in here for at least two weeks," Rocco said as he reached them. "Where have you been?"

"On trial," replied Simeon, nodding toward Ben. "Do you know Ben Corbin?"

"Sure. We've got a case going to trial pretty soon down in Chancery." He gave Ben's shoulder a patronizing pat. "So, Ben, drowning your sorrows after your first battle with Tony Simeon? He's practically made an alcoholic out of me over the years."

"He won," said Simeon.

Rocco stared at Ben. "You won?"

"The judge hasn't issued an order yet," Ben said, "but—"

"But he won," interjected Simeon. "Did you say you've got a trial coming up against him in the near future?"

Rocco nodded dumbly.

"Settle."

Rocco laughed uncertainly. "Uh, thanks for the advice, Tony. See you later, Ben."

Simeon laughed quietly as he watched Rocco retreat to his own table. "There's less to him than meets the eye. He's like a puffer fish: if you can manage to let a little air out of him, you can eat him for lunch anytime."

"Which I take it you've done?" responded Ben.

"He hasn't been willing to take a case to trial against me for five years, but before that he lost eight straight to me."

Ben realized the favor Simeon had just done for him. "Thanks for the vote of confidence."

"You earned it. Let me know if he takes my advice."

"I will. And thanks for calling me the other night and sending me the minutes. I couldn't have won without your help." Ben's voice was casual, but he watched Simeon intently as he spoke.

The older man didn't react visibly. "Not a problem. I hope I didn't wake you with that call."

"I was already awake. Those were some pretty unusual litigation tactics. Why did you do it?"

"I had my ethical and discovery obligations, of course, once I realized that my clients weren't going to produce the minutes. I have a duty to zealously represent them, but that duty doesn't extend to violating the rules on their behalf. If you mean why didn't I simply produce the minutes in discovery, the reason is that it was safer for me to do my duty in a more discreet fashion than usual. Besides"—he winked—"it was more fun to make you do some of the work yourself."

Ben laughed. "I'm glad you enjoyed yourself." He studied the older man. "Was that it, though? Was that really why you did it? This can't be the first time you've had clients like this."

Simeon's smile faded and he looked out the window, squinting slightly in the setting sun. His face was suddenly very old and very tired in the fading light. "No . . . no, it's not."

Simeon was silent for a moment, then looked back at Ben with his bantering smile back in place. "But it is the first time I've been both a secret informant and my opponent's star witness. I've found that the key to keeping my practice interesting as I ossify is to always try something new in each case. And today was definitely a new and interesting experience for me." He raised his glass. "Congratulations on a job well done."

"Likewise." Ben raised his glass in return. "I've got a sneaking suspicion that the case turned out more or less the way you wanted."

"There are other defeats that have bothered me more," the older lawyer acknowledged.

"Do you know what's in the safe-deposit box?" Ben asked suddenly.

"You mean other than the Seiko and the earrings?"

"Other than those."

"No idea whatsoever, but . . ." Simeon looked out the window again. "But it might not have been in my clients' best interests to obtain whatever it is. It might not have been in anybody's best interests."

Ben's heart pounded. "Why do you say that?"

Simeon gave Ben a measuring look. "I am going to tell you this because I think you have a right to know, but I ask that you keep it completely confidential."

"Of course," said Ben.

"They were afraid. They were afraid of whomever they had resold the box to, but they were afraid even before that. All along I've had the feeling that they were dealing with something too serious for them, but that there was too much money involved for them to get out."

"Were they afraid enough to kill Nikolai Zinoviev and Josef Fedorov?"

Simeon chuckled at Ben's directness, but then grew serious. "If they were, then they're probably also afraid enough to kill other people, don't you think?"

A single case file lay open on Elena Kamenev's desk, surrounded by mounds of other files. The open file was titled "Spassky, Sergei." The other files contained the prep materials for twenty-three witness interviews for a complicated extortion scheme that was going to the grand jury by the end of the month. She needed to finish the interviews by the end of the week, and she hadn't even begun to get ready for them. Now it was six o'clock on Tuesday evening and she had no choice. She would have to stay up all night just to be ready for the interviews tomorrow, and the day after didn't look any better.

Realistically, there was very little more that she could do for Sergei at this point. She had interviewed every witness. She had circulated the sketches and descriptions of the suspects she'd obtained from both Sergei and the pot farmers. She had also posted a "missing persons" bulletin with Sergei's picture and description and a notice that he was a potential kidnapping and/or murder victim. And she had pulled and reviewed all the records she could find on Elbek Shishani.

So far, she had found nothing. There were no more leads for her to follow and nothing left on her to-do list for the case. All she could do now was wait for something to turn up—and hope that it wouldn't be Sergei's dead body.

She took a picture out of Sergei's file and looked at it. It came from one of Auntie Olga's photo albums and had been taken at a Spassky family reunion over the Fourth of July weekend. The picture showed a tan and smiling Sergei sitting in a speedboat. His hair was slightly damp and he was wearing swim trunks. He was more muscular than she had guessed from his slender build, and she was surprised to see a tattoo on his right shoulder. Her gaze lingered on his eyes. They were a deep brown that would have looked dark and piercing if he hadn't been smiling. She had never noticed them before because he hid them behind his glasses.

She realized that there were a lot of things she had never noticed about Sergei. He had a reputation as a good agent, and she knew from personal experience that he was a good shot—but beyond that, she had known very little about him until the last few days. He was just a Russian guy who did bank work and whom she sometimes saw around the office. It occurred to her that the scholarly, clean-cut look was probably an asset in the field. Suspects and witnesses would make useful unconscious assumptions about him.

Just like I made assumptions about him. She never would have guessed he would be so much fun to spend time with or that he would drive a sports car and have a tattoo.

She glanced at the clock on her computer screen. It was six thirty. She bit her lip and put the picture down. Then she closed the file, put it back in her cabinet, and did her best to focus on the witness preparation she needed to do.

◆ ◆ ◆

The silent darkness was like a drug. It blurred the line between consciousness and unconsciousness and confused Sergei's sense of time. He could not tell if he had been alone in that room for a few hours or a few days.

After his tormentor vanished, Sergei had apparently been forgotten. He had seen and heard nothing since then. It was so quiet that he guessed he was either underground or in a soundproof room. The complete absence of any light reinforced that guess—even after enough time had passed for his eyes to adjust, he still saw nothing. Not even the faint glow of a covered window or a sliver of light from underneath a closed door.

The deprivation of two of his senses enhanced the others. He was acutely aware of the itching pain from the electrical burns on his back, arms, and legs. The growing sour dryness in his mouth and throat spawned dreams of cool water in his troubled half-sleep.

A sudden noise startled him fully awake as a door opened somewhere behind him. Light poured into the room and blinded him. He heard footsteps walking toward him. A hand grabbed his chin and jerked his head up and sideways, sending waves of sharp pain through his body as his burns rubbed against the chair. "Open your eyes, dog!" a voice ordered in heavily accented Russian. "See your death."

Sergei opened his eyes in a painful squint and saw the muzzle of a pistol a few inches from his face. It was held by a short, wide man with a thick black beard and burning eyes. Sergei tried to struggle, but he was still firmly tied to the chair and was badly weakened by his ordeal. The man jammed the gun against Sergei's forehead. "Now you will die like the filthy beast you are." Sergei watched helplessly as the man's finger tightened on the trigger. The trigger slowly moved back. There was a loud metallic snap as the gun's hammer came down on an empty firing chamber.

Sergei winced involuntarily at the sound, and the man laughed. "You think we will give a clean bullet to a disobedient Russian animal?"

He spat in Sergei's face. "We save you for the battery acid." He laughed again and hit Sergei in the side of the head with the gun barrel, sending the Russian tumbling back into darkness.

Tony Simeon watched Ben's retreating back and smiled. *A good kid,* he decided, *and he's got the makings of a good lawyer.* Corbin had shown a strong courtroom presence and had generally known the right questions to ask. He was a little slow on the uptake at times, but he would get better with age. Most important, he had good instincts. He'd do well.

Tony remembered himself at that age. He'd had good instincts too. He also had the ruthless drive of a barracuda and an uncanny knack for winning. After one brilliant and improbable victory, the judge had invited him back to his chambers. Judge Jenkins had been nearly eighty at the time, a relic of a slower and more genteel era of legal practice. He'd puffed on a gnarled old pipe and poured himself a glass of brandy as Tony waited.

"Mr. Simeon," the old jurist had said at last, "you have remarkable gifts in the courtroom."

"Thank you, Your Honor."

"The question is, what do you want to do with them?"

"Win."

The judge had puffed in silence for a time, wreathed in smoke. "And when you're my age and you look back on your life, is that what you want to see—a neat stack of courtroom victories? Is that *all* you want to see?"

For many years, that had been all Tony really wanted to see—and he had seen it. Win followed win for decades. His reputation and bank account had both grown to impressive proportions. Opposing counsel learned the wisdom of settling early when their opponents retained him. One side or the other called him in virtually every big case filed in Chicago, and his firm paid him essentially whatever he asked for.

Winning had its costs, of course. The time and energy devoured by his cases hadn't left enough of either to make a marriage work, something that had taken two divorces for him to learn. Winning also made close friendships difficult: anyone who knew him well enough to be a true friend also knew that he would sacrifice that friendship if it would give him an advantage—and in the upper echelons of Chicago's legal community, that was bound to happen eventually.

Not all of his clients had been particularly savory, so early in his career he'd made it a rule to never ask questions that might have awkward answers. About fifteen years ago, he had amended this rule to add, "unless the awkward answers implicate Tony Simeon."

Ironically, that change had been caused by Tony's hobby, not his law practice. His one passion outside of the law was art, especially the art of ancient Greece. As his wealth grew, he had begun to collect sculpture and painted vases from the Classical Period. The ancient art market was a shadowy place, abounding in forgeries and treasures from unauthorized digs. It was also subject to a growing body of intricate, conflicting, and generally ignored regulations as the countries that were the source of most antiquities tried to clamp down on what they viewed as black-market trading in these items.

Tony had always had his purchases checked to make sure they were genuine and not subject to an outstanding warrant, but otherwise he'd done little to ensure that every form had been filled out and every permit granted in their countries of origin. That was the dealer's problem, not his.

Then one day he'd opened the *Chicago Tribune* to discover that Allan Robbins, a respected partner from another law firm, was under investigation for allegedly violating the antiquities laws of Turkey. According to the newspaper, he had attempted to donate several Roman marble busts to the Field Museum, which had determined they had come from an illegal dig near the ancient city of Ephesus and had been smuggled out of the country.

As days passed, the scandal worsened. Robbins at first denied that the sculptures had come from looters. Then he claimed ignorance of their origins. Finally, he offered to return them to Turkey. The Customs Service, however, decided to make an example of Robbins and prosecuted him. He reached a plea bargain that kept him out of jail, but he lost his law license and was forced into an early and ignominious retirement.

The day after the lawyer's fate became public, Tony received a call from Dmitry Kolesnikov, an importer from whom Tony had purchased an exquisite statuette of the Titan Prometheus found near the ruins of a Greek temple on the Black Sea. Dmitry had occasionally asked Tony to represent him and his company, the Brothers, but Tony had always demurred. The Brothers were a little too questionable even for Tony. Moreover, they were small fry from his perspective and simply did not have cases big enough to interest him. "I read about that lawyer, Allan Robbins," Dmitry had said. "It was terrible how they destroyed him, don't you think?"

"Yes," Tony replied warily. "I feel very sorry for him."

"As do I," replied Dmitry. "I am calling because I would hate to see something like that happen to you."

"Is there a problem with the item you sold me?"

"Unfortunately, the gentleman from whom we purchased it did not have official permission for his excavation. We could try to get permission now, but the Ukrainians are not likely to grant it. They would probably prosecute us."

"So take back the sculpture and return my money."

"I'm afraid I can't do that. It would be illegal for me to receive undocumented antiquities, but I'm sure none of this will be a problem if we work together."

Tony had suspected something like this was coming. "What did you have in mind?"

What Dmitry had in mind was that Tony would take care of all of the Brothers' legal needs and they would never breathe a word about his statuette. Over the years, he'd helped them with a variety of small matters, from setting up an LLC to reviewing draft contracts to litigating a tax case against the IRS regarding several unexplained wire transfers.

So when the Brothers had asked him to defend a low-level drug dealer in a tiny breach-of-contract case, he'd done so without raising an eyebrow. And when they'd asked him to help them ensure the enforceability of a lucrative agreement with a shadowy group of Chechens for the resale of the contents of a safe-deposit box, he'd had a pretty good idea why they had hired him to defend Nikolai Zinoviev. But he'd made no effort to find out what was inside the box. The less he knew about what these clients did, the better.

When Ben won a big victory, he often celebrated at Alinea, one of Chicago's premier restaurants. If he was lucky, there would be a late cancellation and he could get a table on the same day. Tonight he was lucky.

Alinea was housed in an elegant brick building on the North Side. It offered a single "menu," which was really a complete multicourse meal chosen by the chef. Ben, Noelle, and the Ivanovskys enjoyed an excellent meal and an hour or more of conversation over coffee. They were all in high spirits as they paid the bill and put on their coats. It was drizzling lightly, so Ben and Dr. Ivanovsky went to get their cars, leaving the women in the lobby. As they walked, Ben brought up his conversation with Anthony Simeon at the Metropolitan Club.

"The bottom line is that we need to talk to the police and the FBI," he said as he finished. "He basically warned me that his clients might try to kill you."

"No!" Dr. Ivanovsky insisted. "We have decided before. No police."

Ben had been growing increasingly uncomfortable with that decision. "Yes, but let's look at the facts here. Each time you get close to winning this case, somebody dies or disappears. Now it looks like you might be close to winning again. Who's left? Simeon and I have already done all the damage we can. Judge Harris almost certainly signed the order before he left for the day. There's only one person left whose death can change things: *you*."

"I do not worry," the scientist replied with a dismissive wave.

"Look, you trusted my judgment during this trial, right?"

Dr. Ivanovsky nodded. "Yes."

"And it paid off, right?"

"Yes."

"Then trust me one more time. As your lawyer, I *strongly* advise you to contact the authorities."

"No."

They had reached the crossroads that Ben had feared and expected. He chose his words carefully. "I cannot allow you to use my services to commit a crime. You know that. It would be a crime for you to obtain possession of biological weapons or instructions on how to produce them. If you are not willing to contact the proper authorities, I am afraid I will have to."

Dr. Ivanovsky stared at Ben. His face grew red and the stringy muscles on his neck stood out as he clenched his jaws in shock and fury. Ben braced himself for an outraged tirade, but none came. His client slowly calmed himself and took a deep breath. "You always say nothing is for sure in courts," he said evenly, though banked fires of anger burned behind his eyes. "Okay, so we wait until it is for sure that we win. We will talk tomorrow after we see what the judge has decided. I make no promise, but maybe we call the FBI then."

Ben relaxed and smiled. "Good. Why don't you come to my office at nine o'clock tomorrow morning. We can talk about the order and decide what to do."

"Can I come at ten? There is a thing I must do first."

"Ten is fine. I'll see you then."

All in all, Tony Simeon was satisfied with his life. He enjoyed his work and he was very good at it. He had few friends but many acquaintances. He was never alone unless he wanted to be. The years had rolled by in a comfortable, almost-unnoticed rhythm for nearly four decades.

But that rhythm had stopped suddenly, six weeks ago, in a confusion of squealing tires, a shout, and the awful sound of metal on flesh, a sound that would echo in his mind forever.

He had been walking down Washington Street with one of his partners, Dan Wood, on their way to a hearing. They were deep in conversation, clutching overlapping umbrellas to ward off a bitingly cold October drizzle. Tony slipped on a patch of invisible ice on the sidewalk and fell. Dan stopped and leaned over to help him just as a taxi rounded the corner of LaSalle and Washington going too fast. Its tires lost traction on the slick road and it careened toward them. Tony could see it from where he lay, but it was approaching Dan from behind. Tony shouted and scrambled to the side, but Dan couldn't react fast enough. He had only half turned before the cab hit him in the side with a loud, dull noise like the sound of someone hitting a pillow very hard with a baseball bat.

The collision threw Dan twenty feet down the sidewalk, where he lay in an awkward, unmoving heap. Tony ran over to him and checked for a pulse, but there was none. He called an ambulance on his cell phone, then he stood in the chill rain, looking down at Dan's body. A small crowd of onlookers gathered. He didn't know what else to do, and he was relieved when the ambulance finally came for Dan's remains.

He'd gone back to the office, told the necessary people, and made the necessary phone calls. Then he had sat down at his desk and tried to do some work. But for the first time in his professional life, he'd been unable to focus on the work in front of him.

Six weeks later, not much had changed. He still did his work well and could maintain the same courtroom manner, but the practice of law no longer held any joy or meaning for him. During his divorces and other life crises he had been able to lose himself in the practice of law and forget what went on outside the office and the courtroom. But now it was as if a blazing light had seared the eyes of his mind and soul, leaving him to wander blindly through the empty mansions of his life.

He had told himself that it was the shock of the event, that he would get over it in a day or two—or a week or two. But he hadn't. Every day he came into work and tried to concentrate, and every day the frozen face of Dan Wood stared up at him from the pages of pleadings and cases. And every day the sound of squealing tires and that terrible impact rang in his ears.

◆　◆　◆

"Hello, James. We'd like to talk to you for a minute." Special Agent James Washington looked up and saw two men standing in the doorway of his office, one he recognized and one he didn't. The man he recognized was Fred Giacolone, his CIA liaison. The other man was an older African American with an air of authority and a faint frown, as if his lunch were giving him heartburn.

"Sure," James replied. "What's up?"

Fred closed the door and said, "James, I'd like you to meet Bill Alexander, deputy director for intelligence here at the CIA. Bill has some questions about a file search you ordered last week."

"Fire away," said James, trying not to sound as apprehensive as he felt. Getting a closed-door visit from the deputy director could hardly be good news. James was FBI, but his job was to be a point of contact between the two intelligence agencies. He hoped he hadn't done anything to screw that up.

Deputy Director Alexander looked him in the eyes. "Mr. Washington, why did you request our files on Alexei Zinoviev?"

It was a routine, everyday errand—the kind one forgets almost before it's over. Yet Khalid Mohammed would never forget buying stamps on Wednesday morning.

The day was clear and cold. A bright, small sun shone in a pale-blue sky. Khalid decided it was a perfect day for a brisk walk.

The post office was about half a mile away, meaning the round trip would take about half an hour by foot. That would still leave plenty of time to call in his supply orders before lunchtime, as long as there weren't long lines. Khalid doubted there would be at this time of day and set off at a quick pace, humming to himself as he walked.

As soon as he stepped inside the doors of the post office, he knew that he had guessed wrong about the lines. They snaked around the edge of the wide floor. Refusing to let this unexpected annoyance dampen his good spirits, he looked at his watch and decided that he would wait ten minutes. If he hadn't reached the counter by then, he would walk back to the office, count this as his daily exercise, and pick up the stamps later.

A long and battered cork bulletin board ran along the wall beside the line. It was covered with hundreds of flyers for missing persons, library book sales, wanted criminals, and other government and community announcements. The "wanted" posters were mildly interesting, and Khalid idly scanned them as he waited. They ran the gamut from murderers to forgers to tax cheats. There was even a man wanted for stealing trees.

A ripple ran through the line and it slowly shrugged forward like a giant, lazy caterpillar. Khalid found himself in front of a new collection of faces and crimes. Right in front of him were police sketches of two vaguely familiar faces. According to the posters, they were both wanted "for attempted murder, assault with a deadly weapon, kidnapping, and burglary." He looked more closely at the faces. They looked uncomfortably like the two men he had met just before evening prayers the day before. Khalid doubted that his esteemed neighbors could be criminals, so he carefully read the descriptions under each sketch. They matched— even the injury to the shorter man's hand was described exactly.

Khalid's mind whirled. Could these posters be right? When it came to Muslims, the American government had adopted an "arrest first and ask questions later" policy, or at least that's how it seemed to many people at his mosque. Could he call the FBI, knowing that he might be sending innocent men to prison or deportation? On the other hand, could he *not* call the FBI, knowing that these men might be dangerous criminals who could strike again? He prayed for guidance.

The phone rang in Sergei Spassky's empty office, disturbing the silence that had reigned for most of the past twenty-four hours. The FBI and police had been there earlier in the day looking for clues, but otherwise it had been as still and dark as a tomb. It was a spacious but windowless room in a half-empty office building that Sergei had found quiet or lonely, depending on his mood and the time of day. Stacks of documents and file folders nearly covered the wide desk and matching round table. The phone sat atop one pillar of paper, jangling loudly.

After four rings, voice mail picked up. "You have reached Sergei Spassky of the Spassky Detective Agency. I'm not here right now, but if you leave your name and phone number at the tone, I'll get back to you as soon as possible."

"Hi, Sergei, it's James Washington. Listen, I need to talk to you about that file request you gave me a couple of weeks ago. It's important, so give me a call as soon as you get this message. Thanks. I'll talk to you soon."

Seven hundred miles away, James hung up the phone and debated what to do next. Should he have someone from the Chicago office try to track down Sergei today, or should he wait to see if Sergei called back tomorrow morning? It was after six in Langley, so it would be past five in Chicago. Getting an agent to give up his or her evening based solely on a request from the CIA would be tough and unpleasant. And it would be ten times worse if had to give an "I'm sorry but this is classified and I can't tell you why we need to find him" bureaucratic stiff-arm. James didn't feel like going through that hassle, particularly since the Agency had sat on this for two weeks before suddenly making it his emergency half an hour ago. Besides, Sergei was pretty good about returning phone messages. So James decided to let the matter rest.

CHAPTER FOURTEEN
JUDGMENT DAY

For the first time in a month, it was the sunrise that woke Ben. He had planned on the trial running longer than it had, so his calendar was clear for the day except for his meeting with Dr. Ivanovsky. That wasn't until ten, though, so he had decided to turn off his alarm clock and sleep in for a change.

He felt around in the thick down comforter and determined that he was alone in bed. He was about to call Noelle's name when he noticed the smell of coffee and burning eggs. Smiling, he got out of bed and headed down to the kitchen.

Noelle's back was to him as she set the table, her long brown hair tumbling loose down her flannel nightgown.

"Good morning," he said, announcing his presence.

"Hello," she said, turning around and giving him a hug. "I thought I'd surprise you with some breakfast. The scrambled eggs got a little overdone, though. Want me to go out and get some muffins?"

Ben shook his head. He poked a fork into the skillet of partially blackened eggs and speared a chunk. "These aren't overdone, they're Cajun-style."

He picked up a bottle of Tabasco Sauce, sprinkled it liberally on the clump of carbonized egg on the end of his fork, and took a bite. "Perfect," he announced. He meant it too, more or less. Ben liked to cover most food with large doses of powerful condiments, so Noelle's troubled relationship with frying pans and woks rarely bothered him.

The Corbins spent a relaxing hour eating breakfast, drinking coffee, and chatting. Thanksgiving was two weeks away, and they hadn't yet decided what to do because Ben's schedule had been up in the air. By the time he finished his eggs, they had resolved to spend Thanksgiving Day with his parents in nearby Downers Grove. They would make the picturesque drive to Noelle's family home in Rochester, Minnesota, on Friday, spend the weekend there, and drive back on Monday. And neither of them would take any work.

They left home at nine o'clock and arrived in the office at nine thirty, which would give Ben plenty of time to walk over to the Daley Center, pick up Judge Harris's order, and be back in the office before Dr. Ivanovsky came.

The wide plaza in front of the courthouse was empty—a windswept expanse of cold gray stone and concrete presided over by Picasso's foreboding guardian. Ben hurried across it and into the lobby.

Judge Harris was on the bench, so Ben went around back to the judges' chambers, a row of office suites along the outer wall of the Daley Center. Fortunately, the judge's assistant hadn't decided to slip out for a break while the judge, clerk, and bailiff were all in the courtroom.

"Hi, Marge, I'm here to pick up the judge's order in the Ivanovsky case."

"Oh," she said, seeming a little surprised. "Just a moment, Mr. Corbin. I didn't realize you'd need another copy." She disappeared for a minute, and Ben could hear a copy machine running in the next room. She returned and handed him the still-warm copy. "There you go."

Ben quickly read the order, which covered less than a page:

> *This matter having come before the Court for trial, both parties appearing and presenting evidence and argument, and the Court being duly advised in the premises,*
>
> *IT IS HEREBY ORDERED:*
>
> 1. *That judgment is entered in favor of the Plaintiff, Mikhail Ivanovsky, and against the Defendant, the Estate of Nikolai Zinoviev;*
> 2. *That title to the contents of safe-deposit box #4613 of the LaSalle Street branch of the American Union Bank is hereby vested in the Plaintiff; and*
> 3. *That this is a final and appealable order.*
>
> *Honorable Alfred S. Harris*
> *Circuit Judge*

"Congratulations, Mr. Corbin," she said when Ben looked up. "We were talking about it this morning, and no one could remember the last time someone beat Mr. Simeon."

"Tony Simeon is a great lawyer."

"You must be very excited. I know your client is—he was all smiles when he saw the judge's order."

Ben looked at her in confusion. "My client already saw the order?"

"Yes, he was waiting outside the door at eight thirty. He left as soon as I gave him the order, but I could tell he was thrilled."

He stared at her open-mouthed. His stomach twisted in knots as he recalled Dr. Ivanovsky's comment that there was a *"thing I must do"* before their meeting that morning. And, like an idiot, Ben hadn't pressed his client on what "thing" could be more important than the judgment in this case.

The secretary looked up, startled by the expression on Ben's face. "Is everything all right, Mr. Corbin?"

"I hope so."

He turned and walked out into the hallway. As soon as he found a quiet spot, he called American Union Bank. As the phone rang, he sent up a quick prayer that Dr. Ivanovsky hadn't done anything spectacularly stupid.

"Hello, American Union legal department, Sophie speaking."

"This is Ben Corbin. Could you connect me to Chris Reid?" Reid was the in-house attorney responsible for handling safe-deposit-box legal issues. He had been Ben's contact at the bank throughout the Ivanovsky case.

"One moment."

Ben wiped the sweat from his hands as he waited to be put through. A few seconds later, a man's voice came on the line. "Hi, Ben. Congratulations on your win."

Ben's throat tightened. "How did you know?"

"Dr. Ivanovsky was in here almost an hour ago with a certified copy of the judgment."

"Where is he now?"

"I don't know. He emptied that safe-deposit box and took off." Reid paused. "Is that a problem?"

A knock on the conference-room door interrupted Elena's witness interview. "Come in," she called.

Frank Hernandez, an agent with whom she had worked on several cases, stuck his head in. "There's a phone call for you."

She was about to object that she was busy, but Frank obviously knew that already. If this could wait, he wouldn't have broken in on her interview. She excused herself and left with him.

"What is it?" she asked as they walked down the hall.

"There's a guy on the phone who says he's spotted the suspects in Sergei's case and knows where they are. He sounds credible, but he won't give us any details until he talks to the agent in charge of the investigation. We're tracing the call in case he won't cooperate over the phone."

Her heart raced. "Put him through to my line."

She half walked, half ran to her office, picked up her phone, and pressed the blinking red button. "Hello, Special Agent Elena Kamenev speaking."

"Hello," said a man's voice with a Middle Eastern accent. "As I told Mr. Hernandez, I have information about the two suspects, but there is something I need to know first: What evidence do you have that these men are criminals?"

"I can't tell you our whole case against them, of course," Elena said as she pulled out Sergei's file to see exactly what had already been disclosed publicly, "but I can tell you that we have fingerprint and eyewitness evidence linking them to a home invasion and attempted murder a week ago. The evidence is very solid."

The line was silent for several seconds. "You swear before God that all this is true?"

"Sure," replied Elena, who was agnostic.

"All right. My name is Khalid Mohammed. Here is what I know . . ."

"Allah has blessed us, and the operation has entered the second phase sooner than we expected," Elbek said to Shamil. "The database is no longer necessary. Shut it down and join us by noon." The "database" was the Vainakh Guard's code name for the Russian detective. The phone connection should've been secure, but one could never be too careful.

"That is wonderful news," replied Shamil. We will take care of it and join you shortly."

◆ ◆ ◆

"I'm headed for 436 Ryan Avenue," Elena called to Frank Hernandez as she ran out the door. "Call the city police—I'll need backup."

"I'm on it," he replied.

Elena went to her weapons locker and grabbed her standard-issue Glock pistol. She hesitated for an instant, then took her sniper rifle too. She doubted she would fire it, but the scope might be useful for surveillance.

She jogged to her car and drove quickly through the light mid-morning traffic. Her cell phone rang when she was about halfway there. "Hello?"

"Hi. It's Frank. I just got off the phone with the police. They'll have a black-and-white there in twenty minutes."

"A black-and-white? I need a SWAT team!"

"I know. That's what I told them, but they're short staffed today. They said that they'll pull a team off another assignment—and this is a direct quote—'If this turns out to be something more serious than a couple of pot farmers.'"

Elena switched lanes, nearly hitting a car that was in her blind spot. She waved apologetically as the other driver blared his horn. If a single squad car was all they would give her, then she would have to swallow her irritation and make do with that.

"Well, I hope they know what they're doing. Ask them to meet me at the corner of Edgar and Ryan so we can coordinate before we go in."

She drove past 436 Ryan slowly—but not slowly enough to attract attention—before heading to the rendezvous. It was a single-story brick-and-concrete building with the words "Advanced Gear" painted in large, fading letters over the weathered wooden door, which was the only entrance or exit she could see. Small, chicken-wire-covered windows stared blankly from the walls on either side of the door. There were no vehicles parked along the curb in front, but a cracked concrete driveway led back out of view. There must have been a rear entrance out of view from the street.

She turned the corner and drove back to the rendezvous. The squad car was waiting for her. She parked behind it and walked around to the passenger-side window. The officer inside, the younger of the two, rolled it down and said, "So what've we got?"

"A couple of kidnapping-and-assault suspects, and they may not be alone." She handed copies of the sketches in through the window. "They're armed and dangerous."

"We've got our body armor on," said the driver, knocking on his chest. Elena heard a muffled clank from the steel plate that sat over his heart inside the Kevlar vest. He was a burly, grizzled man of about fifty who had the look of a longtime veteran. "We'll be fine."

Elena wasn't so sure. "I've got a sniper certification and I brought my rifle. I can cover you while you go around back, break in the rear door, and—"

"This isn't a commando raid, young lady," interrupted the older policeman. "I'll go up to the front door and knock. Officer Fitzpatrick here"—he gestured to the younger man—"will be stationed behind the building in case we have any runners."

"Actually, this *is* a commando raid," Elena replied testily. "At least one of the suspects is a former Soviet commando."

"All the more reason for us not to bust in with our guns blazing," the officer persisted. "I've done this kind of thing a hundred times before, and the only times I've ever gotten shot at were when we pulled stunts like that. Nine times out of ten, suspects give up as soon as they see a cop at their front door and another one waiting out back. And the tenth time, they try to jump out of a window or something. Don't worry. We know what we're doing."

There was a knock at the door just as Shamil ended his conversation with General Shishani. Umar and Mamed came running up the stairs and appeared at the old desk where Shamil sat. They had been in the basement, guarding the semiconscious prisoner, but they knew their roles in defending against intruders.

Shamil nodded and gestured for them to take their positions. Mamed ran to cover the back door, while Umar went to the lobby. He quickly crouched down behind two carefully positioned file cabinets. The drawers had all been filled with sand, making them effectively bulletproof. Umar was virtually invisible from the door, but his range of fire covered the entire room.

A second, more forceful knock rattled the old door in its warped jambs.

"Just a moment!" called Shamil in a friendly voice as Umar settled in and positioned himself.

When they were ready, Shamil opened the door and saw a police officer. He was smiling and his gun was in its holster, but he had the shrewd eyes of a man who has spent decades dealing with liars. The shirt inside his open jacket had the stiff, bulky look that told Shamil he was wearing a Kevlar vest. He hoped Umar would notice as well and not waste bullets on chest shots.

"How can I help you?" asked Shamil.

"We're looking for these two men," said the policeman, holding out two sketches. "Have you seen them?"

A tingle of apprehension ran down Shamil's spine and settled in his stomach. One of the drawings was clearly General Shishani—it even had his name and description. The other was his bodyguard, Iljas, though the likeness was not as good. He shook his head and handed the sketches back. "No. I am sorry; I have not seen those men."

"Are you sure?" asked the officer, looking him in the eye. "They were seen coming out of this building."

"That must be a mistake. Those men have never been here."

"Do you mind if I come in and look around?"

"We are very busy now. Tomorrow you can come."

Shamil started to close the door, but the policeman put his hand on it. "It's an emergency."

"Okay. For an emergency, you can come in."

"Thank you," said the officer as Shamil opened the door and stepped aside. "We'll try not to interfere with your operations," he continued, scanning the dimly lit room as he crossed the threshold. His eyes caught the oddly configured file cabinets in the corner and he reached for his gun.

Two quick gunshots flashed from between the cabinets. The first hit the policeman squarely in the forehead, jerking his head back. The second tore through his exposed neck and shattered his spine. His body collapsed backward onto the doorstep.

Shamil signaled Mamed, and seconds later the other policeman lay dead in the alleyway behind the building.

A hundred yards away, Elena Kamenev looked through the scope on her rifle and watched in horror as the policeman flopped down lifelessly. The man who had opened the door reached down to pull in the body. She put a bullet through the top of his head. He fell heavily on top of the officer's body and lay still.

Adrenaline poured into her blood, and her heart raced. Her training kicked in and she automatically slowed her breath to steady her nerves and improve her aim. She chambered the next round, watching the inside of the room carefully. She couldn't see her target and waited for some movement before firing.

It came a split second later—a metallic glint and then the flash of a gunshot. A car window shattered twenty yards to her right, setting off a screeching alarm. She fired at the flash.

Nothing moved in the shadowy interior of the room. She glanced around, looking for other shooters who might be stalking her. Nothing. She took out her cell phone and called Frank Hernandez.

"Hi, Elena," he said. "How'd it go?"

"There's an officer down with a head wound and I'm taking fire," she said quickly. "I need that SWAT team and an ambulance."

She paused. If Sergei was still alive, there was a good chance they would kill him now. She pictured finding him crumpled on the floor with a bullet hole in the back of his head, his skin still warm. She knew better than to go into a situation like this alone, but she couldn't bear the thought of being too late to save him.

"I'm going in." She ended the call before Frank could object.

Slinging her rifle across her back, she took out her pistol and ran out from behind the car where she had been crouching. Gunfire erupted from inside as she ran toward the building. She squeezed off several shots and dove behind a row of mailboxes.

It had been a risk, but worth it. She had covered about thirty yards and had a better angle for shooting into the door. Also, the three-inch gap separating each box from its neighbor provided just enough room for a rifle barrel. Elena holstered her pistol and slipped her sniper rifle between two boxes. She rested the stock on her thumb, providing a steady brace as she looked through the scope. She saw the two file cabinets and an indistinct shape behind them. It moved slightly and she saw that it was a man holding a gun. She fired. The figure collapsed and the gun fell to the floor between the two cabinets.

Elena cautiously poked her head from behind the mailboxes and surveyed the scene inside the doorway. Nothing moved, so she got up and ran toward the building again. The seconds it took to cross the narrow street and weedy lawn seemed an eternity. She reached the door and flattened herself against the wall to the right of it.

Heart pounding, she pulled out her Glock, took a deep breath, and turned into the doorway. She stepped awkwardly to get around the two bodies lying in the entrance. She momentarily lost her balance and nearly tripped. If the lobby had held any living Chechens, she'd be dead.

Fortunately, it didn't. She regained her footing, crossed the lobby to another doorway, and peeked around the corner. The door opened into a long hallway. A man at the other end of the hall turned and saw her at the same instant she saw him. She pulled her head back just as he fired a shot. A cloud of plaster exploded from the wall a few inches from the doorway. Running steps retreated into the building.

Gambling that she wasn't stepping into an ambush, Elena ran through the doorway and down the hall, following the sound of the steps. She reached the door at the other end and saw the man's back disappearing into another doorway.

"Freeze! FBI!" she yelled, but he ignored her and raced down a flight of stairs.

"Help!" a man's voice called from somewhere in the distance. "Down here!" The voice was weak and hoarse, but she recognized it at once—*Sergei!*

The sound of gunfire jolted Sergei more or less awake. Thirst and the aftereffects of a concussion slowed his thoughts. A growing fever also fogged his mind, and at first he thought he was dreaming or hallucinating. But as the shots and yells grew closer and louder, he realized what must be happening.

He heard sounds behind him and twisted his head around in time to see a gun-wielding man come running down the stairs that led to

Sergei's prison. It was the same one who had threatened and pistol-whipped him earlier.

They're going to kill me before I can be rescued. "Help! Down here!" he croaked as loudly as he could.

But the man ignored Sergei. He stepped to the side of the doorway at the bottom of the stairs and pressed himself against the wall, his gun at eye level and pointed toward the staircase, poised to blow the head off of whoever came down next.

I'm bait, Sergei realized, kicking himself for shouting.

A woman's feet appeared on the stairs, cautiously and silently picking their way past nearly invisible booby-trap trip wires. As more of the woman's body appeared, Sergei realized that it was Elena.

"Look out!" Sergei yelled. "Bottom of the stairs on the right!"

The man whipped his gun around and aimed it at Sergei. The detective jerked his body sideways, tipping the chair over. A flash and explosion went off simultaneously behind him, and a bullet whizzed past his right shoulder as he fell. The man fired again and the bullet ricocheted off the steel frame of the chair back. But Sergei didn't notice—he had struck his head on the concrete floor and was unconscious again.

Elena jumped down the remaining stairs while the Chechen was shooting at Sergei. She landed nimbly with her gun aimed at his chest. "Freeze!" she ordered.

He swung the gun back toward her.

Bang!

The man staggered backward, looking down in shock at the bullet hole in his chest. His eyes rolled back in his head and he collapsed, dead before he hit the floor.

Elena ran over to Sergei, who lay motionless on the floor. Fearing the worst, she checked his pulse and breathing and looked for wounds.

Relief poured through her when she found that he was still alive and hadn't been shot. His skin was hot to the touch, however, and angry red streaks spread out from the long burns on his back. And he still hadn't woken up.

"Sergei!" she cried, cradling his head in her hands. "Can you hear me? Sergei!"

He opened his eyes and looked at her blearily. "Elena?" he groaned through dry, cracked lips. "What happened? Did you get him?"

"Yeah, I got him."

"Did you get the other ones? I think . . ." His mind wandered for a few seconds, then he focused again with a visible effort. "Two. Yeah, I think there were two more. Did you get 'em?"

"I got 'em."

He smiled weakly. "Gotta love a woman who can shoot." Then he passed out again.

As soon as Ben hung up the phone after talking to Chris Reid, he dialed Dr. Ivanovsky's home number—but he punched in the numbers too quickly and made a mistake. He hung up and tried again, but no one picked up. It finally occurred to him that maybe his client really was planning to meet him at ten o'clock. Maybe he had already destroyed whatever was in that box and both their lives could go back to normal.

Ben looked at his watch: *10:01.*

He jogged back to his office, praying that he'd find Dr. Ivanovsky in the lobby, drinking too-sweet tea and rereading Judge Harris's order for the 146th time. He'd probably also have a page of handwritten questions to ask Ben. Actually, probably two pages. Ben relaxed a little and grinned as he pictured the scene. It would be typical Ivanovsky.

But Dr. Ivanovsky wasn't in the lobby.

Ben turned to Susan, about to ask her if she'd seen his client, but she spoke first. "Ben, Irina Ivanovsky is on the phone. Do you want to talk to her?"

He paused for a heartbeat. *Why is Irina calling?* "Put her through."

The phone rang as he walked into his office and picked it up. "Hello. Ben Corbin."

"Mr. Corbin, Mikhail—he said I call you," she began in an uncertain, trembling voice. "He said if bad thing happen to him, I call you."

Ben stiffened, every muscle in his body tense. "Bad thing? What happened?"

She started to cry. "Police said they see Mikhail's car by the road. Mikhail is inside. He is—they shoot him many times." She sobbed again.

"The police shot him?"

"No. They shoot him before police come. He is very afraid for many weeks. He said nothing to me, but I am a wife and I see. Now I am so afraid." Her grief overwhelmed her and she said nothing coherent for a time. "I am sorry. Mikhail is . . . I do not know what happens to me if he dies. I must go to hospital now. He is in University Chicago Hospital."

The line went dead and Ben slowly hung up the receiver. As he thought through what he had just heard, fear descended on him like a cold and poisonous mist.

CHAPTER FIFTEEN
COUNCILS OF WAR

Elbek set the small, tightly sealed jar on the table in front of him. It was filled about halfway with a whitish-brown powder so fine that it flowed like thick smoke if the jar was moved. Each particle was incredibly tiny—less than five microns across—and had been painstakingly designed not to clump or stick to other particles. Ordinary dust motes were huge objects by comparison—floating boulders and logs one hundred microns wide or larger. They would irritate the nose or throat and be coughed out. But the powder in the jar would float unnoticed into the tiniest openings in the lungs. There, it would stick to the wall of the lung and begin to breed.

There was enough powder in the jar to start an epidemic that would rage through a city in a few weeks, killing virtually all whom it infected—or so Dr. Umarov had said. He had also said that he could use this powder as seed stock to grow hundreds of pounds of the disease. Elbek would be meeting with the doctor in a few minutes to discuss the status of their preparations, but for now he sat alone at the table with his prize and his thoughts.

Strange that something I have never seen could trigger so many memories.

He remembered the joy of his men when he told them that they were giving up the fight against the Russians, but beginning a much greater war. They were weary of war, of course, but they were much wearier of defeat. Now their general gave them the chance for victory—a small chance, but a real one—and they would follow him into the very gates of hell.

They abandoned their caves and learned the life of border smugglers from Elbek and Hamzat. Their ranks grew as Elbek quietly recruited the best Chechen and Ingush fighters he knew, particularly other disaffected *Spetsnaz* veterans.

Smuggling not only paid the bills, it allowed Elbek and his men to hear news from the underground arms market. They heard many rumors of anthrax, bubonic plague, smallpox, Marburg, and other bio-weapons for sale. None of them had panned out. Either the rumors were false, the germs were too weak for Elbek's purposes, or they had been outbid. Until one day a source in Moscow told him there might be a very interesting weapon for sale in America.

The lights went out and the click and whir of an old-fashioned movie projector started at the back of the room. All eyes turned to the screen. It showed a silent black-and-white image of the inside of a huge metal chamber. It was empty except for twelve rhesus monkeys huddled together on the floor and a sphere mounted on a brace at the top.

The sphere exploded, releasing a pale cloud that spread out ominously over the monkeys. Several of the animals became quite agitated as the cloud slowly descended on them, clinging to each other or racing around looking for a way out. Their mouths moved constantly as they soundlessly screamed and gibbered. The smoky fog thinned as it settled on the floor of the chamber, then vanished altogether, leaving the monkeys seemingly unharmed.

The scene suddenly shifted to a row of cages attended by figures wearing what appeared to be spacesuits. "This is forty-eight hours later," announced a voice at the back of the room.

The camera slowly panned along the lines of cages, which each held a monkey. The monkeys were mostly sitting or lying in their cages, though some of them still moved about. Their eyes appeared to be black, and dark lesions showed through their fur. Most of them had dark, wet spots under their noses and on their hindquarters.

The scene jumped again, showing a wide stainless-steel table. "This is seventy-two hours after they were exposed."

The camera slowly scanned along the table, showing twelve dark, inert lumps. Each one lay in a puddle of blackish liquid.

The film ended suddenly and the lights came back on, revealing eight men and women with ashen faces. They sat around a conference table, silent as the film they had just seen. A ninth man walked briskly to the front of the room as the movie screen disappeared into the ceiling.

"We found this film in storage this morning," he said as he reached the lectern at the end of the conference table. "Fortunately, our A/V people still had the equipment to run it. We now believe that it shows experiments performed in a secret facility on an island in the Aral Sea sometime in early 1985."

"We've known about this thing since 1985?" interrupted the representative from Homeland Security, a short bulldog of a man with thick, close-cropped gray hair. "Why didn't we do anything?"

The first speaker, Bill Alexander of the CIA, pressed his lips together in frustration. "We didn't take it seriously. The intelligence consensus at the time was that the Soviet Union did not have an active biological weapons program, though some of us disputed that."

"Including you," said a woman from the Pentagon.

He smiled. "Including me. You have a long memory, Mary. Even I would have doubted the authenticity of this particular piece of intelligence. The source was not reliable, and not even the greatest pessimists thought that the Soviets had the ability to genetically engineer something like this.

"The gentleman who sold us this film was named Alexei Zinoviev. He claimed that he could obtain a sample of the organism itself and possibly other materials for a price—which he wanted in advance, of course. We told him to bring us the germ first. Then we could talk about the price.

"Mr. Zinoviev disappeared for six months. Then one day he called his handler to arrange a meeting in West Berlin. He claimed he had something 'very big,' but he wouldn't say more. We had agents waiting to meet him at the agreed rendezvous, but he never arrived. Instead, he called us from Chicago and told us to meet him on a bridge there. We sent people as quickly as we could, but by the time we got there he was dead. The police were just fishing him out of the Chicago River."

"KGB?" asked the man from Homeland Security.

"It's certainly possible," acknowledged Deputy Director Alexander, "but they would have been a long way from home. Also, we knew that this gentleman had enemies in Chicago. In any event, he had nothing related to biological weapons on his person or in his hotel room, so we dropped the matter. The analyst who had originally reviewed this film retired, the Cold War ended, and this file was sent into storage.

"Then two weeks ago, a liaison officer from the FBI requested information on Mr. Zinoviev. Once the file was retrieved from the warehouse, it was brought to my attention. I questioned the liaison, who informed me that a former FBI agent in Chicago had called asking for this information."

"We've pulled in this ex-FBI guy for questioning, right?" asked the man from Homeland Security.

"Tom, you know more about that than I do at this point," said Alexander, looking at an athletic Hispanic man of about fifty, who was the FBI representative at the council.

The FBI man nodded. "I just got off the phone with a squad leader in our Chicago office before I came to this meeting. They'd actually been looking for the former agent since he disappeared two days ago. They found him this morning. He'd been kidnapped, interrogated, and tortured by a group of Chechens. He's in the intensive-care unit at a local hospital, but we'll talk to him as soon as we can." He looked at the man from Homeland Security. "It looks like we weren't the only ones who wanted to ask him questions.

"There's more bad news," he continued. "The agent who found and rescued this guy said that he'd been hired by a lawyer representing a retired Russian germ-warfare expert named Mikhail Ivanovsky. Ivanovsky was suing Zinoviev's brother for possession of something that Zinoviev left in a safe-deposit box in Chicago before he died. According to the court file, the case ended this morning with a judgment giving the box to Mr. Ivanovsky. He's already been to the bank and emptied the box. Then he disappeared. We just found him ten minutes ago. He's currently undergoing surgery for multiple bullet wounds."

No one spoke for several seconds as they digested this information and its ramifications. "Has anyone talked to Zinoviev's brother?" asked the woman from the Pentagon.

"He died about three weeks ago."

"It seems like the only person who isn't dead or in the hospital is the lawyer for the germ-warfare expert," said Bill Alexander. "I assume we're looking for him."

◆ ◆ ◆

Elbek's only regret was that Hamzat could not be here for this moment. He had died of pneumonia last January. Yet he had died a happy man, having lived to see the founding of the Vainakh Guard and its growth into a formidable shadow army. But he had not seen Allah's sword of victory delivered into their hands. His eyes had not beheld the key that would unlock the cage that had held all Muslims for centuries.

And now that key sat on the table in front of Elbek. There was much work still to do, but all the pieces were finally in place. It was merely a question of staying hidden until they were ready to strike.

Dr. Umarov walked in. He was a disaffected Uzbek who, despite his youthful appearance, had spent more than twenty years operating a smallpox-production line in Siberia before being summarily laid off when Boris Yeltsin terminated Russia's bioweapons-manufacturing program. "I hope I have not kept you waiting, General."

"Not at all. I arrived early." Elbek held up the vial. "So tell me, Doctor. What *exactly* can we do with this little jar?"

"Hi, Ben," Elena said. "I got your message, and we need to talk to you right away. Your phone line may not be safe. Can you come in?"

"On my way," said Ben. He grabbed his coat, told Susan and Noelle where he was going, and left the office. A cold, wind-whipped rain struck him as he stepped out of the building, but he didn't even consider going back for his umbrella. He had just spent three hours in his office tensely waiting to talk to someone from the FBI. He was not going to wait any longer, whatever the weather.

The FBI offices were in the Dirksen Building, only a few blocks from Ben's office. He walked down Dearborn Street at a pace that was nearly a jog, weaving through the crowd of pedestrians returning from lunch. Questions about the upcoming meeting crowded everything else out of his mind.

The Dirksen Building, a massive federal-office-and-courthouse structure, mirrored the architectural style of the Daley Center—grim glass-and-steel exterior, narrow windows, and a cold, stone-floored lobby.

Ben burst through the doors and hurried across the lobby to the security checkpoint. Once there he was forced to wait impatiently in line. Only one metal detector was working, and it was obstructed by an elderly man who apparently had a metal object in or on his person that neither he nor the security guard could locate.

A hand plucked at Ben's sleeve and a familiar voice said, "Ben! I was just heading back to the office to call you. Could I talk to you for a few minutes?"

Ben turned to see Steve Rocco, his suit and hair immaculate despite the wind and rain. "Uh, not right now, Steve. I'm on my way to a meeting."

"I'm sure it can wait for ten minutes," Rocco said, gently tugging Ben toward a bench. "I've got a settlement proposal that I think you'll find very interesting."

Ben wouldn't budge from the line, which was finally starting to move now that the old man had remembered the steel pin he had in his leg. "No offense, Steve, but I really don't have time. Put your best offer in writing and I'll discuss it with my client and get back to you." He moved forward with the line, leaving a startled Steve Rocco several feet behind him.

Not to be deterred, the prominent attorney followed Ben, little lines of irritation showing around his mouth. "Ben, the window of opportunity on this offer is very short. I need an answer from your client today. I'm sure your meeting is very important, but it can wait ten minutes. Now, if you'll just step over here, we can—"

"Actually, it *can't* wait," interrupted Ben as he reached the checkpoint. "I'm sorry, Steve, but I've got other things on my mind right now. Send your offer to my office and we'll look at it. I'll try to get back to you today, but I can't promise anything."

Two weeks ago, he would have spent the whole afternoon analyzing Rocco's offer and planning how to respond. Now he had forgotten about it by the time he stepped out of the elevator.

He walked into the lobby of the FBI offices, a small room with two receptionists behind bulletproof glass and locked doors that had to be buzzed open. Ben gave his name to the receptionists and paced nervously as he waited for Elena to come get him. A large glass case lined one wall of the lobby. In it were the pictures and names of agents from the office who had died in the line of duty. Ben skimmed over the names and faces, wondering if any new ones would be added after this case was over.

Elena buzzed Ben in and whisked him into a conference room where two men waited. One was a heavyset, dark-skinned man with a large turquoise ring. The other was a small, pale man in a dark suit. "Ben, I'd like you to meet Oleg Ignatev of the CIA and Alberto Gomez of the HMRU, the Bureau's Hazardous Materials Response Unit. We'd like to talk to you about Dr. Ivanovsky, but first I wanted to let you know that we found Sergei. He'll be all right, though he'll need to spend a few days in the hospital." She briefly described her rescue of Sergei and what he had told her about his captors.

"That's great news!" Ben said when she had finished. It was the first good news he'd had all day. "I'd begun to think I'd never see him again."

He glanced at the two CIA men. "I'll bet Sergei's kidnapping had something to do with the Ivanovsky matter. Am I right?"

"We think there might be a connection," acknowledged Agent Gomez. "Sergei told us that you asked him to investigate whether the CIA had a file on a Mr. Zinoviev. Why did you do that?"

"For the reasons I mentioned in the voice mail I left for Elena. Dr. Ivanovsky told me a very disturbing story about a CIA employee named Zinoviev. My client said Zinoviev had stolen biological weapons and committed over a dozen murders in the process. It would have been awkward—and possibly unethical—for me to just call Elena and repeat the whole thing to her. So I decided to try something less direct. Sergei and I figured that if the story was true, you'd have a file on it and ask us the question you just asked me. If it wasn't true, my client's story was wrong and there was nothing to worry about."

"What precisely was your client's story?" asked Agent Ignatev. He had no accent, but enunciated with the careful clarity of someone for whom English is a second language. "Please be as specific as possible."

Ben repeated what Dr. Ivanovsky had told him on the day he'd lost the summary-judgment motion. They had a tape recorder on the table, but Ben noticed that they also took notes occasionally while he spoke, as if they knew most of the story already, but not all of it. Neither man betrayed any surprise or emotion.

Ben's frustration mounted as he spoke. When he finished, he leaned forward and looked each of them in the eye. "So if this is all true, what took you guys so long?"

"We can't comment on that, Mr. Corbin," said Agent Gomez. "This matter is highly classified."

"But it *is* true, right?" persisted Ben. "Maybe not all the details, but the basic story is accurate, isn't it? Otherwise we wouldn't be having this conversation."

"I'm sorry, but we can't comment on any of that."

Ben clenched his jaws and looked each man in the eye. "I have a right to know what's going on. My client and my detective are both in the hospital. Everyone else who has stood in the way of the Brothers and these Chechens has either died or vanished. How do I know I'm not next?"

After a brief pause, Elena said, "We can protect you."

"Thanks," said Ben, "but you can't tell me what's going on?"

Agent Gomez smiled and spread his hands palm up. "I'm afraid not."

"Can you at least tell me who you're protecting me from? I know something about the Brothers, of course, but who are these other guys? I'll sleep better at night if I know."

"No, you won't," replied Agent Gomez.

"How do you feel?" Elena asked.

Sergei lay on his stomach on the hospital bed, an IV needle in his arm and long, narrow bandages on his back and legs. "Like a steak that got left on the grill a little too long. I look like one too, don't I?"

Elena laughed. "I wasn't going to say anything. Seriously, though, you look a lot better than the last time I saw you." Four hours ago, he had been in the back of an ambulance, semi-delirious with fever, dehydration, and the aftereffects of two minor concussions. He'd spent the whole trip to the hospital telling her in rambling detail all that he could remember about his captors.

By now, the powerful antibiotics coursing through his blood had taken effect, and he had been steadily drinking electrolytes to rehydrate his body. His CAT scan had shown no evidence of brain damage, and the neurologist doubted that Sergei would have any nerve damage from his torture.

"I feel a lot better too. They're planning to release me tomorrow, and the doctor says I'll be fine, though I may have some scars." He pushed himself up and sat on the edge of the bed, moving slowly and gingerly. "But it could have been much worse." He paused, and his warm brown eyes held hers. "Thanks."

Elena pulled a chair close and sat down, her knees a few inches from his. "I'm just glad I got there in time."

He smiled and winked. "Me too. So, any new developments?"

"We just finished interviewing Ben," she replied. "I can't give you any classified information, of course, but there's going to be a protective detail guarding him and Noelle within the hour."

"Good. How about the Brothers? Have you found them yet?"

"Not yet."

"Think you will? My guess is they've disappeared, either voluntarily or involuntarily."

She nodded. "These Chechens play pretty rough, and the Brothers probably know that. If I were them, I'd leave Chicago and go to ground somewhere, maybe in Russia."

"That would be smart," said Sergei. A shadow passed over his face. "I wish I'd done the same thing."

"I know." Elena laid a hand on his arm. "It must have been awful for you."

"It was no fun." His face turned grim as he remembered his torment. "The worst part actually came after they'd stopped shocking me. The guy held up that syringe and told me he was going to kill me right then." He dropped his eyes from hers. "I started to lose it when he said that."

"Of course—I think most people would lose it in that situation."

"This isn't the first time I've come close to death or had someone threaten to kill me. I've never been afraid of death. It's always seemed like a challenge—or an enemy to be outwitted. But when I sat tied to that chair staring at that syringe, I was convinced that I was going to die. I had to face death head-on, and I was scared out of my mind. It wasn't so much the thought of *dying* that scared me—you know, how much it would hurt and everything—it was the thought of *being dead*, of . . . of being gone, not existing anymore. Or maybe being someplace else. I felt completely unprepared for whatever would come next." He fell silent for a moment. "It's tough to put into words."

"It will probably take a while for you to put it behind you," Elena said, feeling awkward. "You've been through a lot."

He fidgeted with his sheet. "Yeah. I just wish . . . I don't know. Maybe the best thing is not to think about it anymore."

She wanted to comfort him somehow, but didn't know what to say. She'd never really thought about what lay on the other side of death, and the topic tongue-tied her.

After a few seconds, he looked up and made a dismissive gesture, as if he were shooing away a fly. "But enough about me. *You* were amazing. A rescue like that almost makes the whole thing worthwhile."

She felt herself blush and shrugged modestly. "Well, we're all trained for situations like that. I just happened to be in the right place at the right time. Any one of us could have done it."

He smiled. "You were trained not to go into that building without backup. Not that I'm complaining."

She smiled back. "I'll try not to screw up next time."

"Good. I wouldn't want anything to happen to you."

He put his hand on hers and looked at her, his eyes deep wells of feeling. Then he leaned forward and kissed her.

A letter from Steve Rocco awaited Ben when he arrived back at his office. It was three pages, single-spaced, but the gist was that Rocco's clients were willing to pay five million dollars over five years in return for a full release and a paid-up license to use Circuit Dynamics' technology. That would mean half a million to Ben personally, but he was still convinced that the case was worth a lot more.

He brought Rocco's letter into Noelle's office and handed it to her. She skimmed it and then looked up at him. "So they're finally serious, huh?"

"Yeah, but not serious enough," replied Ben. "I'm going to advise Fred Schultz to stand pat at twenty-five million—at least until they come up to ten. Otherwise we'll take them to trial."

She handed the letter back to him, not even bothering to bring up the cost of trial or what a settlement would mean for their finances. "Now tell me how things went with the FBI."

◆　◆　◆

"Eggs?" Elbek said in confusion. He stood in front of three industrial-size egg incubators full of unnaturally shiny chicken eggs. "What are you doing with all these eggs?"

Dr. Umarov turned to him, his face impossible to read inside the respirator and hood of his biosafety "blue suit." "We are creating death from life. Smallpox only grows in living cells. In the Soviet Union, we used cell cultures from green monkeys and human fetuses. These cannot be bought easily and without attracting attention. So where do we get cells? Eggs. Fertilized chicken eggs are excellent virus factories. We dip the eggs in paraffin, inject them with smallpox, and wait while it multiplies inside them. Then, when the virus concentration is at its highest, we crack open the eggs into this fermenter"—he gestured to a large vat equipped with pipes, valves, and gauges—"and cook them according to my secret recipe."

He paused for a laugh that didn't come.

"That stabilizes the weapon and makes it more virulent," he continued. "Then we dry it in here"—he pointed to a commercial bread oven—"and grind it into powder with this." He gestured to a large milling machine before continuing. "In the Soviet Union, we had another machine to treat the powder so that each particle would repel the others, making the dispersal area larger. But this machine will still make a very effective weapon.

"Finally, we put the powder into weapons. How would you like to deliver it? Bombs? Aerosol containers? Aerial dispersion tanks?"

Dr. Umarov was a hired gun and a non-Chechen. Elbek did not entirely trust him and did not want to tell him more than was absolutely necessary. "We will have a decision for you by the time the powder is ready. When will that be?"

The scientist made some mental calculations. "Two weeks," he replied with a touch of pride. "Maybe even less."

Chapter Sixteen
Two Weeks

"I don't like it," said Noelle as she looked out through the living-room window.

An unmarked blue government sedan was parked on the street in front of their house. In it sat two men who did nothing except watch the streets and occasionally speak into a radio or cell phone. The car had been outside the house every day that week, but never in the same place. Occasionally one or both of the men would get out and stroll around the outside of the house, though they always remained within sight of each other.

At least once a day, they would come inside to check the phone lines for bugs and look through the house. If one of the Corbins tried to strike up a conversation, the men would be polite and friendly but uniformly unwilling to let slip the tiniest scrap of information about exactly what they were watching for.

"I know what you mean," replied Ben. "I appreciate the protection, but I'd like to know what they're protecting us from."

"Is there any way you can make them tell us? I mean, do we have any legal right to know?"

Ben shook his head. "I checked. The only way we can get information out of the FBI or CIA is to negotiate, and we're fresh out of bargaining chips."

Later that day, the phone rang in Ben's office as he was putting together an exhibit list for the upcoming *Circuit Dynamics* trial.

"Hello. Ben Corbin."

"Hello, Ben. It's Agent Ignatev with the CIA. We need your help with a small matter."

"What matter is that?"

"Dr. Ivanovsky's condition has improved to the point where we can ask him questions."

"I had *heard* he was doing better," Ben said with a slight note of sarcasm. He had not been allowed to see or speak to his client for "security reasons."

"He is. In fact, I'd like you to visit him with me and Agent Kamenev."

"I'd be happy to, but how does that help you?"

There was a brief pause. "Well, we'd also like you to try to convince him to talk to us. We're having some, ah, difficulty with him."

Ben laughed. "Somehow I'm not surprised. I can help you—or try to, anyway—but only if you help me first."

"How?" Agent Ignatev asked, suspicion in his voice.

"I'll need you to tell me what's going on and who these Chechens are."

"We told you, that's classified."

"Yes, you did. And I'm telling you that I can't help you until you give me some more information. I'm sure you've done a background check on me and I'm sure it's clean. So why not tell me? I can keep a secret."

"I don't doubt that you can, but I'm not in a position to make that call. Let me talk to some people and get back to you."

"I'll wait to hear from you." If push came to shove, Ben would help them whether they briefed him or not. But he was going to push as hard as he could in the meantime. He was sick of other people deciding how much he needed to know—and deciding wrong. "Remember," he said before the CIA agent could hang up, "I already know about Variant D and the CIA's connection. There's been nothing stopping me from going to the press with that information, but I haven't done it."

"I thought I told you that everything about this investigation is classified," Agent Ignatev said sharply. "Besides, all you have is Dr. Ivanovsky's story. We haven't confirmed any of it."

"Precisely," replied Ben. "Information that I got from former *Soviet* government officials can't possibly be classified information belonging to the *American* government, can it? Look, my only point is that I've kept this secret so far, even though I don't have an obligation to do so."

"We'll call you back."

Twenty minutes later, Ben's phone rang again. "Hello. Ben Corbin."

"Hello, Mr. Corbin," a deep, gravelly voice said. "This is Deputy Director for Intelligence Bill Alexander at the Central Intelligence Agency. I understand that you're insisting on access to classified information before you'll assist us in investigating this matter. Is that correct?"

"Yes."

"In light of your close personal connection to this operation, I have authorized the disclosure of certain information to you, provided that you obligate yourself to keep it strictly confidential."

"Of course."

"Agent Gomez and Agent Ignatev will brief you at the FBI's offices."

"I'm on my way," said Ben. "Thanks."

"One other thing, Mr. Corbin. We'll need you to also agree that any information about this matter, no matter how you obtained it, will be treated as confidential."

Ben smiled—his bluff had worked. "Not a problem."

Elbek walked into the meeting room and surveyed his men. They sat at tables or stood in small groups, talking and laughing. Their conversation was excited and celebratory, but also nervous and uncertain—like soldiers who have won one battle but know they'll have to fight another soon. He smiled inwardly. It was a pleasure to command veterans who could anticipate the course of an operation and were ready to carry out his orders almost before he gave them.

The men saw him and quickly became silent.

"Gentlemen, as you know, we have tasted victory this week. The first stage of our mission is complete. Allah has now given us the weapon with which to strike down our enemies. In two weeks, that weapon will be ready to use." The men glanced at each other, nodding and murmuring in approval.

"But we have also tasted defeat," Elbek continued. "We lost Shamil, Umar, and Mamed. They are in Paradise, but we who remain are diminished. We are also endangered—the interrogation building is compromised, and the prisoner was rescued by the enemy. We cannot tell how much they know or guess about us and our plans.

"In two weeks, none of this will matter. But for now we are vulnerable, and they are searching for us with all their strength. We must make that search as difficult as possible. Here is what we will do . . ."

"Before we get started, I'm going to give you one last chance to bail out," Agent Gomez told Ben. "Having classified information will subject you to a lot of rules and regulations that can be a real pain to follow. What I tell you today will probably give you headaches down the road."

"I'd love to have headaches *down the road*," Ben replied. "That's the point."

"Fair enough," said Agent Gomez with a smile. "Our best guess is that we're dealing with the Vainakh Guard. They're a fairly new group and they operate out of the mountains of southern Chechnya. To our knowledge, this is their first confirmed operation in the US. It's a very disturbing development."

"So what are they?" asked Ben. "Criminals? Terrorists?"

"Both, we think. Unfortunately, we don't know much about them. There's a fair amount of smuggling and arms trading that goes on in that area, and we think they may be involved in it. The Russians also blame them for several attacks on convoys and patrols in the Argun Valley, though these appear to be mainly defensive strikes intended primarily to keep authorities away from their bases and smuggling routes."

"'Arms trading,'" Ben repeated. "Do you think that's what they're doing in Chicago—picking up a new weapon to sell?"

"Could be," said Agent Gomez.

"But they could also use it?"

"It's possible, and I can't think of a group I'd less like to have a weapon like Dr. Ivanovsky described to you. The Vainakh Guard is a new kind of terrorist group, and they're potentially much more dangerous than traditional groups like Hamas or al-Qaeda. Imagine . . ." He searched for the right analogy. "Imagine an inner-city gang: streetwise and tough, but loosely organized and not very well trained. That's Hamas. They recruit religious fanatics and teach them how to make crude bombs, handle outdated assault rifles, do some basic hand-to-hand fighting, and stuff like that. They're kids, really—half-trained, wild-eyed kids.

"Al-Qaeda is on another level. They proved on 9/11 that they're capable of organizing an operation beyond anything Hamas can do. But they're still basically religious fanatics with minimal training.

"Now imagine a professional army. That's the Vainakh Guard. Most of them are former *Spetsnaz* commandos. They're the cream of the crop from the old Red Army, specialists in carrying out guerrilla operations and assassinations in Western societies. They have a decentralized but highly efficient command structure that makes them really tough to infiltrate. Also, any member who's been identified by law enforcement either vanishes or is immediately cut off from the group. They've been giving the Russians fits for years now, though they've kept a low profile and haven't tried any major operations."

"What kinds of things have they done?" asked Ben. He shifted uncomfortably in his seat, despite the fact that it was well cushioned.

Agent Gomez looked down at the file spread in front of him. "Other than what I already described, it's been mostly little stuff—small-scale infiltration of military facilities, breaches of government and business-security systems, and attacks on soft targets in secondary urban centers."

"Soft targets?"

"Targets with light security: shopping centers, train stations, office buildings—that sort of thing. There may be more incidents that we don't know about. These were minor attacks, and they might not all have been picked up as terrorist incidents. Here in the US, a lot of what they do might be classified as vandalism or petty crime."

"So they could have been doing the same thing here for a while, but it just slipped under the radar screen—is that what you mean about this being their first confirmed operation here?" Ben asked.

Agent Gomez nodded.

Ben frowned. "Why would a group like this be into such petty stuff? And if they are, why are they such a threat?"

"Because we do not think they are 'into petty stuff,'" Agent Ignatev interjected, leaning forward and speaking in precise, clipped tones. "We think they have been testing our defenses—seeing how security systems react to certain kinds of incidents, which threats we spot and which ones we miss, how quickly we respond, and so on."

"In which case there's probably a major attack coming, right?" Ben looked at the two agents, hoping they would disagree with him.

"That is why we need to speak to Dr. Ivanovsky as soon as possible," replied Agent Ignatev.

◆　◆　◆

"Ben! It is very, very good to see you!" Dr. Ivanovsky said. His face wore a happy smile that vanished into a bandage covering a bullet wound and surgical incision on the left side of his head. If the shot had struck a few millimeters to the right, it would have killed him or at least left him severely brain damaged. Other bandages on his torso covered other wounds. One bullet had collapsed a lung and nicked an artery, and he had nearly bled to death on the way to the hospital. Another bullet had lodged in his spine, where it was likely to stay for the rest of his life; its location made it impossible to remove safely.

He had hovered near death for twenty-four hours, but had recovered rapidly since then. "He's a tough old guy," one of his surgeons had commented to Ben and Agent Ignatev when they arrived. "Very determined. I think he decided he was going to live, and then he just did it."

Ben walked over to Dr. Ivanovsky's bedside and placed his hand lightly on the old man's shoulder. "It's great to see you too," he said. "I'm glad they finally let me in." He had insisted on meeting alone with Dr. Ivanovsky, at least initially.

"Yes. I argued very much about this. I said, 'I have the right to my lawyer.' And they said, 'You are not arrested; you have no right to speak to your lawyer. Also, this is about terrorism.' But I said, 'This is not Soviet Union! This is America—everyone must have lawyers!' So they let you come. This is good. We have many things to speak about."

"We do indeed. I haven't even heard what happened to you on the morning you were shot. The morning you were supposed to come to my office so we could talk about what to do."

Dr. Ivanovsky looked down. "Yes, okay. I went to the judge's secretary and she gave me the judgment paper. Then I went to the American Union Bank and I showed this paper to them and they took me to the room with the safe-deposit boxes and gave the key to the box to me. I looked inside the box. There was the lab notes on the procedures to make Variant D and a paper with information for a company named Illinois Cryostorage. So I drive there and show them the paper, and they show me the liquid-nitrogen freezer that Nicki's brother rented. Inside is the container of the organisms. So I took everything and I began driving to my friend who has very powerful sealed ovens for making experiments with very hot metals and gases and other things. He said he will let me use the oven, but I did not tell him why. I just explained this is very, very important, and he said okay. I planned to make the container very hot to kill the organisms. Then I planned to bury it someplace that no one will find. The notes I planned to burn."

He glanced up at Ben, then dropped his eyes again. Ben watched him impassively, waiting for him to continue. The Russian shrugged his narrow shoulders. "After this, I remember nothing. I was driving on the road, and then I wake up here with much pain. The doctors say maybe I never remember more because of the injuries."

"I see. And you planned to come to our meeting after burning these notes?"

"Yes, this was my plan," confirmed Dr. Ivanovsky. "I . . . This was my plan." He glanced at Ben again, but said nothing more.

Ben suppressed the urge to point out that his client's plan might have worked a lot better if he had shared it with Ben and asked for his help. "Well, we're meeting now, and the main item on our agenda is still the same: How do we stop this Variant D from escaping? Our only real option at this point is to work with the federal government to—"

"No!" said Dr. Ivanovsky, shaking his head as vigorously as his injuries would allow. "I have explained this to you before. I do not trust the government to have Variant D. But you are right that we must stop it from escaping. This is very, very important. First, you must—"

"Stop. Wait," interrupted Ben. "You can't do this on your own anymore. It's time to turn this over to professionals."

To Ben's surprise, Dr. Ivanovsky nodded. "Yes, I think the same thing. This detective"—he groped for the name—"Spassky. Did you find him? Maybe he can help us to get more professionals."

"*I* didn't find him, but the *FBI* did. They rescued him on the same morning you were shot. Those are the professionals I'm talking about. They helped Sergei Spassky. Why won't you let them help you?"

"Help me?" exploded Dr. Ivanovsky. "They make me prisoner here in my hospital bed. Look outside this room and you see men with guns. They ask me many questions with drugs in my blood making my thoughts confused. This is like in the old Lubyanka."

"Lubyanka?"

"KGB headquarters."

"You really think you're being treated like a KGB prisoner?" Ben asked incredulously.

His client nodded stubbornly.

Ben pointed at the door. "Those men are there to keep terrorists out, not to keep you in. And I'll bet the drugs in your system were put there by the doctors as part of your treatment."

"I am sure KGB had similar explanations. And why they will not let me speak with my lawyer?"

"That bothers me some," Ben conceded.

"You see, I told you—they are all the same!"

"No, but even if they were, so what?" Ben responded. "It would be better for this weapon to be in the hands of the KGB than in the hands of terrorists."

"But best for it to be in my hands and then destroyed," countered Dr. Ivanovsky. "We should not speak of this again. I have decided this."

"You still think you can handle this?" Ben asked in disbelief. "Look at yourself! Look at what you've done! You single-handedly alerted Russian criminals to the fact that the key to an Armageddon bug was sitting in a forgotten safe-deposit box. I managed to stop them from giving the bug to terrorists, but you took care of that too, didn't you? You decided to go behind my back and do things by yourself again—and you not only delivered the bug to the terrorists on a silver platter, you nearly got yourself killed in the process. Don't you think that maybe, just maybe, you should trust someone else's judgment for a change?"

"I have decided it," Dr. Ivanovsky repeated, his face frozen in a stony, defiant frown.

"You have decided?" said Ben. "*You* have decided? And who gave you the right to make that decision? Who gave you the right to make life-or-death decisions for thousands, maybe millions, of people? You think you're God?"

"You have no place to say such things! I am in church every Sunday. I pray to God and—"

"But you don't trust him, do you?" interrupted Ben. "You don't trust the FBI, you don't trust the military, you don't trust me—not when it really matters, anyway—and you don't even trust God, do you? At the end of the day, when things are really on the line, the only person you trust is yourself. Isn't that right?"

"I do not need to answer such questions from you!" shot back Dr. Ivanovsky, almost yelling. "You are my lawyer, and you will help me with this thing or you will not help me. This is all we must speak about."

Ben took a deep breath to calm himself. "I'll help you, but not like this. I will do everything in my power to ensure that Variant D is never used, but the way to do that is to work with the government. Not against them. I will not help you try yet again to handle this on your own. That hasn't worked before, and it won't work now."

"Then we have nothing more to speak about. You are not my lawyer anymore. Go away." He turned to face the wall until Ben left the room.

"That could have gone better," Ben said as he crossed the hospital parking lot with Agent Ignatev and Elena.

"I had hoped that he might be a little more flexible after what happened to him," said Elena.

"So had I," said Ben. "He's stubborn, but he's not stupid. Maybe I pushed him a little too hard. I wish I'd had more time to work on him."

"We do not have more time," replied Agent Ignatev. "If there is a way to get more information from him, you need to try it now."

Ben shook his head. "No, that bridge is burned to the ground. He wouldn't even look at me when I left his hospital room. Have you guys managed to get anything out of the Brothers?"

"Do you know where they are?" asked Elena.

Ben gave a dry smile. "Did you try the Chicago River?"

"Yes."

Anton Brodsky didn't like Vetlugorsk much. It was a small, featureless town made up of small, featureless buildings constructed during the Brezhnev era. Its inhabitants were mostly middle-aged factory workers and their fat, unattractive wives. The town's one redeeming feature was a vodka distillery, which kept the local liquor store and bars well stocked.

Anton had a cousin in Vetlugorsk who had agreed to hide him until Dmitry decided it would be safe for them to return to America—or to at least regroup in one of Russia's larger cities. Anton had no idea when that would be, so he sat in his cousin's extra bedroom day after day, drinking local vodka and watching soap operas. His favorite was

General Hospital. The dubbing was particularly bad and he could make a game out of guessing what the characters were really saying by reading their lips.

Winter had come early to Vetlugorsk this year. The winds howled off the steppe, bringing swirling snow and leaden skies. The townsfolk wrapped themselves with sweaters, coats, and scarves until they were shapeless gray blobs, scurrying along the windy streets like giant woolen tumbleweeds.

The cold and snow were a blessing for Anton, though. While doing his compulsory military service, he had learned to cross-country ski and enjoyed it. He had not been able to ski much when he lived in big cities like Moscow and Chicago, but Vetlugorsk was surrounded by empty, snow-covered fields. His hosts were relieved to have him out of the house for at least part of the day, so they managed to find a set of secondhand skis and ski boots that fit him. He spent hours crisscrossing the stubbled fields and empty white grasslands outside of town.

Most mornings he would pack a couple of sandwiches, a thermos of coffee, a bottle of vodka, a gun, and a box of bullets into a knapsack. He would drive off in the family's second car and spend the short sunlit hours outside. When he got tired of skiing and drinking, he would shoot at the sparse wildlife (mostly crows and rabbits) or road signs until he ran out of bullets. Then he would drive back to the house, turn on the TV, and open a new bottle of vodka.

When he went skiing, he always parked the car along the same lonely stretch of road. And when he came back half-drunk in the early dusk, he never checked for bombs or mechanical tampering. Neither fact escaped the notice of certain watchful eyes.

◆ ◆ ◆

Elena checked her voice mail as she and Oleg Ignatev drove to Anthony Simeon's office to interview him.

"Anything?" Oleg asked her when she turned off her cell phone.

She shook her head. Investigators had found an address scribbled on a scrap of paper in the pocket of one of Sergei's guards. They had raided the building at that address, but it was empty and completely, meticulously clean: no fingerprints, no paper, no hair, no trash. In a word, no evidence. The building was also in a sparsely leased light-industrial park and conveniently had no neighbors to interview. Forensics experts and other investigators had scoured the building and neighborhood for two weeks but didn't find anything. "Whoever cleaned out that building was very thorough. There aren't even tire marks in the parking lot."

Oleg nodded, but remained silent. He was normally an analyst, not an investigator, and therefore had nothing to contribute on this point. "Do you think we will be able to get any additional information from Anthony Simeon?"

"Maybe. When we interviewed him before, we were primarily interested in finding Sergei Spassky. We knew there was a chance that his clients were involved because of Sergei's work on the *Ivanovsky* lawsuit, but that's all we knew. Of course, we didn't know about the link between the Chechens and the Brothers, so we didn't ask him about that."

"And now he is probably the only one left that we can ask."

When they had returned to the Dirksen Building after Ben's failed interview with Dr. Ivanovsky, they had found two overseas transmissions waiting for them. One was from an FBI legat and the other from the CIA station chief in Moscow. Both reported the same information: all three of the remaining Brothers had been killed in nearly simultaneous attacks inside Russia. Their lawyer was now the last lead.

Tony Simeon watched across the conference-room table as Agent Oleg Ignatev and Special Agent Elena Kamenev opened their briefcases and took out notepads and documents.

So both the FBI and the CIA were sending agents to talk to him. That must mean that whatever they wanted to talk about had both domestic and international ramifications. Interesting.

He had generally found that, in interviews and depositions, he could learn more by listening to questions than by asking them. Even the body language and—as here—the identity of the questioner could be revealing.

"How long have you represented the Brothers?" Special Agent Kamenev asked.

"Since they formed their LLC about seven years ago."

"Then you may know the answer to a question that has bothered me for a while: Are any of them actually brothers?" she asked.

He chuckled. "No. They met in a Soviet prison and became blood brothers there. They went into business together when they got out and called their company *Bratstvo*. When they got to the US, they changed it to 'the Brothers.'"

"What exactly did their business do?" asked Agent Ignatev.

Did? Tony took note of the past tense, but his response betrayed nothing. "Import/export trade with Russia—beluga caviar, vodka, little wooden dolls. That sort of thing."

"And what would they send back to Russia?"

"I know they exported computer equipment, because we handled a legal matter once regarding it. I'm not sure what else they sold."

"Did they ever buy or sell weapons?" asked Special Agent Kamenev.

Tony noticed that both of them tensed very slightly as they waited for his answer. "Not to my knowledge."

"You also represented a gentleman named Nikolai Zinoviev," she said, switching subjects. "How did he come to employ you?"

Tony paused for a moment, considering what he could say. "He was referred to me by the Brothers, who pay my bills for representing him and his estate. I can't tell you more without getting into confidential information covered by the attorney-client privilege."

She jotted down a note. "When did you start representing him?"

"On the day that the *Ivanovsky* case was filed."

"What did he and the Brothers tell you about that case?" asked Agent Ignatev.

"I'm sorry, but that's privileged."

"We have very good grounds to believe that they were using your services as part of a conspiracy to commit extremely serious crimes," countered the CIA man.

"Really? What crimes?"

"We're not at liberty to say," said Agent Ignatev.

"Would they happen to involve illegal ownership of biological weapons?"

Yes, said the stunned looks on both of their faces. Elena Kamenev recovered first. "Why do you ask?"

"Because during Dr. Ivanovsky's deposition testimony, we asked him about his background. He mentioned that he had done classified microbiology work for the Soviet Union. I thought there might be a connection."

"Did you have any other reason to believe that biological weapons might be involved?" she asked.

"No."

"When did you last speak to any of the Brothers?" asked Agent Ignatev.

"On the day that the *Ivanovsky* trial ended." That didn't seem to surprise them, and they didn't ask any follow-up questions—both of which reinforced his suspicion that the agents thought his clients had met untimely ends.

"Have you ever had any contact with the person or persons who planned to buy the contents of Mr. Zinoviev's safe-deposit box from the Brothers?" Agent Ignatev asked.

"I was on a conference call with one of them about a month ago, and we sent some documents back and forth, but that's all."

"Do you have any contact information for them?" Elena Kamenev asked. Tony caught the undertone of urgency in her voice and saw that both agents were looking at him intently.

"They never gave me their names, phone numbers, or street addresses. We probably have their e-mails somewhere in our files. I could have my secretary look for it."

"Could you do it now?" she asked.

"Certainly," he replied, a little surprised. The FBI and CIA must have had no idea where to find the people the Brothers had dealt with. Otherwise, the agents wouldn't have been so excited about e-mail addresses that were over a month old.

He dialed his secretary from the conference-room phone. "Rosa, could you find the correspondence file from the Brothers/Zinoviev transaction matter and bring it in here? Thanks." He hung up the phone. "She'll be up with it in a few minutes. Is there anything else I can do for you?"

"Not at the moment," replied Special Agent Kamenev, "but we may want to talk to you later. In the meantime, we can provide you with protection if you like."

Tony was silent for a long time. The situation was worse than he had thought. Whatever had been in that box was dangerous enough to get the attention of both the FBI and the CIA. And whoever now had it was systematically killing anyone who might know where they were. It seemed to be working. The government apparently had no idea where to find them.

And now the killers might be after him. No, *might* was an understatement. If they were smart, they would almost certainly come after him. He had represented the Brothers for years, had been involved in the sale of the safe-deposit box, and had ostensibly attempted to defend that sale in court. The killers would assume that the Brothers had told him everything—or at least they couldn't safely assume otherwise. So they would try to kill him, and they would do it soon. It was the only rational thing for them to do.

And now he needed to decide what the rational thing for him to do was. He saw only one choice, though he didn't like it. He sighed.

"Mr. Simeon?" prompted Special Agent Kamenev.

He looked at her and smiled, his decision made. "No. Thank you. I won't be needing protection."

Elbek sat at a small table with his squad commanders, discussing recent events and planning strategy. They huddled in a corner of what had once been the shipping room of the brewery building they now occupied. Twenty feet away, Dr. Umarov was hard at work cooking his deadly brew in converted fermentation tanks and turning it into particles finer than bath powder.

The bioweapons expert had not been happy when the small army of Chechens had suddenly arrived on his doorstep twelve days ago. *Well, too bad.* Elbek had not been happy about losing his headquarters building, but there was nothing he could do about it. Once the interrogation facility had been compromised, Elbek knew that it was only a matter of time—and likely not much time—before the FBI found the Elk Grove Village building. So they'd had to evacuate and sterilize it, and fall back to their weapons-production lab.

The portion of the old brewery building they could occupy without being exposed to Variant D was small and uncomfortable: a poorly heated, concrete-floored storage/shipping room, a tiny office, and a bathroom. The men grumbled, but not much. This might be a step down from their prior accommodations, but it was several steps up from the icy and drafty caves of the Chechen mountains. Besides, it would be only for two weeks.

And now those two weeks were almost over. In two days, they would move. It was time to make their final plans.

"Squad One will cover Milwaukee, Grand Rapids, Columbus, Indianapolis, and Minneapolis," Elbek informed his lieutenants. "Squad Two will take Hartford, Boston, Pittsburgh, Nashville, and Atlanta. Squad Three has Fresno, Boulder, Austin, Anaheim, and Salt Lake City. Squad Four will deliver the weapons to our contacts in England, France, Germany, and Chechnya."

The four squad leaders took rapid coded notes. This was the first time their general had given them their operational targets.

"You all have the training and expertise to pick your targets once you arrive," Elbek continued, "and you'll probably be able to make better choices than I can now. I trust your judgment. I will leave the operational details to your discretion. Hit shopping malls, train terminals, indoor sporting events—anything with a large concentration of people, a ventilation system, and light security. Any questions so far?"

"Why aren't we attacking New York or Los Angeles or Chicago?" asked the leader of Squad Two, a young man who had only been with the Vainakh Guard for about a year and had not taken part in their initial strategic discussions.

"For two reasons," Elbek explained patiently. "First, the security is tighter in the bigger cities. Second, remember our goal: we want to disable these countries so that they can no longer keep Islam in a cage. That means spreading disease, but it also means spreading fear. Most Americans and Russians don't live near a big city like New York or Moscow, but most of them do live close to a small or medium-size city. Knowing that New York is under attack will not affect the lives of most Americans. They will continue going to jobs and drinking their Coca-Cola as they did before. But if Columbus and Fresno and

Pittsburgh—and maybe the city where they work and shop—are under attack, then they will cower in terror. The great American machine will grind to a halt."

The squad leader nodded. "And at the same time, the Russian and European machines will also grind to a halt. And we will be free."

"Exactly," said Elbek. "But we cannot begin our attack for two more days, and during that time we must remain undiscovered." He turned to the leader of Squad Three, a former *Spetsnaz* captain and professional assassin. "Ibrahim, you said you had news?"

"Yes, sir. I just received a report from Grozny. All three of the Brothers have been located and eliminated."

Elbek nodded. They had been watching the Brothers for some time, so it had not been particularly difficult to track them to their bolt-holes in Russia. After that, it had merely been a matter of finding the right moment to liquidate them.

"Most of the remaining targets are under FBI and police protection and are therefore too dangerous to hit," Ibrahim continued. "But I'm not sure it matters. We have removed all significant threats."

"Are you sure?" asked Elbek. "What about the lawyer? He knows a lot about this. Does he have guards?"

"Actually, he doesn't."

"Curious." Elbek paused, wondering whether the attorney was bait in a trap. Ibrahim should be good enough to spot a trap, though. He weighed the risks for a moment, then made up his mind. "Kill him. Take care of it personally."

"Yes, sir."

CHAPTER SEVENTEEN
THANKSGIVING

The day before Thanksgiving is not the best time to find a contractor for an emergency home-improvement project. Tony Simeon had to call in a favor before he managed to secure the services of Pierre LeGrand, a retired cat burglar who now worked as a security consultant. LeGrand's main client was a group of high-end art galleries primarily owned by Frank Krause, a friend and client of Tony's. Last year, Tony had cancelled a Hawaiian vacation so he could (successfully) defend Krause against charges of tax fraud.

Krause had repeatedly said he "owed Tony one," and today Tony collected. He called Krause, who called LeGrand, who was willing—but not particularly happy—to do the job, no matter what day it was.

Operating on the assumption that his home and office phones were both bugged, Tony had called LeGrand from a pay phone to discuss the new security system he wanted installed. LeGrand couldn't do it that day, but he was willing to work on Thanksgiving in light of the urgency of Tony's request. Tony did not say why the system needed to be installed immediately, and LeGrand did not ask. He respected his clients' privacy, and he had been in business long enough to know that unrevealed security concerns are often the most pressing.

Tony knew better than to return home. He spent the evening in public but inaccessible places. He arranged a long dinner at the Metropolitan Club and arrived early. While waiting for his table, he used the club phone to call the Lyric Opera ticket office and order a ticket to that evening's six-hour performance of Wagner's *Götterdämmerung*. He then called the Palmer House and reserved a room for the night.

After the opera, the streets and sidewalks were deserted, so he took a cab the few blocks to the hotel. He checked in, made a point of telling the desk clerk that he was *not* expecting any guests, and retired for the evening. He left the lights off as he got ready for bed. He also stayed away from the windows. When he lay down on the comfortable bed, he did not sleep.

"Hi, Mom," Ben said into the phone. "I've got some bad news. We won't be able to make it to Thanksgiving dinner tomorrow."

"Oh, that's too bad," Mrs. Corbin replied. "What happened?"

"I've just got too much going on right now. Sorry."

"You can't even take a break for Thanksgiving dinner?" she asked, sounding hurt.

"Sorry, no. I wish I could."

"Will Noelle be coming, at least? I don't want her to have to spend Thanksgiving alone, and her family is all the way in Minnesota."

"Noelle is busy too, unfortunately."

"You two have been busy a lot recently. I thought things were going to calm down after that trial a couple of weeks ago."

"I did too, but some things came up."

"What kind of things came up?" she demanded.

He quickly evaluated whether he could tell her anything without violating the rules laid down by Deputy Director Alexander—and decided he couldn't. "I can't talk about it."

"You can't even tell your own mother?"

Ben squirmed with guilt. "No. It's a . . . uh . . . a national-security matter. I'm sorry."

"Oh my! How did you get mixed up in something like that?"

"I can't talk about that either."

The line was silent for a moment. "Are you in any danger?"

Ben struggled with conflicting impulses. On the one hand, his mother was a champion worrier, so he didn't want to tell her anything that would upset her further. On the other hand, she could usually tell if he was being evasive or misleading.

"The government is providing us protection," he said at last.

Another pause. "And you're protecting us by not coming to our house for dinner tomorrow, aren't you?"

"Don't worry, Mom. Everything will be fine."

Ibrahim Hasiyev drove slowly through Wilmette, getting a feel for the town. The streets were narrow and some were still brick-paved, making a loud thrumming noise under his tires that startled him at first. Stately elms and maples stood in sentinel rows on both sides of most roads. Wide, manicured lawns edged the streets and surrounded the houses like protective moats. A swirling breeze blew in from nearby Lake Michigan, making the few fallen leaves that had escaped the lawn services dance and race over the grass. The homes were mostly old and large—the type built in the early twentieth century by prosperous, but not quite wealthy, professionals with good taste. The kind of homes with good security systems.

A high-quality American residential security system normally meant sensors on downstairs doors and windows and pressure sensors in the entryways and on the stairs. It might also mean outdoor security cameras and possibly pressure sensors under the windows. None of these could be easily disconnected without triggering alarms. However, the police did not always respond quickly to automatic alarms, particularly during the day. They generally assumed the alarms had been set off accidentally. Ibrahim figured that he probably had at least ten minutes between the time he triggered an alarm and the time the police would arrive. Of course, that was a worst-case scenario. He had no intention of setting off any alarms.

Tony Simeon met Pierre LeGrand at the house on Thanksgiving morning. The retired burglar was a small, wiry man about the same age as Tony, with short gray hair and a professional manner. He had already briefly surveyed the house from the outside and had a preliminary opinion.

"You've already got a good off-the-shelf system, at least on the exterior," he said as they walked down a long hedgerow along one side of the backyard. Tony avoided the front of the house. It was too exposed. "Did you have any particular changes that you'd like me to make?"

"Yes, but I would like your professional opinion on something first. If you were going to break into this house, how would you do it?"

LeGrand chuckled and looked around with a calculating eye. "I would come up the driveway," he said, gesturing to the long, winding strip of asphalt that ran up from the street. "Driveways never have alarm sensors, because pressure pads don't work under asphalt or concrete, and alarm companies figure that having sensors on the doors is enough. And I would drive, since you don't have a gate."

"Why wouldn't you walk? I'd be more likely to notice a car than someone coming on foot."

"Maybe, but your neighbors wouldn't. It would look odd for someone to walk thirty yards up the driveway, especially if that someone was staying in shadows and trying not to be seen from the house. Besides, if it were me, I would come when you weren't here, so it wouldn't matter what you could see from the house.

"No, it makes more sense to drive. I would drive a pickup or van with some sort of logo on the side: window washers, yard service, house cleaners. Everybody around here has at least one of those services, so those kinds of vehicles are invisible. Most security systems don't have sensors on the second floor, so I would wear work clothes, put up a ladder, and go through a window."

"What if all the windows were locked?" asked Tony.

"Then it would take me an extra twenty seconds. Window locks are easy to pick if you have the right tools. Anyway, I would have a lookout climb the ladder after me and look busy while I was inside. I'd be inside for no more than fifteen or twenty minutes, and I'd be careful to leave everything just as I found it. It might be weeks before you know you've been robbed by a professional. A really good burglar will only take a few very valuable items—the kinds of things that are usually kept in wall safes or in the backs of jewelry boxes and only come out once a month or less. By then, no police department in the world could catch me."

"I see," said Tony. "What would you do differently if you weren't here to steal?" He paused. "What would you do if you were here to kill?"

"Thank you, Lord, for all the blessings you give us," said Ben as he sat with his head bowed at the head of the dining-room table. "Thank you for the food set before us. Thank you for the guests who have joined us for this meal. And thank you especially for being a mighty fortress, protecting your children from evil. Amen."

"Amen," said Noelle, Elena, Sergei, and Will Conklin together. Will was one of two FBI agents guarding the Corbins. Elena had volunteered to fill in for the other agent, who had a family and was grateful to be able to spend Thanksgiving at home. The Corbins had invited Sergei because he was otherwise likely to spend the holiday in his apartment with his FBI detail. He had accepted gladly, and his protectors had been happy to take the day off.

Sergei had been out of the hospital for over a week and was doing well. Bandages still covered some of the worst burns on his back and legs, but he was fully mobile and had no pain—unless he momentarily forgot his injuries and leaned back in a sofa or chair. He would then be instantly and intensely reminded that he was not completely healed.

Elena and Noelle—mostly Elena—had put together a respectable turkey dinner on short notice, and Sergei had brought a good bottle of Napa Valley Chardonnay. Soon they were all talking, laughing, and coming as close as they could to putting Variant D and the Vainakh Guard out of their minds. The FBI agents didn't drink any wine, and one of them was always looking out the front window or strolling through the backyard, but otherwise a casual observer would not have thought this was anything but a group of good friends gathered for an informal Thanksgiving dinner.

It wouldn't be Thanksgiving in the Midwest without the traditional Detroit Lions game on TV. They were hosting the Bears this year, and the game actually meant something. After several years in the wilderness, both teams were winning again and the Bears led the NFC North. The Lions' running game was weak, but they had a strong-armed young quarterback and two playmaking receivers. The Bears had their trademark smashmouth defense and a pounding running game that wore down opposing defenses.

The game started with a seventy-five-yard touchdown pass for the Lions, delighting Will (who was from Detroit) and drawing groans from Ben and Sergei. After that, the game settled into a bruising defensive struggle, during which the Lions' quarterback became intimately acquainted with the turf of Ford Field. Bruised and dazed by the third quarter, he threw a pair of wobbly interceptions that led to two touchdowns and a four-point Chicago lead.

"Stick a fork in them. They're done," Sergei crowed during replays of the Bears' fullback pushing his way into the end zone for the go-ahead score.

"They'll come back," replied Will. "Or they would, anyway, if the zebras would start calling holding on the Bears' safeties. It's starting to look like professional wrestling out there."

"Wow. The game isn't even over and already the excuses are starting," Ben said with a grin.

Will opened his mouth to continue his defense of the Lions, but before he could say anything, Ben's cell phone rang. Ben glanced at the caller ID and saw an unfamiliar number.

That's odd, he thought. *Who would be calling my cell phone on Thanksgiving?*

Tony Simeon sat in his den as Pierre LeGrand went about his work. The Bears-Lions game was on the TV in front of Tony, but he wasn't really watching. He was thinking about Dan Wood's funeral.

Dan's colleagues and many friends, including Tony, had spoken to the packed church. For once, Tony's silver tongue had failed him. He'd spoken haltingly and briefly, searching for words and struggling to collect his thoughts.

After the eulogies, Pastor Johan Wilhelm had given a brief sermon. Tony knew him well through having served with him on several charitable boards of the sort that offered good business-development prospects. One part of the sermon had stuck in his mind: "We mourn today, but we do not mourn for Dan. We mourn our loss of Dan. We are saddened that the light he brought to this world has gone out—but we mourn him no more than a caterpillar mourns a butterfly."

After the service, Tony had stopped by Pastor Wilhelm's office. It was a large, slightly shabby room crammed with books; it would have served equally well as the office of a college professor.

"Come in, Tony," the pastor said. "What can I do for you?"

"I'd like your advice on what I suppose is a spiritual matter. Dan's death troubled me a great deal."

"Yes, I could tell you were overcome with emotion during your eulogy."

"I was overcome, but not by grief. It was guilt and fear and . . . *Perspective* is the best word that occurs to me."

Pastor Wilhelm looked at Tony over the tops of his glasses. "What do you mean?"

Tony took a deep breath. This weight had sat heavily on his chest since the day of Dan's death. "When I saw that out-of-control cab, my first instinct was to save myself. Perhaps if I'd had a different instinct, I might have saved Dan. That does not speak well of me, and I know it. I know it in the very roots of my being, and I'm afraid of what it means for me." He paused with the ghost of a smile on his lips. "Not all caterpillars become butterflies."

"No, they don't," Pastor Wilhelm had said. "But don't you think you're being too hard on yourself? At worst, you made one split-second wrong decision that I'm sure you would take back if you could. The fate of your soul is not decided by such things."

"So what does decide it?"

"Your faith. Your surrender of yourself to God. That surrender begins with a decision to follow Jesus Christ, but it doesn't end there. It is a process, a struggle that lasts your entire life. During that struggle, you will have bad days. But without the power and mercy of God, you'd have nothing *but* bad days. When you stumble, all you can do is pick yourself up, confess your sin, and pray for forgiveness and the strength to do better in the future." He looked at Tony compassionately. "And try not to get discouraged."

Tony sighed. "The problem isn't that I had a bad day. The problem is that the more I think about what I did, the more certain I am that I was simply doing what came naturally to me. It wasn't a mistake; it was an *instinct*. I chose to save myself instead of Dan because I'm used to choosing myself. What happened on that sidewalk was a test. I failed it, and a good man is dead as a result."

Pastor Wilhelm had given Tony a measuring look and smiled. "Congratulations, Tony! You have just discovered that you are a bad man." Tony had been taken aback and a little offended. "So am I," continued the minister. "So are all of us. Our hope in Christ is not based on *our* goodness, but on his. It is the guilty who need a redeemer, not the innocent."

As difficult as urban surveillance could be, Ibrahim decided, it was child's play compared to suburban surveillance. There was no place to hide on these wide, well-kept lawns and quiet streets. Worse, there was no anonymity. No one would notice a carefully nondescript man walking every few hours along the same stretch of busy city sidewalk, for example. But a stranger wandering around a residential neighborhood would be followed by more than one pair of concerned eyes. On the bright side, at least he was able to confirm that there were no FBI agents lurking outside the target's home.

Ibrahim finally settled on an old brick grade school about a quarter of a mile from the lawyer's home. The school was closed for Thanksgiving and was situated on a small rise that offered a good view of the house. He parked his van out of sight between a dumpster and some bushes. Then he cautiously made his way to the rear door of the school that opened onto the playground. The lock was so old and loose that he almost didn't need to pick it. He was inside in seconds.

His feet made a soft *slap-slap* on the linoleum floor tiles as he jogged along the half-lit halls. Brightly colored announcements and artwork hanging on the walls rustled like autumn leaves as he passed. He looked quickly from side to side as he went, searching for a staircase. *There.*

He took the steps two at a time, then stopped when he reached the top. He quickly surveyed the second floor and walked into a north-facing classroom. No good—a pine tree obscured his sight line to the house unless he stood close to the window. The next room had an unobstructed view, and he quickly went to work.

Twenty small desks were arranged in clusters of four in different parts of the classroom. For his work area, Ibrahim picked a cluster in front of a large bulletin board festooned with construction-paper cut-outs of children's hands decorated to look like turkeys. The cluttered background would break up his silhouette, making him more difficult to see if someone happened to look in through the window.

He set up his tripod and rifle on one of the desks, which bore a hand-printed sign announcing that it belonged to Anna G. He sat down in Anna's chair and looked through the rifle's powerful scope. He trained the crosshairs on the target's front door, made a slight adjustment for the breeze blowing outside, and waited.

At the end of their meeting, Pastor Wilhelm had given Tony the standard materials he provided to those he called "seekers"—C.S. Lewis's *Mere Christianity* and a list of key Bible passages. Tony read through them in one weekend, then went through them again more slowly. A week later, he asked Pastor Wilhelm for other recommendations. He suggested Saint Augustine's *Confessions* and Dietrich Bonhoeffer's *The Cost of Discipleship*, which Tony promptly bought and devoured.

Reading these books made Tony curiously nostalgic. He had never ceased to believe in God, in the same way he had never ceased to believe in chocolate sodas—both had been weekend fixtures during his childhood but had faded from his life as he grew up. Every Sunday morning, his father had packed the family into their well-maintained 1938 Ford Tudor and driven them to Saint Thomas Episcopal Church. They all sat dutifully in hard, dark-varnished pews for an hour and a half. Then they piled back into the car to drive home, where they listened to the Bears game on the radio and Tony's mother prepared Sunday dinner. That was how respectable middle-class families in the Chicago area spent their Sundays in the 1940s.

But when Tony went away to college, he soon discovered that his professors and fellow students viewed his childhood faith as old-fashioned and simplistic. And, truth be told, Tony's childhood faith *was* simplistic. It amounted to little more than a collection of Bible stories, some bromides about loving his neighbor, and a collection of half-explained prohibitions against cards, tobacco, and alcohol—all staples of life at a state college.

Tony hadn't consciously rejected his faith. Rather, he'd simply packed it into a dark corner of his mind and forgotten about it. He had outgrown it in the same way that he had outgrown the suits he used to wear each Sunday to church.

Now, for the first time, Tony saw Christianity presented by men who backed their faith not with simple Sunday-school axioms but with powerful, clearly reasoned arguments.

If they could speak even half as well as they could write, Tony thought on more than one occasion, *they would have made outstanding lawyers.*

A week later, Tony had met Pastor Wilhelm for lunch at the Metropolitan Club. They'd sat at Tony's customary table by the ceiling-to-floor window, low clouds wrapping the club in an opaque white fog. The two men made small talk for several minutes, chatting about mutual friends and a recent charity dinner they had both attended. When their salads arrived, Tony broached the topic he had wanted to discuss.

"Thank you for recommending those books, Pastor. I've read them and found them quite illuminating."

"You're a fast reader."

"Not particularly. One of the advantages of being a senior partner is that junior lawyers are always willing to do anything I don't want to—and probably do it better. So if something important comes up and I decide that I should spend most of my week reading and thinking, I can do that."

"I see. And did something important come up?"

"Yes. In fact, the most important thing possible came up: God. I suppose he has always been there, but I had never seen him. Or, more accurately, I had never looked. And now . . . now I find that he is much more real and near and alive than I ever imagined. And that changes everything. It's really quite inconvenient."

Pastor Wilhelm laughed. "Change is always hard, particularly for men of our age."

"It truly is. I had a terrible time when my doctor told me to quit smoking twenty years ago. I have a feeling this is going to be much worse."

"I'm very happy for you, my friend. You have made the most important decision of your life, and you made it right."

"Thank you, Johan. It's good to have a purpose bigger than winning in court, particularly since I'm not likely to be able to do that for much longer."

"Have you given any thought to what that purpose might be?"

"Yes, I have."

"Would you like to talk about it?"

"I'm sorry, but I can't. At least, not now."

"The work is all done, Mr. Simeon," LeGrand announced. He showed Tony how to operate the new control panels, and they went over what to do in case of an emergency. Then Tony paid LeGrand's bill and the security expert left.

Tony locked the door, watched the new sensors until they showed that LeGrand had turned out of the driveway, and armed the system.

LeGrand had added several new elements to Tony's previous security system. There were now sensors on the upstairs windows, for example. He had also built a novel security device into Tony's driveway.

But the heart of Tony's security system remained unchanged. A dark-wood ceiling-to-floor bookcase lined one wall of his study, and one section of that bookcase opened to reveal what the previous owner of the house had told Tony was a "rum closet" used to hide liquor during Prohibition. Tony planned to use it to hide himself.

He knew that his sophisticated alarms and sensors could not protect him. They could do little more than warn him of approaching danger and notify the police. He needed a way to stay alive during the crucial minutes between the time an alarm went off and the time the police arrived. He doubted that he could outfight or outrun an assassin, so that meant hiding in the stuffy, unlit secret chamber until the police came.

He walked slowly into the study and stood looking absently at the bookshelf. Awards, plaques, and souvenirs from some of his more memorable victories filled several shelves. There was a crystal baseball bat bearing the legend "Heavy Hitter of the Year 1993," the year he had won high-profile lawsuits for both an alderman and the Chicago Bears. A polished mahogany box held a gold-hilted dagger in a black-velvet sheath—a gift from an appreciative client who knew and admired Tony's nickname. Next to it sat two plaques—one for "Biggest Plaintiff's Verdict 1989" for a $100-million award he'd won for one bank against another, and the other for "Biggest Defense Verdict 1993" for his defense of the alderman.

Tony's eyes lingered on the 1993 plaque. After a minute, he reached out and turned it facedown. The alderman had been guilty as sin, and Tony had known it. It was a fraud case in which the plaintiff, another alderman and former friend of the defendant, had accused him of lying during the sale of a business. Tony had won the case not by defending his client (who had a somewhat blemished reputation for truthfulness), but by attacking the plaintiff—a strategy that had taken the opposing attorney completely by surprise. Tony relentlessly undermined the plaintiff's credibility during the trial, turning every mistake or exaggeration into a cunning lie to be exposed to the jury. It had worked, and at the end of the trial the defendant had escaped untouched. The plaintiff, on the other hand, had gone bankrupt from his legal bills and his losses on the business he'd bought.

It had been a brilliant and celebrated victory, one of many in Tony's storied career. The sun had shone long and bright on him, but now its light was fading and he felt the approach of night. He was an old man in a cavernous mansion, alone with his awards and decades-old victories. *Nothing.* In fact, worse than nothing, because many of them represented the triumph of skill over justice.

He turned from the bookcase and saw his statuette of Prometheus standing on a granite plinth, in a Plexiglas case. It was twenty-three inches tall, a remarkably detailed bronze of piercing beauty. The muscular Titan stood against a jagged, Scythian rock, bound with heavy, god-forged chains. His belly had been torn open by Zeus's vengeful eagle, but his bearded face was defiant and proud and his powerful legs held him erect, straining against the torturing bonds.

"I too was bound," murmured Tony, "but I forged my own chains."

He knew that breaking free of those chains wouldn't be easy. There would be no "cheap grace," as Bonhoeffer put it. Soon after his lunch with Pastor Wilhelm, Tony had begun to discover just how expensive grace could be.

Dmitry Kolesnikov had called him to discuss the Ivanovsky case. Dmitry was concerned about Nikolai Zinoviev, who was at the center of the case. They had put off his deposition for as long as they could, but Ben Corbin was entitled to Nicki's testimony, and if he filed a motion to compel, he certainly would win, and Tony would look bad in the eyes of the judge.

Dmitry went off on a seeming tangent about Nicki's drug problem and the risk that he might overdose. "What would happen to the case if he died?" he had asked. "Ivanovsky's testimony would destroy us then, wouldn't it?"

While Dmitry was speaking, Rosa had walked into Tony's office and handed him an urgent message about another case. He skimmed it as they spoke. "Well, for one thing, Ivanovsky wouldn't be able to testify," he'd said without really thinking. "The Dead Man's Rule would keep his testimony out. If you're really worried about Nicki's health, I can recommend a rehab clinic that some of my other clients have used."

"Thank you," Dmitry had said a bit too smoothly. "I'll talk to Nicki and call you back if we decide to go that route. Well, I know you're busy. I won't take up any more of your time."

Tony hung up the phone and turned his entire attention to the message in his hand.

He had forgotten about the conversation completely until three days later—when Nicki died on the day of his deposition. He realized then that Dmitry had known about the Dead Man's Rule all along, likely from his second cousin, a disbarred lawyer who occasionally advised the Brothers. Dmitry had merely called Tony to confirm how the rule would operate in this case.

The attorney-client privilege arguably covered their conversation, because Dmitry hadn't technically used Tony's advice to commit a crime but only to find out what the impact of a crime would be. Even if the privilege didn't apply, Dmitry had carefully avoided saying anything incriminating enough to be useful to the police.

Tony, however, was not without options. All of them had consequences, of course, ranging from disbarment to death, but he was no longer a man who could—or would—turn a blind eye and do nothing. He had put off his decision for as long as possible. Then he had bought voice-altering equipment, and, deep into a sleepless night, he had called Ben Corbin.

Despite all that had happened since, Tony did not regret his decision. *But the game is not over,* he thought with a grim smile. *There's still plenty of time for regret.*

Ibrahim would only get one shot, so it had to be perfect. He had waited all day for that shot, but it hadn't come. First, the man with the LeGrand Security Services van had spent hours installing equipment. Shortly after he'd left, a plumbing contractor had come and dug a trench across the driveway and part of the yard, putting in white PVC pipe and leaving a ridge of raw earth where he had buried the pipe. When he finally moved his van out, Ibrahim could see that he had left a lump of steel plate and asphalt behind where he had torn up the driveway. All the while, Simeon had stayed inside behind shuttered windows.

It was late afternoon now, and still the lawyer had not shown himself. Even if he did, the glare of the low sun on the windows of the house would make a shot difficult unless he were to actually step outside. Ibrahim decided to abandon his primary plan and go with his backup. He methodically and quickly disassembled and packed his sniper rifle, a thin line between his black eyebrows the only sign of frustration that his iron self-discipline allowed to show.

He jogged through the school and out to his van, where he rapidly changed into workman's coveralls and put magnetic stickers on each side of the van that read "Chicagoland Electrical Services—Certified Electricians." He mentally ran through what he would need to do. He had watched the security devices go in and knew how to slip past them. Would there be others that had not just been installed? Maybe. That was one reason why this plan was the backup and not the primary option. He would also have to be careful while driving over that metal plate; he wouldn't want to leave a scrape of paint or other evidence for the FBI. After all, the whole point of this mission was to deprive the Americans of evidence.

Will it work? Tony wondered. In the courtroom and at the negotiating table, he had routinely bet millions—sometimes billions—on his ability to understand and outthink his opponents. Now he was betting his life and more. Much more.

Have I missed something? His mind had begun to slip in recent years. Not much, but he could tell. He wasn't quite as quick on his feet as he had been ten years ago, and he occasionally missed subtle points that would have been obvious to him in his prime. Maybe he had merely grown mentally and emotionally tired of the practice of law—or at least the way he had practiced it. That might explain why he had lost some of his edge. Or it might not.

God, I commit this into your hands, he prayed silently. *I know you haven't missed anything, even if I have.*

He crouched nervously behind a chair in his living room, watching a narrow wedge of driveway through a crack in the shutters. He estimated that he had about thirty seconds from the time an alarm went off until an intruder could get inside and start looking for him, so he made sure that he had chosen a watching post less than thirty seconds from the rum closet.

A white van turned into his driveway and his heart nearly stopped. This was it. He jumped up from behind the chair and ran into the study. As he jerked open the hidden door, he slipped on an area rug and nearly fell. Regaining his balance, he hurried into the secret chamber, pulling the door shut behind him.

It was dark and silent in the little room, and Tony's breath sounded unnaturally loud in his ears. The walls were cold, slightly dank, and close enough to make even a spelunker claustrophobic. The air was stale and smelled faintly of mildew.

Tony had a cell phone on his belt and was tempted to call LeGrand or the police. He resisted. The alarms should be enough, and he didn't want to spring his trap too soon.

Ibrahim parked the van in the lawyer's driveway, making sure that it blocked the nearest neighbor's view of the front door. He suspected that the door would be locked and fitted with alarms, but both problems could be fixed easily enough.

He took out a simple magnetometer and swept along the edge of the door. The needle jumped where he expected it to, near the upper-left corner of the door. He put the device back in his toolbox and took out a thin strip of steel, which he carefully slid between the jamb and the door at the spot where the magnetometer had registered a field. Because the steel was ferrous, it would not interrupt the magnetic field, but it would tell him exactly where the magnet was.

Click. The magnet pulled the strip down to the top of the door and Ibrahim drew it back out. Reaching into his toolbox again, he took out a tube of quick-setting glue and a tiny but powerful magnet. Placing the magnet on the end of the steel strip, he squeezed a drop of glue onto the magnet and slid the strip back between the door and the jamb, positioning his magnet above the alarm system's magnet. Then he lifted it up and pressed it against the sensor until the glue dried, which took slightly less than a minute. He dropped the strip back into his box and grabbed a diamond-bladed power saw—the fastest and quietest model on the market. He quickly sliced through the dead-bolt lock and put his tools away.

He took a deep breath and said a silent prayer to Allah. Then he opened the door. No alarm screeched. No strobe lights flashed. He smiled. Either the alarm system wasn't turned on or he had successfully tricked the door sensor. In any event, he was now past the first barrier.

He cautiously leaned through the doorway and peered inside. The house had a wide entranceway floored with dark walnut, which was mostly covered by a large Persian rug. He scanned the walls, but saw no motion detectors.

Good. Any pressure sensors would be under the rug, and he could just walk around that.

He took out his gun and stepped into the house, feeling a pleasant tension as he shut the door softly behind him. There was nothing quite like the thrill of the hunt.

At the far end of the foyer, a door stood partially open. Ibrahim walked quickly but quietly around the rug and stopped to listen. Silence. He carefully looked around the edge of the door. It led into a high-ceilinged living room with a large marble fireplace and a scattering of elegant, comfortable-looking furniture. The tired light of a November evening came in through a wide picture window, giving the room a peaceful, slightly melancholy look. But Ibrahim cared about only three things in the room: the motion detector in the far corner and the two security-system control panels next to the door. Fortunately, only one of the panels showed the red light indicating that it was armed; the other glowed green.

He unscrewed the cover of the armed panel and attached two wires from a handheld device that looked like an overgrown calculator with wires of various sizes coming out of its top. He spent several nerve-racking minutes typing on the device's small keyboard, expecting his target to walk in at any moment. At last, the numbers he needed appeared on the screen: 42235. He typed them into the security-panel touchpad and pushed the "Enter" button. The panel gave a soft chime and the red light turned green. He quickly disconnected the wires and put the device away.

He would have to move fast now. The lawyer might have heard the chime or there might be another panel elsewhere in the house—in the master bedroom, for example—that also chimed and went green, alerting the lawyer to the presence of an intruder.

He moved through the house with the speed and silence of a cat on the trail of its prey. He rapidly searched the downstairs but found nothing. He went upstairs, checking each bedroom with care, all too aware that his target could be waiting with a shotgun behind any door. But he wasn't. Ibrahim went downstairs again and searched the basement. Still nothing.

There was only one place left to look. Gun at the ready, he went to the garage and eased open the door. In the dim light he could see a silver Jaguar parked on the far side. He walked cautiously around it—and saw something that sent a stab of real fear through his heart: another door.

While doing his surveillance, he had carefully positioned himself so he could see anyone entering or leaving through either the front door or the sliding door that opened onto the patio at the side of the house, but he had not realized that there was a third door tucked away in a little niche between the garage and the main body of the house. It was possible—in fact it now seemed likely—that the lawyer had somehow realized he was being watched, set the security system, and slipped out through this door.

◆ ◆ ◆

What's happening out there? Tony wondered. First he had heard the faint sound of the alarm being disarmed in the next room. He had anticipated that this would happen. Still, a moment of unreasoning fear gripped him when it actually did.

Then he'd listened as the intruder searched the house. Footsteps went through the study, not ten feet from the rum closet. They went upstairs and came back down again a few minutes later. They went back through the study and then faded from Tony's hearing.

There was silence for a long time—or what seemed like a long time until Tony looked down at the glowing hands of his Rolex and saw that he had been in the rum closet for less than twenty minutes.

Had the intruder left? Or was he still on the prowl? Was he hiding somewhere in the house, waiting for Tony to make the next move? Whatever was happening in the rest of the house, Tony knew that his best strategy was to stay put for the duration, however long that might be. He leaned against the concrete wall and tried to relax.

Ibrahim stood in the garage pondering his options. He could reset the security system and wait for the target to return home. Then he remembered the van outside. There was no way the lawyer would miss that. If he left the house to move the van, it would create an unacceptably high risk that he would be seen on the way back.

If he had possessed sufficient foresight, he would have brought the materials necessary to rig a bomb under the lawyer's Jaguar. He silently cursed his stupidity, but at least now he had a plan. It would be a simple matter to put together a car bomb and pay a visit to the parking lot at the train station where the target parked his car on most weekdays. He would need to borrow a tow truck to avoid suspicion about what he was doing under the lawyer's car, but that could be arranged.

For now, he needed to get out of the house as quickly as possible. But first he would cover his tracks. He couldn't hide the fact that he had been there—the sawn-through dead bolt in the front door made that impossible—but he could hide the purpose of his visit by making it appear to be a simple burglary. He holstered his gun and went back into the house. Jogging upstairs, he quickly cased the bedrooms and grabbed a pair of diamond cufflinks and a gold Cartier watch from the night-stand in the master suite. Back downstairs, he walked quickly through the rooms, looking for something small but valuable. He paused briefly in front of the ancient bronze statuette in the study, looking regretfully at the defiant Titan. From his days as a smuggler, Ibrahim had a fair idea of the market value of a perfectly preserved classical Greek artifact, and it would be quite high. Unfortunately, it would take too long to get the statuette out of its sealed case, and it would be difficult to dispose of such a unique item safely on the international market.

Ibrahim scanned the room for other items worth stealing. The bookcase along one wall held an assortment of knickknacks, but few of them looked valuable. One item, however, caught his eye: a gold-hilted dagger with a black-velvet sheath. Ibrahim wouldn't mind keeping that for himself.

As he walked over to the bookshelf, he noticed something he hadn't seen before: the rug in front of the bookcase was bunched and crooked. It was the only imperfection he had seen in the lawyer's immaculate house. His curiosity piqued, he examined the shelves more closely and found a set of well-hidden hinges where one section of shelves ended and another began.

He smiled and drew his gun.

As the rum closet door began to open, Tony threw himself against it. The door burst open and he fell forward into the study. A man he had never seen before tumbled to the floor a few feet from him. The stranger was about forty and had short salt-and-pepper hair. He was a big man, and his baggy coveralls did not disguise his muscular build. His gloved hand held a black semiautomatic pistol.

Tony lunged for the gun, but the man jerked it away and punched him in the face with his free hand. He wasn't able to put much force into the blow because he lay half-sprawled on the floor, but it knocked Tony back while the intruder scrambled to his feet.

Tony got to his hands and knees. He saw a paperweight lying on the floor next to him and hurled it at his opponent. It hit the man in the forehead and he staggered back, cursing in a language that Tony didn't understand.

Tony grabbed a letter opener from his desk and took a step toward the intruder. Blood dripped down the man's face, but he had recovered from the blow. He brought his pistol up and fired.

The shot hit Tony in the left side of the chest. Agony knifed through him. He stumbled and coughed uncontrollably as blood poured into his lung. He steadied himself and looked the man in the eye, knowing what was coming.

The assassin fired again, hitting Tony in the upper chest. The bullet smashed through his spine on the way out and he collapsed backward, falling through the doorway that led from the study into the living room.

As he lay on the floor, he saw the alarm panels beside the front door. His vision was fading, but he could see that all the lights showed green. Despite the pain from his wounds, Tony smiled in victory. He had specifically asked Peter LeGrand to make the driveway alarm light green, not red.

At least that worked, he thought with relief as consciousness slipped away.

Chapter Eighteen
Nightfall

"Mr. Corbin, my name is Pierre LeGrand of LeGrand Security Services," said a tense, French-accented man's voice. "I installed a security system at Tony Simeon's home. It included a custom-built device in the driveway. He asked me to call a list of people if the alarm for that went off. It did, and you're on the list. I need you to meet me at his house right now. The address is 415 Hancock in Wilmette. It's two houses from Fifth and Hancock."

Ben hit the mute button on the TV remote control, cutting off the announcer in midsentence. "Wait—who are you? Is Tony in trouble?"

"I'm Pierre LeGrand of LeGrand Security," the man repeated in irritation. "Tony might be in serious danger. Someone set off a custom-built security device at his home. He told me to inform you if that happened. You are to meet me at Fifth and Hancock *now*."

Ben thought quickly. This didn't feel like a trap. Even if it was, it made sense to play along until he knew more. "Okay. I'm on my way."

"Good. I'll explain more when we're there. I have more calls to make now." The line went dead.

Ben dropped his phone into his pocket and looked at the circle of inquiring faces gathered around him. "That was a man who claimed to be from Tony Simeon's security company. He said his name was Pierre LeGrand."

"I know LeGrand," said Sergei. "I've worked with him a couple of times. He's a sharp guy. What did he want?"

"He said someone broke into Tony's house and they're getting away. He also said Tony might be in trouble."

"Chechens," said Sergei.

Elena and Will nodded. "Where's his house?" asked Noelle.

"Fifth and Hancock. That's less than a mile from here," he added for the benefit of their guests.

"Then we might get there in time to do some good," said Sergei as he headed for the door.

Sergei and Elena took Sergei's car and Will went with the Corbins. Noelle called the police on her cell phone as Ben sped along the empty streets. Will had his gun out and his eyes darted back and forth as they drove, scanning for ambushes and evaluating firing angles.

"The police are already on their way," Noelle announced as she clicked off her phone, "but they won't be here for at least another five minutes."

They turned from Fifth onto Hancock and saw a white van with a LeGrand Security Services sign parked on the north side of the street in front of a stately brick mansion with a long, winding driveway.

The two cars pulled up behind the van and everyone got out. The FBI agents immediately went around to Sergei's trunk and pulled out bulletproof vests, including ones for Ben and Noelle. The unfamiliar body armor felt stiff and heavy to the Corbins, but they were glad to be wearing it.

Ben and Sergei went to talk to LeGrand while Elena and Will checked the house. "I'm Ben Corbin. What's going on?"

"Mr. Simeon had me build a one-of-a-kind system for his driveway," LeGrand said, pointing to the metal plate on the driveway. "If you drive over it, it pops a magnetic bug onto the bottom of your car. Here's the tracker." He handed Ben a device that looked like a bulky laptop computer with a large antenna protruding from the back. It showed a bright dot moving toward the top of the screen. "It looks like he's on I-94 heading north. You're going to have to hurry if you want to catch him. He'll be off the screen in another couple of minutes."

Will and Elena emerged from the house and jogged over. "He's dead," Elena said, her face drawn.

"Murdered?" asked Sergei.

Will nodded. "Multiple fresh gunshot wounds. I could still smell the cordite in the air. I'd say he's been dead less than fifteen minutes."

"If we hurry, we may be able to catch whoever killed him," said Sergei. "We'll take my car. It's faster and it handles better."

"Won't he recognize it?" asked Ben.

"You don't think he also recognizes your car by now?" Sergei replied. "I'm sure they've been watching both of us at least since the trial ended. Anyway, we won't have to get too close to him with this." He gestured to the tracker in Ben's hands.

Ben looked down and saw that the dot had grown fainter and was less than two inches from the top of the screen. "Sounds good. Let's go!"

They all crowded into Sergei's car and drove off, leaving LeGrand to talk to the police. Ben sat in front with the tracker and Noelle was in the back, sandwiched between Elena and Will.

Sergei drove at breakneck speed down the narrow, tree-lined suburban streets as they tried to keep the bug's fading signal on the screen. They all held on tight to the armrests and braced themselves as Sergei squealed around corners and roared through quiet neighborhoods. Ben struggled to keep the tracker on his lap, glad they weren't trying this in his Camry.

After two miles, they reached a four-lane street with few stoplights and little traffic. They all breathed a little easier as Sergei accelerated on the open road and the signal held steady on the monitor.

"I wish Simeon had taken our offer," Elena said. "We could have protected him."

"I don't think he wanted to be protected," Ben replied, "at least not if it meant the Vainakh Guard would escape with Variant D. I think he planned to trap them by using himself as bait."

"He may wind up handing us the whole nest," added Sergei. "I'll bet the guy with the bug on his car is heading back to their base right now. Even if he isn't, he'll lead us to them sooner or later if we put him under surveillance. Simeon's trap may have worked even better than he intended."

"Oh, I'll bet he intended this," said Ben. "Remember who we're talking about. In fact, I'll bet he intended everything except his death, and he was willing to risk that. He saw it coming too. Why else would he give LeGrand a list of numbers to call? He knew he might not be around to make the calls himself."

The car was silent for several seconds as they each thought of the urbane, potbellied old lawyer. "He showed us how to find the cancer," said Sergei at last. "Now it's up to us to remove it."

Ibrahim drove north, scrupulously obeying every traffic rule. He checked his rearview mirror regularly and took measures to make himself difficult to follow. The last thing he wanted was to get pulled over or tailed now. Just because he had accomplished his mission did not mean he could relax.

After a successful mission, a soldier was tempted to loosen up and maybe get a little sloppy. In fact, a favorite Chechen tactic during the wars with the Russians had been to hit them on the night after they had won a victory. Their guard was generally down and they were often in the midst of a drunken celebration. Ibrahim's celebration would wait until he could share it with all Muslims, when the corrupt colonial empires of the West and Russia collapsed.

Still, he could not resist just a little self-congratulation. He had taken down his target despite setbacks that forced him to abandon his primary plan, despite a state-of-the-art residential security system that took considerable skill to evade, and despite surprisingly tough resistance from the target.

Ibrahim touched the lump and cut on his forehead. The lawyer had fought hard, and he had faced his death with courage. He had proven a worthy—if overmatched—opponent, making Ibrahim's victory over him all the sweeter.

A police siren went off behind Sergei's car. He was going about seventy in a thirty-five-mile-an-hour zone and had blown through two red lights, so it was hardly a shock that local law enforcement had taken an interest in him.

"I'll call and explain the situation," volunteered Elena.

"Good idea," said Sergei. "We can't pull over, and we can't have that siren behind us while we're trying to tail this guy."

Elena called the Evanston Police Department, but the desk sergeant and dispatcher both insisted that none of their units were pursuing a black Mustang Cobra convertible. By the time she ended the call, there were two cars behind them. "I'll try the Wilmette department," she yelled over the sirens.

"This is Special Agent Elena Kamenev of the FBI," she shouted into the phone. "There are two black-and-whites chasing a black Mustang west on Lake. Are they yours?"

"They're ours," confirmed the desk sergeant after a brief pause. "Are you in the car?"

"Yes," said Elena with relief. "I need your officers to turn off their sirens and stop following us. They're interfering with a federal investigation."

"Pull over and show them some ID—and explain to them why your investigation requires you to drive through the middle of town like that."

"We can't pull over! We're in the middle of a hot pursuit."

There was a long pause. "The officers behind you say they don't see anything in front of you," the desk sergeant said suspiciously. "What exactly are you pursuing?"

"A car with an electronic bug," replied Elena, her voice growing hoarse with the effort of shouting over the noise of the chase. "It's not right in front of us!"

"Look, you're just going to have to explain all this to the officers at the roadblock."

"What roadblock?" she asked.

Before the desk sergeant could respond, Sergei slammed on the brakes. The car fishtailed and he fought to control it, bringing it to a halt less than a foot from two squad cars parked sideways on the street. Policemen with drawn guns crouched behind the cars. "Out of the car!" one of them ordered. "Hands on your heads!"

Sergei slammed his fist on the dashboard in frustration. As they got out of the car, Will Conklin yelled, "We're FBI! Right now a murderer is escaping, and you're letting it happen!"

"Just keep your hands up," the policeman ordered. He turned to one of the other officers. "Carl, go check their IDs."

An officer holstered his gun and ran around the roadblock. "Back left pocket," Will told him as he approached.

The policeman pulled out Will's wallet and examined it. "Looks genuine," he called to the other officers.

"Mine's in my purse in the backseat," said Elena. "It's the black one."

The officer briefly surveyed the interior of the car, grabbed her purse, and checked her wallet. "This one looks legit too, and they've got some kind of computer with an antenna in the front seat. Looks like it might be electronic surveillance gear." He held it up for the others to see. As he did so, Ben saw that the screen was blank. They had lost the signal.

Elbek stood in the back of the old brewery, watching with satisfaction as Squad One loaded their deadly cargo into the white Dodge Caravan that would take them to their destination. Flying was out of the question, of course, as was any form of transportation that might allow security personnel access to their bags. There was still a chance that they might get stopped, but they could minimize it by driving nondescript vehicles that police were likely to ignore.

Their cargo was surprisingly small: one banker box per vehicle. Each box held twenty-five aerosol dispensers—five for each city they would visit. The dispensers were little more than modified spray bottles designed by Dr. Umarov. The team members would each take one or two bottles and walk around their targets, spraying discreetly. Building-ventilation systems and Dr. Umarov's tiny particles would do the rest.

They carried little else: a change of clothes, some toiletries, small arms and ammunition hidden in the seats, and a five-gallon red plastic jug of gasoline. The gasoline had two purposes. First, it was an emergency supply in case they ran out of fuel somewhere.

The second purpose was more grim. They would do all they could to avoid infecting themselves during their travels, but contracting Variant D was still a significant risk. If one of them began exhibiting symptoms, the others would have to kill him immediately. They would then smash the teeth on the corpse to prevent identification through dental records and burn the remains sufficiently to eliminate fingerprints, scars, tattoos, and facial features. They had to remain anonymous, even in death.

The Wilmette police finally seemed satisfied. They had called the FBI to confirm Will's and Elena's identities. Then they'd called their office to confirm Anthony Simeon's murder. Only then were they willing to release Sergei and his passengers.

The officer in charge didn't exactly apologize, but he did say, "It's too bad this happened. We'll get you onto I-94 and call the state police to let them know what's going on. Tell us if there's anything else we can do to help with your manhunt."

Escorted by police cruisers, Sergei raced for the highway, but no one in his Mustang had any great hope of reacquiring the signal from the bug. The delay at the roadblock had cost them fifteen minutes, which meant their target was now miles—perhaps as many as fifteen to twenty miles—outside of the scanner's range.

Still, there was nothing to do but try. Sergei turned onto the highway and sped north, weaving in and out of traffic and driving down the shoulder while the rest of them held on tight. Semitrailers traveled the road in long convoys, taking advantage of the light holiday traffic to pick up time on their delivery schedules. Sergei threaded his way among the behemoths, drawing occasional air-horn blasts from angry truckers as he cut in front of them. He hardly noticed, though, as his entire attention was focused on the road ahead. He was going about thirty miles an hour faster than the trucks, so driving through them was like negotiating a moving obstacle course. He brushed the fender of one truck and nearly lost control of the car but managed to muscle it away from the guardrail.

"Whoa! We're almost on top of him," said Ben. "He's practically shooting toward us."

"What? Let me see," said Sergei.

"No, no," Elena called from the backseat. "You drive. I'll look." Ben handed the monitor back. "Ben's right. He must have doubled back."

Sergei laughed with relief as he slowed to a more reasonable speed. "I'll bet he's trying to lose tails. Little does he know. Where is he now?"

Elena looked up from the monitor and watched the southbound lanes across the grassy median. "He just passed us." She handed the scanner back to Ben and took out her gun. Will did the same. "It's possible he just spotted us. Drive carefully."

Sergei smiled. "That's the only way I know how to drive." He turned off onto an exit ramp, drove across an overpass, and got back onto the highway heading south. "Ben, get my gun out of the glove compartment. Be ready to hand it to me if anyone starts shooting at us."

Ben opened the glove compartment and gingerly took out the weapon. It had a matte-finish steel slide and black grips bearing the three rings and arrows of the Beretta logo.

They followed the bugged vehicle at a distance of about a half mile—far enough back so that there was no danger of being seen, but not so far that there was any risk of losing the signal again. The chase took them from I-94 onto I-294, a loop of tollway that swung through Chicago's western and southern suburbs.

"He just turned off," Ben said, looking up from the monitor. He scanned the highway signs announcing upcoming exits. "It looks like he took North Avenue." He glanced down at the tracker again. "He's heading west."

Sergei pulled off the highway and turned west on North. He drove into the setting sun—which was at precisely the right position in the sky to make driving nearly impossible. He pulled down the visor and squinted into the glare, hoping he wouldn't crash. They followed the dot on the tracker through several turns into a commercial and light-industrial area of Elmhurst.

"Okay, he stopped," Ben said. "He's straight ahead of us. Maybe five, six hundred yards."

Sergei pulled over and parked partway down the long entranceway to an industrial park. Everyone shaded their eyes and scanned the neighborhood in front of them. Sergei reached across Ben and took a small pair of binoculars out of the glove compartment. "The warehouse and the brewery look like the most likely candidates," he said after examining the scene for a few seconds. He took a deep breath. "It looks like this is it."

"What do we do now?" asked Noelle.

"We call in the cavalry," answered Will, who was already dialing the Elmhurst police. Elena was looking for Agent Gomez's home number.

"And we wait," added Sergei as he put the binoculars down and retrieved his gun from Ben. "Once they've got the area cordoned off and their SWAT units in place, we'll work with the officer in charge to plan strategy."

As they talked, a white minivan drove past the parked Mustang. Because of the glare from the setting sun, no one noticed that the driver of the minivan was staring at them as he passed. They also didn't notice when the van took a corner just a little too fast a block behind them.

Elbek frowned as he saw the Caravan drive back into the brewery parking lot. Something must be wrong. "Why are you back here?" he asked as soon as the driver's door opened.

"The Russian detective is here," the man said frantically. "I saw his car as I drove out. He's watching us with binoculars."

Rage filled Elbek, but he refused to let it cloud his mind. "Is he alone?"

"There were others in the car with him, but I didn't see anyone else nearby."

The sentries hadn't reported anything suspicious, which probably meant that the detective and his friends were alone, at least for the moment. The vans and other vehicles obviously couldn't continue to leave while they were being watched. They also could not simply wait for the watchers to leave, particularly now that one of the vans had driven past them—and likely alerted them that they had been discovered. Something had to be done immediately. He turned to his aide, Yunus. "Go get Ibrahim. I have another problem for him to eliminate."

The sun had almost set. Long shadows streaked the landscape, providing excellent natural camouflage. A chill wind blew through the grassy field as Ibrahim crept toward the car. He carried a pair of rocket-propelled grenades and a grenade launcher in place of his sniper rifle. A grenade explosion surely would attract more attention than rifle shots, but he had no choice. He needed to kill everyone in the car, and he needed to do it quickly. An RPG, though less elegant than a bullet, was the only practical solution.

He stopped about a hundred yards from the car and lay flat, listening and watching. He heard no sound except the deep-throated idling of the Mustang's engine. The car's occupants appeared to be either focused on the buildings in front of them or talking among themselves. Apparently, no one was watching the empty fields on either side of the road.

The grenade launcher was a five-foot-long tube with a pistol grip and trigger about a third of the way from the end that attached to the grenade. Ibrahim slipped the launcher from its sling on his back and took an RPG out of a pouch slung over his shoulder. He attached the

RPG to the launcher, got up on one knee, shouldered the launcher, and took careful aim at the car.

◆ ◆ ◆

"How much longer until the police get here?" Noelle asked nervously.

"They said half an hour or so, and it's been twenty-five minutes," replied Elena. "It takes some time to put together a squad big enough to surround a building full of armed men."

"Yeah, and I'd rather they do this right than do it fast," added Sergei. "This could get very bad very quickly if they go in with too few cops or without the right equipment."

"Can you tell how many of them there are?" asked Ben.

"Not really," said Sergei. "There are five or six of them loading some SUVs and minivans, but—hold on." He squinted through the binoculars again. All the activity outside the brewery had ceased. "That's weird. They're all gone. It's almost like . . ."

"Like they know we're watching them," Ben said.

"Yeah," said Sergei. He removed the binoculars from his eyes and scanned the fields around the car. The wind kept the tall grass in constant motion, making it difficult to see anything moving through it. The long, early-evening shadows also didn't help.

An object in the grass off to the left caught his attention. It seemed like a lump of dirt, but he couldn't be quite sure. He looked through the binoculars—and saw a man suddenly rise to a kneeling position and shoulder a grenade launcher.

"Hold on!" shouted Sergei as he threw the car into gear and slammed the accelerator to the floor. Shouts of surprise and alarm filled the car as its tires spun in the loose gravel on the side of the road.

The RPG shot toward them in a burst of fire and white smoke. It missed the back of the Mustang by two feet and exploded in the field on the other side of the road. The concussion shattered the right rear window on Sergei's car and blew it onto two wheels for an instant.

Sergei kept his foot down and accelerated toward the cluster of buildings ahead. For a split second he considered making a U-turn, but he glanced back and saw that the man already had another RPG ready to launch. If there was a way out, it lay past the hornet's nest in front of them. Also, the Chechens almost certainly would not expect him to drive *toward* their base.

The buildings were only silent silhouettes in the sunset, but Sergei had no doubt that at least one of them was a hive of activity as the Chechens scrambled to deal with the speeding Mustang. He hoped no one else had an armed grenade launcher handy. "Everybody get down," he said. "They'll start shooting any second."

Everyone except Sergei ducked below window level. He crouched over the wheel to present the smallest possible target. For several seconds, nothing happened. The buildings loomed larger, and Sergei spotted a narrow lane between the warehouse and an electronics factory—a perfect shooting gallery if the Chechens could get men to it in time. If they couldn't, it would be an excellent sheltered escape route.

The shooting started when they were about a hundred yards away. The windshield shattered, showering them all with glass. Howling ninety-mile-an-hour wind and the high-pitched buzz of flying bullets filled the car. Sergei ducked even lower, his eyes just above the dashboard. Automatic rifle fire dug a row of divots out of the road just in front of the car and a long crease appeared in the hood. Ben's headrest exploded in a burst of leather scraps and chunks of foam rubber.

Bangs and pings from under the hood told Sergei that bullets were finding their way through the grille. One hit the radiator, sending a blast of hot steam over the front of the car and into Sergei's face. He choked and squinted as he struggled to keep control of the car.

Fifteen yards from the buildings, the front right tire blew out. The wheel jerked in Sergei's hands as the Mustang sheered suddenly to the right, taking them straight toward the brick facade of the warehouse. Sergei yanked the wheel hard to the left, but the car careened off the corner of the warehouse and smashed into the front offices of the factory. It hurtled through the glass-and-steel exterior and the plant manager's office before finally coming to rest between two rows of cubicles. A corner of the roof collapsed behind them with a crash, blowing a cloud of plaster dust and ceiling-tile particles over the wrecked sports car. The engine died and all was suddenly silent.

Chapter Nineteen
Endgame

"Excellent work! You have gained glory for yourselves and Allah," Elbek said to the cluster of men hastily positioned outside the brewery entrance. They had shown good discipline and initiative, grabbing their weapons and racing out the door to join their commander as soon as Ibrahim's ambush failed and the Russian unexpectedly charged them. Elbek was a good shot, but his pistol alone might not have been enough to stop the speeding car. "Go make sure they're dead and see what you can learn." He turned to the most senior of the men. "Movsar, you're in command."

"Yes, sir," he replied. The group jogged toward the electronics factory as Elbek went back into the brewery.

"Yunus!" he called.

His aide quickly appeared from the back, where he had been supervising the loading of the vans and SUVs. "Yes, General?"

"We need to move faster. Much faster. The Americans will be here any moment, and we need to be ready for them. The squads must all be gone, and the building must be ready. I will take over loading and dispatching the squads. I need you to make the final preparations here." Elbek paused and looked his longtime assistant in the eyes. "There is a very good chance that the enemy will arrive before we can leave."

"Yes, General." Yunus betrayed no emotion as he left to arm the explosives that would obliterate the building and all trace of their operation, adding crucial hours, maybe days, to the time it would take the Americans and their allies to discover what was happening. Of course, the building had to be destroyed before the enemy could seize it—no matter who was left inside.

Ben looked around. The chalky dust and pale-gray light of the dying day gave everyone in the car a corpse-like appearance. A trickle of blood, black in the dim light, ran down the side of Sergei's face as he lay slumped over the steering wheel. For an instant, Ben feared that he was the only one left alive. "Is everyone okay?" he asked, his voice loud in the silence.

Sergei groaned and sat up. "I'll live. How are you guys in back?"

"My legs are stuck," said Will in a strained voice. Ben looked over his seat and saw that it had been jammed back almost into Will's lap, trapping his legs.

Noelle was sitting next to Will. She bent over to get a better look at the problem. "It looks like . . ." Her voice trailed off and she sat back, looking sick. "There's bone sticking out, and there's a lot of blood."

Elena leaned over Noelle and examined Will's badly broken legs. "He has to get to a hospital. Will, how do you feel?"

"It hurts pretty bad," he said, his face slick with sweat. "I can take it, but I . . . I'm having trouble focusing. Probably blood loss 'n' shock."

Elena turned to Sergei. "There's no way an ambulance can get in here, and he won't last long without help."

"And none of us will last long if the Chechens show up in force," Sergei replied. He pulled a towel from under his seat and tore it into several long strips. "Here, use this for a tourniquet, and get him as flat as possible," he said as he handed the pieces back to her. "I'm going to go see what they're up to."

The driver's door was completely smashed in, so Sergei climbed out through the smashed driver's-side window. He winced as his burns bumped against the doorframe, reminding him that he still wasn't fully recovered from his last visit with the Chechens.

He walked down the row of cubicles in a half crouch, keeping his head below the level of the partitions. When he reached the end, he took a deep breath and peered around the corner.

A group of five armed men stood looking in through a window, apparently trying to make out the crash scene in the gloom.

Sergei slipped into a cubicle and crouched motionless, listening. After thirty seconds, he heard careful footsteps coming through the hole the car had torn in the exterior wall. He waited ten more seconds and then slipped back out into the walkway between the cubicle rows. The men had their backs to him as they approached the wreck, weapons ready. Sergei wiped his sweaty palms and took out his Beretta.

Just like at the Academy, he told himself.

Bracing himself for the recoil, he squeezed off three shots in rapid succession.

Bang! Bang! Bang!

The first two bullets hit their targets squarely between the shoulder blades, dropping them immediately. By the time Sergei fired the third shot, the men were turning toward him and the third bullet hit one of them in the left shoulder. Sergei dove back behind the cubicles as the remaining Chechens opened fire. He stumbled and fell as bullets tore through the partitions where he would have been had he kept his feet. He heard the familiar sound of a Glock .40 caliber firing from the direction of the car, followed by confused shouting and running. He smiled.

When the Chechens turned to chase him, Elena must have opened up on them with her FBI standard-issue firearm. No wonder they had run.

Sergei carefully poked his head over the top of the cubicles. Three Chechens lay dead; the rest had vanished. One man's eyes were still open, staring at Sergei. He walked quickly past the dead men and back to the car. "Is everyone okay?"

"We're fine," answered Ben, a slight adrenaline quiver in his voice. "Do you think they'll be back?"

Sergei nodded. "And next time we won't take them by surprise." He walked back to the bodies and picked up their weapons. "Here," he said as he handed them to Ben and Noelle, "you'll need these."

He looked over at Will Conklin. The FBI agent was breathing unevenly and his face was pale and strained.

Elena followed his gaze. "I tried to call the police to ask if there was some way they could move faster, but my phone won't work in here."

Sergei tried his phone, which also didn't work. He glanced through a window in the wall that separated the front office from the production lines. Much of the machinery had been left on, and displays and sensors glowed in the darkness. Maybe all that equipment was interfering with the phone signals, or possibly the place was shielded against cell-phone transmissions and other stuff that would interfere with the equipment. "I'll go outside and try."

"While you're at it, see if you can figure out what's going on next door," Elena said. "I'm sure the Chechens have been busy."

Sergei nodded. "I'm sure they have." The Vainakh Guard would no doubt be watching the front of the building, so Sergei headed for the back to look for a door or window. The machines on the factory floor generated just enough little pools of colored light to prevent Sergei's eyes from adjusting to the dark, but not enough to see by. Small hums and whirs masked his steps—and the steps of anyone else who might be there.

If one of them is in here with night-vision gear, I'm dead.

He saw the dim outline of a window ahead, a rectangle of slightly less dark space hanging in the blackness. He walked over to it as quickly as he could, hands in front of him like a child playing blindman's buff. A file cabinet stood under the window. Sergei climbed clumsily onto it, making far too much noise for his comfort. He unlocked the window and slipped through, dropping the few feet to the ground.

Evening was rapidly fading into a moonless and cold night. Sergei found himself beside a long, bare wall of pale limestone, exposed to a sharp wind and—more importantly—sharp eyes that might be able to pick out his silhouette against the light stone.

He spotted a clump of fir bushes at the end of the wall and ran toward it. Gunfire sounded in the distance as he ran—pops like fire-crackers interspersed with the unmistakable rattle of full-auto bursts. It was too far away and in the wrong direction to be a renewed attack on Elena and the rest. The Elmhurst police must have arrived and set up checkpoints or roadblocks on the exits from the industrial park. Good.

Frost rimed the short needles, which jabbed through Sergei's slacks as he wedged himself between the bushes and the building. As soon as he was settled, he dug his cell phone out of his pocket and turned it on, making sure to hide the display light. To his great relief, it showed a strong signal. The sharp scent of bruised pine needles surrounded him as he dialed, causing him to think incongruously of Christmas.

"Elmhurst Police Department," said a woman's voice.

"This is Sergei Spassky. I'm at the Western Industrial Plaza, and I need to talk to the officer in charge out here. I'm working with Elena Kamenev of the FBI. She spoke to your department earlier about putting together a raid out here."

Thirty seconds later, a man's voice came on the line. "This is Captain Thompson."

"Captain, we have a badly injured agent in here. When will your men be ready to make their assault?"

"It could be a while. Our first priority is to reestablish our cordon. We've been intercepting vehicles full of armed suspects coming out along the rear access road, and they've been fighting us. The last one rammed through our roadblock and took out a lot of my men. We stopped them, but there are a lot of officers down and the roadblock is effectively gone. It won't be back up until—"

"—I can get some more men over there, and I had to send the men I had for the raid. So the raid is on hold until we get more reinforcements," the police captain's tinny, fuzzy voice said from the speaker. Even Elbek, whose English was very good, had difficulty understanding it.

A burst of static drowned out the Russian detective's response. "Sorry sir," said the Vainakh Guard's electronics officer over his shoulder. He hurriedly adjusted the knobs on the scanning equipment.

"I need to hear this, soldier!" snapped Elbek. He had found out about the roadblocks ten minutes ago, when Squad One had radioed back a terse message before suddenly going silent. That was a nasty shock, but Elbek had grown used to those during his military career.

He kept sending vehicles out anyway, in the hope that at least one of them would break through. It was a desperate strategy, but he had no choice. The only other options were to wait for the final assault or try to escape on foot across empty fields where infrared cameras would have no trouble spotting them.

"Yes, sir," said the electronics man.

A few seconds later, the signal came back. The police captain was speaking again.

". . . five minutes, maybe ten. It'll take a few minutes to reposition our men, and they'll have to wait for the ambulances to finish. The first priority is to get the injured men stabilized and out of there."

"The first priority has to be to stop any vehicles from getting through," insisted the detective. "They're probably loaded with highly lethal bioweapons. If one of them escapes . . ."

Elbek had heard enough. He ran back to the loading dock where an efficient team was packing the last two minivans. "Get the weapons in those vans and get them out of here now!"

Ben looked down the barrel of the AK-47 in his hands and into the darkness beyond. According to Elena, it was the easiest gun in the world to use. Just point and shoot.

Keep the barrel low; it's going to buck upward when you fire, he reminded himself as he braced against the smashed-in car door for the recoil and silently prayed that he would have no occasion to test Elena's advice.

The gloom deepened by the minute as the last vestiges of twilight faded outside. As night fell around them, the likelihood of a renewed attack increased—as did their opponents' advantage. The growing darkness hid their enemies—but not them. The Chechens knew exactly where they were.

Ben sniffed, and a new fear formed in his mind. "Do you smell gasoline?" he asked in a low, hurried whisper.

"Yes," replied Elena.

"Me too," said Noelle. "I just noticed it."

Something moved outside the building windows, a barely perceptible shadow against the lightless sky. "Sergei?" Ben called.

No answer.

He saw another movement and fired, shattering the windows. A sharp breeze blew in, carrying a strong smell of gas.

They're going to burn us out! Ben realized. Before he could say anything, a wall of flame roared up. Fed by the breeze, tongues of fire licked in through the broken windows, igniting curtains, splintered furniture, and piles of paper.

Elbek and Yunus climbed into the front seat of the lead van. Yunus drove and Elbek sat beside him. Four more men rode with them—two crouching by the open side doors with AK-47s and RPG launchers, and two other heavily armed gunmen in the back, guarding against any attack from the rear. A plain cardboard box sat on the floor in the middle of the van, carefully packed to prevent it from sliding or tipping. The second van was similarly equipped and manned.

They turned onto the access road, and Elbek got his first clear view of the remnant of the police roadblock. It lay a quarter of a mile ahead, where the street ended in a T-intersection with a four-lane road. A burning police cruiser lay on its roof on the shoulder, and two more had been rammed into a deep ditch on the far side of the intersection. A white Dodge Caravan and two white Ford Expeditions were in a parking lot on the far side of the four-lane road, surrounded by a half dozen police. Two ambulances had pulled up to the south of the intersection, and paramedics were carefully removing dead and wounded officers from the wreckage.

Shattered glass and bits of plastic sparkled on the asphalt in the glare of the emergency lights, but the intersection was clear. Ten minutes ago, Elbek had feared that they would all die in a heroic last stand in the brewery, but now he had hope—no, more than hope: a realistic belief—that they would complete their mission.

Once they were past the roadblock, it would be a small matter to abandon the vans, board buses or trains, and vanish. They would need to redivide the Variant D dispensers and revise their target list, but that would not be difficult. It also probably would not matter, because a virulent plague in even one city would likely spread throughout the nation in a matter of weeks as people fled from the disease by car or plane, unwittingly taking the terror with them.

But there still remained the task of getting past the roadblock—which should be simple, but could not be taken for granted. "Yunus, watch the road when you make the turn," said Elbek. "We cannot afford a flat tire." He turned to the men by the doors. "Put two RPGs in the parking lot, then follow with gunfire. We want them to be dead or distracted when we drive past."

"He'll probably die if we try to move him!" Elena shouted over the blaring fire alarm.

The flames raced up the wall and flowed in broad sheets across the ceiling, blackening and consuming the sound-absorbing tiles. The alarms had gone off almost the instant the fire started, but no water came from the sprinkler heads that dotted the ceiling. The collapse of the roof when the Mustang crashed in must have cut off the water supply.

The flickering flames gave an artificial glow of health to Will's unconscious face, but his slack features and increasingly uneven breathing showed that he was failing rapidly. Despite Noelle's and Elena's best efforts with the tourniquets, a steady flow of blood oozed from his legs.

"We'll all die if we stay here!" replied Ben. "I'm going to at least try to get this seat off his legs!" So far, they had left the seat in place for fear of injuring Will further if they moved it. And they couldn't get in a position to lift it without leaving the cover of the wrecked vehicle. But as Will's condition deteriorated and the fire moved closer, doing nothing became a worse and worse option.

Elena sat in undecided silence, but Noelle said, "Okay, we'll cover you."

Ben said a quick prayer, got out of his seat, and scrambled over the car. Elena and Noelle fired short bursts into spots where Chechen snipers might be hiding. He pushed aside a file cabinet and pulled on the driver's-side door. It didn't budge, but the handle snapped off in his hand.

Ben looked around on the floor and spotted a length of pipe that appeared to have fallen from the ceiling. Jamming one end of it into a gap between the edge of the door and the bent car frame, he braced himself against a row of cubicles and pushed the pipe with all his might, painfully aware that his entire body was now exposed to the dark windows beyond the fire. His muscles strained and shook with the effort, and his back prickled with the fear that at any moment bullets could tear through him. But none came—and after several minutes of exhausting labor, the door suddenly popped open, sending Ben sprawling to the floor.

Panting, he got to his knees and crawled to where he could poke his head in between the doorframe and the seat. The thick stench of blood nearly gagged him as he leaned in to examine the situation. The floor of the car had buckled under the force of the crash, ramming the seat back and down over Will's legs. The crash also had partly torn the seat free from the floorboard. Only two bolts now held it down, and one of them was partially sheared through.

He struggled to unscrew the undamaged bolt, but the combination of his sweat and Will's blood made it too slick. He pulled his shirtsleeve over his hand for a better grip, but still the bolt would not move.

He turned back and fished around on the ground for the pipe he had used to pry open the door. It was now bent, but he was still able to wedge it under the frame of the seat nearest to the damaged bolt and work it back and forth to weaken the torn metal. He could feel the heat on his back increasing, but he resisted the temptation to turn around and look at the progress of the fire.

Snap!

The top of the bolt broke off. Ben tipped the seat off of Will's legs, forcing and bending the seat over the remaining bolt so that the seatback leaned against the steering wheel. Will moaned, and the flow of blood from his crushed legs increased. As Elena watched for snipers outside, Noelle and Ben quickly repositioned and tightened the tourniquets. They could reach more effective locations now that the seat was gone, and the bleeding stopped almost completely.

"Whew!" Ben wiped the sweat from his eyes and sat back on his heels. "All right, now I say we—"

He had been going to say "get out of here," but as he looked around, he saw that that was no longer possible. The fire had spread along the walls of the room, which were lined with paper-filled wooden file cabinets that burned like torches. Roaring flames now barred all exits, trapping the little group in a breathlessly hot and shrinking patch of floor.

"Two more coming," Sergei warned the police captain as he watched the two vans depart from the brewery.

"My men aren't there yet," replied the captain. "If you think you can stop them, do it."

"I'll try." Sergei ended the call and put the phone back in his pocket. He took out his Beretta and readied himself. If he could take out the drivers of the vans, they would probably crash. At the very least, they'd be disabled long enough for the police to reestablish the roadblock.

As the first van approached, Sergei jumped up from his hiding place and aimed through the windshield. But before he could fire, a burst of rifle fire erupted from the trailing van. Bullets struck Sergei in the stomach, chest, and left arm, hurling him to the ground.

He lay writhing in pain by the roadside as the vans barreled past. His Kevlar vest had stopped the bullets that hit his torso, though they still had the impact of body blows delivered by a heavyweight boxer. The third shot had snapped the radius of his left arm.

Hauling himself to his knees with every ounce of grit and determination he could muster, Sergei watched helplessly as the vans raced toward the devastated roadblock.

"Those things are armed like tanks," he muttered to himself as he noticed what looked like grenade launchers and automatic rifles in the hands of the men crouched in the side and back doorways of the vehicles.

Tanks! He suddenly remembered one of his great-uncle Peter's stories from World War II. In the depths of winter, the ground had frozen so hard that Russian infantrymen had been able to take out Nazi Panzer and Tiger tanks by firing their rifles into the ground in front of the tanks. The bullets would bounce off the frozen earth and strike the vulnerable gas tanks from below, creating a spectacular and lethal fireball.

Sergei fired rapidly, aiming a few yards behind the rear van. One ricocheting bullet brought sparks from the bumper, so he moved his aim and put the bullets almost directly underneath the van. But he was just guessing where to shoot; he was firing too quickly to aim well, and the angle the bullets took depended largely on pebbles and small imperfections in the surface of the road.

His tenth shot struck the pavement under the rear axle of the second van. If the asphalt had been perfectly flat, the bullet would have bounced up into the engine, probably causing an oil fire. But the asphalt was not flat. It had a small pothole caused by years of heavy truck traffic. The bullet ricocheted off the lip of the pothole at a much shallower angle than it would have off a flat surface and missed the rear van entirely. It struck the lead van instead, passing through the gas tank before lodging in the frame.

Sergei watched in amazed joy as the lead van burst into flame and swerved. The rear van smashed into it and caught fire as well.

He staggered to his feet, hardly feeling the wound in his arm or the deep bruises in his chest and stomach.

"Yes!" he shouted as the fire reached explosives in the vans and a string of large and small explosions rocked the night. "Yes!" He pointed to the burning wrecks. "*Never* start a fight with a Russian, 'cause he's the one who'll finish it!"

WHUMP!

A tremendous blast behind Sergei knocked him from his feet again. Debris rained on him, and he turned to see the brewery vanish in a cloud of fire and dust. The old brick warehouse next door swayed in the shock wave, then collapsed, crushing the western side of the electronics factory—very near where the wreck of his Mustang sat.

The hot wind from the blast swept over Elbek where he lay in the ditch beside the access road. The shock wave rolled him over and brought him back to consciousness. His skull throbbed, and blood matted the hair above his left ear. As he reached to touch the wound, he realized that he must have struck his head on the hard, gravelly ground when he was thrown from the exploding van.

He tried to stand, but pain shot through his right leg and he fell. Ignoring the electric jolts of agony, he pulled up his pant leg. He felt his leg with the rough, expert hands of a veteran soldier—one who knows pain and has learned much practical medicine in the field. He found no broken bones. Based on the pain and swelling, he guessed that it was a severe sprain. He could force himself to walk with that, but not fast.

He scrambled up the side of the ditch and into the cover of the long grass. He then crawled parallel to the road for about twenty yards, which he judged was far enough from the crash site to avoid being found by police searching for bodies and evidence thrown off by the collision and explosions. He lay flat and looked around, assessing the situation.

He heard shouts and glimpsed running figures. A group stopped by the still-burning vans but looked at them only cursorily and left a lone guard before running on. They were probably hunting fugitives or going to find the group trapped in the factory—or whatever was left of them.

Elbek thought furiously. If he could get just one container out of the wreckage of the vans and escape, it would be enough. He could start over, maybe in Chechnya or the lawless mountains of Afghanistan. Or he could go to O'Hare and walk past the check-in counters in the domestic terminals, dispersing an army of unwitting plague-bearers throughout America.

But how could he get to the vans? Even with his bad leg, he could probably eliminate the guard quietly, but then what? The area was swarming with every free police unit from Elmhurst and the surrounding towns, and all of them would be looking for Chechens.

"Looking for Chechens," he murmured to himself. The germ of an idea took root and began to grow. He smiled. Then he started back toward the ruined Caravans, silent and deadly as a panther.

"Lord, please don't let us die in here, not like this," whispered Ben as he looked around. The flames crowded toward them, marching mercilessly down the rows of cubicles. Everyone now choked on the hot fumes from the burning acrylic carpet and plastic office furniture. Their eyes streamed.

The fire alarm suddenly fell silent as the flames melted the wiring, causing a short, but Elena still had to shout to be heard over the roar and crackle of the flames. "We need to stay low! We can breathe down there!"

There was no longer any question about moving Will. They pulled him out of the car, and all four of them lay flat on the thin gray office carpet. The air wasn't quite as hot down there, and they could breathe without gagging on chemical smoke. But they were still no closer to escaping.

"Now what do we do?" asked Noelle.

A huge explosion drowned out Elena's reply and shook the whole building. A split second later, a scorching wind roared through the broken windows, shrieking over their heads as they lay in the shelter of the wrecked car.

A few seconds after, they heard a deep groan followed by a sound like an avalanche. A six-foot-wide piece of masonry smashed through the burning ceiling and landed a few yards in front of them, followed by a hail of bricks and concrete chunks. Then the wall in front of them vanished beneath the collapsing warehouse. A cloud of dust and debris swept over them like a gray wave, leaving them coughing and blinded.

A chill breeze now blew through. It partially cleared the air, and they could see the devastation around them. Wide mounds of rubble lay where the edge of the building had once stood. Pockets of flame flickered here and there in the ruins, but the falling warehouse had mostly snuffed out the inferno in front of them—though the fire continued to rage behind them. Girders and wires hung down from the torn ceiling. Beyond that, they saw a field of ruins where the brewery and warehouse had once stood. It looked very much like old film clips Ben had seen of bombed-out London streets during the Battle of Britain.

They could hear voices shouting outside—and thankfully they were shouting in English.

"Over here!" Ben yelled. He climbed onto the heap of broken brick and waved his arms. "Hey! We've got an injured man in here!"

Thirty seconds later, two police officers from nearby Lombard appeared out of the darkness. Within five minutes paramedics were treating Will as he lay on a stretcher in the parking lot outside the factory.

Elena talked to one of the police officers while Ben and Noelle stood together watching the shattered factory burn. Noelle shivered, and Ben put his arm around her. "Do you want me to see if I can track down a jacket or something?" he asked.

"That's okay," she replied. "For once, I don't mind feeling cold."

◆ ◆ ◆

"So when do the biohazard guys get here?" Sergei asked the EMT who was bandaging and splinting his left arm.

He reloaded his gun one-handed while they talked. He wasn't expecting more action, but he had long ago developed the habit of always keeping his firearm loaded when it was in its holster—whether he planned to use it or not.

"They're over there." She pointed to the lot across from the road-block. A group of figures in blue "space suits" gathered around the captured minivans and SUVs, which were surrounded by a wide cordon marked with black-and-yellow police tape. "I heard those are packed with biological weapons. Is that true?"

"Yeah, and so are those two there." He gestured to the two burned-out wrecks in the middle of the access road. "Someone ought to put a police line around them. There's some really nasty stuff in them."

"I'll call my supervisor and let her know."

"Thanks." Sergei thought he saw something move in one of the vans and craned his neck for a better view. Given the number of different units at the scene and the general chaos, it was very possible that not everyone there knew the danger involved. What if a take-charge police detective started searching the vans, found a container full of suspicious-looking powder, and decided to open it?

A pair of headlights momentarily silhouetted the vans, clearly showing a figure inside one of them. Sergei pulled away from the EMT and ran toward the scorched hulks. "Hold it!" he yelled as he ran. "Hey buddy! Get out of there—that's a biohazard area!"

He arrived just as the figure carefully backed out of the wreckage. As Sergei had suspected, it was an overly independent cop, probably from the Elmhurst department, judging by the uniform, though Sergei couldn't be sure in the gloom.

"Just checking for unexploded ordnance," the man said, his voice nearly drowned out by an approaching helicopter. He had a slight accent and his voice was vaguely familiar. Sergei couldn't quite place him, but thought nothing of it. He knew lots of police officers, and he had met a lot more tonight.

"Okay, just—" Sergei began. But as he spoke, a helicopter's searchlight swept over them. They recognized each other in the same instant. A split second later, their guns blazed simultaneously and they both fell to the pavement.

The gunshots brought officers running, and the searchlight came back to them. In the harsh white light, Sergei could see Elbek Shishani grabbing for his fallen weapon with one hand while he clutched his chest with the other. No blood welled through his fingers, so Sergei knew he also wore body armor.

Pain burned through Sergei's chest where Elbek's bullet had struck, but he brought his gun up and fired into the Chechen's right arm just as he picked up his gun. Elbek dropped the gun and gave a stifled cry. He glared at Sergei with rage-filled eyes and gathered himself to charge. Sergei shot him in the leg and he collapsed again.

Sergei got to his knees as a group of officers arrived. One kicked Elbek's gun away as the others trained their weapons on him.

"It's over," Sergei said as more officers ran up. "It's all over."

"No." Elbek pulled himself up onto his one good leg. His hand held a small bottle. With a quick movement, he hurled it to the street at Sergei's feet. It shattered—and a cloud of extremely fine dust suddenly swirled through the little crowd. "*Now* it's over!"

CHAPTER TWENTY
A RITE FOR THE DEAD

Elbek lay on his bed, staring at the ceiling. He silently recited Koran verses as he waited to die. His nose itched, but he could not scratch it because his arms were tied down with the soft, unyielding restraints used on psychotic patients. If he turned his head, he could catch a glimpse of soldiers standing guard outside the double sets of locked, airtight doors. His room, of course, had no windows to the outside.

He had considered trying to escape, but decided not to bother. Allah would take him soon enough no matter where he was.

The figure in the blue biohazard suit leaned forward and tried again. "Do you really want to die of this Ebola-smallpox hybrid?" The voice was muffled and tinny as it came through the suit's respirator.

Elbek ignored the question and went on reciting scripture.

"Do you know what it will be like?"

Silence.

"First you will develop a fever. Then blisters will form all over your body, literally tearing the top layer of your skin off. The blisters will be on both the outside and the inside, even in your stomach. The Ebola virus will go to work, eating away your tissues and causing massive bleeding. The blisters will fill with blood and begin to bleed. Then you will start to bleed internally and from your orifices. Even your eyes will bleed. Every moment will be agony, and it will take you days to die."

None of this was news to Elbek. He continued to lie in calm silence. He knew they were lying when they implied they could save him if only he talked. Dr. Umarov had been quite certain that this disease could not be cured. If he told them everything he knew, they might be able to prolong his life and ease his passage to Paradise, but that was all. Besides, Elbek could bear a few days of agony much more easily than a lifetime in an American prison.

"All of your men are dead or in custody. Your weapons lab is destroyed, and all of your bioweapons are accounted for. The only thing you accomplish by not talking to us is to make it impossible for us to treat you."

Elbek remained still and expressionless. *No, you're wrong. I also make it impossible for you to treat that filthy Russian and his American friends, and that's worth accomplishing.* He went back to his meditations.

Ben picked up the ringing phone. "Hello. Ben Corbin."

"Hello," said a subdued but familiar voice. "This is Mikhail Ivanovsky. I would like for you to be my lawyer again. I would like for you to come to my room at the hospital now."

At least he's not telling me I must *come,* thought Ben. *That's a start.* Still, he had to stick to his guns. "I'm sorry. I can't represent you unless you're willing to cooperate with the government. We talked about that last time."

"Yes, I remember this talk. I think maybe I will speak to FBI and CIA persons now."

"Maybe?" replied Ben cautiously.

There was a brief silence, then a sigh. "I will speak to them."

"Then I'm on my way."

Ben arrived at the hospital fifteen minutes later to find Elena and Agent Gomez waiting outside Dr. Ivanovsky's room. "He insisted on having you here before he would let us in," explained Elena.

"Of course he did," said Ben with a good-natured smile. "Remember who you're talking about."

They went in and found Dr. Ivanovsky sitting up in bed. Most of his bandages were gone, and he appeared to be in much better health than when Ben had last seen him. "Thank you for coming, Ben," he said. "It is very, very good to see you." He turned to the FBI agents and eyed them suspiciously, but without hostility. "So, okay. Now my lawyer is here. Ask me these questions."

"Some individuals were exposed to Variant D," Elena said urgently. "We need to know how to treat them, and you know more than anyone in the world about how this organism affects humans."

"I know no treatment. What are their symptoms?"

"They don't have any yet."

"No symptoms?" asked the scientist, arching his eyebrows in surprise. "When were they exposed?"

"Three days ago."

"Not one has symptoms?"

Elena shook her head.

"Then this is not Variant D," he said definitively.

"We are certain that it is," countered Agent Gomez, who had worked with the team that analyzed the powder. "We—"

"Then it has lost virulence," replied Dr. Ivanovsky with unshaken confidence. "You have cultured it?"

"Yes. The cultures all show a fast-growing genetically modified variola major," answered Agent Gomez, referring to the scientific name for the most lethal strain of smallpox.

Dr. Ivanovsky sat silent for a moment, his brows furrowed in concentration. He looked up. "You have cultured the exact sample from the exposure?"

"No," admitted Agent Gomez. "That sample was lost. We got ours from one of the other vehicles we captured. We assumed it would be identical, but . . ." He stopped. "There might be some residue left on the container. We'll check that."

"This is sloppy. There must be no sloppiness with such organisms!" Dr. Ivanovsky chastised with the air of a senior scientist rebuking a lab assistant. He thought for a moment. "This sample, was it exposed to chemicals or heat?"

"It most likely came from a burned-out minivan," said Elena, who had heard the whole story in detail while visiting Sergei. "So it was probably in a fire for a while."

"This fire is wonderful news!" Dr. Ivanovsky beamed.

"Why is that?" asked Ben.

"High heat kills the smallpox," Dr. Ivanovsky explained. "Especially Variant D because it is engineered chimera organism, so it is not very stable. I do not think you will need to treat these persons."

After a few more questions, Elena and Agent Gomez broke off their interview with Dr. Ivanovsky. Agent Gomez had some urgent supplemental research to perform. Elena went to talk to the team treating Sergei and the police who were exposed.

When they were alone, Ben turned to Dr. Ivanovsky. "So, why did you change your mind? Was it because the government managed to get Variant D on its own?"

"This is one part," Dr. Ivanovsky began hesitantly, "but there is more. Those things you said to me—they made me very, very angry. So when Father Ivan from Saint Vladimir comes to visit me next, I speak to him about this. I do not speak of Variant D, but I tell him enough of this story to understand. Then I tell him what you said."

"And what did he say?" asked Ben.

"He says, 'Mikhail, did you read *The Brothers Karamazov*?' I say, 'Yes, when I was in school I read this book.' So he asks me, 'Do you remember it?' Have you read this book, Ben?"

"I started it in college, but I got bogged down and never finished it," admitted Ben.

Dr. Ivanovsky nodded sympathetically. "It is a long book with much talking and depression. I tell Father Ivan that this is all I remember. He says, 'There is a very interesting story that one character tells. Would you like me to tell it to you, Mikhail?' I say okay, so he tells me the story. It is about this man who is grand inquisitor in Spain. He is a very important man in the church there. Another man comes to him and tells him that there is a prophet making miracles and healing sick persons in the villages, so the grand inquisitor says he must speak to this man, and the soldiers bring the prophet to him. The grand inquisitor speaks to this prophet alone and he discovers that this is Jesus."

"You mean someone pretending to be Jesus?"

"No, no. It is really Jesus, who has come back from heaven to earth. So the grand inquisitor kills him."

"What? Why?"

"Because the grand inquisitor has a secret," answered Dr. Ivanovsky.

"What was his secret?"

"He does not believe in God."

"But I thought you just said he knew the prophet was Jesus," objected Ben. "How can he not believe in God?"

"I asked this same question to Father Ivan. He says to me, 'This grand inquisitor thinks he is the best one to take care of the poor persons. He thinks his way is best and Jesus will make problems for him. He trusts only him. He does not trust God, so how can he believe?'

"Then he says, 'Mikhail, maybe it would be good for you to trust God more and you less.' I say, 'Okay. I trust God. I do not trust these government persons.' And he says, 'Maybe God works through other persons and not just you. Maybe you should listen to them and trust them some.' Then he says I should pray about this thing and think about it. So I did, and . . ." His voice faltered, and he stopped for a moment. "And I begin to think of Mr. Simeon, who is dead; and Mr. Conklin, who will not walk again for his whole life; and all the police who are dead or hurt. Then I think that maybe Father Ivan is right and maybe it was not so good that I did these things alone and did not trust you one hundred percent. So then I called you."

"I'm glad you did," said Ben, smiling warmly. "There are many words that describe representing you, but *boring* isn't one of them."

Dr. Ivanovsky laughed. "This is true, but maybe I will try to be boring next time."

"Don't start thinking about next time just yet. I've got a feeling we're not quite done with this case."

Snow fell on Elena and Noelle in big, soft flakes that clung to their hair and coats. They stood on Washington Street watching the State Street Macy's Christmas window displays. This year, the displays showed scenes from *A Christmas Carol*, complete with an astounding set of mechanical figures dancing together at the Fezziwigs' Christmas party.

"So, what are you giving Sergei for Christmas?" Noelle asked.

"I haven't decided. Any ideas? What do you think he needs?"

"A car."

Elena laughed. "Yes. He's actually trying to get his insurance company to give him that. Apparently, his policy does not explicitly cover damage caused by terrorist attacks. They may cover it anyway, though—they're starting to get bad publicity."

After the well-attended gunfights, fire, and explosion in Elmhurst, most of the events of the past two months had been widely reported. The intelligence agencies had managed to keep the exact source and nature of Variant D secret, but pretty much everything else had become public knowledge. All the main participants were minor celebrities now. Sergei in particular had been lionized because a news crew had arrived at the industrial park just in time to film his final confrontation with Elbek, which had been conveniently spotlighted by the police helicopter.

"How's he doing, by the way?" asked Noelle. "Ben says he's been kind of quiet since he got out of the hospital."

"He has been . . . thoughtful. Two times in the past month he thought he was going to die, and all he could do was wait for death. That will have an effect on anybody."

"Is he okay?"

"I think so," replied Elena. "Sometimes I'll catch him just staring into space with a kind of sad look. I ask him what's wrong, but he says it's nothing and then he's himself again—except that he seems a little more serious. He's also reading a lot of books about religion and philosophy."

"It sounds like he's searching."

"Maybe he is," replied Elena. She turned away from the window. "And I'm still searching for a gift for him. Any suggestions—other than a car?"

Noelle decided to drop it. If her friend didn't want to talk about spiritual issues, she wasn't going to push. Besides, she wasn't done fishing for information. "Well, that depends on how close you two are. If you like him, but you're not that serious, I'd go with a pen-and-pencil set or something like that. If you're serious, cologne or a sweater. And if you're *really* serious, talking-about-buying-a-ring serious, then you should get him something for his kitchen. Single men never have enough stuff in their kitchens, and what they have is always cheap—like those frying pans that always burn food. Then once you're married, they don't want you to buy new ones until the old ones actually break."

Elena laughed. "Noelle, you would make an excellent investigator."

◆ ◆ ◆

Every pew in the large sanctuary was filled with Chicago heavyweights, gathered to honor Tony Simeon. Half of the aldermen and most of the judiciary were there, as were high executives from many of Chicago's largest corporations. Also present were representatives of the charities and museums that were the primary beneficiaries of Tony's will, since he had no living relatives closer than cousins. A scattering of reporters and photographers sat around the sides and back of the church and in the nave.

The Corbins sat in a side pew next to Sergei and Elena. Irina Ivanovsky sat next to Elena at the very end of the pew, and her husband was in a wheelchair in the aisle next to her. His doctors had refused to release him from the hospital and had ordered him not to leave, but they relented when he remained adamant and started dressing himself. They could not keep him in his bed without physically restraining him, which would have been both illegal and medically riskier than letting him go. They finally reached a compromise with him: he could go to the funeral, but only if a nurse went with him (she sat in the pew behind him), he stayed in a wheelchair, and he promised to come back to the hospital immediately after the funeral ended.

The black-draped bronze casket lay on a table at the front of the sanctuary. Floral arrangements flanked the bier. An easel beside the coffin held a large, not particularly recent picture of Tony.

The service opened with a hymn, followed by two of the Lyric Opera's singers performing the "O Death, Where Is Thy Sting?" segment from Handel's *Messiah*. Then came a short liturgy and several eulogies from eminent judges and lawyers who had known Tony well. But their polished eloquence was muted and overwhelmed by the circumstance in which they found themselves.

One justice of the Illinois Supreme Court said simply, "I hold in my hands five pages of notes for a speech praising Tony Simeon, but now that I stand before you I realize that there is nothing I can say that will speak better of him than the actions of the last days of his life." And he sat down.

Then Pastor Wilhelm ascended to the pulpit to deliver the homily. "I have been acquainted with Tony Simeon for many years, but I only came to know him recently. Tony was a gifted man who had done much in his life, but he told me that he had used his life and his gifts to serve himself. He regretted that, and he regretted having lived his adult life without God.

"Tony came to faith late, but he did so with a strength and courage that awe me as I stand here today. Tony knew the danger that awaited him along the road he chose. He knew the end to which it might lead. Yet he took it nonetheless. He did not rationalize or temporize. He did not look for an easier way. He saw the task that God had set before him, and he did it without flinching or faltering.

"Through Tony, God delivered millions—including, no doubt, many in this church—from a horrible death. Without Tony's sacrifice, there would be many, many more funerals today. And tomorrow. And every tomorrow until there were none left to mourn the dead or bury them.

"God's deliverance will remain with us even though one of today's deliverers is gone. For our lives do not rest in the hands of terrorists, and the hour of our death is not appointed by men. We belong to God, who promises, 'You shall not be afraid of any terror by night, nor of the arrow that flies by day; of the plague that stalks in the darkness, nor of the sickness that lays waste at midday.'

"God delivered Tony too, but he delivered him through death—not from it. Christ defeated death, but he did not destroy it. In the end, we all receive in our bodies the bitter legacy of the first sin. The earthen mouth opens to receive us, and the worms consume us.

"Many people do not see death at all and live happy, carefree lives— until death catches them unawares and unprepared. Others who are wiser see the loneliness, the pain, and the empty darkness of death, and they despair.

"But Christianity is a religion of hope, even in the presence of death." He held out an open hand toward Tony's casket. "Not because we do not see death, but because we see beyond it. We do not hope blindly, but with vision unclouded by fear or despair.

"We know that beyond the wrenching horror of death lies life such as we have never known. The infant in the womb must pass through the trauma of birth to emerge into the light of the sun and the loving embrace of his parents. So too, Tony has passed through the trauma of death and stands now in the light of the Son and the loving embrace of his Father."

EPILOGUE
SETTLEMENT

"Ninety-eight percent of all cases settle, so why hasn't this one?" demanded Judge Ryan. The *Circuit Dynamics* trial was only two weeks away, and the judge had taken Ben, Steve Rocco, and John Weaver back into his chambers for a pretrial conference. Their meeting involved a large dose of arm-twisting aimed at settling the case.

"Your Honor, we've made a good-faith offer," said Rocco. "My client has put $5 million on the table, which is frankly a lot more than this case is worth. The plaintiff hasn't moved off of $25 million."

"They've offered $5 million on a $100-million case, Judge," retorted Ben.

Judge Ryan rubbed his watery blue eyes. "All right. I'll talk to you each separately, plaintiff first. Mr. Rocco, Mr. Weaver, please wait in the courtroom."

Once they were alone, he turned to Ben. "Five million dollars is a lot of money, particularly to a small business like your client."

"That's true," Ben acknowledged, "but $100 million is a lot more."

"It is, but to get it you have to both win and collect. I've seen your evidence, and it's got some holes. I also can tell you that the defendants will almost certainly take every appeal they can if they lose. Your client won't see a penny for years."

"That's why we're willing to accept twenty-five."

"Is that your bottom line?" asked the judge. "Because if it is, we're just wasting our time. You have to be willing to show some flexibility."

"We can show *some* flexibility, Your Honor, but not when they're at $5 million. This is not a case that is going to settle halfway between their position and ours. It just won't." The bottom line Fred Schultz had given him was actually $12 million, but Ben intended to do better than that.

"All right. I'll see what I can do. Send those guys in."

Ben went out to the courtroom and told Rocco and Weaver that the judge was ready to see them. Then he sat down to wait. The judge hadn't pushed very hard, which worried him a little. If the judge didn't apply more pressure on Rocco and Weaver, the case wouldn't settle.

Back in the judge's chambers, pressure was being applied.

"I don't care how strong your case is," Judge Ryan said. "Do you really want to try a case against Ben Corbin less than two months after that business with the terrorists?"

"I don't see what bearing that has on—" began Weaver.

The judge cut him off. "Jurors read papers and watch the news, Counsel. I will guarantee you that someone on your jury will recognize him. By the end of the first trial day, they'll all know the whole story. Only an idiot or a masochist would go up against him at the moment.

"Now—what are you going to do to settle this case? Don't think about how much your damages expert told you it's worth. Think about how much the jury will hit you for when the man who helped save them from terrorists asks them for $100 million dollars plus punitive damages."

◆ ◆ ◆

Ben walked into the Petrograd half an hour after he was supposed to meet Sergei for lunch. He spotted the detective already seated at a table, eating his lunch.

Ben pulled out a chair. "Sorry I'm late. My pretrial conference ran a little longer than I had planned."

"No problem," replied Sergei around a mouthful of *shuba* herring salad. "How did it go?"

A waitress came over as Ben sat down, and he quickly ordered lunch. "The conference went great," he said, turning back to Sergei. "I came in offering twenty-five million, and we settled for twenty plus a license fee of a million a year for the next ten years."

Sergei stopped chewing. "So basically you were willing to take twenty-five, but you got them to give you thirty?"

"Basically, but I was willing to take less than twenty-five."

"Okay, I'm taking you with me when I buy my next car."

Ben laughed. "I've got a sneaking suspicion that you'll do just fine on your own. In fact, I'd like your help with some negotiations I'll be starting shortly."

"That's what I figured from your call. What can I do for you?"

"I've gotten a lot of document and interview requests from the Bureau and the US Attorney's Office for stuff on the *Ivanovsky* case. They haven't said that Dr. Ivanovsky is the target of a criminal investigation, but—"

"But you're worried and you want to know what I think they're doing."

"Yeah."

Sergei nodded. "They probably have opened a file on him. After all, he did break a lot of laws. Trying to obtain bioweapons is serious business, even if his intentions were good. And he did cause the Bureau, the CIA, and several police departments a whole lot of trouble."

"Think they'll indict him?"

"Good question. There's a grand jury hearing evidence against what's left of the Vainakh Guard. It's possible that they're also hearing evidence against Dr. Ivanovsky."

That's what Ben had feared. "I'd like to get this out in the open as soon as possible so we can start dealing with it. Do you think it's worth calling the US Attorney's Office and asking what their intentions are?"

"Sure. Criminal-defense attorneys do it all the time. Sometimes the assistant US attorney in charge of the case will tell you, sometimes they won't. There's no harm in asking, though."

"That's what I was wondering. Thanks."

Just then, Auntie Olga walked up with Ben's lunch. "You must be Ben Corbin," she remarked as she served him. "Sergei has told me a lot about you."

"And you must be Olga," replied Ben. "I understand you hosted the whole Spassky clan for Christmas."

"She even invited Elena," put in Sergei. "She couldn't make it back to Russia because a snowstorm cancelled her flight."

"She's a nice girl, but I don't see why she wants you to eat more Chinese food," said Auntie Olga with a wink.

"Chinese food?" asked Ben.

"Elena gave me a wok for Christmas," Sergei explained.

"Hi, Curt," Ben said into the phone. Curt Grunwald was the assistant US attorney handling the Vainakh Guard investigation. "I just thought

I'd call and touch base with you about a couple of things regarding Dr. Ivanovsky."

"Fire away."

"First, is your office considering criminal charges against my client?"

"Sorry, Ben. I can't tell you anything one way or the other."

"Okay. The second thing I'd like to talk about is the judgment in *Ivanovsky v. Zinoviev*. There's a final and nonappealable judgment that gives my client the rights to a set of lab notes and a sample of Variant D. I believe those are currently in the possession of the federal government."

The line was silent for several seconds. "So? I could get that judgment vacated a dozen different ways."

"Probably, but not quickly and not without giving Dr. Ivanovsky his Fourteenth Amendment due-process rights. At the very least, you would have to explain the whole story to a federal judge, which I suspect you'd rather not do."

"All things being equal, no, I'd rather not. But all things aren't equal here, are they?"

"Nope," said Ben.

"All right. I assume you have a proposal to make."

"I do, but it won't be worth either of our time unless the government is willing to forgo prosecution of Dr. Ivanovsky."

"We might be, under certain circumstances," Grunwald said thoughtfully. "I'll call you back."

Forty-five minutes later, Grunwald was back on the line.

"We're willing to agree not to prosecute," he said, "if we can agree on a few points. First, Dr. Ivanovsky will assign to the United States all rights he has under that judgment. Second, we'll need him to sign a confidentiality agreement similar to the one you signed. Third—"

"Hold on a sec," said Ben as he scribbled. "I take slow notes. By the way, my client has an additional condition."

"What's that?" Grunwald asked warily.

"He'll have to be involved in any further work on Variant D," said Ben, choosing his words carefully. If there was going to be a sticking point, this was it. "As you know, he's concerned that it might be developed into an offensive weapon. This will let him verify that it isn't. Involving him will also give the government access to his extensive—and in many cases unique—knowledge of biodefense and decontamination."

Grunwald chuckled. "The last point on my list says, 'Must make Ivanovsky available to DoD as consultant re Variant D countermeasures.' We'll need to paper this, but I think we have a deal."

Fort Detrick, home to the United States Army Medical Research Institute of Infectious Diseases, is a collection of utilitarian-looking buildings scattered over roughly three square miles outside of Frederick, Maryland. USAMRIID's nerve center is a huge tan building on the fort's grounds, and it was to this building that two large MPs escorted Ben and Dr. Ivanovsky.

Dr. Ivanovsky was there to meet with the team of scientists that was probing the secrets of Variant D. Ben was there at the insistence of Dr. Ivanovsky, who now treated him as something of a security blanket. They spent the morning discussing protocols for storing and handling the organism, a subject that Dr. Ivanovsky and his new colleagues found endlessly fascinating. Only an iron will and four cups of coffee kept Ben awake.

Over lunch, Dr. Ivanovsky asked the head of the USAMRIID team, a general who also had a PhD in molecular biology, "What do you think of this Variant D? It is brilliant, no?"

The man frowned. "No offense to your countrymen, but I think they created an abomination. It's a death sentence hanging over the whole human race. We don't know when the ax will fall, but we need to be ready to catch it when it does. If I was sure that we had the only culture of it, I wouldn't be so worried—at least not about this bug, anyway. I'd heat it in the autoclave and count my blessings that it was dead.

"But you know as well as I do that when the Soviet Union fell apart, so did their bioweapons program. Things disappeared, especially valuable things." He pointed to a partial analysis of Variant D's genome. "Things like this. Every morning when I wake up, I wonder if today will be the day that some terrorist or rogue nation lets loose one of these superbugs. And every night when I go to bed, I thank God that it didn't happen."

"Yes, thank God," said Dr. Ivanovsky, who seemed oddly reassured by the military man's answer. "And trust him, too." He turned to Ben. "This general thinks correctly. You can go home. I am okay now."

AFTERWORD

Not nearly enough of this book is fiction.

The Soviet Union did indeed have a massive and secret biological-weapons program, of which Biopreparat was a part. The scientists who worked there developed a number of genetically engineered germs that are deadlier, more infectious, and less curable than anything humanity has ever faced. When the program was shut down—or at least scaled back—after the collapse of the Soviet Union, dozens of germ factories were simply abandoned. Thousands of scientists with only one market-able skill were suddenly without jobs.

The Ebolapox virus depicted in the story probably exists. Russian scientists admit to having developed the technology to insert Ebola genes into smallpox viruses, but claim they have not actually done so. The former second-in-command at Biopreparat, Dr. Ken Alibek, doubts that claim. But even if his former coworkers have not bred Ebolapox in Russia, some of them may well have done so for Iran, North Korea, or one of several other new employers. Now that the process for breeding this virus is known, it is only a matter of time before someone actually does it—if they have not already.

Shortly before the 9/11 attacks, the Johns Hopkins Center for Civilian Biodefense Strategies led a war-game-style simulation called "Dark Winter." It was intended to study the effects of a terrorist attack like the one plotted by the Vainakh Guard (i.e., simultaneous attacks on multiple American cities). The only significant differences were that (1) the simulated terrorists in Dark Winter used ordinary smallpox—not one of the "superbugs" created by Biopreparat or another secret weapons lab, and (2) the terrorists hit only three targets, shopping malls in widely separated cities. Within three weeks of the simulated attack, the Johns Hopkins scientists projected, smallpox would have spread from those three malls to twenty-five states. Within two months, up to one million Americans would have died and the epidemic would be out of control. After the simulation ended, former senator Sam Nunn, one of the Dark Winter participants, said this in his testimony to Congress: "It's a lucky thing for the United States that—as the Emergency Broadcast Network used to say—'This is just a test, this is not a real emergency.' But, Mr. Chairman, our lack of preparation is a real emergency."

Much has been done since Dark Winter, including the initiation of Project BioShield, a comprehensive federal effort to protect America against bioterrorism. But much remains to be done. Some of the deadliest organisms used in biological weapons have no cure. Further, the Director of National Intelligence's 2015 Worldwide Threat Assessment found that "the time when only a few states had access to the most dangerous technologies is past. Biological and chemical materials and technologies, almost always dual-use, move easily in the globalized economy, as do personnel with the scientific expertise to design and use them."

ACKNOWLEDGMENTS

You would not be holding this book in your hands right now if I had not received help and support from innumerable people. First and foremost, I thank my wife, Anette, who is my muse, sounding board, and biggest fan.

Thank you to Amy Hosford, associate publisher at Waterfall Press, for believing in this book and bringing out a new edition.

Thanks to Sue Brower, agent extraordinaire, for tirelessly advocating for her authors and their stories.

I also owe a special debt of gratitude to those experts who reviewed the portions of the book dealing with Russian crime and biological weapons—subjects with which I happily have no personal experience. Assistant United States Attorney Terry Kinney provided extensive and invaluable feedback on the Russian criminal culture in Chicago. Dr. Nwadiuto Esiobu, professor of microbiology at Florida Atlantic University, who does federally funded work on bioterrorism countermeasures, offered helpful insight on the care and culturing of the virus described in these pages. My fellow Golden Domer, Special

Agent Cathy Viray, was generous with her time and expertise in providing several useful details about the inner workings of the FBI.

Dennis Hillman and Dave Lindstedt edited an earlier version of this book and made invaluable suggestions throughout.

Last, but certainly not least, I appreciate the suggestions and corrections of the Valley Community Church Writers Group and dozens of other test readers.

ABOUT THE AUTHOR

 Bestselling author Rick Acker is supervising deputy attorney general in the California Department of Justice. Most recently, he and his team won a string of unprecedented recoveries against the Wall Street players who created the mortgage securities that triggered the Great Recession. Acker has authored several legal thrillers, including *When the Devil Whistles*, which award-winning author Colleen Coble described as "a legal thriller you won't want to miss." He spends most of his free time with his wife and children. You can learn more about Acker and his books at www.rickacker.com.